HEMINGWAY ON WAR

ERNEST HEMINGWAY

Edited and with an Introduction by
SEÁN HEMINGWAY

Foreword by Patrick Hemingway

SCRIBNER
New York   London   Toronto   Sydney

SCRIBNER
1230 Avenue of the Americas
New York, NY 10020

SCRIBNER and design are trademarks of Macmillan Library Reference USA, Inc., used under license by Simon & Schuster, the publisher of this work.

For information about special discounts for bulk purchases, please contact Simon & Schuster Special Sales: 1-800-456-6798 or business@simonandschuster.com

Text set in Caslon 540

Manufactured in the United States of America

1 3 5 7 9 10 8 6 4 2

The Library of Congress has cataloged the hardcover edition as follows:
Hemingway, Ernest, 1899–1961.
Hemingway on war / Ernest Hemingway : edited and with an introduction by Seán Hemingway ; foreword by Patrick Hemingway.
p. cm.
"A bibliography of Ernest Hemingway's writings on war": p.
1. War stories, American. 2. War. I. Hemingway, Seán A. II. Title.
PS3515.E37A6 2003
813'.52—dc22 2003057393

ISBN 978-0-7432-4329-2

Courage is grace under pressure.
—Ernest Hemingway

Cowardice, as distinguished from panic is almost always simply a lack of ability to suspend the functioning of the imagination. Learning to suspend your imagination and live completely in the very second of the present minute with no before and after is the greatest gift a soldier can acquire.
—From *Men at War*

Contents

Contents

III

Revolution and Civil War in Spain

IV

At the Front Again: The Allied Invasion of Europe

Contents

SELECTED WAR CORRESPONDENCE

V

World War I and Its Aftermath

VI

The Greco-Turkish War

Contents

VII

The Spanish Civil War

VIII

World War II

Foreword

I am sure Ernest Hemingway would be pleased with the selection his grandson Seán has made from his grandfather's writing on war. Any selection implies just that: some things have been left out, but more than enough has been left in to give the twenty-first-century reader the true gen on war as it was waged in the last hundred years.

Hemingway was born in 1899 and had he lived as long as it is possible for a man to live, he could have borne witness to the whole of the deadliest and most war-torn century of which we have a historical record. Sadly, his health began to fail at mid-century and drastically worsened when he was forced to choose by the Cold War between his beloved Finca Vigía and his country. He died just short of completing the second third of the twentieth century.

How much did his going to the wars affect his health and shorten his life? In my opinion, a great deal. As a fortunate American, he chose to go to war rather than, as an unlucky Spaniard or an even unluckier Pole, have it inevitably come to him.

James Joyce, perhaps the greatest writer of the twentieth century, neither went to war nor wrote about it in any way but he did not have Hemingway's initially robust constitution and would not have lasted very long in war. Writers who write of war from personal experience have to have special qualities, and I am not sure any of them succeed without strong drink. I like to think that Karl von Clausewitz would never have made it through the Jena campaign without potato schnapps and we know Ulysses S. Grant needed both cigars and corn whiskey to get him through the Wilderness.

About the earlier wars: the Italian front in 1918 and the Greco-Turkish War in the 1920s I know only from what my father wrote in such stories as "A Way You'll Never Be," but I do remember when I was ten years old in 1938 and in the fifth grade being beside my father at the top of the stairs on the second floor of our home in Key West when he opened and read a telegram informing him of the start of the last big offensive of the Spanish Republic which would end sixteen weeks later in disaster on the Ebro. Papa left us for Spain at once. That was the year my mother, my younger brother, and I went to war, three whole years before Pearl Harbor. My family was, as they say, prematurely antifascist.

Martha Gellhorn, who was a protégée of Mrs. Roosevelt, arranged an invitation for Hemingway to the White House when it was by then very clear that Spain was about to fall to Franco and his German and Italian allies. I remember my father's conversation after that visit, all of us enjoying an excellent meal at the long eighteenth-century Spanish table downstairs in our Key West house in the dining room with the big painting by Joan Miró of his farm outside Barcelona. Papa was telling us that he had come away from his White House evening with a confirmation of his previous dislike of the President. Things had gotten off to a bad start, from my father's point of view, when the President somewhat gratuitously remarked that he had not read any work of fiction since he was an undergraduate at Harvard. Hemingway must have then recalled to mind what he had written not long before in *Green Hills of Africa*, that all countries eventually eroded and that the only things that lasted were the people who had practiced the arts. The rest of the evening the President spent telling about, not listening to, what was going on in Spain. Furthermore, said my father, Mrs. Roosevelt, although undoubtedly a person with deep sympathies for humanity in general, was a poor housekeeper and he had never had to eat a worse meal than what was served him at the White House, especially the squab, which was tougher than rubber.

Only a year or so later, when the great popular success of *For Whom the Bell Tolls* seemed to confirm the wisdom of his having ended his second marriage, Hemingway left Key West and started a new expatriate life in Cuba with Martha Gellhorn, and they both went as journalists to China and the British and Dutch colonies in the Far East. Marty, long after her marriage to my father had ended, wrote a wonderful memoir of their tour together and Papa at the time produced some of his most prescient military journalism, still very happy to work and live together with Marty as he had done during the Spanish Civil War.

Ernest Hemingway loved the sea. He had seafaring ancestors from the age of sail and he and his kid brother, Leicester, once they left Oak Park, the landlocked Chicago suburb where they were born, always made their home within sight of salt water and owned boats, Leicester sail and Ernest power. So when Pearl Harbor brought America into World War II, Papa was uniquely situated to make a highly unconventional contribution to the war effort. From his experience in the Spanish Civil War, he had a wealth of information on the people who now made up the fascist government in that country as well as how they might behave in any Axis intelligence operation against the United States through Latin America, especially Cuba. Despite the snub he had received from President Roosevelt two years before, he contacted Naval Intelligence through the American embassy in Havana, and it accepted his help with intelligence work that led to the arrest of German agents as they tried to disembark in Cuba from Spanish vessels the Falangist political clubs in Spain had helped them travel through Spain to board, vessels which as neutrals could make port in Havana and other destinations in Latin America. Soon afterwards it gave him paramilitary status as captain of his sport-fishing boat, *Pilar,* to play a small part in the large operation to contain and turn back Operation *Paukenschlag,* the all-out U-boat assault on American coastal shipping lanes in the first six months after America's entry into the war.

By the middle of July 1942, the submarine war had mostly shifted to the North Atlantic and Papa felt it was safe enough to bring his two younger sons, Gregory and myself, to spend the rest of our summer vacation with him at Cayo Confites, the tiny offshore island then used by the Cuban military to keep watch on the narrow deepwater channel that separates the northeastern end of Cuba from the southern end of the Bahama Bank. Cayo Confites itself was exactly like that island cartoonists draw with the shipwrecked sailor, but it lacked even a single palm tree, with only the poor unpainted shack that housed the two soldiers who manned a two-way shortwave radio.

Greg and I slept in the two forward bunks on the *Pilar,* which always came in to anchor by the island in the evening after the daytime patrols. During the patrols we were left ashore with our own small skiff, and one day we almost drowned when a summer afternoon line squall caught us goggle fishing a little ways south of the island, swamping our skiff and washing us up on what was, luckily for us, a sandy shore. Goggle fishing was what we called it back then, for the U-boat people had not yet even invented the snorkel, and I think Greg and I were the very first people in the Americas to hunt an underwater coral reef using swimming goggles that had been welded together to give a single plane of vision for both eyes.

Marty and Papa's marriage began to fall apart that summer, and on through what passes for fall and winter in the northern tropics, with a great many home truths harshly expressed by both parties. Marty was probably right. With the buildup of shipments of men and materiel from America to Britain in order to launch the second front the Russians so desperately wanted, the U-boat battles now mostly being fought in the approaches to the British Isles, it was time for two veteran war correspondents to gear up and go to cover together the impending invasion of Western Europe. The trouble was Papa was a little more veteran and a lot more writer than Marty, for he was now an old forty-three years, wise to the ways of both art and warfare and with a bad case of piles, a very unpleasant handicap indeed under combat conditions. He was also well aware that Jim Joyce, who had never heard a shot fired in anger, was sitting out the war in Switzerland and was likely to be hailed as the greatest writer of the twentieth century. Later he would joke about such thoughts to his friends in the 4th American Infantry Division, calling himself Ernie Hemorrhoids, the Poor Man's Pyle, but Marty had to use pretty strong words to get him to take up again the war writing burden and he never forgave her.

World War II was the last war that Ernest Hemingway covered. When asked by his two youngest boys what he had done in that war, he told us he paid for it. This was a sardonic reference to the confiscatory income tax he paid on the sale of *For Whom the Bell Tolls* to the movies. Just as he had been unfortunate in his prescient but premature antifascism, selling the movie rights to his best-selling novel just at the moment the income tax rates rose to over 80 percent for high income brackets in order to instill a real feeling of sacrifice in the home front people and corporations that stood to profit at last, after twelve dry years, from a war economy, left him dangerously exposed financially. He had turned over the domestic income from his first big success, *The Sun Also Rises*, to his first wife, Hadley, at the time of their divorce. He was paying a high alimony rate for the support of his second wife, Pauline, and their two young children, and his foreign rights income had been cut off by the war. Most of his profits from *A Farewell to Arms* had gone to setting up trust funds after his father's suicide for the support of his mother, unmarried sisters, and kid brother, generously added to by G. A. Pfeiffer, Pauline's very rich uncle. His finances had reached their lowest point after the poor sales of *Across the River and Into the Trees*, when my wife, Henrietta, suggested he and his fourth wife, Mary, could make big money reporting on Mr. Truman's war in Korea. To his credit, he did not throw us out of the Finca Vigía, where we were visiting at the time. It was during these same years that poor Robert Capa, whose only profitable trade was photographing war, finally bought the farm in Indo-China.

Papa made a remarkable comeback from his arduous journalistic coverage of the Normandy invasion, the liberation of Paris, and the combat horrors of the Schnee Eifel with *The Old Man and the Sea*, to this day his best-selling book. He was always healthiest and happiest at sea. It pleases me to leave him standing with his last wife, Mary, the only one of his wives who really loved the sea, on the flying bridge of the *Pilar,* out in the Stream off the Moro wearing only a sun hat, white pressed shirt, and black tailored Bermuda shorts that show off his elegant eighteenth-century calves, a cool drink in his left hand, his right hand on the wheel, his head turned back toward the stern, watching the two outrigger baits bounce in the blue water on each side of the boat's twin curling white wake for the first sight of a marlin's wagging bill, dark gray dorsal fin, or scythe-shaped tail, jumping down to the stern deck to snatch the rod from its holder, slacking the reel drag to feed line, then tightening down the drag and hauling the rod back hard four or five times to set the hook that sends the reel screaming and the huge fish high into the air for its first jump.

Patrick Hemingway
Bozeman, Montana
April 2003

Acknowledgments

To Patrick Hemingway, I extend my sincere gratitude and appreciation for considering me for this project; his suggestions for a number of literary works to include in this volume, his answers to my many queries about my grandfather's experiences in war, and his thoughtful Foreword were an invaluable contribution. I offer my sincere thanks to Carol Hemingway, especially for her assistance with passages from *The Fifth Column;* to Michael Katakis for the inspiration for this book and for his good counsel and support; to Megan Desnoyers and James Roth of the Hemingway Archives at the John F. Kennedy Library for their help with research pertaining to unpublished materials in the collection, and to Allan Goodrich and James Hill at the audiovisual archives for indispensable assistance with the photographic material; to the Ernest Hemingway Foundation, Inc., for permission to publish excerpts from the letters, and to J. Gerald Kennedy for facilitating this permission; to Simon & Schuster for permission to reprint excerpts from published works, and to Lydia Zelaya and Jeff Wilson for facilitating this permission; to Charles Scribner III for his enthusiasm and efforts, and to Brant Rumble, John McGhee, and Gillian Blake for their assistance; to Cornell Capa for permission to publish the photographs by his brother, Robert Capa, and to Anna Winand for facilitating this permission; to Getty Images for permission to publish the photograph by Lloyd Arnold, and to Valerie Zars for facilitating this permission; to A. E. Hotchner for permission to publish his photograph from his publication; to Demetri Villard for permission to publish the photograph taken by his father, Henry S. Villard; to President Fidel Castro for thought-provoking discussion about my grandfather and about warfare; to Valerie Hemingway for her specific and valuable comments about Ernest Hemingway in Spain, and for her general support; to Joseph Czapski for his encouragement and helpful suggestions; to Henry Gornowicz for his copy of the film *The Spanish Earth;* and to Patricia Czapski, Gladys Rodriguez, James Nagel, Brendan Hemingway, Robin Smith, Brian Gaisford, Achille Dimatteo, Dominic Tripoli, Angela Hemingway, Steven

Acknowledgments

Gold, George Plimpton, Jenny Phillips, Congressman James McGovern, and, in memoriam, Gregory Hemingway, Jack Hemingway, and John Groth. Finally, as always, I reserve my warmest note of appreciation for my wife, and my muse, Colette, for her critical reading of this text and for her patience and essential support throughout this endeavor.

Introduction

"War is part of the intercourse of the human race," wrote the Prussian philosopher-soldier General Karl von Clausewitz, whom Hemingway considered to be among the greatest military thinkers of all time.[1] This provocative statement has history on its side. Since the dawn of civilization there has been war. In 323 B.C., after waging war for most of his adult life, Alexander the Great of Macedonia had formed an empire the likes of which the world had never seen before. The new kingdom stretched from the fertile plains of northern Greece across western Asia to the Indus River valley. When asked on his deathbed to whom he would leave his empire, Alexander replied, "To the strongest." Soon thereafter, war broke out as the short-lived empire was divided into many smaller kingdoms.[2] This story speaks to the fundamental elements that often lead to war: opportunity, personal ambition, and the struggle for power attained through superior strength. Clausewitz viewed war as a rational instrument of national policy, essentially political in nature. In Hemingway's *Men at War,* his anthology of the best war stories of all time, he divided the stories into sections taken from Clausewitz's magnum opus *On War* that defined what Hemingway believed were the salient elements of war: danger, courage, physical exertion, suffering, uncertainty, chance, friction, resolution, firmness, and staunchness. To Clausewitz's observations, Hemingway added, "War is fought by human beings."

This volume brings together for the first time the most important works of Ernest Hemingway's own writings on war. From his boyhood enlistment in World War I as a volunteer Red Cross ambulance driver to his remarkable career as a war correspondent and writer, Hemingway witnessed and recorded the major conflicts of the first half of the twentieth century. This book includes what I believe are the best short stories, passages from novels, and articles written by my grandfather. They provide a balanced representation from different periods throughout his career. There is much that will be of interest to anyone who wants to understand war and how it was waged in the first half of the twentieth century. His accounts, both fictional and journalistic, represent an extraordinarily rich depiction of war as it evolved into the modern era, through the development of machine warfare to the first deployment of the atomic bomb. Hemingway was a military expert, a student of war in its totality, from machine gun emplacements, tactics, and maneuvers to civilian morale and industrial organization.[3] In my opinion, one of his greatest accomplishments as a writer, and one so evident in the collection of writings in *Hemingway on War,* is his portrayal of the physical and psychological impact of war and its aftermath.

When Ernest Miller Hemingway was born on July 21, 1899, the last major conflict involving the United States of America had been its own civil war, still the bloodiest war ever to be fought on North American soil. Both of Ernest's grandfathers had participated in the war on the Union side and they regaled the young boy with war tales. Like most boys, Ernest had a keen and naïve interest in war. My father, Gregory Hemingway, remembered Papa telling him that he loved to read the Bible when he was seven or eight because it was so full of battles. Ernest's own father, Clarence Hemingway, had also served as a corporal with the First Iowa Volunteer Cavalry and even carried a Confederate musket ball in one thigh. Clarence, however, never allowed the war to be discussed in his presence.[4]

In April of 1917, when the United States entered World War I through its declaration of war on Germany, Ernest Hemingway was in his senior year of high school. Like many of his classmates, he was keen to join the U.S. efforts overseas, but his father strongly opposed his enlistment. After graduation, Hemingway did not go on to college but joined the staff of the *Kansas City Star* as a cub reporter. In spite of defective vision in his left eye, he was able to sign on with the 7th Missouri Infantry, a "Home Guard" unit based in Kansas City. However, this was not enough action for the young reporter, as he wrote to his sister Marcelline, "I can't let a show like this go on without getting into it."[5] By spring of the following year, Hemingway had enlisted for a six-month tour of duty with the American Red Cross as an ambulance driver.[6] He set sail from New York on May 24, 1918, bound for Bordeaux and, after a brief layover in Paris, arrived in northern Italy by train on the seventh of June. He was assigned to Section Four of the American Red Cross and stationed at Schio.

Hemingway's active service for the Red Cross was brief. After little more than two weeks of relative inactivity driving Fiat ambulances at Schio, Ernest volunteered to run a mobile canteen dispensing chocolate and cigarettes to the wounded and the soldiers at the front at Fossalta di

Introduction

Piave. This involved visits to the line of battle by bicycle and by foot and it was on one such trip, on July 8, that Hemingway was severely wounded during an Austrian offensive. While handing out supplies in a forward listening post on the west bank of the Piave River, a projectile from an Austrian Minenwerfer exploded, hurling steel-rod fragments and metal junk in what Hemingway later described as a furnacelike blast: "Then there was a flash, as when a blast-furnace door is swung open, and a roar that started white and went red . . . I tried to breathe, but my breath would not come. The ground was torn up and in front of my head there was a splintered beam of wood. In the jolt of my head I heard somebody crying . . . I tried to but I could not move. I heard the machine guns and rifles firing across the river."[7] Shrapnel from a trench mortar blast had inflicted more than two hundred separate wounds in his legs. Despite his serious injuries, he carried a wounded Italian soldier to safety, but only after a round of heavy machine gun fire tore into his right knee. In recognition of his courage, Hemingway was awarded the Silver Medal of Valor and the Croce di Guerra, and promoted to first lieutenant in the Italian army. While recovering from his wounds in the American Hospital in Milan, he met and fell in love with a tall, dark-haired, and beautiful American nurse named Agnes von Kurowsky. Their brief love affair was to be the inspiration for his novel *A Farewell to Arms*. When Hemingway returned to Oak Park, Illinois, alone in January 1919, he was heralded as a hero and the first American to be wounded at the Italian front.[8]

The following year Hemingway began to write freelance articles for *The Toronto Star*. The war and its impact on his own life weighed heavily on his mind. One of the first pieces that he wrote for *The Toronto Star* was "Popular in Peace—Slacker in War," which begins the selections of journalism in this book. This biting essay satirizes the reassimilation of Canadian draft dodgers who had fled to America during the war, men who were now trying to resume their lives in their native country.

Some months later Ernest met and fell in love with Elizabeth Hadley Richardson, of St. Louis. They were married on September 3, 1921, at the Hemingway family cottage in Upper Michigan and soon moved to Paris, where Ernest continued to work as a freelance reporter for *The Toronto Star*. The present volume includes only five dispatches from this time aside from the reports on the Greco-Turkish War, which are grouped separately. "Fascisti Party Half-Million" is Hemingway's exclusive interview with Benito Mussolini in 1922. Mussolini, "a big, brown-faced man with a high forehead, a slow smiling mouth, and large, expressive hands," sits behind his desk answering Hemingway's questions while stroking the ears of his wolfhound pup. Around this time,

Hemingway made a trip with Hadley to the battlefield where he had been wounded in northern Italy. "A Veteran Visits the Old Front" describes the dissolution he felt in not being able to recognize a single landmark, finding only a rusty mortar shell in one of the hedge groves. "Did Poincaré Laugh in Verdun Cemetery?" is a very different kind of article. Hemingway explains a political smear campaign against the French premier, who was photographed in an apparent moment of disrespect at the cemetery for soldiers who died at one of the bloodiest battles of World War I.

During his time with *The Toronto Star,* Hemingway was assigned to cover the Lausanne Peace Conference in Switzerland, where world leaders were gathering in order to move forward after the devastation of World War I. "Mussolini, Europe's Prize Bluffer" describes Hemingway's second interview with the Fascist dictator, and already reveals the author's strong antifascist sentiments. Hemingway reports how Mussolini, his face now contorted into the famous frown, pretended to read intently a French-English dictionary held upside down! In "War Medals for Sale," one of the last pieces that Hemingway wrote for *The Toronto Star,* he returns to the theme of the veteran soldier, who is here reduced to selling his war medals in peacetime to make ends meet. Is it possible to put a price on valor during times of peace?

In September and October of 1922, Hemingway traveled to Constantinople to report on the Greco-Turkish War, which was coming to a head. Hemingway's less-known coverage of this deep-rooted conflict between Christian and Muslim countries powerfully portrays its climactic moments, when Greece backed down and was forced to move out of Turkey. The tension surrounding the impending invasion of Constantinople is palpable in "Waiting for an Orgy." "A Silent, Ghastly Procession" follows the thousands of Thracian refugees in their somber march along the road to Adrianople—twenty miles of carts, animals, and babies being born, all in freezing rain. The flight of the Thracian refugees would provide material for his later descriptive account of the retreat of the Italians at Caporetto in *A Farewell to Arms.* Hemingway gives an insightful portrayal of Mustafa Kemal, the conquering Turkish general who had raised support for his cause in the name of jihad, a holy war against Christianity, but became a more moderate, businesslike leader upon victory. Kemal became Atatürk, the revered father of modern Turkey.

Hemingway's perceptive article "Afghans: Trouble for Britain" has astonishing parallels in light of the current political situation in Afghanistan, with the American bombing of al-Qaeda sites in retaliation for the terrorist attacks on New York and Washington of September 11, 2001. "Kemal's One Submarine" reports on Allied naval activities in which British destroyers, on the side of the Greeks, cruised the Black Sea in pursuit of a single Turkish submarine provided by Soviet Russia. The Greco-Turkish War stemmed from long-standing disputes partially shrouded in the mists of time. As Hemingway put it, the Greeks lost their second siege of Troy. At the same time, it was fundamentally a war, like so many others, fought over land claimed by two different nations.

Hemingway had a deep appreciation for the Spanish people, having visited Spain many times when he lived in Europe. Spain was the setting of his first novel, *The Sun Also Rises*, and of *Death in the Afternoon*, his treatise on bullfighting, a sport that he followed passionately. So when General Francisco Franco led a revolt of fascists in the Spanish army against the government in July 1936 and the Spanish Civil War began, it was not long before Hemingway agreed to cover the conflict as a correspondent for the North American Newspaper Alliance (NANA). Over the course of the war, Hemingway filed some twenty dispatches for NANA, and wrote and narrated a documentary entitled *The Spanish Earth*. The film, directed by Joris Ivens, was produced in order to raise funds for the Loyalist cause. During this time, Hemingway wrote some of his best fiction about war, including the novel *For Whom the Bell Tolls*, his only full-length play, *The Fifth Column*, and several short stories.

Hemingway has been, I believe, fairly criticized for not portraying an unbiased representation of the Spanish Civil War as a war correspondent, siding as he did so strongly with the Republic against the Nationalists.[9] However, his Spanish dispatches do include fine portrayals of modern warfare, as "A New Kind of War" and "The Chauffeurs of Madrid" attest. These dispatches were written in a new style of reporting that told the public about every facet of the war, especially, and most important, its effects on the common man, woman, and child.[10] Nonetheless, it is the duty of a war correspondent to present both sides in his writing, and Hemingway failed to do this in many of his dispatches. This is most evident in the articles Hemingway did for *Ken* magazine, of which "Dying, Well or Badly" and "A Program for U.S. Realism" are included in this volume. The original "Dying, Well or Badly" was accompanied by extremely graphic images that my uncle, Patrick Hemingway, remembers well and which made an especially strong impression on his father as evidence of the horrors of war. I believe that Hemingway's frank descriptions of the dead sustain the narrative power, especially in light of today's graphically violent imagery. When the Spanish Loyalists lost the war with the Battle of the Ebro in 1938, it was a terrible defeat for

Hemingway. Reflecting on the war, he later wrote, "There is no man alive today who has not cried at a war if he was at it long enough. Sometimes it is after a battle, sometimes it is when someone that you love is killed, sometimes it is from a great injustice to another, sometimes it is at the disbanding of a corps or a unit that has endured and accomplished together and now will never be together again. But all men at war cry sometimes, from Napoleon, the greatest butcher, down."[11]

Hemingway did not believe that being a journalist was as important as writing fiction. In fact, he believed that a writer had only so much creative "juice" and that, after a certain point early in one's career, one should not waste one's talent writing journalism when one could be writing fiction instead. In his own words, "A writer's job is to tell the truth. His standard of fidelity to the truth should be so high that his invention, out of his experience, should produce a truer account than anything factual can be. For facts can be observed badly; but when a good writer is creating something, he has time and scope to make it of an absolute truth."[12] So in early 1941, when Martha Gellhorn, his third wife, wanted Hemingway to go with her to the Orient to report on the Chinese army and its defenses against the Japanese, he was, she later wrote, her "unwilling companion."[13] Still, Hemingway recognized the potential importance of contemporary unrest in the East. As the two selections from *Esquire* magazine show, he closely followed world politics and had predicted another major world war as early as 1935. The Sino-Japanese War had been going on for several years, but the Japanese had now joined Germany and Italy in the Axis powers, and it seemed likely that Japan would start destroying the East, just as its partners were destroying the West, which could easily lead to war with the United States.

Ernest and Martha set out for Hong Kong via Hawaii in January 1941, and spent a month in Hong Kong, where Hemingway interviewed the Japanese as well as the Chinese. From Hong Kong, they traveled to Shaikwan, in mainland China, the headquarters of the 7th War Zone. For a month, they stayed on the front lines and Hemingway immersed himself in studying the organization of the Chinese war zone from its commanders down to its frontline troops. They did not see any action in the combat zone, but were buzzed by a squadron of Japanese fighter planes on one occasion. Later they traveled through various parts of China, seeing the country as well as inspecting the Chinese military system. In Chungking, they met with Generalissimo Chiang Kaishek and his wife, Madame Chiang. Included in this volume is just one of the articles that Hemingway wrote for *PM* magazine shortly after returning from China in May 1941. "Russo-Japanese Pact" gives a sense of the tenuous but significant nature of alliances in war as well as the contempt that allies can feel for each other. Hemingway brilliantly sums up the situation with his story about a British officer who wears a monocle so that he will not see more than he can understand.

In March 1942, Hemingway agreed to edit and write an introduction for *Men at War,* to be published later that year. The book, a masterful compendium on war, is organized in true Hemingway style and remains a significant reference work. Hemingway dedicated *Men at War* to his three sons, John, Patrick, and Gregory, in the hopes that the cumulative experiences from the accounts within would enable them to understand the "truth about war as near as we can come by it." He also noted, however, that "It will not replace experience."[14] Quotes from Hemingway's introduction are interspersed throughout this book.

That same year, Hemingway volunteered to help with the war effort in Cuba by organizing a private spy network to gather information about Nazi sympathizers on the island. The group was code-named the Crook Factory. This venture into espionage led to one of Hemingway's most unusual military exploits—hunting German submarines in the Caribbean. Hemingway convinced the American ambassador to Cuba that his forty-foot fishing boat, the *Pilar,* could be converted into a sub destroyer and that she could easily sink one of the German submarines that were preying on Allied ships in the Straits of Florida. The following summer, in 1943, when my father was twelve and my uncle Patrick was turning fifteen, my father remembered joining Papa on the *Pilar,* which was armed to the teeth: "Two men were stationed in the bow with submachine guns and two in the stern with BARs and hand grenades. Papa steered on the bow and up there with him was 'The Bomb,' a huge explosive device, shaped like a coffin, with handles on each end. The idea was to maneuver the *Pilar* next to a sub—how exactly was not clear—whereupon a pair of over-the-hill jai alai players with more guts than brains would heave 'The Bomb' into the open hatch of the conning tower. And then 'The Bomb' would presumably blow the submarine to kingdom come." Papa was reluctant to take the boys along on sub patrols, but on their way down to Cayo Confites, their base island, my father recalled seeing a whale shark, the largest fish in the sea, sixty feet long, with black and white polka dots on its dorsal side. Since the giant fish was just basking on the surface, and appeared docile and harmless, they pulled up alongside it. The first mate, Gregorio Fuentes, poked it in the side with an oar to see if he could make it move. As my father remembered it, it was like poking the side of a building. "Christ," Gregorio said, "that thing is enormous." "Yes," Papa replied, "almost a third of the size of the sub we are looking for."[15] There certainly were German submarines running throughout the Caribbean and even along the coast of North America at this time. Although Hemingway never closed on one, he did report useful intelligence on U-boat movements.[16]

By the fall of 1943, Hemingway, again at the instigation of his wife, Martha Gellhorn, began to think about covering the war in Europe as a correspondent. In spring of the following year, he signed on with *Collier's* magazine and flew to London. While living at the Dorchester Hotel, he met and began an amorous liaison with his future wife, my godmother, Mary Welsh, who was, at that time, a correspondent for *Time* magazine. Despite suffering a concussion from a car crash after a party given by the photographer Robert Capa, Hemingway flew on reconnaissance missions with the Royal Air Force. Over the course of ten months, he would witness the relentless German bombing of London, the D-day landing at Normandy, the liberation of Paris, and the final breaking of the Siegfried Line by the Allied infantry and their movement into Germany. The three dispatches from this time included in this volume vividly depict pivotal events in the war. "Voyage to Victory" powerfully recalls the D-day landing at Normandy on June 6, 1944. As a civilian correspondent and something of a national treasure, Hemingway was not allowed to land with the infantry at Normandy; nonetheless, he captures the extreme conditions and heroic measures undertaken by the soldiers in order to secure the beaches on that gray, windy day.

While in France, Hemingway joined up with the 22nd regiment of the First Army's 4th Infantry Division, the famous "Ivy Leaf." There he became fast friends with the regimental commander, Colonel "Buck" Lanham. A second concussion left Hemingway recuperating in Mont-Saint-Michel, separated from the division for a couple of days. It was shortly after this that Hemingway made his way to Rambouillet, outside of Paris, and together with a group of French partisans, his so-called irregulars, he gathered intelligence about enemy defenses around the capital city. In a controversial decision, Hemingway, with written military authorization, put aside his correspondent's duties and took up arms for the cause.[17] The article "How We Came to Paris" describes this period and Hemingway's emotional return to the city he loved best in all the world.

When I was a boy, the artist John Groth told me stories of meeting Hemingway during the war while Groth was gathering material for his book of war sketches, *Studio Europe*. Groth, Hemingway, Buck Lanham, and some other soldiers were all having dinner together at Lanham's command post when a German 88 shell landed near the house, spraying plaster and shattering glass all over the dining room. Everyone at the table made a dive for cover—except Ernest. Sitting calmly at the table, he continued eating cheese and drinking wine. Amazed, Groth asked afterwards, "How could you just sit there?" To which Ernest replied, "Groth, if you hit the deck every time you hear a pop, you'll wind up with chronic indigestion." This became a famous wartime anecdote.[18] For Hemingway, the war climaxed at the brutal Battle of Hürtgenwald and the taking of the heavily fortified Siegfried Line. "War in the Siegfried Line," the last article in this volume, describes the final days of that long engagement in the last months of 1944.

Hemingway was back in Cuba at the Finca Vigía, his farmhouse just outside San Francisco de Paula, when World War II finally came to an end with the dropping of the atomic bombs on Hiroshima and Nagasaki. He wrote down his thoughts on the advent of atomic warfare, which were published as the foreword to a book entitled *Treasury for the Free World:*

> We have waged war in the most ferocious and ruthless way that it has ever been waged. We waged it against fierce and ruthless enemies that it was necessary to destroy. Now we have destroyed one of our enemies and forced the capitulation of the other. For the moment we are the strongest power in the world. It is very important that we do not become the most hated. . . . We need to study and understand certain basic problems of our world as they were before Hiroshima to be able to continue, intelligently, to discover how some of them have changed and how they can be settled justly now that a new weapon has become a property of part of the world. We must study them more carefully than ever now and remember that no weapon has ever settled a moral problem. It can impose a solution but it cannot guarantee it to be a just one. . . . An aggressive war is the great crime against everything good in the world. A defensive war, which must necessarily turn to aggressive at the earliest moment, is the necessary great counter-crime. But never think that war, no matter how necessary, nor how justified, is not a crime. Ask the infantry and the dead.

When Ernest Hemingway returned from World War II he was arguably the most famous writer in the world. In 1947, he was awarded the U.S. Bronze Star for his meritorious service as a war correspondent during 1944 in France and Germany. The medal citation stated that "he displayed a broad familiarity with modern military science, interpreting and evaluating the campaigns and operations of friendly and enemy forces, circulating freely under fire in combat areas in order to obtain an accurate picture of conditions. Through his talent of expression, Mr. Hemingway enabled readers to obtain a vivid picture of the difficulties and triumphs of the front-line soldier and his organization in combat."[19] Hemingway's public now expected him to write a novel about World War II that would be bigger in every way than *For Whom the Bell Tolls.* However, it was not until 1950 that he completed his next novel, *Across the River and Into the Trees,* a bittersweet love story set in Venice about an American colonel in the twilight of his life. Although the book has many telling recollections of World War II, many of which are included in this volume, *Across the River and Into the Trees* was a critical failure. It took the writing of his subsequent novella, *The Old Man and the Sea,* and his receipt of the Nobel Prize in Literature in 1954 to regain his "title."

Hemingway would not go to war again but it came to him. The revolution in Cuba in 1959 and the American Cold War diplomacy that ensued forced him to leave the island and his home of twenty-some years. Ernest, however, believed he would return to the Finca Vigía someday. Still, when one visits the house, as my wife and I did recently, there is a strong feeling of the man and his home, a good place where he could write. In many ways, Hemingway was a casualty of that last war—he retreated to Idaho, where he took up residence in a bunkerlike home, a concrete fortress perched on a hill on the outskirts of Ketchum. This is the place where he took his life only two years later after battling depression and the onset of old age, after a lifetime of physical excess, and the fear of not being able to write. To this day the house emits an aura of sadness. It is the final chapter of one extraordinary man's extraordinary life.

The lion's share of this book is devoted to selections of Ernest Hemingway's fiction writings, the medium that counted most to him. Included among these are some of the best writings on the subject of war in the twentieth century. The material is presented roughly chronologically and primarily according to the different wars that Hemingway wrote about: World War I, the Spanish Civil War, and World War II. There are many more short stories and even other novels written by Hemingway that touch on the subject of war. For those interested in reading more, a bibliography of relevant works has been included at the end of this book.

The title of the first section, "May There Be Peace in Our Time," is taken from the Book of Common Prayer, the source for the title of Hemingway's first book of short stories, *In Our Time,* which was published in New York in 1925. The selection of writings begins with a very early and undistinguished short story, "The Mercenaries," that was not published in Hemingway's lifetime and only appeared in *The New York Times Magazine* in 1985. It was written in 1919, shortly after Hemingway returned from the war, and when you compare it with the other stories in this volume, you can see how quickly Hemingway developed his talent for writing.[20] "On the Quai at Smyrna" was also not written from personal experience but it, nonetheless, evokes a strong sense of the Greek retreat through Smyrna at the end of the Greco-Turkish War. Hemingway added this story to the second edition of *In Our Time*, intending it to be a kind of author's introduction to the book. The horrors of the war, mothers clinging to their dead babies and the graphic description of mules being maimed and left to die in the water by the dock, present realities that contrast so markedly with the notion of peace offered in the title of the book.

"A Very Short Story" describes a soldier who falls in love with his nurse while recovering from a battle wound in Italy and is jilted afterwards. The story contains many elements of Hemingway's own love affair with Agnes von Kurowsky during World War I and makes for an interesting comparison to the novel *A Farewell to Arms*. "Soldier's Home" is the troubling story of a young veteran of World War I who has returned home safely and the difficulties that he faces reassimilating to civilian life. In "The Revolutionist," a Hungarian Communist wanders through Italy after having been tortured in and exiled from his own country for his beliefs. The young revolutionist, a lover of art and nature, believes almost religiously in his "world revolution," only to end up in a prison in Switzerland.

In Our Time interspersed the vignettes between short stories. Hemingway wrote to Edmund Wilson that the effect was meant "to give the picture of the whole between examining it in detail. Like looking with your eyes at something, say a passing coastline, and then looking at it with 15X binoculars. Or rather, maybe, looking at it and then going in and living in it—and then coming out and looking at it again."[21] When Nick Adams, the narrator, after having been injured in the spine, turns to the Italian soldier Rinaldi and says, "You and me, we've made a separate peace," he is stating that he is psychologically, as well as physically, ready to stop fighting, and is expressing the disillusionment that can come with being wounded in war.

In some ways, the pieces from *In Our Time* could have been grouped with the later stories in the second section of this collection, as they predominantly relate to World War I and its aftermath. "In Another Country" opens with one of the most powerful sentences ever to begin a war story: "In the fall the war was always there, but we did not go to it any more." Hemingway returns to the theme of the wounded soldier and the hardships and uncertainties of rehabilitation. "Now I Lay Me" presents another aspect of surviving battle, difficulty sleeping at night with the memory of a near-death experience. It is sometimes hard to appreciate today how revolutionary the author's now famous writing style was in those early years. In a highly critical review of *Men Without Women*, his book of short stories that included "In Another Country" and "Now I Lay Me," as well as other notable works such as "The Killers," Virginia Woolf compared Hemingway's laconic writing style to "winter days when the boughs are bare against the sky."[22] Hemingway described his philosophy of writing years later in an interview with George Plimpton: "I always try to write on the principle of the iceberg. There is seven-eighths of it underwater for every part that shows. Anything you know you can eliminate and it only strengthens your iceberg. It is the part that doesn't show. If a writer omits something because he does not know it then there is a hole in the story."[23]

"A Natural History of the Dead" is an unusual experimental story that depicts the dead on a battlefield as a naturalist objectively describes a plant or animal. This gruesome yet tongue-in-cheek portrayal is contrasted with a moving and incredibly perceptive tale of a dispute between a doctor and an artillery officer over the humane treatment in the midst of war of a badly wounded soldier on the verge of death. In "A Way You'll Never Be," Nick Adams is a shell-shocked soldier who has been severely wounded and is supposed to be building morale among the Italian troops by wearing his American uniform.

Along with Erich Maria Remarque's *All Quiet on the Western Front* and the account of the British "Private 19022" (Frederic Manning), *Her Privates We*, Hemingway's *A Farewell to Arms*, first published in 1929, is among the best novels ever written about World War I. It is the story of an American, Frederic Henry, who has volunteered as a lieutenant in the Italian army in 1918. Wounded in the line of duty while, ironically, doing nothing more than eating cheese, Henry recuperates in a hospital in Milan, where he falls in love with his English nurse, Catherine Barkley. He eventually returns to duty and participates in the retreat at Caporetto, one of the major defeats for the Italian army in northern Italy during the war. After abandoning his broken-down vehicle and realizing that he may be shot as a deserter or a suspected Austrian infiltrator because of his foreign accent, Frederic Henry meets Catherine at Lake Maggiore and flees to Switzerland with her. Just three passages from *A Farewell to Arms* are included in this volume; anyone who enjoys these should read the book in its entirety. "Self-Inflicted Wounds," an early episode from the novel, tells of Frederic meeting a wandering Italian-American soldier who has ruptured an old injury in order to avoid combat. Sympathetic to his cause, Frederic advises the soldier to bump his head as well, assuring him that he will take him to the hospital when he returns this way. Upon Frederic's return, however, he finds that the soldier, with a dusty and bleeding head, is being hauled back to the front by his unit, which remains unconvinced by the soldier's false red badge of courage.

"At the Front" sets the stage for "The Retreat from Caporetto" and contains strong words about the glory of war: "I was always embarrassed by the words sacred, glorious, and sacrifice and the expression in vain. We had heard them, sometimes standing in the rain almost out of earshot, so that only the shouted words came through, and had read them, on proclamations that were slapped up by billposters over other proclamations, now for a long time, and I had seen nothing sacred, and the things that were glorious had no glory and the sacrifices were like the stockyards at Chicago if nothing was done with the meat except to bury it. There were many words that you could not stand to hear and finally only the names of places had dignity." In a very careful analysis, Michael Reynolds has shown that Hemingway did considerable research to describe the conditions at the front and provides a historically accurate account of the sequence of events leading up to the retreat.[24] Likewise, in "The Retreat from Caporetto" Hemingway goes way beyond his correspondent's treatment of the Greek retreat of 1922 by including a range of precise topographical and meteorological details.

To give an example of Hemingway's "iceberg philosophy" masterfully executed in *A Farewell to Arms*, Frederic Henry sees a German staff car heading into the city of Udine during the retreat. This car can be identified historically as carrying General von Berrer, commander of the German Alpenkorps, who was killed by the Italian rear guard (the same rear guard that shoots Frederic's companion Aymo) in his staff car as he entered Udine on October 27, 1918. Although the general is never named in *A Farewell to Arms*, Hemingway singles him out in the short story "A Natural History of the Dead."[25] When you have read "The Retreat from Caporetto" you will know a part of World War I and what it was like to have been there.

The selection "Immortal Youth" from *Across the River and Into the Trees* provides an interesting contrast to the passages from *A Farewell to Arms*, looking back as it does on the war in northern Italy many years later. It is a moving recollection by the protagonist of the novel, Colonel Richard Cantwell, who reflects on being seriously wounded during World War I and his first true understanding as a young man that he could and would eventually die. As Hemingway wrote in *A Farewell to Arms:* "If people bring so much courage to this world the world has to kill them to break them, so of course it kills them. The world breaks everyone and afterward many are strong at the broken places. But those that will not break it kills. It kills the very good and the very gentle and the very brave impartially. If you are none of these you can be sure it will kill you too but there will be no special hurry."

Hemingway wrote some of his best war stories during the years of the Spanish Civil War. When "The Butterfly and the Tank" was first published in *Esquire* magazine in 1938, John Steinbeck called it "one of the very few finest stories of all time."[26] Based on an actual incident at Chicote's Bar, Madrid, in the fall of 1937, it is the story of a tragic misunderstanding that leads to the senseless killing of a man. His only crime is to try to bring some levity to the oppressive atmosphere that pervades everyone's lives in the midst of prolonged war. In "Night Before Battle," a tank commander, who knows his orders for battle the coming morning and that the odds of victory are slim, has a feeling that he is going to die "tomorrow." The play *The Fifth Column* presents an entirely different aspect of war: espionage, the systematic use of spies by a government to discover military and political secrets. The title takes its name from the fascist sympathizers in Madrid who were prepared to betray the city, under attack by four columns of the insurgents' army. These spies within the city were considered an invisible fifth column of the army working from within. The protagonist of the play, Philip Rawlings, is an undercover agent working against this fifth column.

By all accounts, *For Whom the Bell Tolls* is Hemingway's masterpiece of the Spanish Civil War. Hemingway achieves a synoptic view of the war and its protagonists in this novel about Robert Jordan, a young American in the International Brigades attached to an antifascist guerrilla unit in the mountains. It is a story of loyalty and courage, love and defeat, and the tragic death of an ideal. Four passages from *For Whom the Bell Tolls* are included in this collection. "Flying Death Machines" is a brief but poignant account of the fascists' Heinkel fighter planes, "wide-finned in silver, roaring, the light mist of their propellers in the sun," which brought strategic warfare into the third dimension. Indeed, the innovative use of the fighter plane by the Germans in Spain as close support for infantry operations was devastatingly effective and served as a proving ground for their World War II tactics.[27] Hemingway wrote to his Russian colleague Ivan Kashkin, "In stories about the war I try to show all the different sides of it, taking it slowly and honestly and examining it from many ways. So never think one story represents my viewpoint because it is much too complicated for that."[28] "Small Town Revolution" is a piercing and frank account of the Loyalist takeover of a small provincial town in Spain. It reveals in incredible detail the brutalities of war and the horrific executions of Nationalist sympathizers by Loyalists.

For Whom the Bell Tolls is so accurate in its details that it might even be used as a textbook on guerrilla warfare. I was in Cuba recently, attending a ceremony to inaugurate a joint American-Cuban project to preserve the remaining papers of Ernest Hemingway at the Finca, and had the rare and fortunate opportunity to spend the day with President Fidel Castro. Castro told me that he had read For Whom the Bell Tolls several times and had committed parts of it to memory. Having had no formal military training, Castro considered it a kind of manual and had learned from it guerrilla tactics that he put to use during the Cuban revolution of 1959. "Guerrilla Warfare," which describes the placement and making of a machine gun blind in the mountains, is one of the passages that Castro specifically recalled as having been instructional for him. "El Sordo's Last Stand," which Hemingway dubbed "The Fight on the Hilltop" when he included it in Men at War, is equally riveting and, as a counterpart to "Small Town Revolution," displays the brutality of the fascists who cut off the heads of Sordo and his band as trophies after their battle.

The last section of fiction in this collection features works relating to World War II, specifically the Allied invasion of 1944. "Black Ass at the Cross Roads," a short story published posthumously, was written sometime between the end of World War II and 1961. The phrase "black ass" is one that Hemingway used for depression, a clinical disease that he himself suffered from at the end of his life. The story is a dark reflection on combat duty by a depressed American soldier who fatally wounds a young German soldier and watches him die.

Across the River and Into the Trees is Hemingway's last major war novel. I believe its critical failure is due in large part to his extremely realistic portrayal of two people in love and the monotonous dialogue that lovers often slip into, filled with the same frequent terms of endearment. Nonetheless, the novel contains remarkable passages on warfare that were written when Hemingway was at the pinnacle of his military expertise. The protagonist, Colonel Cantwell, is partially based on Ernest's old friend and career soldier "Chink" Dorman-Smith, and on Hemingway himself. Cantwell is a cantankerous but distinguished old colonel with a keen mind who likes his martinis dry. He calls them "Montgomerys" because the proportion of gin to vermouth should be fifteen or twenty to one, like the odds, he says, that the British General

Montgomery required to go to battle. "The Taking of Paris" and "The Valhalla Express" offer glimpses of World War II through the eyes of Colonel Cantwell. "Pistol-Slappers" are military officers who enjoy the power of command, but never engage in battle themselves. The image of an officer who does not use his pistol but gets sexual pleasure from feeling it against his thigh is a sharp contrast to the scene during the retreat from Caporetto in *A Farewell to Arms* when Frederic Henry draws and shoots his pistol at two sergeants who desert their posts, killing one of them. A comparison between the necessity of following orders in the army and the need to obey the female in a relationship is played out in "The Chain of Command." In "The Ivy Leaf," the nickname of the U.S. Army's 4th Infantry Division, to which Cantwell (and Hemingway) belonged, Hemingway portrays the deep camaraderie among soldiers, while in "The Dead" he offers a final reflection on the commonplace of death in wars and the difficulty of living with the memory of horrors impossible to communicate to others.

The culminating passage of fiction in this collection is taken from Hemingway's posthumous novel *Islands in the Stream*, which follows the fortunes of Thomas Hudson from his experiences as a painter on Bimini through his antisubmarine activities off the coast of Cuba during World War II. "Losing Your Son to War" describes one of the most painful experiences a parent can have. Hemingway's first son, my uncle Jack, parachuted into Nazi-occupied France as part of the Allied invasion of 1944 and was lost behind enemy lines. Ernest had plenty of time to contemplate Jack's death before it was reported that his son was, in fact, still alive and being held in a prisoner-of-war camp. *Islands in the Stream* presents a much darker, more difficult outcome faced by families across the globe in times of war.

As I write this Introduction, American troops are fighting in Iraq and war again haunts us. It seems impossible that the destruction and devastation of lives could be forgotten: the awful contrasts between peace and war in Hemingway's first book, *In Our Time*, are as relevant today as they were shockingly modern in 1925. Yet as Hemingway once correctly observed, even soldiers "as they get further and further away from a war they have taken part in have the tendency to make it more as they wish it had been rather than how it really was."[29]

Seán Hemingway
Brooklyn, New York
April 2003

Notes

1. Hemingway used this quote as the title of the first chapter division of his war anthology, *Men at War.*
2. Arrian, *Anabasis of Alexander* 7.26.3.
3. Ralph Ingersoll, "Hemingway Interviewed by Ralph Ingersoll," *PM,* June 9, 1941, reprinted in *By-Line: Ernest Hemingway* (New York: Scribner, 1967), p. 304.
4. Carlos Baker, *Ernest Hemingway: A Life Story* (New York: Scribner, 1969), p. 98.
5. Carlos Baker, *supra,* p. 36, n. 4. Copyright © 1969. Printed with permission of the Ernest Hemingway Foundation.
6. James Nagel, "Hemingway and the Italian Legacy," in Henry S. Villard and James Nagel, *Hemingway in Love and War: The Lost Diary of Agnes von Kurowsky* (Boston: Northeastern University Press, 1989), p. 202.
7. Carlos Baker, *supra,* pp. 44–45, n. 4.
8. "Has 227 Wounds, but Is Looking for a Job," *New York Sun,* January 22, 1919, p. 8. It has been shown that, in fact, at least one other American working for the Red Cross was killed at the Italian front before Hemingway was wounded. See Villard and Nagel, *supra,* pp. 22–23, n. 6.
9. See, for example, Philip Knightly, *The First Casualty: From the Crimea to Vietnam: The War Correspondent as Hero, Propagandist, and Myth Maker* (New York and London: Harcourt Brace Jovanovich, 1975), pp. 212–14.
10. Richard Holmes, ed., *The Oxford Companion to Military History* (Oxford and New York: Oxford University Press, 2001), p. 973.
11. Ernest Hemingway, preface to Gustav Regler, *The Great Crusade* (New York and Toronto: Longmans, Green, 1940).
12. Ernest Hemingway, ed., *Men at War* (first published 1942; Bramhall House edition, New York, 1979), p. xiv.
13. Martha Gellhorn, *Travels with Myself and Another* (first published 1978 by Eland; Putnam, 2001), p. 10. Chapter two, "Mr. Ma's Tigers," is an account of their trip to Hong Kong and China.
14. Ernest Hemingway, *supra,* p. xxiii, n. 12.
15. Gregory H. Hemingway, *Papa: A Personal Memoir* (Boston: Houghton Mifflin, 1976), pp. 70–74.
16. Leicester Hemingway describes one near encounter in his book, *My Brother, Ernest Hemingway* (Cleveland: World Publishing Co., 1962), pp. 208–10. The day log of the *Pilar* for 1942, given to the National Archives by Mary Hemingway, and accessible at the Hemingway Room of the Kennedy Library in Boston, also makes clear that contact was not common, but Hemingway keeps detailed records of the territory that he covered and occasionally makes reference to military sightings. See also Jeffrey Meyers, *Hemingway: A Biography* (New York: Da Capo Press, 1999), chapter 18, especially p. 388.
17. A note authorizing Hemingway to requisition small arms and grenades is preserved in the Hemingway Collection at the Kennedy Library in Boston. An official U.S. Army investigation two months later cleared Hemingway of charges of carrying arms that had been made against him. For a transcript of the inquiry, see Robert W. Trogdon, *Ernest Hemingway: A Literary Reference* (New York: Carroll and Graf, 1999), pp. 256–61.
18. This story was widely publicized at the time, as WWII veterans have told me, and

has appeared in many places. See, for example, Carlos Baker, *supra*, p. 427, n. 4; A. E. Hotchner, *Hemingway and His World: An Illustrated Biography* (New York: Viking, 1989), p. 9.

19. Carlos Baker, *supra*, pp. 461–62, n. 4.
20. Peter Griffin, *Along with Youth: Hemingway, the Early Years* (Oxford and New York: Oxford University Press, 1985), p. 104.
21. Ernest Hemingway to Edmund Wilson, Paris, October 18, 1924. Carlos Baker, ed., *Ernest Hemingway, Selected Letters, 1917–1961* (New York: Scribner, 1981), p. 128.
22. Virginia Woolf, "An Essay in Criticism," *New York Herald Tribune Books*, October 9, 1927, pp. 1, 8.
23. "The Art of Fiction XXI: Ernest Hemingway," *Paris Review* 18 (1950), p. 84.
24. Michael Reynolds, *Hemingway's First War: The Making of A Farewell to Arms* (Princeton, N.J.: Princeton University Press, 1976), especially pp. 87–104.
25. Michael Reynolds, *supra*, pp. 121–23, n. 24. Hemingway spells the general's name Behr.
26. Carlos Baker, *supra*, p. 337, n. 4.
27. Major General J. F. C. Fuller, *Machine Warfare* (Washington, D.C.: Infantry Journal, 1943), p. 41.
28. Ernest Hemingway to Ivan Kashkin, Key West, March 23, 1939. Carlos Baker, *supra*, p. 480, n. 21. Copyright © 1981. Printed with permission of the Ernest Hemingway Foundation.
29. Ernest Hemingway, *supra*, pp. xiv–xv, n. 12.

WORKS OF
FICTION

I

May There Be Peace in Our Time

"You and me, we've made a separate peace."
—From *In Our Time*

"I have seen much war in my lifetime and I hate it profoundly."
—From *Men at War*

The Mercenaries

If you are honestly curious about pearl fishing conditions in the Marquesas, the possibility of employment on the projected Trans Gobi Desert Railway, or the potentialities of any of the hot tamale republics, go to the Cafe Cambrinus on Wabash Avenue, Chicago. There at the rear of the dining room where the neo-bohemians struggle nightly with their spaghetti and ravioli is a small smoke-filled room that is a clearinghouse for the camp followers of fortune. When you enter the room, and you will have no more chance than the zoological entrant in the famous camel-needle's eye gymkana of entering the room unless you are approved by Cambrinus, there will be a sudden silence. Then a varying number of eyes will look you over with that detached intensity that comes of a periodic contemplation of death. This inspection is not mere boorishness. If you're recognized favourably, all right; if you are unknown, all right; Cambrinus has passed on you. After a time the talk picks up again. But one time the door was pushed open, men looked up, glances of recognition shot across the room, a man half rose from one of the card tables, his hand behind him, two men ducked to the floor, there was a roar from the doorway, and what had had its genesis in the Malay Archipelago terminated in the back room of the Cambrinus. But that's not this.

I came out of the wind scoured nakedness of Wabash Avenue in January into the cosy bar of the Cambrinus and, armed with a smile from Cambrinus himself, passed through the dining room where the waiters were clearing away the debris of the table d'hotes and sweeping out into the little back room. The two men I had seen in the café before were seated at one of the three tables with half empty bottles of an unlabeled beverage known to the initiates as "Kentucky Brew" before them. They nodded and I joined them.

"Smoke?" asked the taller of the two, a gaunt man with a face the color of half-tanned leather, shoving a package of cheap cigarettes across the table.

"It is possible the gentleman would prefer one of these," smiled the other with a flash of white teeth under a carefully pointed mustache, and

5

pushed a monogrammed cigarette box across to me with a small, well-manicured hand.

"Shouldn't wonder," grunted the big man, his adam's apple rising and falling above his flannel shirt collar. "Can't taste em myself." He took one of his own cigarettes and rolled the end between thumb and forefinger until a tiny mound of tobacco piled up on the table before him, then carefully picked up the stringy wad and tucked it under his tongue, lighting the half-cigarette that remained.

"It is droll, that manner of smoking a cigarette, is it not?" smiled the dark little man as he held a match for me. I noted a crossed-cannon monogram on his box as I handed it back to him.

"Artigliere français?" I questioned.

"Mais oui, Monsieur; le soixante-quinze!" he smiled again, his whole face lighting up.

"Say," broke in the gaunt man, eyeing me thoughtfully; "Artill'ry ain't your trade, is it?"

"No, takes too much brains," I said.

"That's too darn bad. It don't," the leather-faced man replied to my answer and observation.

"Why?" said I.

"There's a good job now." He rolled the tobacco under his tongue and drew a deep inhalation on his cigarette butt. "For gunners. Peru verstus and against Chile. Two hundred dollars a month—"

"In gold," smiled the Frenchman, twisting his mustache.

"In gold," continued the leather-face. "We got the dope from Cambrinus. Artillery officers they want. We saw the consul. He's fat and important and oily. 'War with Chile? Reediculous!' he says. I talked spiggotty to him for awhile and we come to terms. Napoleon here—"

The Frenchman bowed, "Lieutenant Denis Ricaud."

"Napoleon here—," continued leather-face unmoved, "and me are officers in the Royal Republican Peruvian Army with tickets to New York." He tapped his coat pocket. "There we see the Peruvian consul and present papers," he tapped his pocket again, "and are shipped to Peru via way of the Isthmus. Let's have a drink."

He pushed the button under the table and Antonio the squat Sardinian waiter poked his head in the door.

"If you haven't had one, perhaps you'd try a cognac-benedictine?" asked the leather-faced man. I nodded, thinking. "Tre martell-benedictine, Nino. It's all right with Cambrinus."

Antonino nodded and vanished. Ricaud flashed his smile at me, "And you will hear people denounce the absinthe as an evil beverage!"

6

I was puzzling over the drink leather-face had ordered, for there is only one place in the world where people drink that smooth, insidious, brain-rotting mixture. And I was still puzzling when Antonino returned with the drinks, not in liqueur glasses, but in big full cock-tail containers.

"These are mine altogether in toto," said the leather-face, pulling out a roll of bills. "Me and Napoleon are now being emolumated at the rate of two hundred dollars per month—"

"Gold!" smiled Ricaud.

"Gold!" calmly finished leather-face. "Say, my name is Graves, Perry Graves." He looked across the table at me.

"Mine's Rinaldi, Rinaldi Renaldo," I said.

"Wop?" asked Graves, lifting his eyebrows and his adam's apple simultaneously.

"Grandfather was Italian," I replied.

"Wop, eh," said Graves unhearingly, then lifted his glass. "Napoleon, and you, Signor Resolvo, I'd like to propose a toast. You say 'A bas Chile!' Napoleon. You say 'Delenda Chile!' Risotto. I drink 'To Hell with Chile!'" We all sipped our glasses.

"Down with Chile," said Graves meditatively, then in an argumentative tone, "They're not a bad lot, those Chillies!"

"Ever been there?" I asked.

"Nope," said Graves, "a rotten bad lot those dirty Chillies."

"Capitain Graves is a propagandiste to himself," smiled Ricaud, and lit a cigarette.

"We'll rally round the doughnut. The Peruvian doughnut," mused Graves, disembowelling another cigarette. "Follow the doughnut, my boys, my brave boys. Vive la doughnut. Up with the Peruvian doughnut and down with the chile concarne. A dirty rotten lot those Chillies!"

"What is the doughnut, mon cher Graves?" asked Ricaud, puzzled.

"Make the world safe for the doughnut, the grand old Peruvian doughnut. Don't give up the doughnut. Remember the doughnut. Peru expects every doughnut to do his duty," Graves was chanting in a monotone. "Wrap me in the doughnut, my brave boys. No, it doesn't sound right. It ain't got something a slogum ought to have. But those Chillies are a rotten lot!"

"The Capitain is très patriotic, n'est-ce pas? The doughnut is the national symbol of Peru, I take it?" asked Ricaud.

"Never been there. But we'll show those dirty Chillies they can't trample on the grand old Peruvian doughnut though, Napoleon!" said Graves, fiercely banging his fist on the table.

"Really, we should know more of the country at whose disposal we have placed our swords," murmured Ricaud, apologetically. "What I wonder is the flag of Peru?"

"Can't use the sword myself," said Graves dourly, raising his glass. "That reminds me of something. Say, you ever been to Italy?"

"Three years," I replied.

"During the war?" Graves shot a look at me.

"Durante la guerra," I said.

"Good boy! Ever hear of Il Lupo?"

Who in Italy has not heard of Il Lupo, the Wolf? The Italian ace of aces and second only to the dead Baracca. Any school boy can tell the number of his victories and the story of his combat with Baron Von Hauser, the great Austrian pilot. How he brought Von Hauser back alive to the Italian lines, his gun jammed, his observer dead in the cockpit.

"Is he a brave man?" asked Graves, his face tightening up.

"Of course!" I said.

"Certainment!" said Ricaud, who knew the story as well as I did.

"He is not," said Graves, quietly the leather mask of his face crinkled into a smile. "I'll leave it to you Napoleon, and to you, Signor Riposso, if he is a brave man. The war is over—"

"I seem to have heard as much somewheres," murmured Ricaud.

"The war is over," calmly proceeded Graves. "Before it, I was a top kicker of field artillery. At the end I was a captain of field artillery, acting pro tempor for the time being. After awhile, they demoted us all to our pre-war rank and I took a discharge. It's a long tumble from captain to sergeant. You see, I was an officer, but not a gentleman. I could command a battery, but I've got a rotten taste in cigarettes. But I wasn't no worse off than lots of other old non-coms. Some were majors even and lieutenant colonels. Now they're all non-coms again or out. Napoleon here is a gentleman. You can tell it to look at him. But I ain't. That ain't the point of this, and I ain't kicking if that's the way they want to run their army." He raised his glass.

"Down with the Chillies!"

"After the Armistice I rated some leave and got an order of movement good for Italy, and went down through Genoa and Pisa and hit Rome, and a fella said it was good weather in Sicily. That's where I learned to drink this." He noted his glass was empty and pushed the button under the table. "Too much of this ain't good for a man."

I nodded.

"You go across from a place called Villa San Giovani on a ferry to Messina, where you can get a train. One way it goes to Palermo. The other way to Catania. It was just which and together with me which way to go. There was quite a crowd of us standing there where the two trains were waiting, and a woman came up to me and smiled and said, 'You are the American captain, Forbes, going to Taormina?'

"I wasn't, of course, and a gentleman like Napoleon here would have said how sorry he was but that he was not Captain Forbes, but I don't know. I saluted and when I looked at her I admitted that I was that captain enroute on the way to nowheres by Taormina, wherever it should be. She was so pleased, but said that she had not expected me for three or four days, and how was dear Dyonisia?

"I'd been out at the Corso Cavalli in Rome and had won money on a dog named Dyonisia that came from behind in the stretch and won the prettiest race you ever saw, so I said without lying any that Dyonisia was never better in her life. And Bianca, how was she, dear girl? Bianca, so far as I knew, was enjoying the best of health. So all this time we were getting into a first class compartment and the Signora, whose name I hadn't caught, was exclaiming what a funny and lucky thing it was that we had met up. She had known me instantly from Dyonisia's description. And wasn't it fine that the war was over and we could all get a little pleasure again, and what a fine part we Americans had played. That was while some of the Europeans still admitted that the United States had been in the war.

"It's all lemon orchards and orange groves along the right-hand side of the railway, and so pretty that it hurts to look at it. Hills terraced and yellow fruit shining through the green leaves and darker green of olive trees on the hills, and streams on the hills, and streams with wide dry pebbly beds cutting down to the sea and old stone houses, and everything all color. And over on the left-hand side you've got the sea, lots bluer than the Bay of Naples, and the coast of Calabria over across is purple like no other place there is. Well, the Signora was just as good to look at as the scenery. Only she was different. Blue-black hair and a face colored like old ivory and eyes like inkwells and full red lips and one of those smiles, you know what they're like, Signor Riscossa."

"But what has this most pleasant adventure to do with the valor of the Wolf, Capitain?" asked Ricaud, who had his own ideas about the points of women.

"A whole lot, Napoleon," continued Graves. "She had those red lips, you know—"

"To the loup! Curse her red lips!" exclaimed Ricaud, impatiently.

"God bless her red lips, Napoleon. And after awhile the little train stopped at a station called Jardini, and she said that this was our getting off place, and that Taormina was the town up on the hill. There was a car-

9

riage waiting, and we got in and drove up the pipe elbow road to the little town way up above. I was very gallant and dignified. I'd like to have had you see me, Napoleon.

"That evening we had dinner together, and I'm telling you it wasn't no short order chow. First a martell-benedictine and then an antipasto di magro of all kind of funny things you couldn't figure out but that ate great. Then a soup, clear, and after, these little flat fish like baby flounders cooked like those soft-shelled crabs you get at Rousseau's in New Orleans. Roast young turkey with a funny dressing and the Bronte wine that's like melted up rubies. They grow the grapes on Aetna and they're not allowed to ship it out of the country, off the island, you know. For dessert we had these funny crumpily things they call *pasticerria* and black turkish coffee, with a liqueur called cointreau.

"After the meal, we sat out in the garden under the orange trees, jasmine matted on the walls, and the moon making all the shadows blueblack and her hair dusky and her lips red. Away off you could see the moon on the sea and the snow up on the shoulder of Aetna mountain. Everything white as plaster in the moonlight or purple like the Calabria coast, and away down below the lights of Jardini blinking yellow. It seemed she and her husband didn't get along so well. He was a flyer up in Istery of Hystery or somewheres, I didn't care much, with the Wop army of preoccupation, and she was pleased and happy that I had come to cheer her up for a few days. And I was too.

"Well, the next morning we were eating breakfast, or what they call breakfast, rolls, coffee, and oranges, with the sun shining in through the big swinging-door windows, when the door opens and in rushed—an Eyetalian can't come into a room without rushing, excuse me, Signor Disolvo—a good-looking fellow with a scar across his cheek and a beautiful blue theatrical-looking cape and shining black boots and a sword, crying 'Carissima!'

"Then he saw me sitting at the breakfast table, and his 'Carissima!' ended in a sort of gurgle. His face got white, all except that scar that stood out like a bright red welt.

"'What is this?' he said in Eyetalian, and whipped out his sword. Then I placed him. I seen that good-looking, scarred face on the covers of lots of the illustrated magazines. It was the Lupo. The signora was crying among the breakfast dishes, and she was scared. But the Lupo was magnificent. He was doing the dramatic, and he was doing it great. He had anything I ever seen beat.

"'Who are you, you son of a dog?' he said to me. Funny how that expression is international, ain't it, among all countries?

10

"'Captain Perry Graves, at your service,' I said. It was a funny situation, the dashing, handsome, knock em dead Wolf full of righteous wrath, and opposite him old Perry Graves, as homely as you see him now. I didn't look like the side of a triangle, but there was something about me she liked, I guess.

"'Will you give me the satisfaction of a gentleman?' he snapped out.

"'Certainly,' I said, bowing.

"'Here and now?' he said.

"'Surely,' I said, and bowed again.

"'You have a sword?' he asked, in a sweet tone.

"'Excuse me a minute,' I said, and went and got my bag and my belt and gun.

"'You have a sword?' he asked, when I came back.

"'No,' said I.

"'I will get you one,' says he, in his best Lupo manner.

"'I don't wish a sword,' I said.

"'You won't fight me? You dirty dog. I'll cut you down!'"

Graves's face was as hard as his voice was soft.

"'I will fight you here and now,' I said to him. 'You have a pistol, so have I. We will stand facing each other across the table with our left hands touching.' The table wasn't four feet across. 'The Signora will count one, two, three. We will start firing at the count of three. Firing across the table.'

"Then the control of the situation shifted from the handsome Lupo to Perry Graves. Cause just as sure as it was that he would kill me with a sword was the fact that if he killed me at that three foot range with his gun I would take him with me. He knew it too, and he started to sweat. That was the only sign. Big drops of sweat on his forehead. He unbuckled his cape and took out his gun. It was one of those little 7.65 mm. pretty ugly, short little gats.

"We faced across the table and rested our hands on the board, I remember my fingers were in a coffee cup, our right hands with the pistols were below the edge. My big forty-five made a big handful. The Signora was still crying. The Lupo said to her, 'Count, you slut!' She was sobbing hysterically.

"'Emeglio!' called the Lupo. A servant came to the door, his face scared and white. 'Stand at the end of the table,' commanded the Wolf, 'and count slowly and clearly. Una-Dua-Tre!'

"The servant stood at the end of the table. I didn't watch the Wolf's eyes like he did mine. I looked at his wrist where his hand disappeared under the table.

11

"'Una!' said the waiter. I watched the Lupo's hand.

"'Dua!' and his hand shot up. He'd broken under the strain and was going to fire and try and get me before the signal. My old gat belched out and a big forty-five bullet tore his out of his hand as it went off. You see, he hadn't never heard of shooting from the hip.

"The Signora jumped up, screaming, and threw her arms around him. His face was burning red with shame, and his hand was quivering from the sting of the smash. I shoved my gun into the holster and got my musette bag and started for the door, but stopped at the table and drank my coffee standing. It was cold, but I like my coffee in the morning. There wasn't another word said. She was clinging to his neck and crying, and he was standing there, red and ashamed. I walked to the door and opened it, and looked back, and her eye flickered at me over his shoulder. Maybe it was a wink, maybe not. I shut the door and walked out of the courtyard down the road to Jardini. Wolf, hell no, he was a coyote. A coyote, Napoleon, is a wolf that is not a wolf. Now do you think he was a brave man, Signor Disporto?"

I said nothing. I was thinking of how this leather-faced old adventurer had matched his courage against admittedly one of the most fearless men in Europe.

"It is a question of standards," said Ricaud, as the fresh glasses arrived. "Lupo is brave, of course. The adventure of Von Hauser is proof. Also, mon capitain, he is Latin. That you cannot understand, for you have courage without imagination. It is a gift from God, monsieur." Ricaud smiled, shaking his head sadly. "I wish I have it. I have died a thousand times, and I am not a coward. I will die many more before I am buried, but it is, what you call it, Graves, my trade. We go now to a little war. Perhaps a joke war, eh? But one dies as dead in Chile as on Montfaucon. I envy you, Graves, you are American.

"Signor Rinaldi, I like you to drink with me to Capitain Perry Graves, who is so brave he makes the bravest flyer in your country look like a coward!" He laughed, and raised his glass.

"Aw, say, Napoleon!" broke in Graves, embarrassedly, "Let's change that to 'Vive la doughnut!'"

On the Quai at Smyrna

The strange thing was, he said, how they screamed every night at midnight. I do not know why they screamed at that time. We were in the harbor and they were all on the pier and at midnight they started screaming. We used to turn the searchlight on them to quiet them. That always did the trick. We'd run the searchlight up and down over them two or three times and they stopped it. One time I was senior officer on the pier and a Turkish officer came up to me in a frightful rage because one of our sailors had been most insulting to him. So I told him the fellow would be sent on ship and be most severely punished. I asked him to point him out. So he pointed out a gunner's mate, most inoffensive chap. Said he'd been most frightfully and repeatedly insulting; talking to me through an interpreter. I couldn't imagine how the gunner's mate knew enough Turkish to be insulting. I called him over and said, "And just in case you should have spoken to any Turkish officers."

"I haven't spoken to any of them, sir."

"I'm quite sure of it," I said, "but you'd best go on board ship and not come ashore again for the rest of the day."

Then I told the Turk the man was being sent on board ship and would be most severely dealt with. Oh most rigorously. He felt topping about it. Great friends we were.

The worst, he said, were the women with dead babies. You couldn't get the women to give up their dead babies. They'd have babies dead for six days. Wouldn't give them up. Nothing you could do about it. Had to take them away finally. Then there was an old lady, most extraordinary case. I told it to a doctor and he said I was lying. We were clearing them off the pier, had to clear off the dead ones, and this old woman was lying on a sort of litter. They said, "Will you have a look at her, sir?" So I had a look at her and just then she died and went absolutely stiff. Her legs drew up and she drew up from the waist and went quite rigid. Exactly as though she had been dead over night. She was quite dead and absolutely rigid. I told a medical chap about it and he told me it was impossible.

They were all out there on the pier and it wasn't at all like an earth-

13

quake or that sort of thing because they never knew about the Turk. They never knew what the old Turk would do. You remember when they ordered us not to come in to take off any more? I had the wind up when we came in that morning. He had any amount of batteries and could have blown us clean out of the water. We were going to come in, run close along the pier, let go the front and rear anchors and then shell the Turkish quarter of the town. They would have blown us out of water but we would have blown the town simply to hell. They just fired a few blank charges at us as we came in. Kemal came down and sacked the Turkish commander. For exceeding his authority or some such thing. He got a bit above himself. It would have been the hell of a mess.

You remember the harbor. There were plenty of nice things floating around in it. That was the only time in my life I got so I dreamed about things. You didn't mind the women who were having babies as you did those with the dead ones. They had them all right. Surprising how few of them died. You just covered them over with something and let them go to it. They'd always pick out the darkest place in the hold to have them. None of them minded anything once they got off the pier.

The Greeks were nice chaps too. When they evacuated they had all their baggage animals they couldn't take off with them so they just broke their forelegs and dumped them into the shallow water. All those mules with their forelegs broken pushed over into the shallow water. It was all a pleasant business. My word yes a most pleasant business.

A Very Short Story

One hot evening in Padua they carried him up onto the roof and he could look out over the top of the town. There were chimney swifts in the sky. After a while it got dark and the searchlights came out. The others went down and took the bottles with them. He and Luz could hear them below on the balcony. Luz sat on the bed. She was cool and fresh in the hot night.

Luz stayed on night duty for three months. They were glad to let her. When they operated on him she prepared him for the operating table; and they had a joke about friend or enema. He went under the anæsthetic holding tight on to himself so he would not blab about anything during the silly, talky time. After he got on crutches he used to take the temperatures so Luz would not have to get up from the bed. There were only a few patients, and they all knew about it. They all liked Luz. As he walked back along the halls he thought of Luz in his bed.

Before he went back to the front they went into the Duomo and prayed. It was dim and quiet, and there were other people praying. They wanted to get married, but there was not enough time for the banns, and neither of them had birth certificates. They felt as though they were married, but they wanted every one to know about it, and to make it so they could not lose it.

Luz wrote him many letters that he never got until after the armistice. Fifteen came in a bunch to the front and he sorted them by the dates and read them all straight through. They were all about the hospital, and how much she loved him and how it was impossible to get along without him and how terrible it was missing him at night.

After the armistice they agreed he should go home to get a job so they might be married. Luz would not come home until he had a good job and could come to New York to meet her. It was understood he would not drink, and he did not want to see his friends or any one in the States. Only to get a job and be married. On the train from Padua to Milan they quarrelled about her not being willing to come home at once. When they had to say good-bye, in the station at Milan, they kissed good-bye, but

15

were not finished with the quarrel. He felt sick about saying good-bye like that.

He went to America on a boat from Genoa. Luz went back to Pordenone to open a hospital. It was lonely and rainy there, and there was a battalion of *arditi* quartered in the town. Living in the muddy, rainy town in the winter, the major of the battalion made love to Luz, and she had never known Italians before, and finally wrote to the States that theirs had been only a boy and girl affair. She was sorry, and she knew he would probably not be able to understand, but might some day forgive her, and be grateful to her, and she expected, absolutely unexpectedly, to be married in the spring. She loved him as always, but she realized now it was only a boy and girl love. She hoped he would have a great career, and believed in him absolutely. She knew it was for the best.

The major did not marry her in the spring, or any other time. Luz never got an answer to the letter to Chicago about it. A short time after he contracted gonorrhea from a sales girl in a loop department store while riding in a taxicab through Lincoln Park.

Soldier's Home

Krebs went to the war from a Methodist college in Kansas. There is a picture which shows him among his fraternity brothers, all of them wearing exactly the same height and style collar. He enlisted in the Marines in 1917 and did not return to the United States until the second division returned from the Rhine in the summer of 1919.

There is a picture which shows him on the Rhine with two German girls and another corporal. Krebs and the corporal look too big for their uniforms. The German girls are not beautiful. The Rhine does not show in the picture.

By the time Krebs returned to his home town in Oklahoma the greeting of heroes was over. He came back much too late. The men from the town who had been drafted had all been welcomed elaborately on their return. There had been a great deal of hysteria. Now the reaction had set in. People seemed to think it was rather ridiculous for Krebs to be getting back so late, years after the war was over.

At first Krebs, who had been at Belleau Wood, Soissons, the Champagne, St. Mihiel and in the Argonne did not want to talk about the war at all. Later he felt the need to talk but no one wanted to hear about it. His town had heard too many atrocity stories to be thrilled by actualities. Krebs found that to be listened to at all he had to lie, and after he had done this twice he, too, had a reaction against the war and against talking about it. A distaste for everything that had happened to him in the war set in because of the lies he had told. All of the times that had been able to make him feel cool and clear inside himself when he thought of them; the times so long back when he had done the one thing, the only thing for a man to do, easily and naturally, when he might have done something else, now lost their cool, valuable quality and then were lost themselves.

His lies were quite unimportant lies and consisted in attributing to himself things other men had seen, done or heard of, and stating as facts certain apocryphal incidents familiar to all soldiers. Even his lies were not sensational at the pool room. His acquaintances, who had heard

17

detailed accounts of German women found chained to machine guns in the Argonne forest and who could not comprehend, or were barred by their patriotism from interest in, any German machine gunners who were not chained, were not thrilled by his stories.

Krebs acquired the nausea in regard to experience that is the result of untruth or exaggeration, and when he occasionally met another man who had really been a soldier and they talked a few minutes in the dressing room at a dance he fell into the easy pose of the old soldier among other soldiers: that he had been badly, sickeningly frightened all the time. In this way he lost everything.

During this time, it was late summer, he was sleeping late in bed, getting up to walk down town to the library to get a book, eating lunch at home, reading on the front porch until he became bored and then walking down through the town to spend the hottest hours of the day in the cool dark of the pool room. He loved to play pool.

In the evening he practised on his clarinet, strolled down town, read and went to bed. He was still a hero to his two young sisters. His mother would have given him breakfast in bed if he had wanted it. She often came in when he was in bed and asked him to tell her about the war, but her attention always wandered. His father was non-committal.

Before Krebs went away to the war he had never been allowed to drive the family motor car. His father was in the real estate business and always wanted the car to be at his command when he required it to take clients out into the country to show them a piece of farm property. The car always stood outside the First National Bank building where his father had an office on the second floor. Now, after the war, it was still the same car.

Nothing was changed in the town except that the young girls had grown up. But they lived in such a complicated world of already defined alliances and shifting feuds that Krebs did not feel the energy or the courage to break into it. He liked to look at them, though. There were so many good-looking young girls. Most of them had their hair cut short. When he went away only little girls wore their hair like that or girls that were fast. They all wore sweaters and shirt waists with round Dutch collars. It was a pattern. He liked to look at them from the front porch as they walked on the other side of the street. He liked to watch them walking under the shade of the trees. He liked the round Dutch collars above their sweaters. He liked their silk stockings and flat shoes. He liked their bobbed hair and the way they walked.

When he was in town their appeal to him was not very strong. He did not like them when he saw them in the Greek's ice cream parlor. He did not want them themselves really. They were too complicated. There was something else. Vaguely he wanted a girl but he did not want to have to work to get her. He would have liked to have a girl but he did not want to have to spend a long time getting her. He did not want to get into the intrigue and the politics. He did not want to have to do any courting. He did not want to tell any more lies. It wasn't worth it.

He did not want any consequences. He did not want any consequences ever again. He wanted to live along without consequences. Besides he did not really need a girl. The army had taught him that. It was all right to pose as though you had to have a girl. Nearly everybody did that. But it wasn't true. You did not need a girl. That was the funny thing. First a fellow boasted how girls mean nothing to him, that he never thought of them, that they could not touch him. Then á fellow boasted that he could not get along without girls, that he had to have them all the time, that he could not go to sleep without them.

That was all a lie. It was all a lie both ways. You did not need a girl unless you thought about them. He learned that in the army. Then sooner or later you always got one. When you were really ripe for a girl you always got one. You did not have to think about it. Sooner or later it would come. He had learned that in the army.

Now he would have liked a girl if she had come to him and not wanted to talk. But here at home it was all too complicated. He knew he could never get through it all again. It was not worth the trouble. That was the thing about French girls and German girls. There was not all this talking. You couldn't talk much and you did not need to talk. It was simple and you were friends. He thought about France and then he began to think about Germany. On the whole he had liked Germany better. He did not want to leave Germany. He did not want to come home. Still, he had come home. He sat on the front porch.

He liked the girls that were walking along the other side of the street. He liked the look of them much better than the French girls or the German girls. But the world they were in was not the world he was in. He would like to have one of them. But it was not worth it. They were such a nice pattern. He liked the pattern. It was exciting. But he would not go through all the talking. He did not want one badly enough. He liked to look at them all, though. It was not worth it. Not now when things were getting good again.

He sat there on the porch reading a book on the war. It was a history and he was reading about all the engagements he had been in. It was the most interesting reading he had ever done. He wished there were more maps. He looked forward with a good feeling to reading all the really good histories when they would come out with good detail maps. Now he was really learning about the war. He had been a good soldier. That made a difference.

One morning after he had been home about a month his mother came into his bedroom and sat on the bed. She smoothed her apron.

"I had a talk with your father last night, Harold," she said, "and he is willing for you to take the car out in the evenings."

"Yeah?" said Krebs, who was not fully awake. "Take the car out? Yeah?"

"Yes. Your father has felt for some time that you should be able to take the car out in the evenings whenever you wished but we only talked it over last night."

"I'll bet you made him," Krebs said.

"No. It was your father's suggestion that we talk the matter over."

"Yeah. I'll bet you made him," Krebs sat up in bed.

"Will you come down to breakfast, Harold?" his mother said.

"As soon as I get my clothes on," Krebs said.

His mother went out of the room and he could hear her frying something downstairs while he washed, shaved and dressed to go down into the dining-room for breakfast. While he was eating breakfast his sister brought in the mail.

"Well, Hare," she said. "You old sleepy-head. What do you ever get up for?"

Krebs looked at her. He liked her. She was his best sister.

"Have you got the paper?" he asked.

She handed him *The Kansas City Star* and he shucked off its brown wrapper and opened it to the sporting page. He folded *The Star* open and propped it against the water pitcher with his cereal dish to steady it, so he could read while he ate.

"Harold," his mother stood in the kitchen doorway, "Harold, please don't muss up the paper. Your father can't read his *Star* if it's been mussed."

"I won't muss it," Krebs said.

His sister sat down at the table and watched him while he read.

"We're playing indoor over at school this afternoon," she said. "I'm going to pitch."

"Good," said Krebs. "How's the old wing?"

"I can pitch better than lots of the boys. I tell them all you taught me. The other girls aren't much good."

"Yeah?" said Krebs.

"I tell them all you're my beau. Aren't you my beau, Hare?"

"You bet."

"Couldn't your brother really be your beau just because he's your brother?"

"I don't know."

"Sure you know. Couldn't you be my beau, Hare, if I was old enough and if you wanted to?"

"Sure. You're my girl now."

"Am I really your girl?"

"Sure."

"Do you love me?"

"Uh, huh."

"Will you love me always?"

"Sure."

"Will you come over and watch me play indoor?"

"Maybe."

"Aw, Hare, you don't love me. If you loved me, you'd want to come over and watch me play indoor."

Krebs's mother came into the dining-room from the kitchen. She carried a plate with two fried eggs and some crisp bacon on it and a plate of buckwheat cakes.

"You run along, Helen," she said. "I want to talk to Harold." She put the eggs and bacon down in front of him and brought in a jug of maple syrup for the buckwheat cakes. Then she sat down across the table from Krebs.

"I wish you'd put down the paper a minute, Harold," she said.

Krebs took down the paper and folded it.

"Have you decided what you are going to do yet, Harold?" his mother said, taking off her glasses.

"No," said Krebs.

"Don't you think it's about time?" His mother did not say this in a mean way. She seemed worried.

"I hadn't thought about it," Krebs said.

"God has some work for every one to do," his mother said. "There can be no idle hands in His Kingdom."

"I'm not in His Kingdom," Krebs said.

"We are all of us in His Kingdom."

Krebs felt embarrassed and resentful as always.

"I've worried about you so much, Harold," his mother went on. "I know the temptations you must have been exposed to. I know how weak men are. I know what your own dear grandfather, my own father, told us about the Civil War and I have prayed for you. I pray for you all day long, Harold."

Krebs looked at the bacon fat hardening on his plate.

"Your father is worried, too," his mother went on. "He thinks you have lost your ambition, that you haven't got a definite aim in life. Charley Simmons, who is just your age, has a good job and is going to be married. The boys are all settling down; they're all determined to get somewhere; you can see that boys like Charley Simmons are on their way to being really a credit to the community."

Krebs said nothing.

"Don't look that way, Harold," his mother said. "You know we love you and I want to tell you for your own good how matters stand. Your father does not want to hamper your freedom. He thinks you should be allowed to drive the car. If you want to take some of the nice girls out riding with you, we are only too pleased. We want you to enjoy yourself. But you are going to have to settle down to work, Harold. Your father doesn't care what you start in at. All work is honorable as he says. But you've got to make a start at something. He asked me to speak to you this morning and then you can stop in and see him at his office."

"Is that all?" Krebs said.

"Yes. Don't you love your mother, dear boy?"

"No," Krebs said.

His mother looked at him across the table. Her eyes were shiny. She started crying.

"I don't love anybody," Krebs said.

It wasn't any good. He couldn't tell her, he couldn't make her see it. It was silly to have said it. He had only hurt her. He went over and took hold of her arm. She was crying with her head in her hands.

"I didn't mean it," he said. "I was just angry at something. I didn't mean I didn't love you."

His mother went on crying. Krebs put his arm on her shoulder.

"Can't you believe me, mother?"

His mother shook her head.

"Please, please, mother. Please believe me."

"All right," his mother said chokily. She looked up at him. "I believe you, Harold."

Krebs kissed her hair. She put her face up to him.

"I'm your mother," she said. "I held you next to my heart when you were a tiny baby."

Krebs felt sick and vaguely nauseated.

"I know, Mummy," he said. "I'll try and be a good boy for you."

"Would you kneel and pray with me, Harold?" his mother asked.

They knelt down beside the dining-room table and Krebs's mother prayed.

"Now, you pray, Harold," she said.

"I can't," Krebs said.

"Try, Harold."

"I can't."

"Do you want me to pray for you?"

"Yes."

So his mother prayed for him and then they stood up and Krebs kissed his mother and went out of the house. He had tried so to keep his life from being complicated. Still, none of it had touched him. He had felt sorry for his mother and she had made him lie. He would go to Kansas City and get a job and she would feel all right about it. There would be one more scene maybe before he got away. He would not go down to his father's office. He would miss that one. He wanted his life to go smoothly. It had just gotten going that way. Well, that was all over now, anyway. He would go over to the schoolyard and watch Helen play indoor baseball.

The Revolutionist

In 1919 he was travelling on the railroads in Italy, carrying a square of oilcloth from the headquarters of the party written in indelible pencil and saying here was a comrade who had suffered very much under the Whites in Budapest and requesting comrades to aid him in any way. He used this instead of a ticket. He was very shy and quite young and the train men passed him on from one crew to another. He had no money, and they fed him behind the counter in railway eating houses.

He was delighted with Italy. It was a beautiful country, he said. The people were all kind. He had been in many towns, walked much, and seen many pictures. Giotto, Masaccio, and Piero della Francesca he bought reproductions of and carried them wrapped in a copy of *Avanti*. Mantegna he did not like.

He reported at Bologna, and I took him with me up into the Romagna where it was necessary I go to see a man. We had a good trip together. It was early September and the country was pleasant. He was a Magyar, a very nice boy and very shy. Horthy's men had done some bad things to him. He talked about it a little. In spite of Hungary, he believed altogether in the world revolution.

"But how is the movement going in Italy?" he asked.

"Very badly," I said.

"But it will go better," he said. "You have everything here. It is the one country that every one is sure of. It will be the starting point of everything."

I did not say anything.

At Bologna he said good-bye to us to go on the train to Milano and then to Aosta to walk over the pass into Switzerland. I spoke to him about the Mantegnas in Milano. "No," he said, very shyly, he did not like Mantegna. I wrote out for him where to eat in Milano and the addresses of comrades. He thanked me very much, but his mind was already looking forward to walking over the pass. He was very eager to walk over the pass while the weather held good. He loved the mountains in the autumn. The last I heard of him the Swiss had him in jail near Sion.

24

Selected Vignettes

(from *In Our Time*)

CHAPTER I

Everybody was drunk. The whole battery was drunk going along the road in the dark. We were going to the Champagne. The lieutenant kept riding his horse out into the fields and saying to him, "I'm drunk, I tell you, mon vieux. Oh, I am so soused." We went along the road all night in the dark and the adjutant kept riding up alongside my kitchen and saying, "You must put it out. It is dangerous. It will be observed." We were fifty kilometers from the front but the adjutant worried about the fire in my kitchen. It was funny going along that road. That was when I was a kitchen corporal.

CHAPTER II

Minarets stuck up in the rain out of Adrianople across the mud flats. The carts were jammed for thirty miles along the Karagatch road. Water buffalo and cattle were hauling carts through the mud. No end and no beginning. Just carts loaded with everything they owned. The old men and women, soaked through, walked along keeping the cattle moving. The Maritza was running yellow almost up to the bridge. Carts were jammed solid on the bridge with camels bobbing along through them. Greek cavalry herded along the procession. Women and kids were in the carts crouched with mattresses, mirrors, sewing machines, bundles. There was a woman having a kid with a young girl holding a blanket over her and crying. Scared sick looking at it. It rained all through the evacuation.

CHAPTER III

We were in a garden at Mons. Young Buckley came in with his patrol from across the river. The first German I saw climbed up over the garden wall. We waited till he got one leg over and then potted him. He had so much equipment on and looked awfully surprised and fell down into the garden. Then three more came over further down the wall. We shot them. They all came just like that.

CHAPTER IV

It was a frightfully hot day. We'd jammed an absolutely perfect barricade across the bridge. It was simply priceless. A big old wrought-iron grating from the front of a house. Too heavy to lift and you could shoot through it and they would have to climb over it. It was absolutely topping. They tried to get over it, and we potted them from forty yards. They rushed it, and officers came out along and worked on it. It was an absolutely perfect obstacle. Their officers were very fine. We were frightfully put out when we heard the flank had gone, and we had to fall back.

CHAPTER V

They shot the six cabinet ministers at half-past six in the morning against the wall of a hospital. There were pools of water in the courtyard. There were wet dead leaves on the paving of the courtyard. It rained hard. All the shutters of the hospital were nailed shut. One of the ministers was sick with typhoid. Two soldiers carried him downstairs and out into the rain. They tried to hold him up against the wall but he sat down in a puddle of water. The other five stood very quietly against the wall. Finally the officer told the soldiers it was no good trying to make him stand up. When they fired the first volley he was sitting down in the water with his head on his knees.

CHAPTER VI

Nick sat against the wall of the church where they had dragged him to be clear of machine-gun fire in the street. Both legs stuck out awkwardly. He had been hit in the spine. His face was sweaty and dirty. The sun shone on his face. The day was very hot. Rinaldi, big backed, his equipment sprawling, lay face downward against the wall. Nick looked straight ahead brilliantly. The pink wall of the house opposite had fallen out from the roof, and an iron bedstead hung twisted toward the street. Two Austrian dead lay in the rubble in the shade of the house. Up the street were other dead. Things were getting forward in the town. It was going well. Stretcher bearers would be along any time now. Nick turned his head carefully and looked at Rinaldi. "Senta Rinaldi. Senta. You and me we've made a separate peace." Rinaldi lay still in the sun breathing with difficulty. "Not patriots." Nick turned his head carefully away smiling sweatily. Rinaldi was a disappointing audience.

CHAPTER VII

While the bombardment was knocking the trench to pieces at Fossalta, he lay very flat and sweated and prayed oh jesus christ get me out of here. Dear jesus please get me out. Christ please please please christ. If you'll only keep me from getting killed I'll do anything you say. I believe in you and I'll tell every one in the world that you are the only one that matters. Please please dear jesus. The shelling moved further up the line. We went to work on the trench and in the morning the sun came up and the day was hot and muggy and cheerful and quiet. The next night back at Mestre he did not tell the girl he went upstairs with at the Villa Rossa about Jesus. And he never told anybody.

27

II

The War to End Wars

"When you go to war as a boy you have this great illusion of immortality. Other people get killed; not you. It can happen to other people; but not to you. Then when you are badly wounded the first time you lose that illusion and you know it can happen to you. After being severely wounded two weeks before my nineteenth birthday I had a bad time until I figured out that nothing could happen to me that had not happened to all men before me. Whatever I had to do men had always done. If they had done it then I could do it too and the best thing was not to worry about it."

—From *Men at War*

In Another Country

In the fall the war was always there, but we did not go to it any more. It was cold in the fall in Milan and the dark came very early. Then the electric lights came on, and it was pleasant along the streets looking in the windows. There was much game hanging outside the shops, and the snow powdered in the fur of the foxes and the wind blew their tails. The deer hung stiff and heavy and empty, and small birds blew in the wind and the wind turned their feathers. It was a cold fall and the wind came down from the mountains.

We were all at the hospital every afternoon, and there were different ways of walking across the town through the dusk to the hospital. Two of the ways were alongside canals, but they were long. Always, though, you crossed a bridge across a canal to enter the hospital. There was a choice of three bridges. On one of them a woman sold roasted chestnuts. It was warm, standing in front of her charcoal fire, and the chestnuts were warm afterward in your pocket. The hospital was very old and very beautiful, and you entered through a gate and walked across a courtyard and out a gate on the other side. There were usually funerals starting from the courtyard. Beyond the old hospital were the new brick pavilions, and there we met every afternoon and were all very polite and interested in what was the matter, and sat in the machines that were to make so much difference.

The doctor came up to the machine where I was sitting and said: "What did you like best to do before the war? Did you practise a sport?"

I said: "Yes, football."

"Good," he said. "You will be able to play football again better than ever."

My knee did not bend and the leg dropped straight from the knee to the ankle without a calf, and the machine was to bend the knee and make it move as in riding a tricycle. But it did not bend yet, and instead the machine lurched when it came to the bending part. The doctor said: "That will all pass. You are a fortunate young man. You will play football again like a champion."

31

In the next machine was a major who had a little hand like a baby's. He winked at me when the doctor examined his hand, which was between two leather straps that bounced up and down and flapped the stiff fingers, and said: "And will I too play football, captain-doctor?" He had been a very great fencer, and before the war the greatest fencer in Italy.

The doctor went to his office in a back room and brought a photograph which showed a hand that had been withered almost as small as the major's, before it had taken a machine course, and after was a little larger. The major held the photograph with his good hand and looked at it very carefully. "A wound?" he asked.

"An industrial accident," the doctor said.

"Very interesting, very interesting," the major said, and handed it back to the doctor.

"You have confidence?"

"No," said the major.

There were three boys who came each day who were about the same age I was. They were all three from Milan, and one of them was to be a lawyer, and one was to be a painter, and one had intended to be a soldier, and after we were finished with the machines, sometimes we walked back together to the Café Cova, which was next door to the Scala. We walked the short way through the communist quarter because we were four together. The people hated us because we were officers, and from a wine-shop some one called out, "A basso gli ufficiali!" as we passed. Another boy who walked with us sometimes and made us five wore a black silk handkerchief across his face because he had no nose then and his face was to be rebuilt. He had gone out to the front from the military academy and been wounded within an hour after he had gone into the front line for the first time. They rebuilt his face, but he came from a very old family and they could never get the nose exactly right. He went to South America and worked in a bank. But this was a long time ago, and then we did not any of us know how it was going to be afterward. We only knew then that there was always the war, but that we were not going to it any more.

We all had the same medals, except the boy with the black silk bandage across his face, and he had not been at the front long enough to get any medals. The tall boy with a very pale face who was to be a lawyer had been a lieutenant of Arditi and had three medals of the sort we each had only one of. He had lived a very long time with death and was a little detached. We were all a little detached, and there was nothing that held us together except that we met every afternoon at the hospital. Although, as we walked to the Cova through the tough part of town, walking in the dark, with light and singing coming out of the wine-shops, and sometimes having to walk into the street when the men and women would crowd together on the sidewalk so that we would have had to jostle them to get by, we felt held together by there being something that had happened that they, the people who disliked us, did not understand.

We ourselves all understood the Cova, where it was rich and warm and not too brightly lighted, and noisy and smoky at certain hours, and there were always girls at the tables and the illustrated papers on a rack on the wall. The girls at the Cova were very patriotic, and I found that the most patriotic people in Italy were the café girls—and I believe they are still patriotic.

The boys at first were very polite about my medals and asked me what I had done to get them. I showed them the papers, which were written in very beautiful language and full of *fratellanza* and *abnegazione*, but which really said, with the adjectives removed, that I had been given the medals because I was an American. After that their manner changed a little toward me, although I was their friend against outsiders. I was a friend, but I was never really one of them after they had read the citations, because it had been different with them and they had done very different things to get their medals. I had been wounded, it was true; but we all knew that being wounded, after all, was really an accident. I was never ashamed of the ribbons, though, and sometimes, after the cocktail hour, I would imagine myself having done all the things they had done to get their medals; but walking home at night through the empty streets with the cold wind and all the shops closed, trying to keep near the street lights, I knew that I would never have done such things, and I was very much afraid to die, and often lay in bed at night by myself, afraid to die and wondering how I would be when I went back to the front again.

The three with the medals were like hunting-hawks; and I was not a hawk, although I might seem a hawk to those who had never hunted; they, the three, knew better and so we drifted apart. But I stayed good friends with the boy who had been wounded his first day at the front, because he would never know now how he would have turned out; so he could never be accepted either, and I liked him because I thought perhaps he would not have turned out to be a hawk either.

The major, who had been the great fencer, did not believe in bravery, and spent much time while we sat in the machines correcting my grammar. He had complimented me on how I spoke Italian, and we talked together very easily. One day I had said that Italian seemed such an easy

33

language to me that I could not take a great interest in it; everything was so easy to say. "Ah, yes," the major said. "Why, then, do you not take up the use of grammar?" So we took up the use of grammar, and soon Italian was such a difficult language that I was afraid to talk to him until I had the grammar straight in my mind.

The major came very regularly to the hospital. I do not think he ever missed a day, although I am sure he did not believe in the machines. There was a time when none of us believed in the machines, and one day the major said it was all nonsense. The machines were new then and it was we who were to prove them. It was an idiotic idea, he said, "a theory, like another." I had not learned my grammar, and he said I was a stupid impossible disgrace, and he was a fool to have bothered with me. He was a small man and he sat straight up in his chair with his right hand thrust into the machine and looked straight ahead at the wall while the straps thumped up and down with his fingers in them.

"What will you do when the war is over if it is over?" he asked me. "Speak grammatically!"

"I will go to the States."

"Are you married?"

"No, but I hope to be."

"The more of a fool you are," he said. He seemed very angry. "A man must not marry."

"Why, Signor Maggiore?"

"Don't call me 'Signor Maggiore.'"

"Why must not a man marry?"

"He cannot marry. He cannot marry," he said angrily. "If he is to lose everything, he should not place himself in a position to lose that. He should not place himself in a position to lose. He should find things he cannot lose."

He spoke very angrily and bitterly, and looked straight ahead while he talked.

"But why should he necessarily lose it?"

"He'll lose it," the major said. He was looking at the wall. Then he looked down at the machine and jerked his little hand out from between the straps and slapped it hard against his thigh. "He'll lose it," he almost shouted. "Don't argue with me!" Then he called to the attendant who ran the machines. "Come and turn this damned thing off."

He went back into the other room for the light treatment and the massage. Then I heard him ask the doctor if he might use his telephone and he shut the door. When he came back into the room, I was sitting in another machine. He was wearing his cape and had his cap on, and he came directly toward my machine and put his arm on my shoulder.

"I am so sorry," he said, and patted me on the shoulder with his good hand. "I would not be rude. My wife has just died. You must forgive me."

"Oh—" I said, feeling sick for him. "I am *so* sorry."

He stood there biting his lower lip. "It is very difficult," he said. "I cannot resign myself."

He looked straight past me and out through the window. Then he began to cry. "I am utterly unable to resign myself," he said and choked. And then crying, his head up looking at nothing, carrying himself straight and soldierly, with tears on both his cheeks and biting his lips, he walked past the machines and out the door.

The doctor told me that the major's wife, who was very young and whom he had not married until he was definitely invalided out of the war, had died of pneumonia. She had been sick only a few days. No one expected her to die. The major did not come to the hospital for three days. Then he came at the usual hour, wearing a black band on the sleeve of his uniform. When he came back, there were large framed photographs around the wall, of all sorts of wounds before and after they had been cured by the machines. In front of the machine the major used were three photographs of hands like his that were completely restored. I do not know where the doctor got them. I always understood we were the first to use the machines. The photographs did not make much difference to the major because he only looked out of the window.

Now I Lay Me

That night we lay on the floor in the room and I listened to the silk-worms eating. The silk-worms fed in racks of mulberry leaves and all night you could hear them eating and a dropping sound in the leaves. I myself did not want to sleep because I had been living for a long time with the knowledge that if I ever shut my eyes in the dark and let myself go, my soul would go out of my body. I had been that way for a long time, ever since I had been blown up at night and felt it go out of me and go off and then come back. I tried never to think about it, but it had started to go since, in the nights, just at the moment of going off to sleep, and I could only stop it by a very great effort. So while now I am fairly sure that it would not really have gone out, yet then, that summer, I was unwilling to make the experiment.

I had different ways of occupying myself while I lay awake. I would think of a trout stream I had fished along when I was a boy and fish its whole length very carefully in my mind; fishing very carefully under all the logs, all the turns of the bank, the deep holes and the clear shallow stretches, sometimes catching trout and sometimes losing them. I would stop fishing at noon to eat my lunch; sometimes on a log over the stream; sometimes on a high bank under a tree, and I always ate my lunch very slowly and watched the stream below me while I ate. Often I ran out of bait because I would take only ten worms with me in a tobacco tin when I started. When I had used them all I had to find more worms, and sometimes it was very difficult digging in the bank of the stream where the cedar trees kept out the sun and there was no grass but only the bare moist earth and often I could find no worms. Always though I found some kind of bait, but one time in the swamp I could find no bait at all and had to cut up one of the trout I had caught and use him for bait.

Sometimes I found insects in the swamp meadows, in the grass or under ferns, and used them. There were beetles and insects with legs like grass stems, and grubs in old rotten logs; white grubs with brown pinching heads that would not stay on the hook and emptied into nothing in the cold water, and wood ticks under logs where sometimes I found angle-worms that slipped into the ground as soon as the log was raised. Once I used a salamander from under an old log. The salamander was very small and neat and agile and a lovely color. He had tiny feet that tried to hold on to the hook, and after that one time I never used a salamander, although I found them very often. Nor did I use crickets, because of the way they acted about the hook.

Sometimes the stream ran through an open meadow, and in the dry grass I would catch grasshoppers and use them for bait and sometimes I would catch grasshoppers and toss them into the stream and watch them float along swimming on the stream and circling on the surface as the current took them and then disappear as a trout rose. Sometimes I would fish four or five different streams in the night; starting as near as I could get to their source and fishing them down stream. When I had finished too quickly and the time did not go, I would fish the stream over again, starting where it emptied into the lake and fishing back up stream, trying for all the trout I had missed coming down. Some nights too I made up streams, and some of them were very exciting, and it was like being awake and dreaming. Some of those streams I still remember and think that I have fished in them, and they are confused with streams I really know. I gave them all names and went to them on the train and sometimes walked for miles to get to them.

But some nights I could not fish, and on those nights I was cold-awake and said my prayers over and over and tried to pray for all the people I had ever known. That took up a great amount of time, for if you try to remember all the people you have ever known, going back to the earliest thing you remember—which was, with me, the attic of the house where I was born and my mother and father's wedding-cake in a tin box hanging from one of the rafters, and, in the attic, jars of snakes and other specimens that my father had collected as a boy and preserved in alcohol, the alcohol sunken in the jars so the backs of some of the snakes and specimens were exposed and had turned white—if you thought back that far, you remembered a great many people. If you prayed for all of them, saying a Hail Mary and an Our Father for each one, it took a long time and finally it would be light, and then you could go to sleep, if you were in a place where you could sleep in the daylight.

On those nights I tried to remember everything that had ever happened to me, starting with just before I went to the war and remembering back from one thing to another. I found I could only remember back to that attic in my grandfather's house. Then I would start there and remember this way again, until I reached the war.

I remember, after my grandfather died we moved away from that house and to a new house designed and built by my mother. Many things that were not to be moved were burned in the backyard and I remember those jars from the attic being thrown in the fire, and how they popped in the heat and the fire flamed up from the alcohol. I remember the snakes burning in the fire in the backyard. But there were no people in that, only things. I could not remember who burned the things even, and I would go on until I came to people and then stop and pray for them.

About the new house I remember how my mother was always cleaning things out and making a good clearance. One time when my father was away on a hunting trip she made a good thorough cleaning out in the basement and burned everything that should not have been there. When my father came home and got down from his buggy and hitched the horse, the fire was still burning in the road beside the house. I went out to meet him. He handed me his shotgun and looked at the fire. "What's this?" he asked.

"I've been cleaning out the basement, dear," my mother said from the porch. She was standing there smiling, to meet him. My father looked at the fire and kicked at something. Then he leaned over and picked something out of the ashes. "Get a rake, Nick," he said to me. I went to the basement and brought a rake and my father raked very carefully in the ashes. He raked out stone axes and stone skinning knives and tools for making arrow-heads and pieces of pottery and many arrow-heads. They had all been blackened and chipped by the fire. My father raked them all out very carefully and spread them on the grass by the road. His shotgun in its leather case and his game-bags were on the grass where he had left them when he stepped down from the buggy.

"Take the gun and the bags in the house, Nick, and bring me a paper," he said. My mother had gone inside the house. I took the shotgun, which was heavy to carry and banged against my legs, and the two game-bags and started toward the house. "Take them one at a time," my father said. "Don't try and carry too much at once." I put down the game-bags and took in the shotgun and brought out a newspaper from the pile in my father's office. My father spread all the blackened, chipped stone implements on the paper and then wrapped them up. "The best arrow-heads went all to pieces," he said. He walked into the house with the paper package and I stayed outside on the grass with the two game-bags. After a while I took them in. In remembering that, there were only two people, so I would pray for them both.

Some nights, though, I could not remember my prayers even. I could only get as far as "On earth as it is in heaven" and then have to start all over and be absolutely unable to get past that. Then I would have to recognize that I could not remember and give up saying my prayers that night and try something else. So on some nights I would try to remember all the animals in the world by name and then the birds and then fishes and then countries and cities and then kinds of food and the names of all the streets I could remember in Chicago, and when I could not remember anything at all any more I would just listen. And I do not remember a night on which you could not hear things. If I could have a light I was not afraid to sleep, because I knew my soul would only go out of me if it were dark. So, of course, many nights I was where I could have a light and then slept because I was nearly always tired and often very sleepy. And I am sure many times too that I slept without knowing it—but I never slept knowing it, and on this night I listened to the silk-worms. You can hear silk-worms eating very clearly in the night and I lay with my eyes open and listened to them.

There was only one other person in the room and he was awake too. I listened to him being awake, for a long time. He could not lie as quietly as I could because, perhaps, he had not had as much practice being awake. We were lying on blankets spread over straw and when he moved the straw was noisy, but the silk-worms were not frightened by any noise we made and ate on steadily. There were the noises of night seven kilometres behind the lines outside but they were different from the small noises inside the room in the dark. The other man in the room tried lying quietly. Then he moved again. I moved too, so he would know I was awake. He had lived ten years in Chicago. They had taken him for a soldier in nineteen fourteen when he had come back to visit his family, and they had given him me for an orderly because he spoke English. I heard him listening, so I moved again in the blankets.

"Can't you sleep, Signor Tenente?" he asked.

"No."

"I can't sleep, either."'

"What's the matter?"

"I don't know. I can't sleep."

"You feel all right?"

"Sure. I feel good. I just can't sleep."

"You want to talk a while?" I asked.

"Sure. What can you talk about in this damn place."

"This place is pretty good," I said.

"Sure," he said. "It's all right."

"Tell me about out in Chicago," I said.

"Oh," he said, "I told you all that once."

"Tell me about how you got married."

"I told you that."

"Was the letter you got Monday—from her?"

"Sure. She writes me all the time. She's making good money with the place."

"You'll have a nice place when you go back."

"Sure. She runs it fine. She's making a lot of money."

"Don't you think we'll wake them up, talking?" I asked.

"No. They can't hear. Anyway, they sleep like pigs. I'm different," he said. "I'm nervous."

"Talk quiet," I said. "Want a smoke?"

We smoked skilfully in the dark.

"You don't smoke much, Signor Tenente."

"No. I've just about cut it out."

"Well," he said, "it don't do you any good and I suppose you get so you don't miss it. Did you ever hear a blind man won't smoke because he can't see the smoke come out?"

"I don't believe it."

"I think it's all bull, myself," he said. "I just heard it somewhere. You know how you hear things."

We were both quiet and I listened to the silk-worms.

"You hear those damn silk-worms?" he asked. "You can hear them chew."

"It's funny," I said.

"Say, Signor Tenente, is there something really the matter that you can't sleep? I never see you sleep. You haven't slept nights ever since I been with you."

"I don't know, John," I said. "I got in pretty bad shape along early last spring and at night it bothers me."

"Just like I am," he said. "I shouldn't have ever got in this war. I'm too nervous."

"Maybe it will get better."

"Say, Signor Tenente, what did you get in this war for, anyway?"

"I don't know, John. I wanted to, then."

"Wanted to," he said. "That's a hell of a reason."

"We oughtn't to talk out loud," I said.

"They sleep just like pigs," he said. "They can't understand the English language, anyway. They don't know a damn thing. What are you going to do when it's over and we go back to the States?"

"I'll get a job on a paper."

"In Chicago?"

40

"Maybe."

"Do you ever read what this fellow Brisbane writes? My wife cuts it out for me and sends it to me."

"Sure."

"Did you ever meet him?"

"No, but I've seen him."

"I'd like to meet that fellow. He's a fine writer. My wife don't read English but she takes the paper just like when I was home and she cuts out the editorials and the sports page and sends them to me."

"How are your kids?"

"They're fine. One of the girls is in the fourth grade now. You know, Signor Tenente, if I didn't have the kids I wouldn't be your orderly now. They'd have made me stay in the line all the time."

"I'm glad you've got them."

"So am I. They're fine kids but I want a boy. Three girls and no boy. That's a hell of a note."

"Why don't you try and go to sleep?"

"No, I can't sleep now. I'm wide awake now, Signor Tenente. Say, I'm worried about you not sleeping though."

"It'll be all right, John."

"Imagine a young fellow like you not to sleep."

"I'll get all right. It just takes a while."

"You got to get all right. A man can't get along that don't sleep. Do you worry about anything? You got anything on your mind?"

"No, John, I don't think so."

"You ought to get married, Signor Tenente. Then you wouldn't worry."

"I don't know."

"You ought to get married. Why don't you pick out some nice Italian girl with plenty of money? You could get any one you want. You're young and you got good decorations and you look nice. You been wounded a couple of times."

"I can't talk the language well enough."

"You talk it fine. To hell with talking the language. You don't have to talk to them. Marry them."

"I'll think about it."

"You know some girls, don't you?"

"Sure."

"Well, you marry the one with the most money. Over here, the way they're brought up, they'll all make you a good wife."

"I'll think about it."

41

"Don't think about it, Signor Tenente. Do it."

"All right."

"A man ought to be married. You'll never regret it. Every man ought to be married."

"All right," I said. "Let's try and sleep a while."

"All right, Signor Tenente. I'll try it again. But you remember what I said."

"I'll remember it," I said. "Now let's sleep a while, John."

"All right," he said. "I hope you sleep, Signor Tenente."

I heard him roll in his blankets on the straw and then he was very quiet and I listened to him breathing regularly. Then he started to snore. I listened to him snore for a long time and then I stopped listening to him snore and listened to the silk-worms eating. They ate steadily, making a dropping in the leaves. I had a new thing to think about and I lay in the dark with my eyes open and thought of all the girls I had ever known and what kind of wives they would make. It was a very interesting thing to think about and for a while it killed off trout-fishing and interfered with my prayers. Finally, though, I went back to trout-fishing, because I found that I could remember all the streams and there was always something new about them, while the girls, after I had thought about them a few times, blurred and I could not call them into my mind and finally they all blurred and all became rather the same and I gave up thinking about them almost altogether. But I kept on with my prayers and I prayed very often for John in the nights and his class was removed from active service before the October offensive. I was glad he was not there, because he would have been a great worry to me. He came to the hospital in Milan to see me several months after and was very disappointed that I had not yet married, and I know he would feel very badly if he knew that, so far, I have never married. He was going back to America and he was very certain about marriage and knew it would fix up everything.

A Natural History of the Dead

It has always seemed to me that the war has been omitted as a field for the observations of the naturalist. We have charming and sound accounts of the flora and fauna of Patagonia by the late W. H. Hudson, the Reverend Gilbert White has written most interestingly of the Hoopoe on its occasional and not at all common visits to Selborne, and Bishop Stanley has given us a valuable, although popular, *Familiar History of Birds*. Can we not hope to furnish the reader with a few rational and interesting facts about the dead? I hope so.

When that persevering traveller, Mungo Park, was at one period of his course fainting in the vast wilderness of an African desert, naked and alone, considering his days as numbered and nothing appearing to remain for him to do but to lie down and die, a small moss-flower of extraordinary beauty caught his eye. "Though the whole plant," says he, "was no larger than one of my fingers, I could not contemplate the delicate confirmation of its roots, leaves and capsules without admiration. Can that Being who planted, watered and brought to perfection, in this obscure part of the world, a thing which appears of so small importance, look with unconcern upon the situation and suffering of creatures formed after his own image? Surely not. Reflections like these would not allow me to despair; I started up and, disregarding both hunger and fatigue, travelled forward, assured that relief was at hand; and I was not disappointed."

With a disposition to wonder and adore in like manner, as Bishop Stanley says, can any branch of Natural History be studied without increasing that faith, love and hope which we also, every one of us, need in our journey through the wilderness of life? Let us therefore see what inspiration we may derive from the dead.

In war the dead are usually the male of the human species although this does not hold true with animals, and I have frequently seen dead mares among the horses. An interesting aspect of war, too, is that it is only there that the naturalist has an opportunity to observe the dead of mules. In twenty years of observation in civil life I had never seen a dead mule and had begun to entertain doubts as to whether these animals were really mortal. On rare occasions I had seen what I took to be dead mules, but on close approach these always proved to be living creatures who seemed to be dead through their quality of complete repose. But in war these animals succumb in much the same manner as the more common and less hardy horse.

Most of those mules that I saw dead were along mountain roads or lying at the foot of steep declivities whence they had been pushed to rid the road of their encumbrance. They seemed a fitting enough sight in the mountains where one was accustomed to their presence and looked less incongruous there than they did later, at Smyrna, where the Greeks broke the legs of all their baggage animals and pushed them off the quay into the shallow water to drown. The numbers of broken-legged mules and horses drowning in the shallow water called for a Goya to depict them. Although, speaking literally, one can hardly say that they called for a Goya since there has only been one Goya, long dead, and it is extremely doubtful if these animals, were they able to call, would call for pictorial representation of their plight but, more likely, would, if they were articulate, call for some one to alleviate their condition.

Regarding the sex of the dead it is a fact that one becomes so accustomed to the sight of all the dead being men that the sight of a dead woman is quite shocking. I first saw inversion of the usual sex of the dead after the explosion of a munition factory which had been situated in the countryside near Milan, Italy. We drove to the scene of the disaster in trucks along poplar-shaded roads, bordered with ditches containing much minute animal life, which I could not clearly observe because of the great clouds of dust raised by the trucks. Arriving where the munition plant had been, some of us were put to patrolling about those large stocks of munitions which for some reason had not exploded, while others were put at extinguishing a fire which had gotten into the grass of an adjacent field; which task being concluded, we were ordered to search the immediate vicinity and surrounding field for bodies. We found and carried to an improvised mortuary a good number of these and, I must admit, frankly, the shock it was to find that these dead were women rather than men. In those days women had not yet commenced to wear their hair cut short, as they did later for several years in Europe and America, and the most disturbing thing, perhaps because it was the most unaccustomed, was the presence and, even more disturbing, the occasional absence of this long hair. I remember that after we had searched quite thoroughly for the complete dead we collected fragments. Many

44

of these were detached from a heavy, barbed-wire fence which had surrounded the position of the factory and from the still existent portions of which we picked many of these detached bits which illustrated only too well the tremendous energy of high explosive. Many fragments we found a considerable distance away in the fields, they being carried farther by their own weight.

On our return to Milan I recall one or two of us discussing the occurrence and agreeing that the quality of unreality and the fact that there were no wounded did much to rob the disaster of a horror which might have been much greater. Also the fact that it had been so immediate and that the dead were in consequence still as little unpleasant as possible to carry and deal with made it quite removed from the usual battlefield experience. The pleasant, though dusty, ride through the beautiful Lombard countryside also was a compensation for the unpleasantness of the duty and on our return, while we exchanged impressions, we all agreed that it was indeed fortunate that the fire which broke out just before we arrived had been brought under control as rapidly as it had and before it had attained any of the seemingly huge stocks of unexploded munitions. We agreed too that the picking up of the fragments had been an extraordinary business; it being amazing that the human body should be blown into pieces which exploded along no anatomical lines, but rather divided as capriciously as the fragmentation in the burst of a high explosive shell.

A naturalist, to obtain accuracy of observation, may confine himself in his observations to one limited period and I will take first that following the Austrian offensive of June, 1918, in Italy as one in which the dead were present in their greatest numbers, a withdrawal having been forced and an advance later made to recover the ground lost so that the positions after the battle were the same as before except for the presence of the dead. Until the dead are buried they change somewhat in appearance each day. The color change in Caucasian races is from white to yellow, to yellow-green, to black. If left long enough in the heat the flesh comes to resemble coal-tar, especially where it has been broken or torn, and it has quite a visible tarlike iridescence. The dead grow larger each day until sometimes they become quite too big for their uniforms, filling these until they seem blown tight enough to burst. The individual members may increase in girth to an unbelievable extent and faces fill as taut and globular as balloons. The surprising thing, next to their progressive corpulence, is the amount of paper that is scattered about the dead. Their ultimate position, before there is any question of burial, depends on the location of the pockets in the uniform. In the Austrian army these pockets were in the back of the breeches and the dead, after a short time, all consequently lay on their faces, the two hip pockets pulled out and, scattered around them in the grass, all those papers their pockets had contained. The heat, the flies, the indicative positions of the bodies in the grass, and the amount of paper scattered are the impressions one retains. The smell of a battlefield in hot weather one cannot recall. You can remember that there was such a smell, but nothing ever happens to you to bring it back. It is unlike the smell of a regiment, which may come to you suddenly while riding in the street car and you will look across and see the man who has brought it to you. But the other thing is gone as completely as when you have been in love; you remember things that happened, but the sensation cannot be recalled.

One wonders what that persevering traveller, Mungo Park, would have seen on a battlefield in hot weather to restore his confidence. There were always poppies in the wheat in the end of June and in July, and the mulberry trees were in full leaf and one could see the heat waves rise from the barrels of the guns where the sun struck them through the screens of leaves; the earth was turned a bright yellow at the edge of holes where mustard gas shells had been and the average broken house is finer to see than one that has been shelled, but few travellers would take a good full breath of that early summer air and have any such thoughts as Mungo Park about those formed in His own image.

The first thing that you found about the dead was that, hit badly enough, they died like animals. Some quickly from a little wound you would not think would kill a rabbit. They died from little wounds as rabbits die sometimes from three or four small grains of shot that hardly seem to break the skin. Others would die like cats; a skull broken in and iron in the brain, they lie alive two days like cats that crawl into the coal bin with a bullet in the brain and will not die until you cut their heads off. Maybe cats do not die then, they say they have nine lives, I do not know, but most men die like animals, not men. I'd never seen a natural death, so called, and so I blamed it on the war and like the persevering traveller, Mungo Park, knew that there was something else; that always absent something else, and then I saw one.

The only natural death I've ever seen, outside of loss of blood, which isn't bad, was death from Spanish influenza. In this you drown in mucus, choking, and how you know the patient's dead is: at the end he turns to be a little child again, though with his manly force, and fills the sheets as full as any diaper with one vast, final, yellow cataract that flows and dribbles on after he's gone. So now I want to see the death of any self-called

Humanist* because a persevering traveller like Mungo Park or me lives on and maybe yet will live to see the actual death of members of this literary sect and watch the noble exits that they make. In my musings as a naturalist it has occurred to me that while decorum is an excellent thing some must be indecorous if the race is to be carried on since the position prescribed for procreation is indecorous, highly indecorous, and it occurred to me that perhaps that is what these people are, or were: the children of decorous cohabitation. But regardless of how they started I hope to see the finish of a few, and speculate how worms will try that long preserved sterility; with their quaint pamphlets gone to bust and into foot-notes all their lust.

While it is, perhaps, legitimate to deal with these self-designated citizens in a natural history of the dead, even though the designation may mean nothing by the time this work is published, yet it is unfair to the other dead, who were not dead in their youth of choice, who owned no magazines, many of whom had doubtless never even read a review, that one has seen in the hot weather with a half-pint of maggots working where their mouths have been. It was not always hot weather for the dead, much of the time it was the rain that washed them clean when they lay in it and made the earth soft when they were buried in it and sometimes then kept on until the earth was mud and washed them out and you had to bury them again. Or in the winter in the mountains you had to put them in the snow and when the snow melted in the spring some one else had to bury them. They had beautiful burying grounds in the mountains, war in the mountains is the most beautiful of all war, and in one of them, at a place called Pocol, they buried a general who was shot through the head by a sniper. This is where those writers are mistaken who write books called *Generals Die in Bed*, because this general died in a trench dug in snow, high in the mountains, wearing an Alpini hat with an eagle feather in it and a hole in front you couldn't put your little finger in and a hole in back you could put your fist in, if it were a small fist and you wanted to put it there, and much blood in the snow. He was a damned fine general, and so was General von Behr who commanded the Bavarian Alpenkorps troops at the battle of Caporetto and was killed in his staff car by the Italian rearguard as he drove into Udine ahead of his troops, and the titles of all such books should be *Generals Usually Die in Bed*, if we are to have any sort of accuracy in such things.

*The reader's indulgence is requested for this mention of an extinct phenomenon. The reference, like all references to fashion, dates the story but it is retained because of its mild historical interest and because its omission would spoil the rhythm.

In the mountains too, sometimes, the snow fell on the dead outside the dressing station on the side that was protected by the mountain from any shelling. They carried them into a cave that had been dug into the mountainside before the earth froze. It was in this cave that a man whose head was broken as a flower-pot may be broken, although it was all held together by membranes and a skillfully applied bandage now soaked and hardened, with the structure of his brain disturbed by a piece of broken steel in it, lay a day, a night, and a day. The stretcher-bearers asked the doctor to go in and have a look at him. They saw him each time they made a trip and even when they did not look at him they heard him breathing. The doctor's eyes were red and the lids swollen, almost shut from tear gas. He looked at the man twice; once in daylight, once with a flashlight. That too would have made a good etching for Goya, the visit with the flashlight, I mean. After looking at him the second time the doctor believed the stretcher-bearers when they said the soldier was still alive.

"What do you want me to do about it?" he asked.

There was nothing they wanted done. But after a while they asked permission to carry him out and lay him with the badly wounded.

"No. No. No!" said the doctor, who was busy. "What's the matter? Are you afraid of him?"

"We don't like to hear him in there with the dead."

"Don't listen to him. If you take him out of there you will have to carry him right back in."

"We wouldn't mind that, Captain Doctor."

"No," said the doctor. "No. Didn't you hear me say no?"

"Why don't you give him an overdose of morphine?" asked an artillery officer who was waiting to have a wound in his arm dressed.

"Do you think that is the only use I have for morphine? Would you like me to have to operate without morphine? You have a pistol, go out and shoot him yourself."

"He's been shot already," said the officer. "If some of you doctors were shot you'd be different."

"Thank you very much," said the doctor waving a forceps in the air. "Thank you a thousand times. What about these eyes?" He pointed the forceps at them. "How would you like these?"

"Tear gas. We call it lucky if it's tear gas."

"Because you leave the line," said the doctor. "Because you come running here with your tear gas to be evacuated. You rub onions in your eyes."

"You are beside yourself. I do not notice your insults. You are crazy."

48

The stretcher-bearers came in.

"Captain Doctor," one of them said.

"Get out of here!" said the doctor.

They went out.

"I will shoot the poor fellow," the artillery officer said. "I am a humane man. I will not let him suffer."

"Shoot him then," said the doctor. "Shoot him. Assume the responsibility. I will make a report. Wounded shot by lieutenant of artillery in first curing post. Shoot him. Go ahead shoot him."

"You are not a human being."

"My business is to care for the wounded, not to kill them. That is for gentlemen of the artillery."

"Why don't you care for him then?"

"I have done so. I have done all that can be done."

"Why don't you send him down on the cable railway?"

"Who are you to ask me questions? Are you my superior officer? Are you in command of this dressing post? Do me the courtesy to answer."

The lieutenant of artillery said nothing. The others in the room were all soldiers and there were no other officers present.

"Answer me," said the doctor holding a needle up in his forceps. "Give me a response."

"F— yourself," said the artillery officer.

"So," said the doctor. "So, you said that. All right. All right. We shall see."

The lieutenant of artillery stood up and walked toward him.

"F— yourself," he said. "F— yourself. F— your mother. F— your sister. . . ."

The doctor tossed the saucer full of iodine in his face. As he came toward him, blinded, the lieutenant fumbled for his pistol. The doctor skipped quickly behind him, tripped him and, as he fell to the floor, kicked him several times and picked up the pistol in his rubber gloves. The lieutenant sat on the floor holding his good hand to his eyes.

"I'll kill you!" he said. "I'll kill you as soon as I can see."

"I am the boss," said the doctor. "All is forgiven since you know I am the boss. You cannot kill me because I have your pistol. Sergeant! Adjutant! Adjutant!"

"The adjutant is at the cable railway," said the sergeant.

"Wipe out this officer's eyes with alcohol and water. He has got iodine in them. Bring me the basin to wash my hands. I will take this officer next."

"You won't touch me."

49

"Hold him tight. He is a little delirious."

One of the stretcher-bearers came in.

"Captain Doctor."

"What do you want?"

"The man in the dead-house——"

"Get out of here."

"Is dead, Captain Doctor. I thought you would be glad to know."

"See, my poor lieutenant? We dispute about nothing. In time of war we dispute about nothing."

"F— you," said the lieutenant of artillery. He still could not see. "You've blinded me."

"It is nothing," said the doctor. "Your eyes will be all right. It is nothing. A dispute about nothing."

"Ayee! Ayee! Ayee!" suddenly screamed the lieutenant. "You have blinded me! You have blinded me!"

"Hold him tight," said the doctor. "He is in much pain. Hold him very tight."

A Way You'll Never Be

The attack had gone across the field, been held up by machine-gun fire from the sunken road and from the group of farm houses, encountered no resistance in the town, and reached the bank of the river. Coming along the road on a bicycle, getting off to push the machine when the surface of the road became too broken, Nicholas Adams saw what had happened by the position of the dead.

They lay alone or in clumps in the high grass of the field and along the road, their pockets out, and over them were flies and around each body or group of bodies were the scattered papers.

In the grass and the grain, beside the road, and in some places scattered over the road, there was much material: a field kitchen, it must have come over when things were going well; many of the calf-skin-covered haversacks, stick bombs, helmets, rifles, sometimes one butt-up, the bayonet stuck in the dirt, they had dug quite a little at the last; stick bombs, helmets, rifles, intrenching tools, ammunition boxes, star-shell pistols, their shells scattered about, medical kits, gas masks, empty gas-mask cans, a squat, tripodded machine gun in a nest of empty shells, full belts protruding from the boxes, the water-cooling can empty and on its side, the breech block gone, the crew in odd positions, and around them, in the grass, more of the typical papers.

There were mass prayer books, group postcards showing the machine-gun unit standing in ranked and ruddy cheerfulness as in a football picture for a college annual; now they were humped and swollen in the grass; propaganda postcards showing a soldier in Austrian uniform bending a woman backward over a bed; the figures were impressionistically drawn; very attractively depicted and had nothing in common with actual rape in which the woman's skirts are pulled over her head to smother her, one comrade sometimes sitting upon the head. There were many of these inciting cards which had evidently been issued just before the offensive. Now they were scattered with the smutty postcards, photographic; the small photographs of village girls by village

51

photographers, the occasional pictures of children, and the letters, letters, letters. There was always much paper about the dead and the débris of this attack was no exception.

These were new dead and no one had bothered with anything but their pockets. Our own dead, or what he thought of, still, as our own dead, were surprisingly few, Nick noticed. Their coats had been opened too and their pockets were out, and they showed, by their positions, the manner and the skill of the attack. The hot weather had swollen them all alike regardless of nationality.

The town had evidently been defended, at the last, from the line of the sunken road and there had been few or no Austrians to fall back into it. There were only three bodies in the street and they looked to have been killed running. The houses of the town were broken by the shelling and the street had much rubble of plaster and mortar and there were broken beams, broken tiles, and many holes, some of them yellow-edged from the mustard gas. There were many pieces of shell, and shrapnel balls were scattered in the rubble. There was no one in the town at all.

Nick Adams had seen no one since he had left Fornaci, although, riding along the road through the over-foliaged country, he had seen guns hidden under screens of mulberry leaves to the left of the road, noticing them by the heat-waves in the air above the leaves where the sun hit the metal. Now he went on through the town, surprised to find it deserted, and came out on the low road beneath the bank of the river. Leaving the town there was a bare open space where the road slanted down and he could see the placid reach of the river and the low curve of the opposite bank and the whitened, sun-baked mud where the Austrians had dug. It was all very lush and over-green since he had seen it last and becoming historical had made no change in this, the lower river.

The battalion was along the bank to the left. There was a series of holes in the top of the bank with a few men in them. Nick noticed where the machine guns were posted and the signal rockets in their racks. The men in the holes in the side of the bank were sleeping. No one challenged. He went on and as he came around a turn in the mud bank a young second lieutenant with a stubble of beard and red-rimmed, very blood-shot eyes pointed a pistol at him.

"Who are you?"

Nick told him.

"How do I know this?"

Nick showed him the tessera with photograph and identification and the seal of the third army. He took hold of it.

"I will keep this."

"You will not," Nick said. "Give me back the card and put your gun away. There. In the holster."

"How am I to know who you are?"

"The tessera tells you."

"And if the tessera is false? Give me that card."

"Don't be a fool," Nick said cheerfully. "Take me to your company commander."

"I should send you to battalion headquarters."

"All right," said Nick. "Listen, do you know the Captain Paravicini? The tall one with the small mustache who was an architect and speaks English?"

"You know him?"

"A little."

"What company does he command?"

"The second."

"He is commanding the battalion."

"Good," said Nick. He was relieved to know that Para was all right. "Let us go to the battalion."

As Nick had left the edge of the town three shrapnel had burst high and to the right over one of the wrecked houses and since then there had been no shelling. But the face of this officer looked like the face of a man during a bombardment. There was the same tightness and the voice did not sound natural. His pistol made Nick nervous.

"Put it away," he said. "There's the whole river between them and you."

"If I thought you were a spy I would shoot you now," the second lieutenant said.

"Come on," said Nick. "Let us go to the battalion." This officer made him very nervous.

The Captain Paravicini, acting major, thinner and more English-looking than ever, rose when Nick saluted from behind the table in the dugout that was battalion headquarters.

"Hello," he said. "I didn't know you. What are you doing in that uniform?"

"They've put me in it."

"I am very glad to see you, Nicolo."

"Right. You look well. How was the show?"

"We made a very fine attack. Truly. A very fine attack. I will show you. Look."

He showed on the map how the attack had gone.

"I came from Fornaci," Nick said. "I could see how it had been. It was very good."

"It was extraordinary. Altogether extraordinary. Are you attached to the regiment?"

"No. I am supposed to move around and let them see the uniform."

"How odd."

"If they see one American uniform that is supposed to make them believe others are coming."

"But how will they know it is an American uniform?"

"You will tell them."

"Oh. Yes, I see. I will send a corporal with you to show you about and you will make a tour of the lines."

"Like a bloody politician," Nick said.

"You would be much more distinguished in civilian clothes. They are what is really distinguished."

"With a homburg hat," said Nick.

"Or with a very furry fedora."

"I'm supposed to have my pockets full of cigarettes and postal cards and such things," Nick said. "I should have a musette full of chocolate. These I should distribute with a kind word and a pat on the back. But there weren't any cigarettes and postcards and no chocolate. So they said to circulate around anyway."

"I'm sure your appearance will be very heartening to the troops."

"I wish you wouldn't," Nick said. "I feel badly enough about it as it is. In principle, I would have brought you a bottle of brandy."

"In principle," Para said and smiled, for the first time, showing yellowed teeth. "Such a beautiful expression. Would you like some Grappa?"

"No, thank you," Nick said.

"It hasn't any ether in it."

"I can taste that still," Nick remembered suddenly and completely.

"You know I never knew you were drunk until you started talking coming back in the camions."

"I was stinking in every attack," Nick said.

"I can't do it," Para said. "I took it in the first show, the very first show, and it only made me very upset and then frightfully thirsty."

"You don't need it."

"You're much braver in an attack than I am."

"No," Nick said. "I know how I am and I prefer to get stinking. I'm not ashamed of it."

"I've never seen you drunk."

"No?" said Nick. "Never? Not when we rode from Mestre to Portogrande that night and I wanted to go to sleep and used the bicycle for a blanket and pulled it up under my chin?"

"That wasn't in the lines."

"Let's not talk about how I am," Nick said. "It's a subject I know too much about to want to think about it any more."

"You might as well stay here a while," Paravicini said. "You can take a nap if you like. They didn't do much to this in the bombardment. It's too hot to go out yet."

"I suppose there is no hurry."

"How are you really?"

"I'm fine. I'm perfectly all right."

"No. I mean really."

"I'm all right. I can't sleep without a light of some sort. That's all I have now."

"I said it should have been trepanned. I'm no doctor but I know that."

"Well, they thought it was better to have it absorb, and that's what I got. What's the matter? I don't seem crazy to you, do I?"

"You seem in top-hole shape."

"It's a hell of a nuisance once they've had you certified as nutty," Nick said. "No one ever has any confidence in you again."

"I would take a nap, Nicolo," Paravicini said. "This isn't battalion headquarters as we used to know it. We're just waiting to be pulled out. You oughtn't to go out in the heat now—it's silly. Use that bunk."

"I might just lie down," Nick said.

Nick lay on the bunk. He was very disappointed that he felt this way and more disappointed, even, that it was so obvious to Captain Paravicini. This was not as large a dugout as the one where that platoon of the class of 1899, just out at the front, got hysterics during the bombardment before the attack, and Para had had him walk them two at a time outside to show them nothing would happen, he wearing his own chin strap tight across his mouth to keep his lips quiet. Knowing they could not hold it when they took it. Knowing it was all a bloody balls—if he can't stop crying, break his nose to give him something else to think about. I'd shoot one but it's too late now. They'd all be worse. Break his nose. They've put it back to five-twenty. We've only got four minutes more. Break that other silly bugger's nose and kick his silly ass out of here. Do you think they'll go over? If they don't, shoot two and try to scoop the others out some way. Keep behind them, sergeant. It's no use to walk ahead and find there's nothing coming behind you. Bail them out as you go. What a bloody balls. All right. That's right. Then, looking at the watch, in that quiet tone, that valuable quiet tone, "Savoia." Making it cold, no time to get it, he couldn't find his own after the cave-in, one whole end had caved in; it was that started them; making it cold up that slope the only time he hadn't done it stinking. And after they came back the *teleferica* house burned, it seemed, and some of the wounded got down four days later and some did not get down, but we went up and we went back and we came down—we always came down. And there was Gaby Delys, oddly enough, with feathers on; you called me baby doll a year ago tadada you said that I was rather nice to know tadada with feathers on, with feathers off, the great Gaby, and my name's Harry Pilcer, too, we used to step out of the far side of the taxis when it got steep going up the hill and he could see that hill every night when he dreamed with Sacré Cœur, blown white, like a soap bubble. Sometimes his girl was there and sometimes she was with some one else and he could not understand that, but those were the nights the river ran so much wider and stiller than it should and outside of Fossalta there was a low house painted yellow with willows all around it and a low stable and there was a canal, and he had been there a thousand times and never seen it, but there it was every night as plain as the hill, only it frightened him. That house meant more than anything and every night he had it. That was what he needed but it frightened him especially when the boat lay there quietly in the willows on the canal, but the banks weren't like this river. It was all lower, as it was at Portogrande, where they had seen them come wallowing across the flooded ground holding the rifles high until they fell with them in the water. Who ordered that one? If it didn't get so damned mixed up he could follow it all right. That was why he noticed everything in such detail to keep it all straight so he would know just where he was, but suddenly it confused without reason as now, he lying in a bunk at battalion headquarters, with Para commanding a battalion and he in a bloody American uniform. He sat up and looked around; they all watching him. Para was gone out. He lay down again.

The Paris part came earlier and he was not frightened of it except when she had gone off with some one else and the fear that they might take the same driver twice. That was what frightened about that. Never about the front. He never dreamed about the front now any more but what frightened him so that he could not get rid of it was that long yellow house and the different width of the river. Now he was back here at the river, he had gone through that same town, and there was no house. Nor was the river that way. Then where did he go each night and what was the peril, and why would he wake, soaking wet, more frightened than he had ever been in a bombardment, because of a house and a long stable and a canal?

He sat up; swung his legs carefully down; they stiffened any time they were out straight for long; returned the stares of the adjutant, the signallers and the two runners by the door and put on his cloth-covered trench helmet.

"I regret the absence of the chocolate, the postal-cards and cigarettes," he said. "I am, however, wearing the uniform."

"The major is coming back at once," the adjutant said. In that army an adjutant is not a commissioned officer.

"The uniform is not very correct," Nick told them. "But it gives you the idea. There will be several millions of Americans here shortly."

"Do you think they will send Americans down here?" asked the adjutant.

"Oh, absolutely. Americans twice as large as myself, healthy, with clean hearts, sleep at night, never been wounded, never been blown up, never had their heads caved in, never been scared, don't drink, faithful to the girls they left behind them, many of them never had crabs, wonderful chaps. You'll see."

"Are you an Italian?" asked the adjutant.

"No, American. Look at the uniform. Spagnolini made it but it's not quite correct."

"A North or South American?"

"North," said Nick. He felt it coming on now. He would quiet down.

"But you speak Italian."

"Why not? Do you mind if I speak Italian? Haven't I a right to speak Italian?"

"You have Italian medals."

"Just the ribbons and the papers. The medals come later. Or you give them to people to keep and the people go away; or they are lost with your baggage. You can purchase others in Milan. It is the papers that are of importance. You must not feel badly about them. You will have some yourself if you stay at the front long enough."

"I am a veteran of the Eritrea campaign," said the adjutant stiffly. "I fought in Tripoli."

"It's quite something to have met you," Nick put out his hand. "Those must have been trying days. I noticed the ribbons. Were you, by any chance, on the Carso?"

"I have just been called up for this war. My class was too old."

"At one time I was under the age limit," Nick said. "But now I am reformed out of the war."

"But why are you here now?"

"I am demonstrating the American uniform," Nick said. "Don't you think it is very significant? It is a little tight in the collar but soon you will see untold millions wearing this uniform swarming like locusts. The grasshopper, you know, what we call the grasshopper in America, is really a locust. The true grasshopper is small and green and comparatively feeble. You must not, however, make a confusion with the seven-year locust or cicada which emits a peculiar sustained sound which at the moment I cannot recall. I try to recall it but I cannot. I can almost hear it and then it is quite gone. You will pardon me if I break off our conversation?"

"See if you can find the major," the adjutant said to one of the two runners. "I can see you have been wounded," he said to Nick.

"In various places," Nick said. "If you are interested in scars I can show you some very interesting ones but I would rather talk about grasshoppers. What we call grasshoppers that is; and what are, really, locusts. These insects at one time played a very important part in my life. It might interest you and you can look at the uniform while I am talking."

The adjutant made a motion with his hand to the second runner who went out.

"Fix your eyes on the uniform. Spagnolini made it, you know. You might as well look, too," Nick said to the signallers. "I really have no rank. We're under the American consul. It's perfectly all right for you to look. You can stare, if you like. I will tell you about the American locust. We always preferred one that we called the medium-brown. They last the best in the water and fish prefer them. The larger ones that fly making a noise somewhat similar to that produced by a rattlesnake rattling his rattlers, a very dry sound, have vivid colored wings, some are bright red, others yellow barred with black, but their wings go to pieces in the water and they make a very blowsy bait, while the medium-brown is a plump, compact, succulent hopper that I can recommend as far as one may well recommend something you gentlemen will probably never encounter. But I must insist that you will never gather a sufficient supply of these insects for a day's fishing by pursuing them with your hands or trying to hit them with a bat. That is sheer nonsense and a useless waste of time. I repeat, gentlemen, that you will get nowhere at it. The correct procedure, and one which should be taught all young officers at every small-arms course if I had anything to say about it, and who knows but what I will have, is the employment of a seine or net made of common mosquito netting. Two officers holding this length of netting at alternate ends, or let us say one at each end, stoop, hold the bottom extremity of the net in one hand and the top extremity in the other and run into the wind. The hoppers, flying with the wind, fly against the length of netting and are imprisoned in its folds. It is no trick at all to catch a very great quantity indeed, and no officer, in my opinion, should be without a length of mosquito netting suitable for the improvisation of one of these grasshopper seines. I hope I have made myself clear, gentlemen. Are there any questions? If there is anything in the course you do not understand please ask questions. Speak up. None? Then I would like to close on this note. In the words of that great soldier and gentleman, Sir Henry Wilson: Gentlemen, either you must govern or you must be governed. Let me repeat it. Gentlemen, there is one thing I would like to have you remember. One thing I would like you to take with you as you leave this room. Gentlemen, either you must govern—or you must be governed. That is all, gentlemen. Good-day."

He removed his cloth-covered helmet, put it on again and, stooping, went out the low entrance of the dugout. Para, accompanied by the two runners, was coming down the line of the sunken road. It was very hot in the sun and Nick removed the helmet.

"There ought to be a system for wetting these things," he said. "I shall wet this one in the river." He started up the bank.

"Nicolo," Paravicini called. "Nicolo. Where are you going?"

"I don't really have to go." Nick came down the slope, holding the helmet in his hands. "They're a damned nuisance wet or dry. Do you wear yours all the time?"

"All the time," said Para. "It's making me bald. Come inside."

Inside Para told him to sit down.

"You know they're absolutely no damned good," Nick said. "I remember when they were a comfort when we first had them, but I've seen them full of brains too many times."

"Nicolo," Para said. "I think you should go back. I think it would be better if you didn't come up to the line until you had those supplies. There's nothing here for you to do. If you move around, even with something worth giving away, the men will group and that invites shelling. I won't have it."

"I know it's silly," Nick said. "It wasn't my idea. I heard the brigade was here so I thought I would see you or some one else I knew. I could have gone to Zenzon or to San Dona. I'd like to go to San Dona to see the bridge again."

"I won't have you circulating around to no purpose," Captain Paravicini said.

"All right," said Nick. He felt it coming on again.

59

"You understand?"

"Of course," said Nick. He was trying to hold it in.

"Anything of that sort should be done at night."

"Naturally," said Nick. He knew he could not stop it now.

"You see, I am commanding the battalion," Para said.

"And why shouldn't you be?" Nick said. Here it came. "You can read and write, can't you?"

"Yes," said Para gently.

"The trouble is you have a damned small battalion to command. As soon as it gets to strength again they'll give you back your company. Why don't they bury the dead? I've seen them now. I don't care about seeing them again. They can bury them any time as far as I'm concerned and it would be much better for you. You'll all get bloody sick."

"Where did you leave your bicycle?"

"Inside the last house."

"Do you think it will be all right?"

"Don't worry," Nick said. "I'll go in a little while."

"Lie down a little while, Nicolo."

"All right."

He shut his eyes, and in place of the man with the beard who looked at him over the sights of the rifle, quite calmly before squeezing off, the white flash and clublike impact, on his knees, hot-sweet choking, coughing it onto the rock while they went past him, he saw a long, yellow house with a low stable and the river much wider than it was and stiller. "Christ," he said, "I might as well go."

He stood up.

"I'm going, Para," he said. "I'll ride back now in the afternoon. If any supplies have come I'll bring them down tonight. If not I'll come at night when I have something to bring."

"It is still hot to ride," Captain Paravicini said.

"You don't need to worry," Nick said. "I'm all right now for quite a while. I had one then but it was easy. They're getting much better. I can tell when I'm going to have one because I talk so much."

"I'll send a runner with you."

"I'd rather you didn't. I know the way."

"You'll be back soon?"

"Absolutely."

"Let me send——"

"No," said Nick. "As a mark of confidence."

"Well, *ciao* then."

"*Ciao*," said Nick. He started back along the sunken road toward where he had left the bicycle. In the afternoon the road would be shady once he had passed the canal. Beyond that there were trees on both sides that had not been shelled at all. It was on that stretch that, marching, they had once passed the Terza Savoia cavalry regiment riding in the snow with their lances. The horses' breath made plumes in the cold air. No, that was somewhere else. Where was that?

"I'd better get to that damned bicycle," Nick said to himself. "I don't want to lose the way to Fornaci."

Self-Inflicted Wounds

(from *A Farewell to Arms*)

I came back the next afternoon from our first mountain post and stopped the car at the *smistimento* where the wounded and sick were sorted by their papers and the papers marked for the different hospitals. I had been driving and I sat in the car and the driver took the papers in. It was a hot day and the sky was very bright and blue and the road was white and dusty. I sat in the high seat of the Fiat and thought about nothing. A regiment went by in the road and I watched them pass. The men were hot and sweating. Some wore their steel helmets but most of them carried them slung from their packs. Most of the helmets were too big and came down almost over the ears of the men who wore them. The officers all wore helmets; better-fitting helmets. It was half of the brigata Basilicata. I identified them by their red and white striped collar mark. There were stragglers going by long after the regiment had passed—men who could not keep up with their platoons. They were sweaty, dusty and tired. Some looked pretty bad. A soldier came along after the last of the stragglers. He was walking with a limp. He stopped and sat down beside the road. I got down and went over.

"What's the matter?"

He looked at me, then stood up.

"I'm going on."

"What's the trouble?"

"—— the war."

"What's wrong with your leg?"

"It's not my leg. I got a rupture."

"Why don't you ride with the transport?" I asked. "Why don't you go to the hospital?"

"They won't let me. The lieutenant said I slipped the truss on purpose."

"Let me feel it."

"It's way out."

"Which side is it on?"

"Here."

I felt it.

"Cough," I said.

"I'm afraid it will make it bigger. It's twice as big as it was this morning."

"Sit down," I said. "As soon as I get the papers on these wounded I'll take you along the road and drop you with your medical officers."

"He'll say I did it on purpose."

"They can't do anything," I said. "It's not a wound. You've had it before, haven't you?"

"But I lost the truss."

"They'll send you to a hospital."

"Can't I stay here, Tenente?"

"No, I haven't any papers for you."

The driver came out of the door with the papers for the wounded in the car.

"Four for 105. Two for 132," he said. They were hospitals beyond the river.

"You drive," I said. I helped the soldier with the rupture up on the seat with us.

"You speak English?" he asked.

"Sure."

"How you like this goddam war?"

"Rotten."

"I say it's rotten. Jesus Christ, I say it's rotten."

"Were you in the States?"

"Sure. In Pittsburgh. I knew you was an American."

"Don't I talk Italian good enough?"

"I knew you was an American all right."

"Another American," said the driver in Italian looking at the hernia man.

"Listen, lootenant. Do you have to take me to that regiment?"

"Yes."

"Because the captain doctor knew I had this rupture. I threw away the goddam truss so it would get bad and I wouldn't have to go to the line again."

"I see."

"Couldn't you take me no place else?"

"If it was closer to the front I could take you to a first medical post. But back here you've got to have papers."

"If I go back they'll make me get operated on and then they'll put me in the line all the time."

63

I thought it over.

"You wouldn't want to go in the line all the time, would you?" he asked.

"No."

"Jesus Christ, ain't this a goddam war?"

"Listen," I said. "You get out and fall down by the road and get a bump on your head and I'll pick you up on our way back and take you to a hospital. We'll stop by the road here, Aldo." We stopped at the side of the road. I helped him down.

"I'll be right here, lieutenant," he said.

"So long," I said. We went on and passed the regiment about a mile ahead, then crossed the river, cloudy with snow-water and running fast through the spiles of the bridge, to ride along the road across the plain and deliver the wounded at the two hospitals. I drove coming back and went fast with the empty car to find the man from Pittsburgh. First we passed the regiment, hotter and slower than ever: then the stragglers. Then we saw a horse ambulance stopped by the road. Two men were lifting the hernia man to put him in. They had come back for him. He shook his head at me. His helmet was off and his forehead was bleeding below the hair line. His nose was skinned and there was dust on the bloody patch and dust in his hair.

"Look at the bump, lieutenant!" he shouted. "Nothing to do. They come back for me."

At the Front

(from *A Farewell to Arms*)

He said there were Croats in the lines opposite us now and some Magyars. Our troops were still in the attacking positions. There was no wire to speak of and no place to fall back to if there should be an Austrian attack. There were fine positions for defense along the low mountains that came up out of the plateau but nothing had been done about organizing them for defense. What did I think about the Bainsizza anyway?

I had expected it to be flatter, more like a plateau. I had not realized it was so broken up.

"Alto piano," Gino said, "but no piano."

We went back to the cellar of the house where he lived. I said I thought a ridge that flattened out on top and had a little depth would be easier and more practical to hold than a succession of small mountains. It was no harder to attack up a mountain than on the level, I argued. "That depends on the mountains," he said. "Look at San Gabriele."

"Yes," I said, "but where they had trouble was at the top where it was flat. They got up to the top easy enough."

"Not so easy," he said.

"Yes," I said, "but that was a special case because it was a fortress rather than a mountain, anyway. The Austrians had been fortifying it for years." I meant tactically speaking in a war where there was some movement a succession of mountains were nothing to hold as a line because it was too easy to turn them. You should have possible mobility and a mountain is not very mobile. Also, people always over-shoot downhill. If the flank were turned, the best men would be left on the highest mountains. I did not believe in a war in mountains. I had thought about it a lot, I said. You pinched off one mountain and they pinched off another but when something really started every one had to get down off the mountains.

What were you going to do if you had a mountain frontier? he asked.

I had not worked that out yet, I said, and we both laughed. "But," I said, "in the old days the Austrians were always whipped in the quadrilateral around Verona. They let them come down onto the plain and whipped them there."

"Yes," said Gino. "But those were Frenchmen and you can work out military problems clearly when you are fighting in somebody else's country."

"Yes," I agreed, "when it is your own country you cannot use it so scientifically."

"The Russians did, to trap Napoleon."

"Yes, but they had plenty of country. If you tried to retreat to trap Napoleon in Italy you would find yourself in Brindisi."

"A terrible place," said Gino. "Have you ever been there?"

"Not to stay."

"I am a patriot," Gino said. "But I cannot love Brindisi or Taranto."

"Do you love the Bainsizza?" I asked.

"The soil is sacred," he said. "But I wish it grew more potatoes. You know when we came here we found fields of potatoes the Austrians had planted."

"Has the food really been short?"

"I myself have never had enough to eat but I am a big eater and I have not starved. The mess is average. The regiments in the line get pretty good food but those in support don't get so much. Something is wrong somewhere. There should be plenty of food."

"The dogfish are selling it somewhere else."

"Yes, they give the battalions in the front line as much as they can but the ones in back are very short. They have eaten all the Austrians' potatoes and chestnuts from the woods. They ought to feed them better. We are big eaters. I am sure there is plenty of food. It is very bad for the soldiers to be short of food. Have you ever noticed the difference it makes in the way you think?"

"Yes," I said. "It can't win a war but it can lose one."

"We won't talk about losing. There is enough talk about losing. What has been done this summer cannot have been done in vain."

I did not say anything. I was always embarrassed by the words sacred, glorious, and sacrifice and the expression in vain. We had heard them, sometimes standing in the rain almost out of earshot, so that only the shouted words came through, and had read them, on proclamations that were slapped up by billposters over other proclamations, now for a long time, and I had seen nothing sacred, and the things that were glorious had no glory and the sacrifices were like the stockyards at Chicago if nothing was done with the meat except to bury it. There were many words that you could not stand to hear and finally only the names of places had dignity. Certain numbers were the same way and certain dates and these with the names of the places were all you could say and have them mean anything. Abstract words such as glory, honor, courage, or hallow were obscene beside the concrete names of villages, the numbers of roads, the names of rivers, the numbers of regiments and the dates. Gino was a patriot, so he said things that separated us sometimes, but he was also a fine boy and I understood his being a patriot. He was born one. He left with Peduzzi in the car to go back to Gorizia.

It stormed all that day. The wind drove down the rain and everywhere there was standing water and mud. The plaster of the broken houses was gray and wet. Late in the afternoon the rain stopped and from out number two post I saw the bare wet autumn country with clouds over the tops of the hills and the straw screening over the roads wet and dripping. The sun came out once before it went down and shone on the bare woods beyond the ridge. There were many Austrian guns in the woods on that ridge but only a few fired. I watched the sudden round puffs of shrapnel smoke in the sky above a broken farmhouse near where the line was; soft puffs with a yellow white flash in the centre. You saw the flash, then heard the crack, then saw the smoke ball distort and thin in the wind. There were many iron shrapnel balls in the rubble of the houses and on the road beside the broken house where the post was, but they did not shell near the post that afternoon. We loaded two cars and drove down the road that was screened with wet mats and the last of the sun came through in the breaks between the strips of mattings. Before we were out on the clear road behind the hill the sun was down. We went on down the clear road and as it turned a corner into the open and went into the square arched tunnel of matting the rain started again.

The wind rose in the night and at three o'clock in the morning with the rain coming in sheets there was a bombardment and the Croatians came over across the mountain meadows and through patches of woods and into the front line. They fought in the dark in the rain and a counter-attack of scared men from the second line drove them back. There was much shelling and many rockets in the rain and machine-gun and rifle fire all along the line. They did not come again and it was quieter and between the gusts of wind and rain we could hear the sound of a great bombardment far to the north.

The wounded were coming into the post, some were carried on stretchers, some walking and some were brought on the backs of men that came across the field. They were wet to the skin and all were scared. We filled two cars with stretcher cases as they came up from the cellar of the post and as I shut the door of the second car and fastened it I felt the rain on my face turn to snow. The flakes were coming heavy and fast in the rain.

When daylight came the storm was still blowing but the snow had stopped. It had melted as it fell on the wet ground and now it was raining again. There was another attack just after daylight but it was unsuccessful. We expected an attack all day but it did not come until the sun was going down. The bombardment started to the south below the long wooded ridge where the Austrian guns were concentrated. We expected a bombardment but it did not come. It was getting dark. Guns were firing from the field behind the village and the shells, going away, had a comfortable sound.

We heard that the attack to the south had been unsuccessful. They did not attack that night but we heard that they had broken through to the north. In the night word came that we were to prepare to retreat. The captain at the post told me this. He had it from the Brigade. A little while later he came from the telephone and said it was a lie. The Brigade had received orders that the line of the Bainsizza should be held no matter what happened. I asked about the break through and he said that he had heard at the Brigade that the Austrians had broken through the twenty-seventh army corps up toward Caporetto. There had been a great battle in the north all day.

"If those bastards let them through we are cooked," he said.

"It's Germans that are attacking," one of the medical officers said. The word Germans was something to be frightened of. We did not want to have anything to do with the Germans.

"There are fifteen divisions of Germans," the medical officer said. "They have broken through and we will be cut off."

"At the Brigade, they say this line is to be held. They say they have not broken through badly and that we will hold a line across the mountains from Monte Maggiore."

"Where do they hear this?"

"From the Division."

"The word that we were to retreat came from the Division."

"We work under the Army Corps," I said. "But here I work under you. Naturally when you tell me to go I will go. But get the orders straight."

"The orders are that we stay here. You clear the wounded from here to the clearing station."

"Sometimes we clear from the clearing station to the field hospitals too," I said. "Tell me, I have never seen a retreat—if there is a retreat how are all the wounded evacuated?"

"They are not. They take as many as they can and leave the rest."

"What will I take in the cars?"

"Hospital equipment."

"All right," I said.

The next night the retreat started. We heard that Germans and Austrians had broken through in the north and were coming down the mountain valleys toward Cividale and Udine. The retreat was orderly, wet and sullen. In the night, going slowly along the crowded roads we passed troops marching under the rain, guns, horses pulling wagons, mules, motor trucks, all moving away from the front. There was no more disorder than in an advance.

The Retreat from Caporetto

(from *A Farewell to Arms*)

At noon we were stuck in a muddy road about, as nearly as we could figure, ten kilometres from Udine. The rain had stopped during the forenoon and three times we had heard planes coming, seen them pass overhead, watched them go far to the left and heard them bombing on the main highroad. We had worked through a network of secondary roads and had taken many roads that were blind, but had always, by backing up and finding another road, gotten closer to Udine. Now, Aymo's car, in backing so that we might get out of a blind road, had gotten into the soft earth at the side and the wheels, spinning, had dug deeper and deeper until the car rested on its differential. The thing to do now was to dig out in front of the wheels, put in brush so that the chains could grip, and then push until the car was on the road. We were all down on the road around the car. The two sergeants looked at the car and examined the wheels. Then they started off down the road without a word. I went after them.

"Come on," I said. "Cut some brush."

"We have to go," one said.

"Get busy," I said, "and cut brush."

"We have to go," one said. The other said nothing. They were in a hurry to start. They would not look at me.

"I order you to come back to the car and cut brush," I said. The one sergeant turned. "We have to go on. In a little while you will be cut off. You can't order us. You're not our officer."

"I order you to cut brush," I said. They turned and started down the road.

"Halt," I said. They kept on down the muddy road, the hedge on either side. "I order you to halt," I called. They went a little faster. I opened up my holster, took the pistol, aimed at the one who had talked the most, and fired. I missed and they both started to run. I shot three times and dropped one. The other went through the hedge and was out of sight. I fired at him through the hedge as he ran across the field. The pistol clicked empty and I put in another clip. I saw it was too far to shoot at the second sergeant. He was far across the field, running, his head held low. I commenced to reload the empty clip. Bonello came up.

"Let me go finish him," he said. I handed him the pistol and he walked down to where the sergeant of engineers lay face down across the road. Bonello leaned over, put the pistol against the man's head and pulled the trigger. The pistol did not fire.

"You have to cock it," I said. He cocked it and fired twice. He took hold of the sergeant's legs and pulled him to the side of the road so he lay beside the hedge. He came back and handed me the pistol.

"The son of a bitch," he said. He looked toward the sergeant. "You see me shoot him, Tenente?"

"We've got to get the brush quickly," I said. "Did I hit the other one at all?"

"I don't think so," Aymo said. "He was too far away to hit with a pistol."

"The dirty scum," Piani said. We were all cutting twigs and branches. Everything had been taken out of the car. Bonello was digging out in front of the wheels. When we were ready Aymo started the car and put it into gear. The wheels spun round throwing brush and mud. Bonello and I pushed until we could feel our joints crack. The car would not move.

"Rock her back and forth, Barto," I said.

He drove the engine in reverse, then forward. The wheels only dug in deeper. Then the car was resting on the differential again, and the wheels spun freely in the holes they had dug. I straightened up.

"We'll try her with a rope," I said.

"I don't think it's any use, Tenente. You can't get a straight pull."

"We have to try it," I said. "She won't come out any other way."

Piani's and Bonello's cars could only move straight ahead down the narrow road. We roped both cars together and pulled. The wheels only pulled sideways against the ruts.

"It's no good," I shouted. "Stop it."

Piani and Bonello got down from their cars and came back. Aymo got down. The girls were up the road about forty yards sitting on a stone wall.

"What do you say, Tenente?" Bonello asked.

"We'll dig out and try once more with the brush," I said. I looked down the road. It was my fault. I had led them up here. The sun was almost out from behind the clouds and the body of the sergeant lay beside the hedge.

"We'll put his coat and cape under," I said. Bonello went to get them. I cut brush and Aymo and Piani dug out in front and between the wheels. I cut the cape, then ripped it in two, and laid it under the wheel in the mud, then piled brush for the wheels to catch. We were ready to start and Aymo got up on the seat and started the car. The wheels spun and we pushed and pushed. But it wasn't any use.

"It's ——ed," I said. "Is there anything you want in the car, Barto?"

Aymo climbed up with Bonello, carrying the cheese and two bottles of wine and his cape. Bonello, sitting behind the wheel, was looking through the pockets of the sergeant's coat.

"Better throw the coat away," I said. "What about Barto's virgins?"

"They can get in the back," Piani said. "I don't think we are going far."

I opened the back door of the ambulance.

"Come on," I said. "Get in." The two girls climbed in and sat in the corner. They seemed to have taken no notice of the shooting. I looked back up the road. The sergeant lay in his dirty long-sleeved underwear. I got up with Piani and we started. We were going to try to cross the field. When the road entered the field I got down and walked ahead. If we could get across, there was a road on the other side. We could not get across. It was too soft and muddy for the cars. When they were finally and completely stalled, the wheels dug in to the hubs, we left them in the field and started on foot for Udine.

When we came to the road which led back toward the main highway I pointed down it to the two girls.

"Go down there," I said. "You'll meet people." They looked at me. I took out my pocket-book and gave them each a ten-lira note. "Go down there," I said, pointing. "Friends! Family!"

They did not understand but they held the money tightly and started down the road. They looked back as though they were afraid I might take the money back. I watched them go down the road, their shawls close around them, looking back apprehensively at us. The three drivers were laughing.

"How much will you give me to go in that direction, Tenente?" Bonello asked.

"They're better off in a bunch of people than alone if they catch them," I said.

"Give me two hundred lire and I'll walk straight back toward Austria," Bonello said.

"They'd take it away from you," Piani said.

"Maybe the war will be over," Aymo said. We were going up the road as fast as we could. The sun was trying to come through. Beside the road were mulberry trees. Through the trees I could see our two big moving-vans of cars stuck in the field. Piani looked back too.

"They'll have to build a road to get them out," he said.

"I wish to Christ we had bicycles," Bonello said.

"Do they ride bicycles in America?" Aymo asked.

"They used to."

"Here it is a great thing," Aymo said. "A bicycle is a splendid thing."

"I wish to Christ we had bicycles," Bonello said. "I'm no walker."

"Is that firing?" I asked. I thought I could hear firing a long way away.

"I don't know," Aymo said. He listened.

"I think so," I said.

"The first thing we will see will be the cavalry," Piani said.

"I don't think they've got any cavalry."

"I hope to Christ not," Bonello said. "I don't want to be stuck on a lance by any —— cavalry."

"You certainly shot that sergeant, Tenente," Piani said. We were walking fast.

"I killed him," Bonello said. "I never killed anybody in this war, and all my life I've wanted to kill a sergeant."

"You killed him on the sit all right," Piani said. "He wasn't flying very fast when you killed him."

"Never mind. That's one thing I can always remember. I killed that —— of a sergeant."

"What will you say in confession?" Aymo asked.

"I'll say, 'Bless me, father, I killed a sergeant.'" They all laughed.

"He's an anarchist," Piani said. "He doesn't go to church."

"Piani's an anarchist too," Bonello said.

"Are you really anarchists?" I asked.

"No, Tenente. We're socialists. We come from Imola."

"Haven't you ever been there?"

"No."

"By Christ it's a fine place, Tenente. You come there after the war and we'll show you something."

"Are you all socialists?"

"Everybody."

"Is it a fine town?"

"Wonderful. You never saw a town like that."

"How did you get to be socialists?"

"We're all socialists. Everybody is a socialist. We've always been socialists."

"You come, Tenente. We'll make you a socialist too."

Ahead the road turned off to the left and there was a little hill and, beyond a stone wall, an apple orchard. As the road went uphill they ceased talking. We walked along together all going fast against time.

* * *

Later we were on a road that led to a river. There was a long line of abandoned trucks and carts on the road leading up to the bridge. No one was in sight. The river was high and the bridge had been blown up in the centre; the stone arch was fallen into the river and the brown water was going over it. We went on up the bank looking for a place to cross. Up ahead I knew there was a railway bridge and I thought we might be able to get across there. The path was wet and muddy. We did not see any troops; only abandoned trucks and stores. Along the river bank there was nothing and no one but the wet brush and muddy ground. We went up to the bank and finally we saw the railway bridge.

"What a beautiful bridge," Aymo said. It was a long plain iron bridge across what was usually a dry river-bed.

"We'd better hurry and get across before they blow it up," I said.

"There's nobody to blow it up," Piani said. "They're all gone."

"It's probably mined," Bonello said. "You cross first, Tenente."

"Listen to the anarchist," Aymo said. "Make him go first."

"I'll go," I said. "It won't be mined to blow up with one man."

"You see," Piani said. "That is brains. Why haven't you brains, anarchist?"

"If I had brains I wouldn't be here," Bonello said.

"That's pretty good, Tenente," Aymo said.

"That's pretty good," I said. We were close to the bridge now. The sky had clouded over again and it was raining a little. The bridge looked long and solid. We climbed up the embankment.

"Come one at a time," I said and started across the bridge. I watched the ties and the rails for any trip-wires or signs of explosive but I saw nothing. Down below the gaps in the ties the river ran muddy and fast. Ahead across the wet countryside I could see Udine in the rain. Across the bridge I looked back. Just up the river was another bridge. As I watched, a yellow mud-colored motor car crossed it. The sides of the bridge were high and the body of the car, once on, was out of sight. But I saw the heads of the driver, the man on the seat with him, and the two men on the rear seat. They all wore German helmets. Then the car was over the bridge and out of sight behind the trees and the abandoned vehicles on the road. I waved to Aymo who was crossing and to the others to come on. I climbed down and crouched beside the railway embankment. Aymo came down with me.

"Did you see the car?" I asked.

"No. We were watching you."

"A German staff car crossed on the upper bridge."

"A staff car?"

"Yes."

"Holy Mary."

The others came and we all crouched in the mud behind the embankment, looking across the rails at the bridge, the line of trees, the ditch and the road.

"Do you think we're cut off then, Tenente?"

"I don't know. All I know is a German staff car went along that road."

"You don't feel funny, Tenente? You haven't got strange feelings in the head?"

"Don't be funny, Bonello."

"What about a drink?" Piani asked. "If we're cut off we might as well have a drink." He unhooked his canteen and uncorked it.

"Look! Look!" Aymo said and pointed toward the road. Along the top of the stone bridge we could see German helmets moving. They were bent forward and moved smoothly, almost supernaturally, along. As they came off the bridge we saw them. They were bicycle troops. I saw the faces of the first two. They were ruddy and healthy-looking. Their helmets came low down over their foreheads and the side of their faces. Their carbines were clipped to the frame of the bicycles. Stick bombs hung handle down from their belts. Their helmets and their gray uniforms were wet and they rode easily, looking ahead and to both sides. There were two—then four in line, then two, then almost a dozen; then another dozen—then one alone. They did not talk but we could not have heard them because of the noise from the river. They were gone out of sight up the road.

"Holy Mary," Aymo said.

"They were Germans," Piani said. "Those weren't Austrians."

"Why isn't there somebody here to stop them?" I said. "Why haven't they blown the bridge up? Why aren't there machine-guns along this embankment?"

"You tell us, Tenente," Bonello said.

I was very angry.

"The whole bloody thing is crazy. Down below they blow up a little bridge. Here they leave a bridge on the main road. Where is everybody? Don't they try and stop them at all?"

"You tell us, Tenente," Bonello said. I shut up. It was none of my business; all I had to do was to get to Pordenone with three ambulances. I had failed at that. All I had to do now was get to Pordenone. I probably could not even get to Udine. The hell I couldn't. The thing to do was to be calm and not get shot or captured.

"Didn't you have a canteen open?" I asked Piani. He handed it to me. I took a long drink. "We might as well start," I said. "There's no hurry though. Do you want to eat something?"

"This is no place to stay," Bonello said.

"All right. We'll start."

"Should we keep on this side—out of sight?"

"We'd be better off on top. They may come along this bridge too. We don't want them on top of us before we see them."

We walked along the railroad track. On both sides of us stretched the wet plain. Ahead across the plain was the hill of Udine. The roofs fell away from the castle on the hill. We could see the campanile and the clock-tower. There were many mulberry trees in the fields. Ahead I saw a place where the rails were torn up. The ties had been dug out too and thrown down the embankment.

"Down! down!" Aymo said. We dropped down beside the embankment. There was another group of bicyclists passing along the road. I looked over the edge and saw them go on.

"They saw us but they went on," Aymo said.

"We'll get killed up there, Tenente," Bonello said.

"They don't want us," I said. "They're after something else. We're in more danger if they should come on us suddenly."

"I'd rather walk here out of sight," Bonello said.

"All right. We'll walk along the tracks."

"Do you think we can get through?" Aymo asked.

"Sure. There aren't very many of them yet. We'll go through in the dark."

"What was that staff car doing?"

"Christ knows," I said. We kept on up the tracks. Bonello tired of walking in the mud of the embankment and came up with the rest of us. The railway moved south away from the highway now and we could not see what passed along the road. A short bridge over a canal was blown up but we climbed across on what was left of the span. We heard firing ahead of us.

We came up on the railway beyond the canal. It went on straight toward the town across the low fields. We could see the line of the other railway ahead of us. To the north was the main road where we had seen the cyclists; to the south there was a small branch-road across the fields with thick trees on each side. I thought we had better cut to the south and work around the town that way and across country toward Campoformio and the main road to the Tagliamento. We could avoid the main line of the retreat by keeping to the secondary roads beyond Udine. I knew there were plenty of side-roads across the plain. I started down the embankment.

"Come on," I said. We would make for the side-road and work to the south of the town. We all started down the embankment. A shot was fired at us from the side-road. The bullet went into the mud of the embankment.

"Go on back," I shouted. I started up the embankment, slipping in the mud. The drivers were ahead of me. I went up the embankment as fast as I could go. Two more shots came from the thick brush and Aymo, as he was crossing the tracks, lurched, tripped and fell face down. We pulled him down on the other side and turned him over. "His head ought to be uphill," I said. Piani moved him around. He lay in the mud on the side of the embankment, his feet pointing downhill, breathing blood irregularly. The three of us squatted over him in the rain. He was hit low in the back of the neck and the bullet had ranged upward and come out under the right eye. He died while I was stopping up the two holes. Piani laid his head down, wiped at his face, with a piece of the emergency dressing, then let it alone.

"The ——," he said.

"They weren't Germans," I said. "There can't be any Germans over there."

"Italians," Piani said, using the word as an epithet, "Italiani!" Bonello said nothing. He was sitting beside Aymo, not looking at him. Piani picked up Aymo's cap where it had rolled down the embankment and put it over his face. He took out his canteen.

"Do you want a drink?" Piani handed Bonello the canteen.

"No," Bonello said. He turned to me. "That might have happened to us any time on the railway tracks."

"No," I said. "It was because we started across the field."

Bonello shook his head. "Aymo's dead," he said. "Who's dead next, Tenente? Where do we go now?"

"Those were Italians that shot," I said. "They weren't Germans."

"I suppose if they were Germans they'd have killed all of us," Bonello said.

"We are in more danger from Italians than Germans," I said. "The rear guard are afraid of everything. The Germans know what they're after."

"You reason it out, Tenente," Bonello said.

"Where do we go now?" Piani asked.

"We better lie up some place till it's dark. If we could get south we'd be all right."

"They'd have to shoot us all to prove they were right the first time," Bonello said. "I'm not going to try them."

"We'll find a place to lie up as near to Udine as we can get and then go through when it's dark."

"Let's go then," Bonello said. We went down the north side of the embankment. I looked back. Aymo lay in the mud with the angle of the embankment. He was quite small and his arms were by his side, his puttee-wrapped legs and muddy boots together, his cap over his face. He looked very dead. It was raining. I had liked him as well as any one I ever knew. I had his papers in my pocket and would write to his family. Ahead across the fields was a farmhouse. There were trees around it and the farm buildings were built against the house. There was a balcony along the second floor held up by columns.

"We better keep a little way apart," I said. "I'll go ahead." I started toward the farmhouse. There was a path across the field.

Crossing the field, I did not know but that some one would fire on us from the trees near the farmhouse or from the farmhouse itself. I walked toward it, seeing it very clearly. The balcony of the second floor merged into the barn and there was hay coming out between the columns. The courtyard was of stone blocks and all the trees were dripping with the rain. There was a big empty two-wheeled cart, the shafts tipped high up in the rain. I came to the courtyard, crossed it, and stood under the shelter of the balcony. The door of the house was open and I went in. Bonello and Piani came in after me. It was dark inside. I went back to the kitchen. There were ashes of a fire on the big open hearth. The pots hung over the ashes, but they were empty. I looked around but I could not find anything to eat.

"We ought to lie up in the barn," I said. "Do you think you could find anything to eat, Piani, and bring it up there?"

"I'll look," Piani said.

"I'll look too," Bonello said.

"All right," I said. "I'll go up and look at the barn." I found a stone stairway that went up from the stable underneath. The stable smelt dry and pleasant in the rain. The cattle were all gone, probably driven off when they left. The barn was half full of hay. There were two windows in the roof, one was blocked with boards, the other was a narrow dormer window on the north side. There was a chute so that hay might be pitched down to the cattle. Beams crossed the opening down into the main floor where the hay-carts drove in when the hay was hauled in to be pitched up. I heard the rain on the roof and smelled the hay and, when I went down, the clean smell of dried dung in the stable. We could pry a board loose and see out of the south window down into the courtyard. The other window looked out on the field toward the north. We could get out of either window onto the roof and down, or go down the hay chute if the stairs were impractical. It was a big barn and we could hide in the hay if we heard any one. It seemed like a good place. I was sure we could have gotten through to the south if they had not fired on us. It was impossible that there were Germans there. They were coming from the north and down the road from Cividale. They could not have come through from the south. The Italians were even more dangerous. They were frightened and firing on anything they saw. Last night on the retreat we had heard that there had been many Germans in Italian uniforms mixing with the retreat in the north. I did not believe it. That was one of those things you always heard in the war. It was one of the things the enemy always did to you. You did not know any one who went over in German uniform to confuse them. Maybe they did but it sounded difficult. I did not believe the Germans did it.

I did not believe they had to. There was no need to confuse our retreat. The size of the army and the fewness of the roads did that. Nobody gave any orders, let alone Germans. Still, they would shoot us for Germans. They shot Aymo. The hay smelled good and lying in a barn in the hay took away all the years in between. We had lain in hay and talked and shot sparrows with an air-rifle when they perched in the triangle cut high up in the wall of the barn. The barn was gone now and one year they had cut the hemlock woods and there were only stumps, dried tree-tops, branches and fireweed where the woods had been. You could not go back. If you did not go forward what happened? You never got back to Milan. And if you got back to Milan what happened? I listened to the firing to the north toward Udine. I could hear machine-gun firing. There was no shelling. That was something. They must have gotten some troops along the road. I looked down in the half-light of the hay-barn and saw Piani standing on the hauling floor. He had a long sausage, a jar of something and two bottles of wine under his arm.

"Come up," I said. "There is the ladder." Then I realized that I should help him with the things and went down. I was vague in the head from lying in the hay. I had been nearly asleep.

"Where's Bonello?" I asked.

"I'll tell you," Piani said. We went up the ladder. Up on the hay we set the things down. Piani took out his knife with the corkscrew and drew the cork on a wine bottle.

"They have sealing-wax on it," he said. "It must be good." He smiled.

"Where's Bonello?" I asked.

Piani looked at me.

"He went away, Tenente," he said. "He wanted to be a prisoner."

I did not say anything.

"He was afraid we would get killed."

I held the bottle of wine and did not say anything.

"You see we don't believe in the war anyway, Tenente."

"Why didn't you go?" I asked.

"I did not want to leave you."

"Where did he go?"

"I don't know, Tenente. He went away."

"All right," I said. "Will you cut the sausage?"

Piani looked at me in the half-light.

"I cut it while we were talking," he said. We sat in the hay and ate the sausage and drank the wine. It must have been wine they had saved for a wedding. It was so old that it was losing its color.

"You look out of this window, Luigi," I said. "I'll go look out the other window."

We had each been drinking out of one of the bottles and I took my bottle with me and went over and lay flat on the hay and looked out the narrow window at the wet country. I do not know what I expected to see but I did not see anything except the fields and the bare mulberry trees and the rain falling. I drank the wine and it did not make me feel good. They had kept it too long and it had gone to pieces and lost its quality and color. I watched it get dark outside; the darkness came very quickly. It would be a black night with the rain. When it was dark there was no use watching any more, so I went over to Piani. He was lying asleep and I did not wake him but sat down beside him for a while. He was a big man and he slept heavily. After a while I woke him and we started.

That was a very strange night. I do not know what I had expected, death perhaps and shooting in the dark and running, but nothing happened. We waited, lying flat beyond the ditch along the main road while a German battalion passed, then when they were gone we crossed the road and went on to the north. We were very close to Germans twice in the rain but they did not see us. We got past the town to the north without seeing any Italians, then after a while came on the main channels of the retreat and walked all night toward the Tagliamento. I had not realized how gigantic the retreat was. The whole country was moving, as well as the army. We walked all night, making better time than the vehicles. My leg ached and I was tired but we made good time. It seemed so silly for Bonello to have decided to be taken prisoner. There was no danger. We had walked through two armies without incident. If Aymo had not been killed there would never have seemed to be any danger. No one had bothered us when we were in plain sight along the railway. The killing came suddenly and unreasonably. I wondered where Bonello was.

"How do you feel, Tenente?" Piani asked. We were going along the side of a road crowded with vehicles and troops.

"Fine."

"I'm tired of this walking."

"Well, all we have to do is walk now. We don't have to worry."

"Bonello was a fool."

"He was a fool all right."

"What will you do about him, Tenente?"

"I don't know."

"Can't you just put him down as taken prisoner?"

"I don't know."

"You see if the war went on they would make bad trouble for his family."

"The war won't go on," a soldier said. "We're going home. The war is over."

"Everybody's going home."

"We're all going home."

"Come on, Tenente," Piani said. He wanted to get past them.

"Tenente? Who's a Tenente? A basso gli ufficiali! Down with the officers!"

Piani took me by the arm. "I better call you by your name," he said. "They might try and make trouble. They've shot some officers." We worked up past them.

"I won't make a report that will make trouble for his family." I went on with our conversation.

"If the war is over it makes no difference," Piani said. "But I don't believe it's over. It's too good that it should be over."

"We'll know pretty soon," I said.

"I don't believe it's over. They all think it's over but I don't believe it."

"Viva la Pace!" a soldier shouted out. "We're going home!"

"It would be fine if we all went home," Piani said. "Wouldn't you like to go home?"

"Yes."

"We'll never go. I don't think it's over."

"Andiamo a casa!" a soldier shouted.

"They throw away their rifles," Piani said. "They take them off and drop them down while they're marching. Then they shout."

"They ought to keep their rifles."

"They think if they throw away their rifles they can't make them fight."

In the dark and the rain, making our way along the side of the road I could see that many of the troops still had their rifles. They stuck up above the capes.

"What brigade are you?" an officer called out.

"Brigata di Pace," some one shouted. "Peace Brigade!" The officer said nothing.

"What does he say? What does the officer say?"

"Down with the officer. Viva la Pace!"

"Come on," Piani said. We passed two British ambulances, abandoned in the block of vehicles.

"They're from Gorizia," Piani said. "I know the cars."

"They got further than we did."

"They started earlier."

"I wonder where the drivers are?"

"Up ahead probably."

"The Germans have stopped outside Udine," I said. "These people will all get across the river."

"Yes," Piani said. "That's why I think the war will go on."

"The Germans could come on," I said. "I wonder why they don't come on."

"I don't know. I don't know anything about this kind of war."

"They have to wait for their transport I suppose."

"I don't know," Piani said. Alone he was much gentler. When he was with the others he was a very rough talker.

"Are you married, Luigi?"

"You know I am married."

"Is that why you did not want to be a prisoner?"

"That is one reason. Are you married, Tenente?"

"No."

"Neither is Bonello."

"You can't tell anything by a man's being married. But I should think a married man would want to get back to his wife," I said. I would be glad to talk about wives.

"Yes."

"How are your feet?"

"They're sore enough."

Before daylight we reached the bank of the Tagliamento and followed down along the flooded river to the bridge where all the traffic was crossing.

"They ought to be able to hold at this river," Piani said. In the dark the flood looked high. The water swirled and it was wide. The wooden bridge was nearly three-quarters of a mile across, and the river, that usually ran in narrow channels in the wide stony bed far below the bridge, was close under the wooden planking. We went along the bank and then worked our way into the crowd that were crossing the bridge. Crossing slowly in the rain a few feet above the flood, pressed tight in the crowd, the box of an artillery caisson just ahead, I looked over the side and watched the river. Now that we could not go our own pace I felt very tired. There was no exhilaration in crossing the bridge. I wondered what it would be like if a plane bombed it in the daytime.

"Piani," I said.

"Here I am, Tenente." He was a little ahead in the jam. No one was talking. They were all trying to get across as soon as they could: thinking only of that. We were almost across. At the far end of the bridge there were officers and carabinieri standing on both sides flashing lights. I saw them silhouetted against the sky-line. As we came close to them I saw one of the officers point to a man in the column. A carabiniere went in after him and came out holding the man by the arm. He took him away from the road. We came almost opposite them. The officers were scrutinizing every one in the column, sometimes speaking to each other, going forward to flash a light in some one's face. They took some one else out just before we came opposite. I saw the man. He was a lieutenant-colonel. I saw the stars in the box on his sleeve as they flashed a light on him. His hair was gray and he was short and fat. The carabiniere pulled him in behind the line of officers. As we came opposite I saw one or two of them look at me. Then one pointed at me and spoke to a carabiniere. I saw the carabiniere start for me, come through the edge of the column toward me, then felt him take me by the collar.

"What's the matter with you?" I said and hit him in the face. I saw his face under the hat, upturned mustaches and blood coming down his cheek. Another one dove in toward us.

"What's the matter with you?" I said. He did not answer. He was watching a chance to grab me. I put my arm behind me to loosen my pistol.

"Don't you know you can't touch an officer?"

The other one grabbed me from behind and pulled my arm up so that it twisted in the socket. I turned with him and the other one grabbed me around the neck. I kicked his shins and got my left knee into his groin.

"Shoot him if he resists," I heard some one say.

"What's the meaning of this?" I tried to shout but my voice was not very loud. They had me at the side of the road now.

"Shoot him if he resists," an officer said. "Take him over back."

"Who are you?"

"You'll find out."

"Who are you?"

"Battle police," another officer said.

"Why don't you ask me to step over instead of having one of these airplanes grab me?"

They did not answer. They did not have to answer. They were battle police.

"Take him back there with the others," the first officer said. "You see. He speaks Italian with an accent."

"So do you, you ——," I said.

"Take him back with the others," the first officer said. They took me down behind the line of officers below the road toward a group of people in a field by the river bank. As we walked toward them shots were fired. I saw flashes of the rifles and heard the reports. We came up to the group. There were four officers standing together, with a man in front of them with a carabiniere on each side of him. A group of men were standing guarded by carabinieri. Four other carabinieri stood near the questioning officers, leaning on their carbines. They were wide-hatted carabinieri. The two who had me shoved me in with the group waiting to be questioned. I looked at the man the officers were questioning. He was the fat gray-haired little lieutenant-colonel they had taken out of the column. The questioners had all the efficiency, coldness and command of themselves of Italians who are firing and are not being fired on.

"Your brigade?"

He told them.

"Regiment?"

He told them.

"Why are you not with your regiment?"

He told them.

"Do you not know that an officer should be with his troops?" He did. That was all. Another officer spoke.

"It is you and such as you that have let the barbarians onto the sacred soil of the fatherland."

"I beg your pardon," said the lieutenant-colonel.

"It is because of treachery such as yours that we have lost the fruits of victory."

"Have you ever been in a retreat?" the lieutenant-colonel asked.

"Italy should never retreat."

We stood there in the rain and listened to this. We were facing the officers and the prisoner stood in front and a little to one side of us.

"If you are going to shoot me," the lieutenant-colonel said, "please shoot me at once without further questioning. The questioning is stupid." He made the sign of the cross. The officers spoke together. One wrote something on a pad of paper.

"Abandoned his troops, ordered to be shot," he said.

Two carabinieri took the lieutenant-colonel to the river bank. He walked in the rain, an old man with his hat off, a carabinieri on either side. I did not watch them shoot him but I heard the shots. They were questioning some one else. This officer too was separated from his troops. He was not allowed to make an explanation. He cried when they read the sentence from the pad of paper, and they were questioning another when they shot him. They made a point of being intent on questioning the next man while the man who had been questioned before was being shot. In this way there was obviously nothing they could do about it. I did not know whether I should wait to be questioned or make a break now. I was obviously a German in Italian uniform. I saw how their minds worked; if they had minds and if they worked. They were all young men and they were saving their country. The second army was being re-formed beyond the Tagliamento. They were executing officers of the rank of major and above who were separated from their troops. They were also dealing summarily with German agitators in Italian uniform. They wore steel helmets. Only two of us had steel helmets. Some of the carabinieri had them. The other carabinieri wore the wide hat. Airplanes we called them. We stood in the rain and were taken out one at a time to be questioned and shot. So far they had shot every one they had questioned. The questioners had that beautiful detachment and devotion to stern justice of men dealing in death without being in any danger of it. They were questioning a full colonel of a line regiment. Three more officers had just been put in with us.

"Where was his regiment?"

I looked at the carabinieri. They were looking at the newcomers. The others were looking at the colonel. I ducked down, pushed between two men, and ran for the river, my head down. I tripped at the edge and went in with a splash. The water was very cold and I stayed under as long as I could. I could feel the current swirl me and I stayed under until I thought I could never come up. The minute I came up I took a breath and went down again. It was easy to stay under with so much clothing and my boots. When I came up the second time I saw a piece of timber ahead of me and reached it and held on with one hand. I kept my head behind it and did not even look over it. I did not want to see the bank. There were shots when I ran and shots when I came up the first time. I heard them when I was almost above water. There were no shots now. The piece of timber swung in the current and I held it with one hand. I looked at the bank. It seemed to be going by very fast. There was much wood in the stream. The water was very cold. We passed the brush of an island above the water. I held onto the timber with both hands and let it take me along. The shore was out of sight now.

Immortal Youth

(from *Across the River and Into the Trees*)

But he continued to look and it was all as wonderful to him and it moved him as it had when he was eighteen years old and had seen it first, understanding nothing of it and only knowing that it was beautiful. The winter had come very cold that year and all the mountains were white beyond the plain. It was necessary for the Austrians to try to break through at the angle where the Sile River and the old bed of the Piave were the only lines of defense.

If you had the old bed of the Piave then you had the Sile to fall back on if the first line did not hold. Beyond the Sile there was nothing but bare-assed plain and a good road network into the Veneto plain and the plains of Lombardy, and the Austrians attacked again and again and again late through the winter, to try to get onto this fine road that they were rolling on now which led straight to Venice. That winter the Colonel, who was a lieutenant then, and in a foreign army, which had always made him slightly suspect afterwards in his own army, and had done his career no good, had a sore throat all winter. This sore throat was from being in the water so much. You could not get dry and it was better to get wet quickly and stay wet.

The Austrian attacks were ill-coordinated, but they were constant and exasperated and you first had the heavy bombardment which was supposed to put you out of business, and then, when it lifted, you checked your positions and counted the people. But you had no time to care for wounded, since you knew that the attack was coming immediately, and then you killed the men who came wading across the marshes, holding their rifles above the water and coming as slow as men wade, waist deep.

If they did not lift the shelling when it started, the Colonel, then a lieutenant, often thought, I do not know what we would be able to do. But they always lifted it and moved it back ahead of the attack. They went by the book.

If we had lost the old Piave and were on the Sile they would move it back to the second and third lines; although such lines were quite untenable, and they should have brought all their guns up very close and whammed it in all the time they attacked and until they breached us. But thank God, some high fool always controls it, the Colonel thought, and they did it piecemeal.

All that winter, with a bad sore throat, he had killed men who came, wearing the stick bombs hooked up on a harness under their shoulders with the heavy, calf hide packs and the bucket helmets. They were the enemy.

But he never hated them; nor could have any feeling about them. He commanded with an old sock around his throat, which had been dipped in turpentine, and they broke down the attacks with rifle fire and with the machine guns which still existed, or were usable, after the bombardment. He taught his people to shoot, really, which is a rare ability in continental troops, and to be able to look at the enemy when they came, and, because there was always a dead moment when the shooting was free, they became very good at it.

But you always had to count and count fast after the bombardment to know how many shooters you would have. He was hit three times that winter, but they were all gift wounds; small wounds in the flesh of the body without breaking bone, and he had become quite confident of his personal immortality since he knew he should have been killed in the heavy artillery bombardment that always preceded the attacks. Finally he did get hit properly and for good. No one of his other wounds had ever done to him what the first big one did. I suppose it is just the loss of the immortality, he thought. Well, in a way, that is quite a lot to lose.

III

Revolution and Civil War in Spain

"The slow, heavy-laden, undramatic movement forwards. The men in echelon in columns of six. In the ultimate loneliness of what is known as contact. Where each man knows there is only himself and five other men, and before him all the great unknown. This is the moment that all the rest of war prepares for, when six men go forward into death to walk across a stretch of land and by their presence on it prove—this earth is ours."

—From *The Spanish Earth*

The Butterfly and the Tank

On this evening I was walking home from the censorship office to the Florida Hotel and it was raining. So about halfway home I got sick of the rain and stopped into Chicote's for a quick one. It was the second winter of shelling in the siege of Madrid and everything was short including tobacco and people's tempers and you were a little hungry all the time and would become suddenly and unreasonably irritated at things you could do nothing about such as the weather. I should have gone on home. It was only five blocks more, but when I saw Chicote's doorway I thought I would get a quick one and then do those six blocks up the Gran Via through the mud and rubble of the streets broken by the bombardment.

The place was crowded. You couldn't get near the bar and all the tables were full. It was full of smoke, singing, men in uniform, and the smell of wet leather coats, and they were handing drinks over a crowd that was three deep at the bar.

A waiter I knew found a chair from another table and I sat down with a thin, white-faced, Adam's-appled German I knew who was working at the censorship and two other people I did not know. The table was in the middle of the room a little on your right as you go in.

You couldn't hear yourself talk for the singing and I ordered a gin and angostura and put it down against the rain. The place was really packed and everybody was very jolly; maybe getting just a little bit too jolly from the newly made Catalan liquor most of them were drinking. A couple of people I did not know slapped me on the back and when the girl at our table said something to me, I couldn't hear it and said, "Sure."

She was pretty terrible looking now I had stopped looking around and was looking at our table; really pretty terrible. But it turned out, when the waiter came, that what she had asked me was to have a drink. The fellow with her was not very forceful looking but she was forceful enough for both of them. She had one of those strong, semi-classical faces and was built like a lion tamer; and the boy with her looked as though he ought to be wearing an old school tie. He wasn't though. He was wear-

91

ing a leather coat just like all the rest of us. Only it wasn't wet because they had been there since before the rain started. She had on a leather coat too and it was becoming to the sort of face she had.

By this time I was wishing I had not stopped into Chicote's but had gone straight on home where you could change your clothes and be dry and have a drink in comfort on the bed with your feet up, and I was tired of looking at both of these young people. Life is very short and ugly women are very long and sitting there at the table I decided that even though I was a writer and supposed to have an insatiable curiosity about all sorts of people, I did not really care to know whether these two were married, or what they saw in each other, or what their politics were, or whether he had a little money, or she had a little money, or anything about them. I decided they must be in the radio. Any time you saw really strange looking civilians in Madrid they were always in the radio. So to say something I raised my voice above the noise and asked, "You in the radio?"

"We are," the girl said. So that was that. They were in the radio.

"How are you comrade?" I said to the German.

"Fine. And you?"

"Wet," I said, and he laughed with his head on one side.

"You haven't got a cigarette?" he asked. I handed him my next to the last pack of cigarettes and he took two. The forceful girl took two and the young man with the old school tie face took one.

"Take another," I shouted.

"No thanks," he answered and the German took it instead.

"Do you mind?" he smiled.

"Of course not," I said. I really minded and he knew it. But he wanted the cigarettes so badly that it did not matter. The singing had died down momentarily, or there was a break in it as there is sometimes in a storm, and we could all hear what we said.

"You been here long?" the forceful girl asked me. She pronounced it bean as in bean soup.

"Off and on," I said.

"We must have a serious talk," the German said. "I want to have a talk with you. When can we have it?"

"I'll call you up," I said. This German was a very strange German indeed and none of the good Germans liked him. He lived under the delusion that he could play the piano, but if you kept him away from pianos he was all right unless he was exposed to liquor, or the opportunity to gossip, and nobody had even been able to keep him away from those two things yet.

Gossip was the best thing he did and he always knew something new and highly discreditable about anyone you could mention in Madrid, Valencia, Barcelona, and other political centers.

Just then the singing really started in again, and you cannot gossip very well shouting, so it looked like a dull afternoon at Chicote's and I decided to leave as soon as I should have bought a round myself.

Just then it started. A civilian in a brown suit, a white shirt, black tie, his hair brushed straight back from a rather high forehead, who had been clowning around from table to table, squirted one of the waiters with a flit gun. Everybody laughed except the waiter who was carrying a tray full of drinks at the time. He was indignant.

"*No hay derecho,*" the waiter said. This means, "You have no right to do that," and is the simplest and the strongest protest in Spain.

The flit gun man, delighted with his success, and not seeming to give any importance to the fact that it was well into the second year of the war, that he was in a city under siege where everyone was under a strain, and that he was one of only four men in civilian clothes in the place, now squirted another waiter.

I looked around for a place to duck to. This waiter, also, was indignant and the flit gun man squirted him twice more, lightheartedly. Some people still thought it was funny, including the forceful girl. But the waiter stood, shaking his head. His lips were trembling. He was an old man and he had worked in Chicote's for ten years that I knew of.

"*No hay derecho,*" he said with dignity.

People had laughed, however, and the flit gun man, not noticing how the singing had fallen off, squirted his flit gun at the back of a waiter's neck. The waiter turned, holding his tray.

"*No hay derecho,*" he said. This time it was no protest. It was an indictment and I saw three men in uniform start from a table for the flit gun man and the next thing all four of them were going out the revolving door in a rush and you heard a smack when someone hit the flit gun man on the mouth. Somebody else picked up the flit gun and threw it out the door after him.

The three men came back in looking serious, tough and very righteous. Then the door revolved and in came the flit gun man. His hair was down in his eyes, there was blood on his face, his necktie was pulled to one side and his shirt was torn open. He had the flit gun again and as he pushed, wild-eyed and white-faced, into the room he made one general, unaimed, challenging squirt with it, holding it toward the whole company.

I saw one of the three men start for him and I saw this man's face. There were more men with him now and they forced the flit gun man back between two tables on the left of the room as you go in, the flit gun man struggling wildly now, and when the shot went off I grabbed the forceful girl by the arm and dove for the kitchen door.

The kitchen door was shut and when I put my shoulder against it it did not give.

"Get down here behind the angle of the bar," I said. She knelt there.

"Flat," I said and pushed her down. She was furious.

Every man in the room except the German, who lay behind a table, and the public-school-looking boy who stood in a corner drawn up against the wall, had a gun out. On a bench along the wall three over-blonde girls, their hair dark at the roots, were standing on tiptoe to see and screaming steadily.

"I'm not afraid," the forceful one said. "This is ridiculous."

"You don't want to get shot in a café brawl," I said. "If that flit king has any friends here this can be very bad."

But he had no friends, evidently, because people began putting their pistols away and somebody lifted down the blonde screamers and every-one who had started over there when the shot came, drew back away from the flit man who lay, quietly, on his back on the floor.

"No one is to leave until the police come," someone shouted from the door.

Two policemen with rifles, who had come in off the street patrol, were standing by the door and at this announcement I saw six men form up just like the line-up of a football team coming out of a huddle and head out through the door. Three of them were the men who had first thrown the flit king out. One of them was the man who shot him. They went right through the policemen with the rifles like good interference taking out an end and a tackle. And as they went out one of the police-men got his rifle across the door and shouted, "No one can leave. Absolutely no one."

"Why did those men go? Why hold us if anyone's gone?"

"They were mechanics who had to return to their air field," someone said.

"But if anyone's gone it's silly to hold the others."

"Everyone must wait for the Seguridad. Things must be done legally and in order."

"But don't you see that if any person has gone it is silly to hold the others?"

"No one can leave. Everyone must wait."

"It's comic," I said to the forceful girl.

"No it's not. It's simply horrible."

94

We were standing up now and she was staring indignantly at where the flit king was lying. His arms were spread wide and he had one leg drawn up.

"I'm going over to help that poor wounded man. Why has no one helped him or done anything for him?"

"I'd leave him alone," I said. "You want to keep out of this."

"But it's simply inhuman. I've nurse's training and I'm going to give him first aid."

"I wouldn't," I said. "Don't go near him."

"Why not?" She was very upset and almost hysterical.

"Because he's dead," I said.

When the police came they held everybody there for three hours. They commenced by smelling of all the pistols. In this manner they would detect one which had been fired recently. After about forty pistols they seemed to get bored with this and anyway all you could smell was wet leather coats. Then they sat at a table placed directly behind the late flit king, who lay on the floor looking like a grey wax caricature of himself, with grey wax hands and a grey wax face, and examined people's papers.

With his shirt ripped open you could see the flit king had no undershirt and the soles of his shoes were worn through. He looked very small and pitiful lying there on the floor. You had to step over him to get to the table where two plain clothes policemen sat and examined everyone's identification papers. The husband lost and found his papers several times with nervousness. He had a safe conduct pass somewhere but he had mislaid it in a pocket but he kept on searching and perspiring until he found it. Then he would put it in a different pocket and have to go searching again. He perspired heavily while doing this and it made his hair very curly and his face red. He now looked as though he should have not only an old school tie but one of those little caps boys in the lower forms wear. You have heard how events age people. Well this shooting had made him look about ten years younger.

While we were waiting around I told the forceful girl I thought the whole thing was a pretty good story and that I would write it sometime. The way the six had lined up in single file and rushed that door was very impressive. She was shocked and said that I could not write it because it would be prejudicial to the cause of the Spanish Republic. I said that I had been in Spain for a long time and that they used to have a phenomenal number of shootings in the old days around Valencia under the monarchy, and that for hundreds of years before the Republic people had been cutting each other with large knives called *navajas* in Andalucia,

95

and that if I saw a comic shooting in Chicote's during the war I could write about it just as though it had been in New York, Chicago, Key West or Marseilles. It did not have anything to do with politics. She said I shouldn't. Probably a lot of other people will say I shouldn't too. The German seemed to think it was a pretty good story however, and I gave him the last of the Camels. Well, anyway, finally, after about three hours the police said we could go.

They were sort of worried about me at the Florida because in those days, with the shelling, if you started for home on foot and didn't get there after the bars were closed at seven-thirty, people worried. I was glad to get home and I told the story while we were cooking supper on an electric stove and it had quite a success.

Well, it stopped raining during the night, and the next morning it was a fine, bright, cold early winter day and at twelve forty-five I pushed open the revolving doors at Chicote's to try a little gin and tonic before lunch. There were very few people there at that hour and two waiters and the manager came over to the table. They were all smiling.

"Did they catch the murderer?" I asked.

"Don't make jokes so early in the day," the manager said. "Did *you* see him shot?"

"Yes," I told him.

"Me too," he said. "I was just here when it happened." He pointed to a corner table. "He placed the pistol right against the man's chest when he fired."

"How late did they hold people?"

"Oh until past two this morning."

"They only came for the *fiambre*," using the Spanish slang word for corpse, the same used on menus for cold meat, "at eleven o'clock this morning."

"But you don't know about it yet," the manager said.

"No. He doesn't know," a waiter said.

"It is a very rare thing," another waiter said. "*Muy raro.*"

"And sad too," the manager said. He shook his head.

"Yes. Sad and curious," the waiter said. "Very sad."

"Tell me."

"It is a very rare thing," the manager said.

"Tell me. Come on tell me."

The manager leaned over the table in great confidence.

"In the flit gun, you know," he said. "He had *eau de cologne.* Poor fellow."

"It was not a joke in such bad taste, you see?" the waiter said.

"It was really just gaiety. No one should have taken offense," the manager said. "Poor fellow."

"I see," I said. "He just wanted everyone to have a good time."

"Yes," said the manager. "It was really just an unfortunate misunderstanding."

"And what about the flit gun?"

"The police took it. They have sent it around to his family."

"I imagine they will be glad to have it," I said.

"Yes," said the manager. "Certainly. A flit gun is always useful."

"Who was he?"

"A cabinet maker."

"Married?"

"Yes, the wife was here with the police this morning."

"What did she say?"

"She dropped down by him and said, 'Pedro, what have they done to thee, Pedro? Who has done this to thee? Oh, Pedro.'"

"Then the police had to take her away because she could not control herself," the waiter said.

"It seems he was feeble of the chest," the manager said. "He fought in the first days of the movement. They said he fought in the Sierra but he was too weak in the chest to continue."

"And yesterday afternoon he just went out on the town to cheer things up," I suggested.

"No," said the manager. "You see it is very rare. Everything is *muy raro*. This I learn from the police who are very efficient if given time. They have interrogated comrades from the shop where he worked. This they located from the card of his syndicate which was in his pocket. Yesterday he bought the flit gun and *agua de colonia* to use for a joke at a wedding. He had announced this intention. He bought them across the street. There was a label on the cologne bottle with the address. The bottle was in the washroom. It was there he filled the flit gun. After buying them he must have come in here when the rain started."

"I remember when he came in," a waiter said.

"In the gaiety, with the singing, he became gay too."

"He was gay all right," I said. "He was practically floating around."

The manager kept on with the relentless Spanish logic.

"That is the gaiety of drinking with a weakness of the chest," he said.

"I don't like this story very well," I said.

"Listen," said the manager. "How rare it is. His gaiety comes in contact with the seriousness of the war like a butterfly—"

"Oh very like a butterfly," I said. "Too much like a butterfly."

"I am not joking," said the manager. "You see it? Like a butterfly and a tank."

This pleased him enormously. He was getting into the real Spanish metaphysics.

"Have a drink on the house," he said. "You must write a story about this."

I remembered the flit gun man with his grey wax hands and his grey wax face, his arms spread wide and his legs drawn up and he did look a little like a butterfly; not too much, you know. But he did not look very human either. He reminded me more of a dead sparrow.

"I'll take gin and Schweppes quinine tonic water," I said.

"You must write a story about it," the manager said. "Here. Here's luck."

"Luck," I said. "Look, an English girl last night told me I shouldn't write about it. That it would be very bad for the cause."

"What nonsense," the manager said. "It is very interesting and important, the misunderstood gaiety coming in contact with the deadly seriousness that is here always. To me it is the rarest and most interesting thing which I have seen for some time. You must write it."

"All right," I said. "Sure. Has he any children?"

"No," he said. "I asked the police. But you must write it and you must call it The Butterfly and the Tank."

"All right," I said. "Sure. But I don't like the title much."

"The title is very elegant," the manager said. "It is pure literature."

"All right," I said. "Sure. That's what we'll call it. The Butterfly and the Tank."

And I sat there on that bright cheerful morning, the place smelling clean and newly aired and swept, with the manager who was an old friend and who was now very pleased with the literature we were making together and I took a sip of the gin and tonic water and looked out the sandbagged window and thought of the wife kneeling there and saying, "Pedro. *Pedro*, who has done this to thee, Pedro?" And I thought that the police would never be able to tell her that even if they had the name of the man who pulled the trigger.

Night Before Battle

At this time we were working in a shell smashed house that overlooked the Casa del Campo in Madrid. Below us a battle was being fought. You could see it spread out below you and over the hills, could smell it, could taste the dust of it, and the noise of it was one great slithering sheet of rifle and automatic rifle fire rising and dropping, and in it came the crack of the guns and the bubbly rumbling of the outgoing shells fired from the batteries behind us, the thud of their bursts, and then the rolling yellow clouds of dust. But it was just too far to film well. We had tried working closer but they kept sniping at the camera and you could not work.

The big camera was the most expensive thing we had and if it was smashed we were through. We were making the film on almost nothing and all the money was in the cans of film and the cameras. We could not afford to waste film and you had to be awfully careful of the cameras.

The day before we had been sniped out of a good place to film from and I had to crawl back holding the small camera to my belly, trying to keep my head lower than my shoulders, hitching along on my elbows, the bullets whocking into the brick wall over my back and twice spurting dirt over me.

Our heaviest attacks were made in the afternoon, God knows why, as the fascists then had the sun at their backs, and it shone on the camera lenses and made them blink like a helio and the Moors would open up on the flash. They knew all about helios and officers' glasses, from the Riff and if you wanted to be properly sniped, all you had to do was use a pair of glasses without shading them adequately. They could shoot too, and they had kept my mouth dry all day.

In the afternoon we moved up into the house. It was a fine place to work and we made a sort of a blind for the camera on a balcony with the broken latticed curtains; but, as I said, it was too far.

It was not too far to get the pine studded hillside, the lake and the outline of the stone farm buildings that disappeared in the sudden smashes of stone dust from the hits by high explosive shells, nor was it too far to get the clouds of smoke and dirt that thundered up on the hill crest as the bombers droned over. But at eight hundred to a thousand yards the tanks looked like small mud-colored beetles bustling in the trees and spitting tiny flashes and the men behind them were toy men who lay flat, then crouched and ran, and then dropped to run again, or to stay where they lay, spotting the hillside as the tanks moved on. Still we hoped to get the shape of the battle. We had many close shots and would get others with luck and if we could get the sudden fountainings of earth, the puffs of shrapnel, the rolling clouds of smoke and dust lit by the yellow flash and white blossoming of grenades that is the very shape of battle we would have something that we needed.

So when the light failed we carried the big camera down the stairs, took off the tripod, made three loads, and then one at a time, sprinted across the fire-swept corner of the Paseo Rosales into the lee of the stone wall of the stables of the old Montana Barracks. We knew we had a good place to work and we felt cheerful. But we were kidding ourselves plenty that it was not too far.

"Come on let's go to Chicote's," I said when we had come up the hill to the Hotel Florida.

But they had to repair a camera, to change film and seal up what we had made so I went alone. You were never alone in Spain and it felt good for a change.

As I started to walk down the Gran Via to Chicote's in the April twilight I felt happy, cheerful and excited. We had worked hard, and I thought well. But walking down the street alone, all my elation died. Now that I was alone and there was no excitement, I knew we had been too far away and any fool could see the offensive was a failure. I had known it all day but you are often deceived by hope and optimism. But remembering how it looked now, I knew this was just another blood bath like the Somme. The people's army was on the offensive finally. But it was attacking in a way that could do only one thing: destroy itself. And as I put together now what I had seen all day and what I had heard, I felt plenty bad.

I knew in the smoke and din of Chicote's that the offensive was a failure and I knew it even stronger when I took my first drink at the crowded bar. When things are all right and it is you that is feeling low a drink can make you feel better. But when things are really bad and you are all right, a drink just makes it clearer. Now, in Chicote's it was so crowded that you had to make room with your elbows to get your drink to your mouth. I had one good long swallow and then someone jostled me so that I spilled part of the glass of whisky and soda. I looked around angrily and the man who had jostled me laughed.

"Hello fish face," he said.

"Hello you goat."

"Let's get a table," he said. "You certainly looked sore when I bumped you."

"Where did you come from?" I asked. His leather coat was dirty and greasy, his eyes were hollow and he needed a shave. He had the big Colt automatic that had belonged to three other men that I had known of, and that we were always trying to get shells for, strapped to his leg. He was very tall and his face was smoke-darkened and grease-smudged. He had a leather helmet with a heavy leather padded ridge longitudinally over the top and a heavily padded leather rim.

"Where'd you come from?"

"Casa del Campo," he said, pronouncing it in a sing-song mocking way we had heard a page boy use in calling in the lobby of a hotel in New Orleans one time and still kept as a private joke.

"There's a table," I said as two soldiers and two girls got up to go. "Let's get it."

We sat at this table in the middle of the room and I watched him raise his glass. His hands were greasy and the forks of both thumbs black as graphite from the back spit of the machine gun. The hand holding the drink was shaking.

"Look at them." He put out the other hand. It was shaking too. "Both the same," he said in that same comic lilt. Then, seriously, "You been down there?"

"We're making a picture of it."

"Photograph well?"

"Not too."

"See us?"

"Where?"

"Attack on the farm. Three twenty-five this afternoon."

"Oh, yes."

"Like it?"

"Nope."

"Me either," he said. "Listen the whole thing is just as crazy as a bedbug. Why do they want to make a frontal attack against positions like those? Who in hell thought it up?"

"An S. O. B. named Largo Caballero," said a short man with thick glasses who was sitting at the table when we came over to it. "The first time they let him look through a pair of field glasses he became a general. This is his masterpiece."

We both looked at the man who spoke. Al Wagner, the tank man,

101

looked at me and raised what had been his eyebrows before they were burnt off. The little man smiled at us.

"If anyone around here speaks English you're liable to get shot Comrade," Al said to him.

"No," said the little short man. "Largo Caballero is liable to be shot. He ought to be shot."

"Listen Comrade," said Al. "Just speak a little quieter will you? Somebody might overhear you and think we were with you."

"I know what I'm talking about," said the short man with the very thick glasses. I looked at him carefully. He gave you a certain feeling that he did.

"Just the same it isn't always a good thing to say what you know," I said. "Have a drink?"

"Certainly," he said. "It's all right to talk to you. I know you. You're all right."

"I'm not *that* all right," I said. "And this is a public bar."

"A public bar is the only private place there is. Nobody can hear what we say here. What is your unit, Comrade?"

"I've got some tanks about eight minutes from here on foot," Al told him. "We are through for the day and I have the early part of this evening off."

"Why don't you ever get washed?" I said.

"I plan to," said Al. "In your room. When we leave here. Have you got any mechanic's soap?"

"No."

"That's all right," he said. "I've got a little here with me in my pocket that I've been saving."

The little man with the thick lensed glasses was looking at Al intently.

"Are you a party member, Comrade?" he asked.

"Sure," said Al.

"I know Comrade Henry here is not," the little man said.

"I wouldn't trust him then," Al said. "I never do."

"You bastid," I said. "Want to go?"

"No," Al said. "I need another drink very badly."

"I know all about Comrade Henry," the little man said. "Now let me tell you something more about Largo Caballero."

"Do we have to hear it?" Al asked. "Remember I'm in the people's army. You don't think it will discourage me do you?"

"You know his head is swelled so badly now he's getting sort of mad. He is Prime Minister and War Minister and nobody can even talk to him anymore. You know he's just a good honest trade union leader somewhere between the late Sam Gompers and John L. Lewis but this man Araquistain who invented him?"

"Take it easy," said Al. "I don't follow."

"Oh Araquistain invented him. Araquistain who is Ambassador in Paris now. He made him up you know. He called him the Spanish Lenin and then the poor man tried to live up to it and somebody let him look through a pair of field glasses and he thought he was Clausewitz."

"You said that before," Al told him coldly. "What do you base it on?"

"Why three days ago in the Cabinet meeting he was talking military affairs. They were talking about this business we've got now and Jesus Hernandez, just ribbing him you know, asked him what was the difference between tactics and strategy. Do you know what the old boy said?"

"No," Al said. I could see this new Comrade was getting a little on his nerves.

"He said, 'In tactics you attack the enemy from in front. In strategy you take him from the sides.' Now isn't that something?"

"You better run along, Comrade," Al said. "You're getting so awfully discouraged."

"But we'll get rid of Largo Caballero," the short Comrade said. "We'll get rid of him right after his offensive. This last piece of stupidity will be the end of him."

"O.K. Comrade," Al told him. "But I've got to attack in the morning."

"Oh you are going to attack again?"

"Listen Comrade. You can tell me any sort of crap you want because it's interesting and I'm grown up enough to sort things out. But don't ask me any questions, see? Because you'll be in trouble."

"I just meant it personally. Not as information."

"We don't know each other well enough to ask personal questions, Comrade," Al said. "Why don't you just go to another table and let Comrade Henry and me talk. I want to ask him some things."

"*Salud* Comrade," the little man said, standing up. "We'll meet another time."

"Good," said Al. "Another time."

We watched him go over to another table. He excused himself, some soldiers made room for him, and as we watched we could see him starting to talk. They all looked interested.

"What do you make of that little guy?" Al asked.

"I don't know."

"Me either," Al said. "He certainly had this offensive sized up." He took a drink and showed his hand. "See? It's all right now. I'm not any rummy either. I never take a drink before an attack."

"How was it today?"

"You saw it. How did it look?"

"Terrible."

"That's it. That's the word for it all right. It was terrible. I guess he's using strategy and tactics both now because we are attacking from straight in front and from both sides. How's the rest of it going?"

"Duran took the new race track. The *hipódromo*. We've narrowed down on the corridor that runs up into University City. Up above we crossed the Coruña road. And we're stopped at the Cerro de Aguilar since yesterday morning. We were up that way this morning. Duran lost over half his brigade, I heard. How is it with you?"

"Tomorrow we're going to try those farm houses and the church again. The church on the hill, the one they call the hermit, is the objective. The whole hillside is cut by those gullies and it's all enfiladed at least three ways by machine-gun posts. They're dug deep all through there and it's well done. We haven't got enough artillery to give any kind of real covering fire to keep them down and we haven't heavy artillery to blow them out. They've got anti-tanks in those three houses and an anti-tank battery by the church. It's going to be murder."

"When's it for?"

"Don't ask me. I've got no right to tell you that."

"If we have to film it, I meant," I said. "The money from the film all goes for ambulances. We've got the Twelfth Brigade in the counterattack at the Argada Bridge. And we've got the Twelfth again in that attack last week by Pingarrón. We got some good tank shots there."

"The tanks were no good there," Al said.

"I know," I said, "but they photographed very well. What about tomorrow?"

"Just get out early and wait," he said. "Not too early."

"How you feel now?"

"I'm awfully tired," he said. "And I've got a bad headache. But I feel a lot better. Let's have another one and then go up to your place and get a bath."

"Maybe we ought to eat first."

"I'm too dirty to eat. You can hold a place and I'll go get a bath and join you at the Gran Via."

"I'll go up with you."

"No. It's better to hold a place and I'll join you." He leaned his head forward on the table. "Boy I got a headache. It's the noise in those buckets. I never hear it any more but it does something to your ears just the same."

"Why don't you go to bed?"

"No. I'd rather stay up with you for a while and then sleep when I get back down there. I don't want to wake up twice."

"You haven't got the horrors, have you?"

"No," he said. "I'm fine. Listen, Hank. I don't want to talk a lot of crap but I think I'm going to get killed tomorrow."

I touched the table three times with my finger tips.

"Everybody feels like that. I've felt like that plenty of times."

"No," he said. "It's not natural with me. But where we've got to go tomorrow doesn't make sense. I don't even know that I can get them up there. You can't make them move if they won't go. You can shoot them afterwards. But at the time if they won't go they won't go. If you shoot them they still won't go."

"Maybe it will be all right."

"No. We've got good infantry tomorrow. They'll go anyway. Not like those yellow bastids we had the first day."

"Maybe it will be all right."

"No," he said. "It won't be all right. But it will be just exactly as good as I can make it. I can make them start all right and I can take them up to where they will have to quit one at a time. Maybe they can make it. I've got three I can rely on. If only one of the good ones doesn't get knocked out at the start."

"Who are your good ones?"

"I've got a big Greek from Chicago that will go anywhere. He's just as good as they come. I've got a Frenchman from Marseille that's got his left shoulder in a cast with two wounds still draining that asked to come out of the hospital in the Palace Hotel for this show and has to be strapped in and I don't know how he can do it. Just technically I mean. He'd break your bloody heart. He used to be a taxi driver." He stopped. "I'm talking too much. Stop me if I talk too much."

"Who's the third one?" I asked.

"The third one? Did I say I had a third one?"

"Sure."

"Oh yes," he said. "That's me."

"What about the others?"

"They're mechanics, but they couldn't learn to soldier. They can't size up what's happening. And they're all afraid to die. I tried to get them over it," he said. "But it comes back on them every attack. They look like tank men when you see them by the tanks with the helmets on. They look like tank men when they get in. But when they shut the traps down there's really nothing inside. They aren't tank men. And so far we haven't had time to make new ones."

"Do you want to take the bath?"

"Let's sit here a little while longer," he said. "It's nice here."

"It's funny all right; with a war right down the end of the street so you can walk to it, and then leave it and come here."

"And then walk back to it," Al said.

"What about a girl? There's two American girls at the Florida. Newspaper correspondents. Maybe you could make one."

"I don't want to have to talk to them. I'm too tired."

"There's the two Moor girls from Ceuta at that corner table."

He looked over at them. They were both dark and bushy headed. One was large and one was small and they certainly both looked strong and active.

"No," said Al. "I'm going to see plenty Moors tomorrow without having to fool with them tonight."

"There's plenty of girls," I said. "Manolita's at the Florida. That Seguridad bird she lives with has gone to Valencia and she's being true to him with everybody."

"Listen, Hank, what are you trying to promote me?"

"I just wanted to cheer you up."

"Grow up," he said. "What's one more?"

"One more."

"I don't mind dying a bit," he said. "Dying is just a lot of crap. Only it's wasteful. The attack is wrong and it's wasteful. I can handle tanks good now. If I had time I could make good tankists too. And if we had tanks that were a little bit faster the anti-tanks wouldn't bother them the way it does when you haven't got the mobility. Listen, Hank, they aren't what we thought they were though: Do you remember when everybody thought if we only had tanks?"

"They were good at Guadalajara."

"Sure. But those were the old boys. They were soldiers. And it was against Italians."

"But what's happened?"

"A lot of things. The mercenaries signed up for six months. Most of them were Frenchmen. They soldiered good for five but now all they want to do is live through the last month and go home. They aren't worth a damn now. The Russians that came out as demonstrators when the government bought the tanks were perfect. But they're pulling them back now for China they say. The new Spaniards are some of them good and some not. It takes six months to make a good tank man, I mean to know anything. And be able to size up and work intelligently you have to have a talent. We've been having to make them in six weeks and there aren't so many with a talent."

"They make fine flyers."

"They'll make fine tank guys too. But you have to get the ones with a vocation for it. It's sort of like being a priest. You have to be cut out for it. Especially now they've got so much anti-tank."

They had pulled down the shutters in Chicote's and now they were locking the door. No one would be allowed in now. But you had a half an hour more before they closed.

"I like it here," said Al. "It isn't so noisy now. Remember that time I met you in New Orleans when I was on a ship and we went in to have a drink in the Monteleone bar and that kid that looked just like Saint Sebastian was paging people with that funny voice like he was singing and I gave him a quarter to page Mr. B. F. Slob?"

"That's the same way you said 'Casa del Campo.'"

"Yeah," he said. "I laugh every time I think of that." Then he went on, "You see, now, they're not frightened of tanks anymore. Nobody is. We aren't either. But they're still useful. Really useful. Only with the anti-tank now they're so damn vulnerable. Maybe we ought to be in something else. *Not really*. Because they're still useful. But the way they are now you've got to have a vocation for them. You got to have a lot of political development to be a good tank man now."

"You're a good tank man."

"I'd like to be something else tomorrow," he said. "I'm talking awfully wet but you have a right to talk wet if it isn't going to hurt anybody else. You know I like tanks too, only we don't use them right because the infantry don't know enough yet. They just want the old tank ahead to give them some cover while they go. That's no good. Then they get to depending on the tanks and they won't move without them. Sometimes they won't even deploy."

"I know."

"But you see if you had tankists that knew their stuff they'd go out ahead and develop the machine-gun fire and then drop back behind the infantry and fire on the gun and knock it out and give the infantry covering fire when they attacked. And other tanks could rush the machine-gun posts as though they were cavalry. And they could straddle a trench and enfilade and put flanking fire down it. And they could bring up infantry when it was right to or cover their advance when that was best."

107

"But instead?"

"Instead it's like it will be tomorrow. We have so damned few guns that we're just used as slightly mobile armored artillery units. And as soon as you are standing still and being light artillery, you've lost your mobility and that's your safety and they start sniping at you with the anti-tanks. And if we're not that we're just sort of iron perambulators to push ahead of the infantry. And lately you don't know whether the perambulator will push or whether the guys inside will push them. And you never know if there's going to be anybody behind you when you get there."

"How many are you now to a brigade?"

"Six to a battalion. Thirty to a brigade. That's in principle."

"Why don't you come along now and get the bath and we'll go and eat?"

"All right. But don't you start taking care of me or thinking I'm worried or anything because I'm not. I'm just tired and I wanted to talk. And don't give me any pep talk either because we've got a political commissar and I know what I'm fighting for and I'm not worried. But I'd like things to be efficient and used as intelligently as possible."

"What made you think I was going to give you any pep talk?"

"You started to look like it."

"All I tried to do was see if you wanted a girl and not to talk too wet about getting killed."

"Well I don't want any girl tonight and I'll talk just as wet as I please unless it does damage to others. Does it damage you?"

"Come on and get the bath," I said. "You can talk just as bloody wet as you want."

"Who do you suppose that little guy was that talked as though he knew so much?"

"I don't know," I said. "But I'm going to find out."

"He made me gloomy," said Al. "Come on. Let's go."

The old waiter with the bald head unlocked the outside door of Chicote's and let us out into the street.

"How is the offensive, Comrades?" he said at the door.

"It's O.K., Comrade," said Al. "It's all right."

"I am happy," said the waiter. "My boy is in the One Hundred and Forty-fifth Brigade. Have you seen them?"

"I am of the tanks," said Al. "This Comrade makes a cinema. Have you seen the Hundred and Forty-fifth?"

"No," I said.

"They are up the Extremadura road," the old waiter said. "My boy is political commissar of the machine-gun company of his battalion. He is my youngest boy. He is twenty."

"What party are you Comrade?" Al asked him.

"I am of no party," the waiter said. "But my boy is a Communist."

"So am I," said Al. "The offensive, Comrade, has not yet reached a decision. It is very difficult. The fascists hold very strong positions. You, in the rear-guard, must be as firm as we will be at the front. We may not take these positions now but we have proved we now have an army capable of going on the offensive and you will see what it will do."

"And the Extremadura road?" asked the old waiter, still holding to the door. "Is it very dangerous there?"

"No," said Al. "It's fine up there. You don't need to worry about him up there."

"God bless you," said the waiter. "God guard you and keep you."

Outside in the dark street, Al said, "Jees he's kind of confused politically, isn't he?"

"He is a good guy," I said. "I've known him for a long time."

"He seems like a good guy," Al said. "But he ought to get wise to himself politically."

The room at the Florida was crowded. They were playing the gramophone and it was full of smoke and there was a crap game going on the floor. Comrades kept coming in to use the bathtub and the room smelt of smoke, soap, dirty uniforms, and steam from the bathroom.

The Spanish girl called Manolita, very neat, demurely dressed, with a sort of false French chic, with much joviality, much dignity and closely set cold eyes, was sitting on the bed talking with an English newspaper man. Except for the gramophone it wasn't very noisy.

"It *is* your room isn't it?" the English newspaper man said.

"It's in my name at the desk," I said. "I sleep in it sometimes."

"But whose is the whisky?" he asked.

"Mine," said Manolita. "They drank that bottle so I got another."

"You're a good girl, daughter," I said. "That's three I owe you."

"Two," she said. "The other was a present."

There was a huge cooked ham, rosy and white edged in a half opened tin on the table beside my typewriter and a comrade would reach up, cut himself a slice of ham with his pocket knife, and go back to the crap game. I cut myself a slice of ham.

"You're next on the tub," I said to Al. He had been looking around the room.

"It's nice here," he said. "Where did the ham come from?"

"We bought it from the *intendencia* of one of the brigades," she said. "Isn't it beautiful?"

"Who's we?"

"He and I," she said, turning her head toward the English correspondent. "Don't you think he's cute?"

"Manolita has been most kind," said the Englishman. "I hope we're not disturbing you."

"Not at all," I said. "Later on I might want to use the bed but that won't be until much later."

"We can have a party in my room," Manolita said. "You aren't cross are you, Henry?"

"Never," I said. "Who are the comrades shooting craps?"

"I don't know," said Manolita. "They came in for baths and then they stayed to shoot craps. Everyone has been very nice. You know my bad news?"

"No."

"It's very bad. You knew my fiancé who was in the police and went to Barcelona?"

"Yes. Sure."

Al went into the bathroom.

"Well he was shot in an accident and I haven't any one I can depend on in police circles and he never got me the papers he had promised me and today I heard I was going to be arrested."

"Why?"

"Because I have no papers and they say I hang around with you people and with people from the brigades all the time so I am probably a spy. If my fiancé had not gotten himself shot it would have been all right. Will you help me?"

"Sure," I said. "Nothing will happen to you if you're all right."

"I think I'd better stay with you to be sure."

"And if you're not all right that would be fine for me wouldn't it?"

"Can't I stay with you?"

"No. If you get in trouble call me up. I never heard you ask anybody any military questions. I think you're all right."

"I'm *really* all right," she said then, leaning over, away from the Englishman. "You think it's all right to stay with him? Is *he* all right?"

"How do I know?" I said. "I never saw him before."

"You're being cross," she said. "Let's not think about it now but everyone be happy and go out to dinner."

I went over to the crap game.

"You want to go out to dinner?"

"No, Comrade," said the man handling the dice without looking up. "You want to get in the game?"

"I want to eat."

"We'll be here when you get back," said another crap shooter. "Come on, roll, I've got you covered."

"If you run into any money bring it up here to the game."

There was one in the room I knew beside Manolita. He was from the Twelfth Brigade and he was playing the gramophone. He was a Hungarian, a sad Hungarian, not one of the cheerful kind.

"*Salud Camarade,*" he said. "Thank you for your hospitality."

"Don't you shoot craps?" I asked him.

"I haven't that sort of money," he said. "They are aviators with contracts. Mercenaries . . . They make a thousand dollars a month. They were on the Teruel front and now they have come here."

"How did they come up here?"

"One of them knows you. But he had to go out to his field. They came for him in a car and the game had already started."

"I'm glad you came up," I said. "Come up any time and make yourself at home."

"I came to play the new discs," he said. "It does not disturb you?"

"No. It's fine. Have a drink."

"A little ham," he said.

One of the crap shooters reached up and cut a slice of ham.

"You haven't seen this guy Henry around that owns the place have you?" he asked me.

"That's me."

"Oh," he said. "Sorry. Want to get in the game?"

"Later on," I said.

"O.K.," he said. Then his mouth full of ham, "Listen you tar heel bastid. Make your dice hit the wall and bounce."

"Won't make no difference to you, Comrade," said the man handling the dice.

Al came out of the bathroom. He looked all clean except for some smudges around his eyes.

"You can take those off with a towel," I said.

"What?"

"Look at yourself once more in the mirror."

"It's too steamy," he said. "To hell with it, I feel clean."

"Let's eat," I said. "Come on Manolita. You know each other?"

I watched her eyes run over Al.

"How are you?" Manolita said.

"I say that is a sound idea," the Englishman said. "Do let's eat. But where?"

"Is that a crap game?" Al said.

"Didn't you see it when you came in?"

"No," he said. "All I saw was the ham."

"It's a crap game."

"You go and eat," Al said. "I'm staying here."

As we went out there were six of them on the floor and Al Wagner was reaching up to cut a slice of ham.

"What do you do, Comrade?" I heard one of the flyers say to Al.

"Tanks."

"Tell me they aren't any good any more," said the flyer.

"Tell you a lot of things," Al said. "What you got there? Some dice?"

"Want to look at them?"

"No," said Al. "I want to handle them."

We went down the hall, Manolita, me and the tall Englishman, and found the boys had left already for the Gran Via restaurant. The Hungarian had stayed behind to replay the new discs. I was very hungry and the food at the Gran Via was lousy. The two who were making the film had already eaten and gone back to work on the bad camera.

This restaurant was in the basement and you had to pass a guard and go through the kitchen and down a stairs to get to it. It was a racket.

They had a millet and water soup, yellow rice with horse meat in it, and oranges for dessert. There had been another dish of chickpeas with sausage in it that everybody said was terrible but it had run out. The newspaper men all sat at one table and the other tables were filled with officers and girls from Chicote's, people from the censorship, which was then in the telephone building across the street, and various unknown citizens.

The restaurant was run by an anarchist syndicate and they sold you wine that was all stamped with the label of the royal cellars and the date it had been put in the bins. Most of it was so old that it was either corked or just plain faded out and gone to pieces. You can't drink labels and I sent three bottles back as bad before we got a drinkable one. There was a row about this.

The waiters didn't know the different wines. They just brought you a bottle of wine and you took your chances. They were as different from the Chicote's waiters as black from white. These waiters were all snotty, all over-tipped and they regularly had special dishes such as lobster or chicken that they sold extra for gigantic prices. But these had all been bought up before we got there so we just drew the soup, the rice and the oranges. The place always made me angry because the waiters were a crooked lot of profiteers and it was about as expensive to eat in, if you had one of the special dishes, as 21 or the Colony in New York.

We were sitting at the table with a bottle of wine that just wasn't bad, you know you could taste it starting to go, but it wouldn't justify making a row about, when Al Wagner came in. He looked around the room, saw us and came over.

"What's the matter?" I said.

"They broke me," he said.

"It didn't take very long."

"Not with those guys," he said. "That's a big game. What have they got to eat?"

I called a waiter over.

"It's too late," he said. "We can't serve anything now."

"This comrade is in the tanks," I said. "He has fought all day and he will fight tomorrow and he hasn't eaten."

"That's not my fault," the waiter said. "It's too late. There isn't anything more. Why doesn't the comrade eat with his unit? The army has plenty of food."

"I asked him to eat with me."

"You should have said something about it. It's too late now. We are not serving anything any more."

"Get the headwaiter."

The headwaiter said the cook had gone home and there was no fire in the kitchen. He went away. They were angry because we had sent the bad wine back.

"The hell with it," said Al. "Let's go somewhere else."

"There's no place you can eat at this hour. They've got food. I'll just have to go over and suck up to the headwaiter and give him some more money."

I went over and did just that and the sullen waiter brought a plate of cold sliced meats, then half a spiny lobster with mayonnaise, and a salad of lettuce and lentils. The headwaiter sold this out of his private stock which he was holding out either to take home, or sell to late comers.

"Cost you much?" Al asked.

"No," I lied.

"I'll bet it did," he said. "I'll fix up with you when I get paid."

"What do you get now?"

"I don't know yet. It was ten pesetas a day but they've raised it now I'm an officer. But we haven't got it yet and I haven't asked."

"Comrade," I called the waiter. He came over, still angry that the headwaiter had gone over his head and served Al. "Bring another bottle of wine please."

"What kind?"

"Any that is not too old so that the red is faded."

"It's all the same."

I said the equivalent of like hell it is in Spanish, and the waiter brought over a bottle of Château Mouton-Rothschild 1906 that was just as good as the last claret we had was rotten.

"Boy that's wine," Al said. "What did you tell him to get that?"

"Nothing. He just made a lucky draw out of the bin."

"Most of that stuff from the palace stinks."

"It's too old. This is a hell of a climate on wine."

"There's that wise comrade," Al nodded across at another table.

The little man with the thick glasses that had talked to us about Largo Caballero was talking with some people I knew were very big shots indeed.

"I guess he's a big shot," I said.

"When they're high enough up they don't give a damn what they say. But I wish he would have waited until after tomorrow. It's kind of spoiled tomorrow for me."

I filled his glass.

"What he said sounded pretty sensible," Al went on. "I've been thinking it over. But my duty is to do what I'm ordered to do."

"Don't worry about it and get some sleep."

"I'm going to get in that game again if you'll let me take a thousand pesetas," Al said. "I've got a lot more than that coming to me and I'll give you an order on my pay."

"I don't want any order. You can pay me when you get it."

"I don't think I'm going to draw it," Al said. "I certainly sound wet, don't I? And I know gambling's bohemianism too. But in a game like that is the only time I don't think about tomorrow."

"Did you like that Manolita girl? She liked you."

"She's got eyes like a snake."

"She's not a bad girl. She's friendly and she's all right."

"I don't want any girl. I want to get back in that crap game."

Down the table Manolita was laughing at something the new Englishman had said in Spanish. Most of the people had left the table.

"Let's finish the wine and go," Al said. "Don't you want to get in that game?"

"I'll watch you for a while," I said and called the waiter over to bring us the bill.

"Where you go?" Manolita called down the table.

"To the room."

"We come by later on," she said. "This man is very funny."

"She is making most awful sport of me," the Englishman said. "She picks up my errors in Spanish. I say, doesn't *leche* mean milk?"

"That's one interpretation of it."

"*Does* it mean something beastly too?"

"I'm afraid so," I said.

"You know it *is* a beastly language," he said. "Now Manolita, stop pulling my leg. I say stop it."

"I'm not pulling your leg," Manolita laughed. "I never touched your leg. I am just laughing about the *leche.*"

"But it *does* mean milk. Didn't you just hear Edwin Henry say so?"

Manolita started to laugh again and we got up to go.

"He's a silly piece of work," Al said. "I'd almost like to take her away because he's so silly."

"You can never tell about an Englishman," I said. It was such a profound remark that I knew we had ordered too many bottles. Outside, in the street, it was turning cold and in the moonlight the clouds were passing very big and white across the wide, building-sided canyon of the Gran Via and we walked up the sidewalk with the day's fresh shell holes neatly cut in the cement, their rubble still not swept away, on up the rise of the hill toward the Plaza Callao where the Florida Hotel faced down the other little hill where the wide street ran that ended at the front.

We went past the two guards in the dark outside the door of the hotel and listened a minute in the doorway as the shooting down the street strengthened into a roll of firing, then dropped off.

"If it keeps up I guess I ought to go down," Al said listening.

"That wasn't anything," I said. "Anyway that was off to the left by Carabanchel."

"It sounded straight down in the Campo."

"That's the way the sound throws here at night. It always fools you."

"They aren't going to counterattack us tonight," Al said. "When they've got those positions and we are up that creek they aren't going to leave their positions to try to kick us out of that creek."

"What creek?"

"You know the name of that creek."

"Oh. *That* creek."

"Yeah. Up that creek without a paddle."

"Come on inside. You didn't have to listen to that firing. That's the way it is every night."

We went inside, crossed the lobby, passing the night watchman at the concierge's desk and the night watchman got up and went with us to the elevator. He pushed a button and the elevator came down. In it was a man with a white curly sheep's wool jacket, the wool worn outside, a pink bald head, and a pink, angry face. He had six bottles of champagne under his arms and in his hands and he said, "What the hell's the idea of bringing the elevator down?"

"You've been riding in the elevator for an hour," the night watchman said.

"I can't help it," said the wooly jacket man. Then to me, "Where's Frank?"

"Frank who?"

"You know Frank," he said. "Come on help me with this elevator."

"You're drunk," I said to him. "Come on skip it and let us get upstairs."

"So would you be drunk," said the white woolly jacket man. "So would you be drunk Comrade old Comrade. Listen, where's Frank?"

"Where do you think he is?"

"In this fellow Henry's room where the crap game is."

"Come on with us," I said. "Don't fool with those buttons. That's why you stop it all the time."

"I can fly anything," said the woolly jacket man. "And I can fly this old elevator. Want me to stunt it?"

"Skip it," Al said to him. "You're drunk. We want to get to the crap game."

"Who are you? I'll hit you with a bottle full of champagne wine."

"Try it," said Al. "I'd like to cool you, you rummy fake Santa Claus."

"A rummy fake Santa Claus," said the bald man. "A rummy fake Santa Claus. And that's the thanks of the Republic."

We had gotten the elevator stopped at my floor and were walking down the hall. "Take some bottles," said the bald man. Then, "Do you know why I'm drunk?"

"No."

"Well I won't tell you. But you'd be surprised. A rummy fake Santa Claus. Well well well. What are you in, Comrade?"

"Tanks."

"And you, Comrade?"

"Making a picture."

"And I'm a rummy fake Santa Claus. Well. Well. Well. I repeat. Well. Well. Well."

"Go and drown in it," said Al. "You rummy fake Santa Claus."

We were outside the room now. The man in the white woolly coat took hold of Al's arm with his thumb and forefinger.

"You amuse me, Comrade," he said. "You truly amuse me."

I opened the door. The room was full of smoke and the game looked just as when we had left it except the ham was all gone off the table and the whisky all gone out of the bottle.

"It's Baldy," said one of the crap shooters.

"How do you do, Comrades," said Baldy bowing. "How do you do? How do you do? How do you do?"

The game broke up and they all started to shoot questions at him.

"I have made my report, Comrades," Baldy said. "And here is a little champagne wine. I am no longer interested in any but the picturesque aspects of the whole affair."

"Where did your wing men muck off to?"

"It wasn't their fault," said Baldy. "I was engaged in contemplating a terrific spectacle and I was ob-*livious* of the fact that I had any wing men until all of those Fiats started coming down over, past and under me and I realized that my trusty little air-o-plane no longer had any tail."

"Jees I wish you weren't drunk," said one of the flyers.

"But I *am* drunk," said Baldy. "And I hope all you gentlemen and comrades will join me because I am very happy tonight even though I have been insulted by an ignorant tank man who has called me a rummy fake Santa Claus."

"I wish you were sober," the other flyer said. "How'd you get back to the field?"

"Don't ask me any questions," Baldy said with great dignity. "I returned in a staff car of the Twelfth Brigade. When I alighted with my trusty par-a-chute there was a tendency to regard me as a criminal fascist due to my inability to master the Lanish Spanguage. But all difficulties were smoothed away when I convinced them of my identity and I was treated with rare consideration. Oh boy you ought to have seen that Junker when she started to burn. That's what I was watching when the Fiats dove on me. Oh boy I wish I could tell you."

"He shot a tri-motor Junker down today over the Jarama and his wingmen mucked off on him and he got shot down and bailed out," one of the flyers said. "You know him. Baldy Jackson."

"How far did you drop before you pulled your rip cord, Baldy?" asked another flyer.

"All of six thousand feet and I think my diaphragm is busted loose in front from when she came taut. I thought it would cut me in two.

There must have been fifteen Fiats and I wanted to get completely clear. I had to fool with the chute plenty to get down on the right side of the river. I had to slip her plenty and I hit pretty hard. The wind was good."

"Frank had to go back to Alcalá," another flyer said. "We started a crap game. We got to get back there before daylight."

"I am in no mood to toy with the dice," said Baldy. "I am in a mood to drink champagne wine out of glasses with cigarette butts in them."

"I'll wash them," said Al.

"For Comrade Fake Santa Claus," said Baldy. "For old Comrade Claus."

"Skip it," said Al. He picked up the glasses and took them to the bathroom.

"Is he in the tanks?" asked one of the flyers.

"Yes. He's been there since the start."

"They tell me the tanks aren't any good anymore," a flyer said.

"You told him that once," I said. "Why don't you lay off? He's been working all day."

"So have we. But I mean really they aren't any good, are they?"

"Not so good. But he's good."

"I guess he's all right. He looks like a nice fellow. What kind of money do they make?"

"They got ten pesetas a day," I said. "Now he gets a lieutenant's pay."

"Spanish lieutenant?"

"Yes."

"I guess he's nuts all right. Or has he got politics?"

"He's got politics."

"Oh well," he said. "That explains it. Say Baldy you must have had a hell of a time bailing out with that wind pressure with the tail gone."

"Yes, Comrade," said Baldy.

"How did you feel?"

"I was thinking all the time, Comrade."

"Baldy, how many bailed out of the Junker?"

"Four," said Baldy, "out of a crew of six. I was sure I'd killed the pilot. I noticed when he quit firing. There's a co-pilot that's a gunner too and I'm pretty sure I got him too. I must have because he quit firing too. But maybe it was the heat. Anyhow four came out. Would you like me to describe the scene? I can describe the scene very well."

He was sitting on the bed now with a large water glass of champagne in his hand and his pink head and pink face were moist with sweat.

"Why doesn't anyone drink to me?" asked Baldy. "I would like all

118

comrades to drink to me and then, I will describe the scene in all its horror and its beauty."

We all drank.

"Where was I?" asked Baldy.

"Just coming out of the McAlester Hotel," a flyer said. "In all your horror and your beauty—don't clown, Baldy. Oddly enough we're interested."

"I will describe it," said Baldy. "But first I must have more champagne wine." He had drained the glass when we drank to him.

"If he drinks like that he'll go to sleep," another flyer said. "Only give him half a glass."

Baldy drank it off.

"I will describe it," he said. "After another little drink."

"Listen Baldy take it easy will you? This is something we want to get straight. You got no ship now for a few days but we're flying tomorrow and this is important as well as interesting."

"I made my report," said Baldy. "You can read it out at the field. They'll have a copy."

"Come on, Baldy, snap out of it."

"I will describe it eventually," said Baldy. He shut and opened his eyes several times then said "Hello Comrade Santa Claus," to Al. "I will describe it eventually. All you comrades have to do is listen."

And he described it.

"It was very strange and very beautiful," Baldy said and drank off the glass of champagne.

"Cut it out, Baldy," a flyer said.

"I have experienced profound emotions," Baldy said. "Highly profound emotions. Emotions of the deepest dye."

"Let's get back to Alcalá," one flyer said. "That pink head isn't going to make sense. What about the game?"

"He's going to make sense," another flyer said. "He's just winding up."

"Are you criticizing me?" asked Baldy. "Is *that* the thanks of the Republic?"

"Listen Santa Claus," Al said. "What was it like?"

"Are you asking me?" Baldy stared at him. "Are *you* putting questions to me? Have you ever been in action, Comrade?"

"No," said Al. "I got these eyebrows burnt off when I was shaving."

"Keep your drawers on, Comrade," said Baldy. "I will describe the strange and beautiful scene. I'm a writer you know as well as a flyer."

He nodded his head in confirmation of his own statement.

"He writes for the Meridian, Mississippi, *Argus*," said a flyer. "All the time. They can't stop him."

"I have talent as a writer," said Baldy. "I have a fresh and original talent for description. I have a newspaper clipping which I have lost which says so. Now I will launch myself on the description."

"O.K. What did it look like?"

"Comrades," said Baldy. "You can't describe it." He held out his glass.

"What did I tell you?" said a flyer. "He couldn't make sense in a month. He never could make sense."

"You," said Baldy, "you unfortunate little fellow. All right. When I banked out of it I looked down and of course she had been pouring back smoke but she was holding right on her course to get over the mountains. She was losing altitude fast and I came up and over and dove on her again. There were still wingmen then and she'd lurched and started to smoke twice as much and then the door of the cockpit came open and it was just like looking into a blast furnace, and then they started to come out. I'd half rolled, dove, and then pulled up out of it and I was looking back and down and they were coming out of her, out through the blast furnace door, dropping out trying to get clear, and the chutes opened up and they looked like great big beautiful morning glories opening up and she was just one big thing of flame now like you never saw and going round and round and there were four chutes just as beautiful as anything you could see just pulling slow against the sky and then one started to burn at the edge and as it burned the man started to drop fast and I was watching him when the bullets started to come by and the Fiats right behind them and the bullets and the Fiats."

"You're a writer all right," said one flyer. "You ought to write for *War Aces*. Do you mind telling me in plain language what happened?"

"No," said Baldy. "I'll tell you. But you know, no kidding, it was something to see. And I never shot down any big tri-motor Junkers before and I'm happy."

"Everybody's happy, Baldy. Tell us what happened, really."

"O.K.," said Baldy. "I'll just drink a little wine and then I'll tell you."

"How were you when you sighted them?"

"We were in a left echelon of V's. Then we went into a left echelon of echelons and dove onto them with all four guns until you could have touched them before we rolled out of it. We crippled three others. The Fiats were hanging up in the sun. They didn't come down until I was sightseeing all by myself."

"Did your wing men muck off?"

"No. It was my fault. I started watching the spectacle and they were gone. There isn't any formation for watching spectacles. I guess they went on and picked up the echelon. I don't know. Don't ask me. And I'm tired. I was elated. But now I'm tired."

"You're sleepy you mean. You're rum-dumb and sleepy."

"I am simply tired," said Baldy. "A man in my position has the right to be tired. And if I become sleepy I have the right to be sleepy. Don't I Santa Claus?" he said to Al.

"Yeah," said Al. "I guess you have the right to be sleepy. I'm even sleepy myself. Isn't there going to be any crap game?"

"We got to get him out to Alcalá and we've got to get out there too," a flyer said. "Why? You lost money in the game?"

"A little," said Al.

"You want to try to pass for it once?" the flyer asked him.

"I'll shoot a thousand," Al said.

"I'll fade you," the flyer said. "You guys don't make much, do you?"

"No," said Al. "We don't make much."

He laid the thousand peseta note down on the floor, rolled the dice between his palms so they clicked over and over, and shot them out on the floor with a snap. Two ones showed.

"They're still your dice," the flyer said picking up the bill and looking at Al.

"I don't need them," said Al. He stood up.

"Need any dough?" the flyer asked him. Looking at him curiously.

"Got no use for it," Al said.

"We've got to get the hell out to Alcalá," the flyer said. "We'll have a game some night soon. We'll get hold of Frank and the rest of them. We could get up a pretty good game. Can we give you a lift?"

"Yes. Want a ride?"

"No," Al said. "I'm walking. It's just down the street."

"Well, we're going out to Alcalá. Does anybody know the password for tonight?"

"Oh, the chauffeur will have it. He'll have gone by and picked it up before dark."

"Come on Baldy. You drunken sleepy bum."

"Not me," said Baldy. "I am a potential ace of the people's army."

"Takes ten to be an ace. Even if you count Italians. You've only got one, Baldy."

"It wasn't Italians," said Baldy. "It was Germans. And you didn't see her when she was all hot like that inside. She was a raging inferno."

121

"Carry him out," said a flyer. "He's writing for that Meridian, Mississippi, paper again. Well, so long. Thanks for having us up in the room."

They all shook hands and they were gone. I went to the head of the stairs with them. The elevator was no longer running and I watched them go down the stairs. One was on each side of Baldy and he was nodding his head slowly. He was really sleepy now.

In their room the two I was working on the picture with were still working over the bad camera. It was delicate, eye-straining work and when I asked, "Do you think you'll get her?" the tall one said, "Yes. Sure. We have to. I make a piece now which was broken."

"What was the party?" asked the other. "We work always on this damn camera."

"American flyers," I said. "And a fellow I used to know who's in tanks."

"Goot fun? I am sorry not to be there."

"All right," I said. "Kind of funny."

"You must get sleep. We must all be up early. We must be fresh for tomorrow."

"How much more have you got on that camera?"

"There it goes again. Damn such shape springs."

"Leave him alone. We finish it. Then we all sleep. What time you call us?"

"Five?"

"All right. As soon as is light."

"Good night."

"*Salud*. Get some sleep."

"*Salud*," I said. "We've got to be closer tomorrow."

"Yes," he said. "I have thought so too. Much closer. I am glad you know."

Al was asleep in the big chair in the room with the light on his face. I put a blanket over him but he woke.

"I'm going down."

"Sleep here. I'll set the alarm and call you."

"Something might happen with the alarm," he said. "I better go down. I don't want to get there late."

"I'm sorry about the game."

"They'd have broke me anyway," he said. "Those guys are poisonous with dice."

"You had the dice there on that last play."

"They're poisonous fading you too. They're strange guys too. I guess they don't get overpaid. I guess if you are doing it for dough there isn't enough dough to pay for doing it."

"Want me to walk down with you?"

"No," he said, standing up, and buckling on the big web-belted Colt he had taken off when he came back after dinner to the game. "No, I feel fine now. I've got my perspective back again. All you need is a perspective."

"I'd like to walk down."

"No. Get some sleep. I'll go down and I'll get a good five hours' sleep before it starts."

"That early?"

"Yeah. You won't have any light to film by. You might as well stay in bed." He took an envelope out of his leather coat and laid it on the table. "Take this stuff, will you, and send it to my brother in N.Y. His address is on the back of the envelope."

"Sure. But I won't have to send it."

"No," he said. "I don't think you will now. But there's some pictures and stuff they'll like to have. He's got a nice wife. Want to see her picture?"

He took it out of his pocket. It was inside his identity book.

It showed a pretty, dark girl standing by a rowboat on the shore of a lake.

"Up in the Catskills," said Al. "Yeah. He's got a nice wife. She's a Jewish girl. Yes," he said. "Don't let me get wet again. So long, kid. Take it easy. I tell you truly I feel O.K. now. And I didn't feel good when I came out this afternoon."

"Let me walk down."

"No. You might have trouble coming back through the Plaza de España. Some of those guys are nervous at night. Good night. See you tomorrow night."

"That's the way to talk."

Upstairs in the room above mine, Manolita and the Englishman were making quite a lot of noise. So she evidently hadn't been arrested.

"That's right. That's the way to talk," Al said. "Takes you sometimes three or four hours to get so you can do it though."

He'd put the leather helmet on now with the raised padded ridge and his face looked dark and I noticed the dark hollows under his eyes.

"See you tomorrow night at Chicote's," I said.

"That's right," he said, and wouldn't look me in the eye. "See you tomorrow night at Chicote's."

"What time?"

"Listen, that's enough," he said. "Tomorrow night at Chicote's. We don't have to go into the time." And he went out.

If you hadn't known him pretty well and if you hadn't seen the terrain where he was going to attack tomorrow, you would have thought he was very angry about something. I guess somewhere inside of himself he was angry, very angry. You get angry about a lot of things and you, yourself, dying uselessly is one of them. But then I guess angry is about the best way that you can be when you attack.

Espionage and Counter-Espionage

(from *The Fifth Column*)

ACT TWO • SCENE ONE

A room in Seguridad headquarters. There is a plain table, bare except for a green-shaded lamp. The windows are all closed and shuttered. Behind the table a short man with a very thin-lipped, hawk-nosed ascetic-looking face is sitting. He has very thick eyebrows. PHILIP *sits on a chair beside the table. The hawk-faced man is holding a pencil. On a chair in front of the table a* MAN *is sitting. He is crying with very deep shaking sobs.* ANTONIO (*the hawk-nosed man*) *is looking at him very interestedly. It is the* FIRST COMRADE *from Scene 3, Act 1. He is bareheaded, his tunic is off, and his braces, which hold up his baggy I.B. trousers, hang down along his trousers. As the curtain rises* PHILIP *stands up and looks at the* FIRST COMRADE.

PHILIP. [*In a tired voice*] I'd like to ask you one more thing.

FIRST COMRADE. Don't ask me. Please don't ask me. I don't want you to ask me.

PHILIP. Were you asleep?

FIRST COMRADE. [*Choking*] Yes.

PHILIP. [*In a very tired flat voice*] You know the penalty for that?

FIRST COMRADE. Yes.

PHILIP. Why didn't you say so at the start and save a lot of trouble? I wouldn't have you shot for that. I'm just disappointed in you now. Do you think people shoot people for fun?

FIRST COMRADE. I should have told you. I was frightened.

PHILIP. Yeah. You should have told me.

FIRST COMRADE. Truly, Comrade Commissar.

PHILIP. [*To* ANTONIO, *coldly*] You think he was asleep?

ANTONIO. How do I know? Do you want me to question him?

125

PHILIP. No, *mi Coronel*, no. We want information. We don't want a confession.

[*To the* FIRST COMRADE]

Listen, what did you dream about when you went to sleep?

FIRST COMRADE. [*Checks himself sobbing, hesitates, then goes on*] I don't remember.

PHILIP. Just try to. Take your time. I only want to be sure, you see. Don't try to lie. I'll know if you lie.

FIRST COMRADE. I remember now. I was against the wall and my rifle was between my legs when I leaned back, and I remember.

[*He chokes*]

In the dream I—I thought it was my girl and she was doing something—kind of funny—to me. I don't know what it was. It was just in a dream.

[*He chokes*]

PHILIP. [*To* ANTONIO] You satisfied now?

ANTONIO. I do not understand it completely.

PHILIP. Well, I guess nobody really understands it completely, but he's convinced me.

[*To the* FIRST COMRADE]

What's your girl's name?

FIRST COMRADE. Alma.

PHILIP. O.K. When you write her tell her she brought you a lot of luck.

[*To* ANTONIO]

As far as I'm concerned you can take him out. He reads the *Worker.* He knows Joe North. He's got a girl named Alma. He's got a good record with the Brigade, and he went to sleep and let a citizen slip who shot a boy named Wilkinson by mistake for me. The thing to do is to give him lots of strong coffee to keep him awake and keep rifles out from between his legs. Listen, Comrade, I'm sorry if I spoke roughly to you in the performance of my duty.

ANTONIO. I would like to put a few questions.

PHILIP. Listen, *mi Coronel*. If I wasn't good at this you wouldn't have let me go on doing it so long. This boy is all right. You know we are none of us *exactly* what you would call all *right*. But this boy is pretty all right. He just went to sleep, and I'm not justice you know. I'm just working for

126

you, and the cause, and the Republic and one thing and another. And we used to have a President named Lincoln in America, you know, who commuted sentences of sentries to be shot for sleeping, you know. So I think if it's all right with you we'll just sort of commute his sentence. He comes from the Lincoln Battalion you see—and it's an awfully good battalion. It's such a good battalion and it's done such things that it would break your damn heart if I tried to tell you about it. And if I was in it I'd feel decent and proud instead of the way I feel doing what I am. But I'm not, see? I'm a sort of a second-rate cop pretending to be a third-rate newspaperman—But listen Comrade Alma—

[*Turning to prisoner*]

If you ever go to sleep again on duty when you are working for me I'll shoot you myself, see? You *hear* me? And write it to Alma.

ANTONIO. [*Ringing. Two* ASSAULT GUARDS *come in*] Take him away. You speak very confusedly, Philip. But you have a certain amount of credit to exhaust.

FIRST COMRADE. Thank you, Comrade Commissar.

PHILIP. Oh, don't say thank you in a war. This is a war. You don't say thank you in it. But you're welcome, see? And when you write to Alma tell her she brought you a lot of luck.

[FIRST COMRADE *goes out with* ASSAULT GUARDS]

ANTONIO. Yes, and now. This man got away from room 107 and shot this boy by mistake for you, and who is this man?

PHILIP. Oh, I don't know. Santa Claus, I guess. He's got a number. They have A numbered one to ten, and B numbered one to ten, and C numbered one to ten, and they shoot people and they blow up things and they do everything you're overly familiar with. And they work very hard, and aren't really awfully efficient. But they kill a lot of people that they shouldn't kill. The trouble is they've worked it out so well on the lines of the old Cuban A.B.C. that unless you get somebody outside that they deal with, it doesn't mean anything. It's just like cutting the heads off boils instead of listening to a Fleischman's Yeast Program. You know, correct me if I become confusing.

ANTONIO. And why do you not take this man with a sufficient force?

PHILIP. Because I cannot afford to make much noise and scare others that we need much more. This one is just a killer.

ANTONIO. Yes. There are plenty of fascists left in a town of a million people, and they work inside. Those who have the courage to. We must have twenty thousand active here.

PHILIP. More. Double that. But when you catch them they won't talk. Except the politicians.

ANTONIO. Politicians. Yes, politicians. I have seen a politician on the floor in that corner of the room unable to stand up when it was time to go out. I have seen a politician walk across that floor on his knees and put his arms around my legs and kiss my feet. I watched him slobber on my boots when all he had to do was such a simple thing as die. I have seen many die, and I have never seen a politician die well.

PHILIP. I don't like to see them die. It's O.K. I guess, if you like to see it. But I don't like it. Sometimes I don't know how you stick it. Listen, who dies well?

ANTONIO. You know. Don't be naïve.

PHILIP. Yes. I suppose I know.

ANTONIO. I could die all right. I don't ask any one to do something that is impossible.

PHILIP. You're a specialist. Look, Tonico. Who dies well? Go ahead, say it. Go ahead. Do you good to talk about your trade. Talk about it you know. Then next thing you know, forget it. Simple, eh? Tell me about in the first days of the movement.

ANTONIO. [*Rather proudly*] You want to hear? You mean definite people?

PHILIP. No. I know a couple of definite people. I mean sort of by classes.

ANTONIO. Fascists, real fascists, the young ones; very well. Sometimes with very much style. They are mistaken, but they have much style. Soldiers, yes, the majority all right. Priests all my life I am against. The church fights us. We fight the church. I am a Socialist for many years. We are the oldest revolutionary party in Spain. But to die—

[*He shakes his hand in the quick triple flip of the wrist that is the Spanish gesture of supreme admiration*]

To die? Priests? Terrific. You know; just simple priests. I don't mean bishops.

PHILIP. And Antonio. Sometimes there must have been mistakes, eh? When you had to work in a hurry perhaps. Or you know, just mistakes, we all make mistakes. I just made a little one yesterday. Tell me, Antonio, were there ever any mistakes?

ANTONIO. Oh, yes. Certainly. Mistakes. Oh, yes. Mistakes. Yes. Yes. Very regrettable mistakes. A very few.

PHILIP. And how did the mistakes die?

ANTONIO. [*Proudly*] All very well.

PHILIP. Ah——

[It is noise a boxer might make when he is hit with a hard body punch]

And this trade we're in now. You know, what's the silly name they call it? Counter-espionage. It doesn't ever get on your nerves?

ANTONIO. *[Simply]* No.

PHILIP. With me it's on the nerves now for a long time.

ANTONIO. But you've only been doing it for a little while.

PHILIP. Twelve bloody months, my boy, in this country. And before that, Cuba. Ever been in Cuba?

ANTONIO. Yes.

PHILIP. That's where I got sucked in on all this.

ANTONIO. How were you sucked in?

PHILIP. Oh, people started trusting me that should have known better. And I suppose because they should have known better I started getting, you know, sort of trustworthy. You know, not elaborately, just sort of moderately trustworthy. And then they trust you a little more and you do it all right. And then you know, you get to believing in it. Finally I guess you get to liking it. I have a sort of a feeling I don't explain it very well.

ANTONIO. You're a good boy. You work well. Everybody trusts you very much.

PHILIP. Too bloody much. And I'm tired too, and I'm worried right now. You know what I'd like? I'd like to never kill another son-of-a-bitch, I don't care who or for what, as long as I live. I'd like to never have to lie. I'd like to know who I'm with when I wake up. I'd like to wake up in the same place every morning for a week straight. I'd like to marry a girl named Bridges that you don't know. But don't mind if I use the name because I like to say it. And I'd like to marry her because she's got the longest, smoothest, straightest legs in the world, and I don't have to listen to her when she talks if it doesn't make too good sense. But I'd like to see what the kids would look like.

ANTONIO. She is the tall blonde with that correspondent?

PHILIP. Don't talk about her like that. She isn't any tall blonde with some correspondent. That's my girl. And if I talk too much or take up your valuable time, why, stop me. You know I'm a very extraordinary fellow. I can talk either English or American. Was brought up in one, raised in the other. That's what I make my living at.

ANTONIO. *[Soothingly]* I know. You are tired, Philip.

PHILIP. Well, now I'm talking American. Bridges is the same way. Only I'm not sure she can talk American. You see she learned her English at college and from the cheap or literary type of Lord, but you know what's funny, you see. I just like to hear her talk. I don't care what she says. I'm relaxed now, you see. I haven't had anything to drink since breakfast, and I'm a lot drunker than I am when I drink, and that's a bad sign. Is it all right for one of your operatives to relax, *mi Coronel?*

ANTONIO. You ought to go to bed. You're tired out, Philip, and you have much work to do.

PHILIP. That's right. I'm tired out and I have much work to do. I'm waiting to meet a comrade at Chicote's. Name of Max. I have, and I do not exaggerate, very much work to do. Max, whom I believe you know and who, to show what a distinguished man he is, has no hind name, while my back name is Rawlings exactly the same as when I started. Which shows you I haven't gotten *very* far in this business. What was I saying?

ANTONIO. About Max.

PHILIP. Max. That's it. Max. Well he's a day overdue now. He's been navigating now for about two weeks, say circulating to avoid confusion, behind the fascist lines. It's his specialty. And he says, and he doesn't lie. I lie. But not right now. Anyway, I'm very tired, see, and I'm also disgusted with my job, and I'm nervous as a bastard because I'm worried and I don't worry easy.

ANTONIO. Go on. Don't be temperamental.

PHILIP. He says, that is Max says, and where he is now I wish to hell I knew, that he has a place located, an observation post, you know. Watch them fall, and say it's the wrong place. One of those. Well, he says that the German head of the siege artillery that shells this town comes there and a lovely politician. You know a museum piece. He comes there too. And *Max* thinks. And *I* think he is screwball. But he thinks better. I think *faster*, but he thinks better. That we can bag those citizens. Now listen very carefully, *mi Coronel*, and correct me instantly. *I* think it sounds very romantic. But *Max* says, and he's a German and very practical, and he'd just as soon go behind the fascist lines as you would go to get a shave, or what shall we say. Well *he* says it's perfectly practical. So *I* thought. And I'm sort of drunk now on drinking nothing for so long. That we would sort of suspend the other projects that we have been working on, temporarily, and try to get these two people for you. I don't think the German is of much practical use to you, but he has a very high exchange value indeed, and this project sort of, in a way, appeals to Max. Lay it to nationalism, I say. But if we get this other citizen you've got something, *mi Coronel*. Because he is very, *very* terrific. I mean *terrific*. He, you see, is *outside* the town. But he knows who is *inside* the town. And then you just sort of bring him into good voice and *you* know who is inside the town. Because they all communicate with him. I talk too much, don't I?

ANTONIO. Philip.

PHILIP. Yes, Mi Coronel.

ANTONIO. Philip, now go to Chicote's and get drunk like a good boy and do your work, and come or call when you have news.

PHILIP. And what do I talk, *mi Coronel*, American or English?

ANTONIO. What you like. Do not talk silly. But go now, please, because we are good friends and I like you very much, but I am very busy. Listen, is it true about the observation post?

PHILIP. Yeah.

ANTONIO. What a thing.

PHILIP. Very fancy, though. Awfully, *awfully* fancy, *mi Coronel*.

ANTONIO. Go, please, and start.

PHILIP. And I talk either English or American?

ANTONIO. What's all that about? Go.

PHILIP. Then I'll talk English. Christ, I can lie so much easier in English, it's pitiful.

ANTONIO. GO. GO. GO. GO. GO.

PHILIP. Yes, *mi Coronel*. Thank you for the instructive little talk. I'll go to Chicote's now. *Salud, mi Coronel.*

[*He salutes, looks at his watch and goes*]

ANTONIO. [*At the desk, looks after him. Then rings. Two* ASSAULT GUARDS *come in. They salute*] Now just bring me in that man you took out before. I want to talk to him a little while alone by myself.

CURTAIN

ACT THREE • SCENE TWO

Interior of an artillery observation post in a shelled house on the top of the Extremadura road.

It is located in the tower of what has been a very pretentious house and access to it is by a ladder which replaces the circular iron stairway which has been smashed and hangs, broken and twisted. You see the ladder against the tower and at its top, the back of the observation post which faces toward Madrid. It is night and the sacks which plug its windows have been removed and looking out through them you see nothing but darkness because the lights of Madrid have been extinguished. There are large-scale military maps on the walls with

131

*the positions marked with colored tacks and tapes, and on a plain
table there is a field telephone. There is an extra large size, single, German model, long tube telemeter opposite the narrow opening in the
wall to the right of the table and a chair beside it. There is an ordi-
nary-sized double tube telemeter at the other opening with a chair at
its base. There is another plain table with a telephone on the right of
the room. At the foot of the ladder is a* SENTRY *with fixed bayonet, and
at the top of the ladder in the room, where there is just enough height
for him to stand straight with his rifle and bayonet, there is another*
SENTRY. *As the curtain rises, you see the scene as described with the*
TWO SENTRIES *at their posts. Two* SIGNALLERS *are bending over the
larger table. After the curtain is up, you see the lights of a motor which
shine brightly on the ladder at the base of the tower. They come closer
and closer and almost blind the* SENTRY.

SENTRY. Cut those lights!

[*The lights shine on, illuminating the* SENTRY *with a blinding light*]

SENTRY. [*Presenting his rifle, pulling back the bolt, and shoving it forward
with a click*] Cut those lights!

[*He says it very slowly, clearly and dangerously, and it is obvious that he
will fire. The lights go off and* THREE MEN, *two of them in officer's uniform,
one large and stout, the other rather thin and elegantly dressed, with riding boots which shine in the flashlight the stout man carries, and a* CIVIL-
IAN, *cross the stage from the left where they have left the motor car off stage;
and approach the ladder*]

SENTRY. [*Giving the first half of the password*] The Victory——
THIN OFFICER. [*Snappily and disdainfully*] To those who deserve it.
SENTRY. Pass.
THIN OFFICER. [*To* CIVILIAN] Just climb up here.
CIVILIAN. I've been here before.

[*The three of them climb the ladder. At the top of the ladder the* SENTRY, *seeing the insignia on the cap of the large, stout officer, presents arms. The* SIG-
NALLERS *remain seated at their telephones. The large officer goes over to the
table followed by the* CIVILIAN *and the shiny-booted officer who is obviously
his* AIDE]

LARGE OFFICER. What's the matter with these signallers?
AIDE. [*To* SIGNALLERS] Come along! Stand to attention there! What's
the matter with you?

132

[SIGNALLERS *stand to attention rather wearily*]

At ease!

[*The* SIGNALLERS *sit down. The* LARGE OFFICER *is studying the map. The* CIVILIAN *looks out of the telemeter and sees nothing in the darkness*]

CIVILIAN. The bombardment's for midnight?
AIDE. What time is the shoot for, Sir?

[*Speaking to the* LARGE OFFICER]

LARGE OFFICER. [*Speaking with a German accent*] You talk too much!
AIDE. I'm sorry, sir. Would you care to have a look at these?

[*He hands him a sheaf of typed orders clipped together.* LARGE OFFICER *takes them and glances at them. Hands them back*]

LARGE OFFICER. [*In heavy voice*] I am familiar with them. I wrote them.
AIDE. Quite, sir. I thought perhaps you wished to verify them.
LARGE OFFICER. I heff verified them!

[*One of the phones rings.* SIGNALLER *at table takes it and listens*]

SIGNALLER. Yes. No. Yes. All right.

[*He nods to the* LARGE OFFICER]

For you, sir.

[LARGE OFFICER *takes the phone*]

LARGE OFFICER. Hello. Yes. That is right. Are you a fool? No? As ordered. By salvos means by salvos.

[*He hangs up the receiver and looks at his watch*]
[*To* AIDE]

What time have you?
AIDE. Twelve minus one, sir.
LARGE OFFICER. I deal with fools here. You cannot say that you command where there is no discipline. Signallers who sit at table when a General comes in. Artillery brigadiers who ask for explanations of orders. What time did you say it was?
AIDE. [*Looking at his watch*] Twelve minus thirty seconds, sir.
SIGNALLER. The brigade called six times, sir!
LARGE OFFICER. [*Lighting a cigar*] What time?
AIDE. Minus fifteen, sir.

LARGE OFFICER. What minus fifteen what?

AIDE. Twelve minus fifteen seconds, sir.

[*Just then you hear the guns. They are a very different sound from the incoming shells. There is a sharp, cracking boom, boom, boom, boom, as a kettle drum would make struck sharply before a microphone and then whish, whish, whish, whish, chu, chu, chu, chu, chu—chu—as the shells go away followed by a distant burst. Another battery closer and louder commences firing and then they are firing all along the line in quick, pounding thuds and the air is full of the noise the departing projectiles make. Through the open window you see the skyline of Madrid lit now by the flashes. The LARGE OFFICER is standing at the big telemeter. The CIVILIAN at the two-branched one. The AIDE is looking over the CIVILIAN'S shoulder*]

CIVILIAN. God, what a beautiful sight!

AIDE. We'll kill plenty of them tonight. The Marxist bastards. This catches them in their holes.

CIVILIAN. It's wonderful to see it.

GENERAL. Is it satisfactory?

[*He does not remove his eyes from the telemeter*]

CIVILIAN. It's beautiful! How long will it go on?

GENERAL. We're giving them an hour. Then ten minutes without. Then fifteen minutes more.

CIVILIAN. No shells will light in the Salamanca quarter, will they? That's where nearly all our people are.

GENERAL. A few will land there.

CIVILIAN. But why?

GENERAL. Errors by Spanish batteries.

CIVILIAN. Why by Spanish batteries?

GENERAL. Spanish batteries are not so good as ours.

[*The CIVILIAN does not answer and the firing keeps up although the batteries are not firing with the speed with which they commenced. There is an incoming whistling rush, then a roar, and a shell has landed just short of the observation post*]

GENERAL. They answer now a little.

[*There are no lights in the observation post now except that of the gun flashes and the light of the cigarette the SENTRY at the foot of the ladder is smoking. As you watch you see the glow of this cigarette describe half an arc in the dark, and there is a thud clearly heard by the audience as the SENTRY falls.*]

You hear the sound of two blows. Another shell comes in with the same sort of screaming rush, and at its burst you see in the flash two men climbing the ladder]

GENERAL. [*Speaking from the telemeter*] Ring me Garabitas.

[SIGNALLER *rings. Then rings again*]

SIGNALLER. Sorry, sir. The wire's gone.
GENERAL. [*To the other* SIGNALLER] Get me through to the Division.
SIGNALLER. I have no wire, sir.
GENERAL. Put some one to trace your wire!
SIGNALLER. Yes, sir.

[*He rises in the dark*]

GENERAL. What's that man smoking for? What sort of an army out of the chorus of *Carmen* is this?

[*You see the cigarette in the mouth of the* SENTRY *at the top of the ladder describe a long parabola toward the ground as though he had tossed it away, and there is the solid noise of a body falling. A flashlight illuminates the three men by the telemeters and the two* SIGNALLERS]

PHILIP. [*From inside the open door at the top of the ladder. In a low, very quiet voice*] Put your hands up and don't try anything heroic, or I'll blow your heads off!

[*He is holding a short automatic rifle which was slung over his back as he climbed up the ladder*]

I mean all five of you! *KEEP* them up there, you fat bastard!

[MAX *has a hand grenade in his right hand, the flashlight in his left*]

MAX. You make a noise, you move, and everybody is dead. You hear?
PHILIP. Who do you want?
MAX. Only the fat one and the townsman. Tie me up the rest. You have also good adhesive tape?
PHILIP. *Da.*
MAX. You see. We are all Russians. Everybody is Russians in Madrid! Hurry up, Tovarich, and tape good the mouths, because I have to throw this thing before we go. You see the pin is pulled already!

[*Just before the curtain goes down, as* PHILIP *is advancing toward them with the short automatic rifle, you see the men's white faces in the flashlight.*

135

The batteries are still firing. From below and beyond the house comes a voice—"Cut out that light!"]

MAX. O.K. soldier, in just a minute!

CURTAIN

ACT THREE • SCENE THREE

As the curtain rises you see the same room in Seguridad headquarters that was shown in Act II, Scene I. ANTONIO, *of the Comisariato de Vigilancia, is sitting behind the table.* PHILIP *and* MAX, *muddy and much the worse for wear, are seated in the two chairs.* PHILIP *still has the automatic rifle slung over his back. The* CIVILIAN *from the observation post, his beret gone, his trench coat ripped clean up the back, one sleeve hanging loose, is standing before the table with an* ASSAULT GUARD *on either side of him.*

ANTONIO. [*To the two* ASSAULT GUARDS] You can go!

[*They salute and go out to the right, carrying their rifles at trail*]
[*To* PHILIP]

What became of the other?
PHILIP. We lost him coming in.
MAX. He was too heavy and he would not walk.
ANTONIO. It would have been a wonderful capture.
PHILIP. You can't do these things as they do them in the cinema.
ANTONIO. Still, if we could have had him!
PHILIP. I'll draw you a little map and you can send out there and find him.
ANTONIO. Yes?
MAX. He was a soldier and he would never have talked. I would have liked the questioning of him, but such a business is useless.
PHILIP. When we're through here I'll draw you a little map and you can send out for him. No one will have moved him. We left him in a likely spot.
CIVILIAN. [*In an hysterical voice*] You *murdered* him.
PHILIP. [*Contemptuously*] Shut up, will you?
MAX. I promise you, he would not have ever talked. I know such men.

136

PHILIP. You see, we didn't expect to find two of these sportsmen at the same time. And this other specimen was oversized and he wouldn't walk finally. He made a sort of sit-down strike. And I don't know whether you've ever tried coming in at night from up there. There are a couple of very odd spots. So you see we didn't really have any bloody choice in the matter.

CIVILIAN. [*Hysterically*] So you murdered him! I saw you do it.

PHILIP. Just quiet down, will you? No one asked you for your opinion.

MAX. You want us now?

ANTONIO. No.

MAX. I think I like to go. This isn't what I like very much. It makes too much remember.

PHILIP. You need me?

ANTONIO. No.

PHILIP. You don't need to worry. You'll get everything—the lists, the locations, everything. This thing has been running it.

ANTONIO. Yes.

PHILIP. You don't need to worry about his talking. He's the talkative type.

ANTONIO. He is a politician. Yes. I have talked to many politicians.

CIVILIAN. [*Hysterically*] You'll never make me talk! Never! Never! Never!

[MAX *and* PHILIP *look at each other*—PHILIP *grins*]

PHILIP. [*Very quietly*] You're talking now. Haven't you noticed it?

CIVILIAN. No! No!

MAX. If it is all right I will go.

[*He stands up*]

PHILIP. I'll run along too, I think.

ANTONIO. You do not want to stay to hear it?

MAX. Please, no.

ANTONIO. It will be very interesting.

PHILIP. It's that we are tired.

ANTONIO. It will be very interesting.

PHILIP. I'll be by tomorrow.

ANTONIO. I would like you very much to stay.

MAX. Please. If you do not mind. As a favor.

CIVILIAN. What are you going to do to me?

ANTONIO. Nothing. Only that you should answer some questions.

CIVILIAN. I'll never talk.
ANTONIO. Oh, yes, you will!
MAX. Please. Please. I go now!

CURTAIN

ACT THREE • SCENE FOUR

Same as Act I, Scene III, but it is late afternoon. As the curtain rises, you see the two rooms. DOROTHY BRIDGES' *room is dark.* PHILIP'S *is lighted, with the curtains drawn.* PHILIP *is lying face down on the bed.* ANITA *is sitting on a chair by the bed.*

ANITA. Philip!
PHILIP. [*Not turning or looking toward her*] What's the matter?
ANITA. Please, Philip.
PHILIP. Please bloody what?
ANITA. Where is whiskey?
PHILIP. Under the bed.
ANITA. Thank you.

[*She looks under the bed. Then crawls part way under*]

No find.
PHILIP. Try the closet then. Somebody's been in here cleaning up again.
ANITA. [*Goes to the closet and opens it. She looks carefully inside*] Is all empty bottles.
PHILIP. You're just a little discoverer. Come here.
ANITA. I want find a whiskey.
PHILIP. Look in the night table.

[ANITA *goes over to the night table by the bed and opens the door—she brings out a bottle of whiskey. Goes for a glass into the bathroom, and pours a whiskey into it and adds water from the carafe by the bed*]

ANITA. Philip. Drink this feel better.

[PHILIP *sits up and looks at her*]

PHILIP. Hello, Black Beauty. How did you get in here?
ANITA. From the pass key.
PHILIP. Well.

138

ANITA. I no see you. I plenty worried. I come here they say you inside. I knock door no answer. I knock more. No answer. I say open me up with the pass key.

PHILIP. And they did?

ANITA. I said you sent for me.

PHILIP. Did I?

ANITA. No.

PHILIP. Thoughtful of you to come though.

ANITA. Philip you still that big blonde?

PHILIP. I don't know. I'm sort of mixed up about that. Things are getting sort of complicated. Every night I ask her to marry me, and every morning I tell her I don't mean it. I think, probably, things can't go on like that. No. They can't go on like that.

[ANITA *sits down by him and pats his head and smooths his hair back*]

ANITA. You feel plenty bad. I know.

PHILIP. Want me to tell you a secret?

ANITA. Yes.

PHILIP. I never felt worse.

ANITA. Is a disappoint. Was think you tell how you catch all the people of the Fifth Column.

PHILIP. I didn't catch them. Only caught one man. Disgusting specimen he was, too.

[*There is a knock on the door. It is the* MANAGER]

MANAGER. Excuse profoundly if disturbation——

PHILIP. Keep it clean you know. There's ladies present.

MANAGER. I mean only to enter and see if every *thing* in order. Control possible actions of young lady in case your absence or incapacity. Also desire offer sincerest warmest greetings congratulations admirable performance feat of counterespionage resulting announcement evening papers arrest three hundred members Fifth Column.

PHILIP. That's in the paper?

MANAGER. With details of arrestations of every type of reprehensible engaged in shooting, plotting assassinations—sabotaging, communicating with enemy, every form of delights.

PHILIP. Of delights?

MANAGER. Is a French word, spells out D-E-L-I-T-S, meaning offenses.

PHILIP. And that's all in the paper?

MANAGER. Absolutely, Mr. Philip.

PHILIP. And where do I come in?

MANAGER. Oh, everybody knows you were engaged in prosecution of such investigations.

PHILIP. Just how do they know?

MANAGER. [*Reproachfully*] Mr. Philip. Is Madrid. In Madrid everybody knows everything often before occurrence of same. After occurrence sometimes is discussions as to who actually did. But before occurrence all the world knows clearly who must do. I offer congratulations now in order to precede reproaches of unsatisfiables who ask, "Ah ha! Only 300? Where are the others?"

PHILIP. Don't be so gloomy. I suppose I'll have to be leaving now though.

MANAGER. Mr. Philip, I have thought of that and I come here, make what hope will result as excellent proposition. If you leave is useless to carry tinned goods as baggage.

[There is a knock on the door. It is MAX]

MAX. Salud camaradas.

EVERY ONE. Salud.

PHILIP. [*To* MANAGER] Run along now, Comrade Stamp Collector. We can talk about that later.

MAX. [*To* PHILIP] *Wie gehts?*

PHILIP. *Gut.* Not too *gut.*

ANITA. O.K. I take bath?

PHILIP. More than O.K., darling. But keep the door shut, will you?

ANITA. [*From bathroom*] Is warm water.

PHILIP. That's a good sign. Shut the door, please.

[ANITA *shuts the door.* MAX *comes over by the bed and sits down on a chair.* PHILIP *is sitting on the bed with his legs hanging over*]

PHILIP. Want anything?

MAX. No, Comrade. You were there?

PHILIP. Oh, yes. I stayed all through it. Every bit of it. All of it. They needed to know something and they called me back.

MAX. How was he?

PHILIP. Cowardly. But it only came out a little at a time for a while.

MAX. And then?

PHILIP. Oh, and then finally he was spilling it out faster than a stenographer could take it. I have a strong stomach, you know.

MAX [*Ignoring this*] I see in the paper about the arrests. Why do they publish such things?

PHILIP. I don't know, my boy. Why do they? I'll bite.

MAX. It is good for morale. But it is also very good to get every one. Did they bring in—the—ah——

PHILIP. Oh, yes. The corpse you mean? They fetched him in from where we left him, and Antonio had him placed in a chair in the corner and I put a cigarette in his mouth and lit it and it was all very jolly. Only the cigarette wouldn't stay lighted, of course.

MAX. I am very happy I did not have to stay.

PHILIP. I stayed. And then I left. And then I came back. Then I left and they called me back again. I've been there until an hour ago and now I'm through. For today, that is. Finished my work for the day. Something else to do tomorrow.

MAX. We did very good job.

PHILIP. As good as we could. It was very brilliant and very flashy, and there were probably many holes in the net and a big part of the haul got away. But they can haul again. You have to send me some place else though. I'm no good here any more. Too many people know what I'm doing. *Not* because I talk, either. It just gets that way.

MAX. There are many places to send. But you still have some work to do here.

PHILIP. I know. But ship me out as quickly as you can, will you? I'm getting on the jumpy side.

MAX. What about the girl in the other room?

PHILIP. Oh, I'm going to break it off with her.

MAX. I do not ask that.

PHILIP. No. But you would sooner or later. There's no sense babying me along. We're in for fifty years of undeclared wars and I've signed up for the duration. I don't exactly remember when it was, but I signed up all right.

MAX. So have we all. There is no question of signing. There is no need to talk with bitterness.

PHILIP. I'm not bitter. I just don't want to fool myself. Nor let things get a hold in part of me where no things should get hold. This thing was getting pretty well in. Well, I know how to cure it.

MAX. How?

PHILIP. I'll show you how.

MAX. Remember, Philip, I am a kind man.

PHILIP. Oh, quite. So am I. You ought to watch me work sometime.

[*While they have been talking you see the door of 109 open and* DOROTHY BRIDGES *comes in. She turns up the lights, takes off her street coat and puts*

141

on the silver fox cape. Standing, she turns in it before the mirror. She looks very beautiful this evening. She goes to the phonograph and puts on the Chopin Mazurka and sits in a chair by the reading light with a book]

PHILIP. There she is. She's come, what do you call the place, home—now.

MAX. Philip, Comrade, you do not have to. I tell you truly I see no signs that she interferes with your work in any way.

PHILIP. No, but I do. And you would damned soon.

MAX. I leave it to you as before. But remember to be kind. To us to whom dreadful things have been done, kindness in all *possible* things is of great importance.

PHILIP. I'm very kind, too, you know. Oh, am I kind! I'm terrific!

MAX. No, I do not know that you are kind. I would like you to be.

PHILIP. Just wait in here, will you?

[PHILIP *goes out of the door and knocks on the door of 109. He pushes it open after knocking and goes in]*

DOROTHY. Hello, beloved.

PHILIP. Hello. How have you been?

DOROTHY. I'm very well and very happy now you're here. Where have you been? You never came in last night. Oh, I'm so *glad* you're here.

PHILIP. Have you a drink?

DOROTHY. Yes, darling.

[*She makes him a whiskey and water. In the other room* MAX *is sitting in a chair staring at the electric stove]*

DOROTHY. Where were you, Philip?

PHILIP. Just around. Checking up on things.

DOROTHY. And how were things?

PHILIP. Some were good, you know. And some were not so good. I suppose they evened up.

DOROTHY. And you don't have to go out tonight?

PHILIP. I don't know.

DOROTHY. Philip, beloved, what's the matter?

PHILIP. Nothing's the matter.

DOROTHY. Philip, let's go away from here. I don't have to stay here. I've sent away three articles. We could go to that place near Saint-Tropez and the rains haven't started yet and it would be lovely there now with no people. Then afterwards we could go to ski.

PHILIP. [*Very bitterly*] Yes, and afterwards to Egypt and make love happily in all the hotels, and a thousand breakfasts come up on trays in the thousand fine mornings of the next three years; or the ninety of the next three months; or however long it took you to be tired of me, or me of you. And all we'd do would be amuse ourselves. We'd stay at the Crillon, or the Ritz, and in the fall when the leaves were off the trees in the Bois and it was sharp and cold, we'd drive out to Auteuil steeplechasing, and keep warm by those big coal braziers in the paddock, and watch them take the water jump and see them coming over the bullfinch and the old stone wall. That's it. And nip into the bar for a champagne cocktail and afterwards ride back in to dinner at La Rue's and weekends go to shoot pheasants in the Sologne. Yes, yes, that's it. And fly out to Nairobi and the old Mathaiga Club, and in the spring a little spot of salmon fishing. Yes, yes, that's it. And every night in bed together. Is that it?

DOROTHY. Oh, darling, think how it would be! Have you *that* much money?

PHILIP. I did have. Till I got into this business.

DOROTHY. And we'll do all that and Saint Moritz, too?

PHILIP. Saint Moritz? Don't be vulgar. Kitzbühel you mean. You meet people like Michael Arlen at Saint Moritz.

DOROTHY. But you wouldn't have to meet him, darling. You could cut him. And will we really do all that?

PHILIP. Do you want to?

DOROTHY. Oh, darling!

PHILIP. Would you like to go to Hungary, too, some fall? You can take an estate there very cheaply and only pay for what you shoot. And on the Danube flats you have great flights of geese. And have you ever been to Lamu where the long white beach is, with the dhows beached on their sides, and the wind in the palms at night? Or what about Malindi where you can surfboard on the beach and the northeast monsoon cool and fresh, and no pajamas, and no sheets at night. You'd like Malindi.

DOROTHY. I know I would, Philip.

PHILIP. And have you ever been out to the Sans Souci in Havana on a Saturday night to dance in the Patio under the royal palms? They're gray and they rise like columns and you stay up all night there and play dice, or the wheel, and drive in to Jaimanitas for breakfast in the daylight. And everybody knows every one else and it's very pleasant and gay.

DOROTHY. Can we go there?

PHILIP. No.

DOROTHY. Why not, Philip?

PHILIP. We won't go anywhere.

DOROTHY. Why not, darling?

PHILIP. You can go if you like. I'll draw you up an itinerary.

DOROTHY. But why can't we go together?

PHILIP. You can go. But I've been to all those places and I've left them all behind. And where I go now I go alone, or with others who go there for the same reason I go.

DOROTHY. And I can't go there?

PHILIP. No.

DOROTHY. And why can't I go wherever it is? I could learn and I'm *not* afraid.

PHILIP. One reason is I don't know where it is. And another is I wouldn't take you.

DOROTHY. Why not?

PHILIP. Because you're useless, really. You're uneducated, you're useless, you're a fool and you're lazy.

DOROTHY. Maybe the others. But I'm not useless.

PHILIP. Why aren t you useless?

DOROTHY. You know—or you ought to know.

[*She is crying*]

PHILIP. Oh, yes. *That.*

DOROTHY. Is that all it means to you?

PHILIP. That's a commodity you shouldn't pay too high a price for.

DOROTHY. So I'm a commodity?

PHILIP. Yes, a very handsome commodity. The most beautiful I ever had.

DOROTHY. Good. I'm glad to hear you say it. And I'm glad it's daylight. Now get out of here. You conceited, *conceited* drunkard. You ridiculous, puffed-up, posing braggart. You commodity, you. Did it ever occur to you that you're a commodity, too? A commodity one shouldn't pay too high a price for?

PHILIP. [*Laughing*] No. But I see it the way you put it.

DOROTHY. Well, you are. You're a perfectly vicious commodity. Never home. Out all night. Dirty, muddy, disorderly. You're a *terrible* commodity. I just liked the package it was put up in. That was all. I'm glad you're going away.

PHILIP. Really?

DOROTHY. Yes, *really.* You and your commodity. But you didn't have to mention all those places if we weren't ever going to them.

PHILIP. I'm very sorry. That wasn't kind.

DOROTHY. Oh, don't be kind either. You're frightful when you're

144

kind. Only kind people should try being kind. You're horrible when
you're kind. And you didn't have to mention them in the daytime.

PHILIP. I'm sorry.

DOROTHY. Oh, don't be sorry. You're at your *worst* when you're sorry.
I can't *stand* you sorry. Just get out.

PHILIP. Well, good-bye.

[*He puts his arms around her to kiss her*]

DOROTHY. Don't kiss me either. You'll kiss me and then you'll go right
in to commodities. I know you.

[PHILIP *holds her tight and kisses her*]

Oh, Philip, Philip, Philip.

PHILIP. Good-bye.

DOROTHY. You—you—you don't want the commodity?

PHILIP. I can't afford it.

[DOROTHY *twists away from him*]

DOROTHY. Then, go then.

PHILIP. Good-bye.

DOROTHY. Oh, get out.

[PHILIP *goes out the door and into his room.* MAX *is still sitting in the chair.
In the other room* DOROTHY *rings the bell for the maid*]

MAX. So?

[PHILIP *stands there looking into the electric stove.* MAX *looks into the stove
too. In the other room* PETRA *has come to the door*]

PETRA. Yes, Señorita.

[DOROTHY *is sitting on the bed. Her head is up but there are tears running
down her cheeks.* PETRA *goes over to her*]

What is it, Señorita?

DOROTHY. Oh, Petra, he's bad just as you said he was. He's bad, bad, bad.
And like a damn fool I thought we were going to be happy. But he's bad.

PETRA. Yes, Señorita.

DOROTHY. But oh, Petra, the trouble is I *love* him.

[PETRA *stands there by the bed with* DOROTHY. *In Room 110* PHILIP
*stands in front of the night table. He pours himself a whiskey and puts
water in it*]

145

PHILIP. Anita.

ANITA. [*From inside the bathroom*] Yes, Philip.

PHILIP. Anita, come out whenever you've finished your bath.

MAX. I go.

PHILIP. No. Stay around.

MAX. No. No. No. Please, I go.

PHILIP. [*In a very dry flat voice*] Anita, was the water hot?

ANITA. [*From inside the bathroom*] Was lovely bath.

MAX. I go. Please, please, please, I go.

CURTAIN

Flying Death Machines

(from *For Whom the Bell Tolls*)

They stood in the mouth of the cave and watched them. The bombers were high now in fast, ugly arrow-heads beating the sky apart with the noise of their motors. They *are* shaped like sharks, Robert Jordan thought, the wide-finned, sharp-nosed sharks of the Gulf Stream. But these, wide-finned in silver, roaring, the light mist of their propellers in the sun, these do not move like sharks. They move like no thing there has ever been. They move like mechanized doom.

You ought to write, he told himself. Maybe you will again some time. He felt Maria holding to his arm. She was looking up and he said to her, "What do they look like to you, *guapa?*"

"I don't know," she said. "Death, I think."

"They look like planes to me," the woman of Pablo said. "Where are the little ones?"

"They may be crossing at another part," Robert Jordan said. "Those bombers are too fast to have to wait for them and have come back alone. We never follow them across the lines to fight. There aren't enough planes to risk it."

Just then three Heinkel fighters in V formation came low over the clearing coming toward them, just over the tree tops, like clattering, wing-tilting, pinch-nosed ugly toys, to enlarge suddenly, fearfully to their actual size; pouring past in a whining roar. They were so low that from the cave mouth all of them could see the pilots, helmeted, goggled, a scarf blowing back from behind the patrol leader's head.

"*Those* can see the horses," Pablo said.

"Those can see thy cigarette butts," the woman said. "Let fall the blanket."

No more planes came over. The others must have crossed farther up the range and when the droning was gone they went out of the cave into the open.

The sky was empty now and high and blue and clear.

147

"It seems as though they were a dream that you wake from," Maria said to Robert Jordan. There was not even the last almost unheard hum that comes like a finger faintly touching and leaving and touching again after the sound is gone almost past hearing.

Small Town Revolution

(from *For Whom the Bell Tolls*)

"It was early in the morning when the *civiles* surrendered at the barracks," Pilar began.

"You had assaulted the barracks?" Robert Jordan asked.

"Pablo had surrounded it in the dark, cut the telephone wires, placed dynamite under one wall and called on the *guardia civil* to surrender. They would not. And at daylight he blew the wall open. There was fighting. Two *civiles* were killed. Four were wounded and four surrendered.

"We all lay on roofs and on the ground and at the edge of walls and of buildings in the early morning light and the dust cloud of the explosion had not yet settled, for it rose high in the air and there was no wind to carry it, and all of us were firing into the broken side of the building, loading and firing into the smoke, and from within there was still the flashing of rifles and then there was a shout from in the smoke not to fire more, and out came the four *civiles* with their hands up. A big part of the roof had fallen in and the wall was gone and they came out to surrender.

"'Are there more inside?' Pablo shouted.

"'There are wounded.'

"'Guard these,' Pablo said to four who had come up from where we were firing. 'Stand there. Against the wall,' he told the *civiles*. The four *civiles* stood against the wall, dirty, dusty, smoke-grimed, with the four who were guarding them pointing their guns at them and Pablo and the others went in to finish the wounded.

"After they had done this and there was no longer any noise of the wounded, neither groaning, nor crying out, nor the noise of shooting in the barracks, Pablo and the others came out and Pablo had his shotgun over his back and was carrying in his hand a Mauser pistol.

"'Look, Pilar,' he said. 'This was in the hand of the officer who killed himself. Never have I fired a pistol. You,' he said to one of the guards, 'show me how it works. No. Don't show me. Tell me.'

"The four *civiles* had stood against the wall, sweating and saying

149

nothing while the shooting had gone on inside the barracks. They were all tall men with the faces of *guardias civiles*, which is the same model of face as mine is. Except that their faces were covered with the small stubble of this their last morning of not yet being shaved and they stood there against the wall and said nothing.

" 'You,' said Pablo to the one who stood nearest him. 'Tell me how it works.'

" 'Pull the small lever down,' the man said in a very dry voice. 'Pull the receiver back and let it snap forward.'

" 'What is the receiver?' asked Pablo, and he looked at the four *civiles*. 'What is the receiver?'

" 'The block on top of the action.'

"Pablo pulled it back, but it stuck. 'What now?' he said. 'It is jammed. You have lied to me.'

" 'Pull it farther back and let it snap lightly forward,' the *civil* said, and I have never heard such a tone of voice. It was grayer than a morning without sunrise.

"Pablo pulled and let go as the man had told him and the block snapped forward into place and the pistol was cocked with the hammer back. It is an ugly pistol, small in the round handle, large and flat in the barrel, and unwieldy. All this time the *civiles* had been watching him and they had said nothing.

" 'What are you going to do with us?' one asked him.

" 'Shoot thee,' Pablo said.

" 'When?' the man asked in the same gray voice.

" 'Now,' said Pablo.

" 'Where?' asked the man.

" 'Here,' said Pablo. 'Here. Now. Here and now. Have you anything to say?'

" '*Nada*,' said the *civil*. 'Nothing. But it is an ugly thing.'

" 'And you are an ugly thing,' Pablo said. 'You murderer of peasants. You who would shoot your own mother.'

" 'I have never killed any one,' the *civil* said. 'And do not speak of my mother.'

" 'Show us how to die. You, who have always done the killing.'

" 'There is no necessity to insult us,' another *civil* said. 'And we know how to die.'

" 'Kneel down against the wall with your heads against the wall,' Pablo told them. The *civiles* looked at one another.

" 'Kneel, I say,' Pablo said. 'Get down and kneel.'

" 'How does it seem to you, Paco?' one *civil* said to the tallest, who had spoken with Pablo about the pistol. He wore a corporal's stripes on his sleeves and was sweating very much although the early morning was still cool.

"'It is as well to kneel,' he answered. 'It is of no importance.'

"'It is closer to the earth,' the first one who had spoken said, trying to make a joke, but they were all too grave for a joke and no one smiled.

"'Then let us kneel,' the first *civil* said, and the four knelt, looking very awkward with their heads against the wall and their hands by their sides, and Pablo passed behind them and shot each in turn in the back of the head with the pistol, going from one to another and putting the barrel of the pistol against the back of their heads, each man slipping down as he fired. I can hear the pistol still, sharp and yet muffled, and see the barrel jerk and the head of the man drop forward. One held his head still when the pistol touched it. One pushed his head forward and pressed his forehead against the stone. One shivered in his whole body and his head was shaking. Only one put his hands in front of his eyes, and he was the last one, and the four bodies were slumped against the wall when Pablo turned away from them and came toward us with the pistol still in his hand.

"'Hold this for me, Pilar,' he said. 'I do not know how to put down the hammer,' and he handed me the pistol and stood there looking at the four guards as they lay against the wall of the barracks. All those who were with us stood there too, looking at them, and no one said anything.

"We had won the town and it was still early in the morning and no one had eaten nor had any one drunk coffee and we looked at each other and we were all powdered with dust from the blowing up of the barracks, as powdered as men are at a threshing, and I stood holding the pistol and it was heavy in my hand and I felt weak in the stomach when I looked at the guards dead there against the wall; they all as gray and as dusty as we were, but each one was now moistening with his blood the dry dirt by the wall where they lay. And as we stood there the sun rose over the far hills and shone now on the road where we stood and on the white wall of the barracks and the dust in the air was golden in that first sun and the peasant who was beside me looked at the wall of the barracks and what lay there and then looked at us and then at the sun and said, '*Vaya*, a day that commences.'

"'Now let us go and get coffee,' I said.

"'Good, Pilar, good,' he said. And we went up into the town to the Plaza, and those were the last people who were shot in the village."

"What happened to the others?" Robert Jordan asked. "Were there no other fascists in the village?"

"*Qué va*, were there no other fascists? There were more than twenty. But none was shot."

"What was done?"

"Pablo had them beaten to death with flails and thrown from the top of the cliff into the river."

"All twenty?"

"I will tell you. It is not so simple. And in my life never do I wish to see such a scene as the flailing to death in the plaza on the top of the cliff above the river.

"The town is built on the high bank above the river and there is a square there with a fountain and there are benches and there are big trees that give a shade for the benches. The balconies of the houses look out on the plaza. Six streets enter on the plaza and there is an arcade from the houses that goes around the plaza so that one can walk in the shade of the arcade when the sun is hot. On three sides of the plaza is the arcade and on the fourth side is the walk shaded by the trees beside the edge of the cliff with, far below, the river. It is three hundred feet down to the river.

"Pablo organized it all as he did the attack on the barracks. First he had the entrances to the streets blocked off with carts as though to organize the plaza for a *capea*. For an amateur bullfight. The fascists were all held in the *Ayuntamiento*, the city hall, which was the largest building on one side of the plaza. It was there the clock was set in the wall and it was in the buildings under the arcade that the club of the fascists was. And under the arcade on the sidewalk in front of their club was where they had their chairs and tables for their club. It was there, before the movement, that they were accustomed to take the apéritifs. The chairs and the tables were of wicker. It looked like a café but was more elegant."

"But was there no fighting to take them?"

"Pablo had them seized in the night before he assaulted the barracks. But he had already surrounded the barracks. They were all seized in their homes at the same hour the attack started. That was intelligent. Pablo is an organizer. Otherwise he would have had people attacking him at his flanks and at his rear while he was assaulting the barracks of the *guardia civil*.

"Pablo is very intelligent but very brutal. He had this of the village well planned and well ordered. Listen. After the assault was successful, and the last four guards had surrendered, and he had shot them against the wall, and we had drunk coffee at the café that always opened earliest in the morning by the corner from which the early bus left, he proceeded to the organization of the plaza. Carts were piled exactly as for a *capea* except that the side toward the river was not enclosed. That was left open. Then Pablo ordered the priest to confess the fascists and give them the necessary sacraments."

"Where was this done?"

"In the *Ayuntamiento*, as I said. There was a great crowd outside and while this was going on inside with the priest, there was some levity outside and shouting of obscenities, but most of the people were very serious and respectful. Those who made jokes were those who were already drunk from the celebration of the taking of the barracks and there were useless characters who would have been drunk at any time.

"While the priest was engaged in these duties, Pablo organized those in the plaza into two lines.

"He placed them in two lines as you would place men for a rope pulling contest, or as they stand in a city to watch the ending of a bicycle road race with just room for the cyclists to pass between, or as men stood to allow the passage of a holy image in a procession. Two meters was left between the lines and they extended from the door of the *Ayuntamiento* clear across the plaza to the edge of the cliff. So that, from the doorway of the *Ayuntamiento*, looking across the plaza, one coming out would see two solid lines of people waiting.

"They were armed with flails such as are used to beat out the grain and they were a good flail's length apart. All did not have flails, as enough flails could not be obtained. But most had flails obtained from the store of Don Guillermo Martín, who was a fascist and sold all sorts of agricultural implements. And those who did not have flails had heavy herdsman's clubs, or ox-goads, and some had wooden pitchforks; those with wooden tines that are used to fork the chaff and straw into the air after the flailing. Some had sickles and reaping hooks but these Pablo placed at the far end where the lines reached the edge of the cliff.

"These lines were quiet and it was a clear day, as today is clear, and there were clouds high in the sky, as there are now, and the plaza was not yet dusty for there had been a heavy dew in the night, and the trees cast a shade over the men in the lines and you could hear the water running from the brass pipe in the mouth of the lion and falling into the bowl of the fountain where the women bring the water jars to fill them.

"Only near the *Ayuntamiento*, where the priest was complying with his duties with the fascists, was there any ribaldry, and that came from those worthless ones who, as I said, were already drunk and were crowded around the windows shouting obscenities and jokes in bad taste in through the iron bars of the windows. Most of the men in the lines were waiting quietly and I heard one say to another, 'Will there be women?'

"And another said, 'I hope to Christ, no.'

"Then one said, 'Here is the woman of Pablo. Listen, Pilar. Will there be women?'

"I looked at him and he was a peasant dressed in his Sunday jacket and sweating heavily and I said, 'No, Joaquín. There are no women. We are not killing the women. Why should we kill their women?'

"And he said, 'Thanks be to Christ, there are no women and when does it start?'

"And I said, 'As soon as the priest finishes.'

" 'And the priest?'

" 'I don't know,' I told him and I saw his face working and the sweat coming down on his forehead. 'I have never killed a man,' he said.

" 'Then you will learn,' the peasant next to him said. 'But I do not think one blow with this will kill a man,' and he held his flail in both hands and looked at it with doubt.

" 'That is the beauty of it,' another peasant said. 'There must be many blows.'

" '*They* have taken Valladolid. *They* have Avila,' some one said. 'I heard that before we came into town.'

" '*They* will never take *this* town. *This* town is ours. We have struck ahead of them,' I said. 'Pablo is not one to wait for them to strike.'

" 'Pablo is able,' another said. 'But in this finishing off of the *civiles* he was egoistic. Don't you think so, Pilar?'

" 'Yes,' I said. 'But now all are participating in this.'

" 'Yes,' he said. 'It is well organized. But why do we not hear more news of the movement?'

" 'Pablo cut the telephone wires before the assault on the barracks. They are not yet repaired.'

" 'Ah,' he said. 'It is for this we hear nothing. I had my news from the roadmender's station early this morning.'

" 'Why is this done thus, Pilar?' he said to me.

" 'To save bullets,' I said. 'And that each man should have his share in the responsibility.'

" 'That it should start then. That it should start.' And I looked at him and saw that he was crying.

" 'Why are you crying, Joaquín?' I asked him. 'This is not to cry about.'

" 'I cannot help it, Pilar,' he said. 'I have never killed any one.'

"If you have not seen the day of revolution in a small town where all know all in the town and always have known all, you have seen nothing. And on this day most of the men in the double line across the plaza wore the clothes in which they worked in the fields, having come into town

154

hurriedly, but some, not knowing how one should dress for the first day of a movement, wore their clothes for Sundays or holidays, and these, seeing that the others, including those who had attacked the barracks, wore their oldest clothes, were ashamed of being wrongly dressed. But they did not like to take off their jackets for fear of losing them, or that they might be stolen by the worthless ones, and so they stood, sweating in the sun and waiting for it to commence.

"Then the wind rose and the dust was now dry in the plaza for the men walking and standing and shuffling had loosened it and it commenced to blow and a man in a dark blue Sunday jacket shouted 'Agua! Agua!' and the caretaker of the plaza, whose duty it was to sprinkle the plaza each morning with a hose, came and turned the hose on and commenced to lay the dust at the edge of the plaza, and then toward the center. Then the two lines fell back and let him lay the dust over the center of the plaza; the hose sweeping in wide arcs and the water glistening in the sun and the men leaning on their flails or the clubs or the white wood pitchforks and watching the sweep of the stream of water. And then, when the plaza was nicely moistened and the dust settled, the lines formed up again and a peasant shouted, 'When do we get the first fascist? When does the first one come out of the box?'

"'Soon,' Pablo shouted from the door of the *Ayuntamiento*. 'Soon the first one comes out.' His voice was hoarse from shouting in the assault and from the smoke of the barracks.

"'What's the delay?' some one asked.

"'They're still occupied with their sins,' Pablo shouted.

"'Clearly, there are twenty of them,' a man said.

"'More,' said another.

"'Among twenty there are many sins to recount.'

"'Yes, but I think it's a trick to gain time. Surely facing such an emergency one could not remember one's sins except for the biggest.'

"'Then have patience. For with more than twenty of them there are enough of the biggest sins to take some time.'

"'I have patience,' said the other. 'But it is better to get it over with. Both for them and for us. It is July and there is much work. We have harvested but we have not threshed. We are not yet in the time of fairs and festivals.'

"'But this will be a fair and festival today,' another said. 'The Fair of Liberty and from this day, when these are extinguished, the town and the land are ours.'

"'We thresh fascists today,' said one, 'and out of the chaff comes the freedom of this pueblo.'

" 'We must administer it well to deserve it,' said another. 'Pilar,' he said to me, 'when do we have a meeting for organization?'

" 'Immediately after this is completed,' I told him. 'In the same building of the *Ayuntamiento*.'

"I was wearing one of the three-cornered patent leather hats of the *guardia civil* as a joke and I had put the hammer down on the pistol, holding it with my thumb to lower it as I pulled on the trigger as seemed natural, and the pistol was held in a rope I had around my waist, the long barrel stuck under the rope. And when I put it on the joke seemed very good to me, although afterwards I wished I had taken the holster of the pistol instead of the hat. But one of the men in the line said to me, 'Pilar, daughter. It seems to me bad taste for thee to wear that hat. Now we have finished with such things as the *guardia civil*.'

" 'Then,' I said, 'I will take it off.' And I did.

" 'Give it to me,' he said. 'It should be destroyed.'

"And as we were at the far end of the line where the walk runs along the cliff by the river, he took the hat in his hand and sailed it off over the cliff with the motion a herdsman makes throwing a stone underhand at the bulls to herd them. The hat sailed far out into space and we could see it smaller and smaller, the patent leather shining in the clear air, sailing down to the river. I looked back over the square and at all the windows and all the balconies there were people crowded and there was the double line of men across the square to the doorway of the *Ayuntamiento* and the crowd swarmed outside against the windows of that building and there was the noise of many people talking, and then I heard a shout and some one said 'Here comes the first one,' and it was Don Benito Garcia, the Mayor, and he came out bareheaded walking slowly from the door and down the porch and nothing happened; and he walked between the line of men with the flails and nothing happened. He passed two men, four men, eight men, ten men and nothing happened and he was walking between that line of men, his head up, his fat face gray, his eyes looking ahead and then flickering from side to side and walking steadily. And nothing happened.

"From a balcony some one cried out, '*Qué pasa, cobardes?* What is the matter, cowards?' and still Don Benito walked along between the men and nothing happened. Then I saw a man three men down from where I was standing and his face was working and he was biting his lips and his hands were white on his flail. I saw him looking toward Don Benito, watching him come on. And still nothing happened. Then, just before Don Benito came abreast of this man, the man raised his flail high so that it struck the man beside him and smashed a blow at Don Benito that hit him on the side of the head and Don Benito looked at him and the man struck again and shouted, 'That for you, *Cabron*,' and the blow hit Don Benito in the face and he raised his hands to his face and they beat him until he fell and the man who had struck him first called to others to help him and he pulled on the collar of Don Benito's shirt and others took hold of his arms and with his face in the dust of the plaza, they dragged him over the walk to the edge of the cliff and threw him over and into the river. And the man who hit him first was kneeling by the edge of the cliff looking over after him and saying, 'The Cabron! The Cabron! Oh, the Cabron!' He was a tenant of Don Benito and they had never gotten along together. There had been a dispute about a piece of land by the river that Don Benito had taken from this man and let to another and this man had long hated him. This man did not join the line again but sat by the cliff looking down where Don Benito had fallen.

"After Don Benito no one would come out. There was no noise now in the plaza as all were waiting to see who it was that would come out. Then a drunkard shouted in a great voice, '*Qué salga el toro!* Let the bull out!'

"Then some one from by the windows of the *Ayuntamiento* yelled, 'They won't move! They are all praying!'

"Another drunkard shouted, 'Pull them out. Come on, pull them out. The time for praying is finished.'

"But none came out and then I saw a man coming out of the door.

"It was Don Federico González, who owned the mill and feed store and was a fascist of the first order. He was tall and thin and his hair was brushed over the top of his head from one side to the other to cover a baldness and he wore a nightshirt that was tucked into his trousers. He was barefooted as when he had been taken from his home and he walked ahead of Pablo holding his hands above his head, and Pablo walked behind him with the barrels of his shotgun pressing against the back of Don Federico González until Don Federico entered the double line. But when Pablo left him and returned to the door of the *Ayuntamiento*, Don Federico could not walk forward, and stood there, his eyes turned up to heaven and his hands reaching up as though they would grasp the sky.

"'He has no legs to walk,' some one said.

"'What's the matter, Don Federico? Can't you walk?' some one shouted to him. But Don Federico stood there with his hands up and only his lips were moving.

"'Get on,' Pablo shouted to him from the steps. 'Walk.'

"Don Federico stood there and could not move. One of the drunkards

157

poked him in the backside with a flail handle and Don Federico gave a quick jump as a balky horse might, but still stood in the same place, his hands up, and his eyes up toward the sky.

"Then the peasant who stood beside me said, 'This is shameful. I have nothing against him but such a spectacle must terminate.' So he walked down the line and pushed through to where Don Federico was standing and said, 'With your permission,' and hit him a great blow alongside of the head with a club.

"Then Don Federico dropped his hands and put them over the top of his head where the bald place was and with his head bent and covered by his hands, the thin long hairs that covered the bald place escaping through his fingers, he ran fast through the double line with flails falling on his back and shoulders until he fell and those at the end of the line picked him up and swung him over the cliff. Never did he open his mouth from the moment he came out pushed by the shotgun of Pablo. His only difficulty was to move forward. It was as though he had no command of his legs.

"After Don Federico, I saw there was a concentration of the hardest men at the end of the lines by the edge of the cliff and I left there and I went to the Arcade of the *Ayuntamiento* and pushed aside two drunkards and looked in the window. In the big room of the *Ayuntamiento* they were all kneeling in a half circle praying and the priest was kneeling and praying with them. Pablo and one named *Cuatro Dedos*, Four Fingers, a cobbler, who was much with Pablo then, and two others were standing with shotguns and Pablo said to the priest, 'Who goes now?' and the priest went on praying and did not answer him.

"'Listen, you,' Pablo said to the priest in his hoarse voice, 'who goes now? Who is ready now?'

"The priest would not speak to Pablo and acted as though he were not there and I could see Pablo was becoming very angry.

"'Let us all go together,' Don Ricardo Montalvo, who was a land owner, said to Pablo, raising his head and stopping praying to speak.

"'*Qué va*,' said Pablo. 'One at a time as you are ready.'

"'Then I go now,' Don Ricardo said. 'I'll never be any more ready.' The priest blessed him as he spoke and blessed him again as he stood up, without interrupting his praying, and held up a crucifix for Don Ricardo to kiss and Don Ricardo kissed it and then turned and said to Pablo, 'Nor ever again as ready. You *Cabron* of the bad milk. Let us go.'

"Don Ricardo was a short man with gray hair and a thick neck and he had a shirt on with no collar. He was bow-legged from much horseback riding. 'Good-by,' he said to all those who were kneeling. 'Don't be sad.

To die is nothing. The only bad thing is to die at the hands of this *canalla*. Don't touch me,' he said to Pablo. 'Don't touch me with your shotgun.'

"He walked out of the front of the *Ayuntamiento* with his gray hair and his small gray eyes and his thick neck looking very short and angry. He looked at the double line of peasants and he spat on the ground. He could spit actual saliva which, in such a circumstance, as you should know, *Inglés*, is very rare and he said, '*Arriba España!* Down with the miscalled Republic and I obscenity in the milk of your fathers.'

"So they clubbed him to death very quickly because of the insult, beating him as soon as he reached the first of the men, beating him as he tried to walk with his head up, beating him until he fell and chopping at him with reaping hooks and the sickles, and many men bore him to the edge of the cliff to throw him over and there was blood now on their hands and on their clothing, and now began to be the feeling that these who came out were truly enemies and should be killed.

"Until Don Ricardo came out with that fierceness and calling those insults, many in the line would have given much, I am sure, never to have been in the line. And if any one had shouted from the line, 'Come, let us pardon the rest of them. Now they have had their lesson,' I am sure most would have agreed.

"But Don Ricardo with all his bravery did a great disservice to the others. For he aroused the men in the line and where, before, they were performing a duty and with no great taste for it, now they were angry, and the difference was apparent.

"'Let the priest out and the thing will go faster,' some one shouted.

"'Let out the priest.'

"'We've had three thieves, let us have the priest.'

"'Two thieves,' a short peasant said to the man who had shouted. 'It was two thieves with Our Lord.'

"'Whose Lord?' the man said, his face angry and red.

"'In the manner of speaking it is said Our Lord.'

"'He isn't my Lord; not in joke,' said the other. 'And thee hadst best watch thy mouth if thou dost not want to walk between the lines.'

"'I am as good a Libertarian Republican as thou,' the short peasant said. 'I struck Don Ricardo across the mouth. I struck Don Federico across the back. I missed Don Benito. But I say Our Lord is the formal way of speaking of the man in question and that it was two thieves.'

"'I obscenity in the milk of thy Republicanism. You speak of Don this and Don that.'

"'Here are they so called.'

"'Not by me, the *cabrones*. And thy Lord— Hi! Here comes a new one!'

"It was then that we saw a disgraceful sight, for the man who walked out of the doorway of the *Ayuntamiento* was Don Faustino Rivero, the oldest son of his father, Don Celestino Rivero, a land owner. He was tall and his hair was yellow and it was freshly combed back from his forehead for he always carried a comb in his pocket and he had combed his hair now before coming out. He was a great annoyer of girls, and he was a coward, and he had always wished to be an amateur bullfighter. He went much with gypsies and with bullfighters and with bull raisers and delighted to wear the Andalucian costume, but he had no courage and was considered a joke. One time he was announced to appear in an amateur benefit fight for the old people's home in Avila and to kill a bull from on horseback in the Andalucian style, which he had spent much time practising, and when he had seen the size of the bull that had been substituted for him in place of the little one, weak in the legs, he had picked out himself, he had said he was sick and, some said, put three fingers down his throat to make himself vomit.

"When the lines saw him, they commenced to shout, '*Hola*, Don Faustino. Take care not to vomit.'

"'Listen to me, Don Faustino. There are beautiful girls over the cliff.'

"'Don Faustino. Wait a minute and we will bring out a bull bigger than the other.'

"And another shouted, 'Listen to me, Don Faustino. Hast thou ever heard speak of death?'

"Don Faustino stood there, still acting brave. He was still under the impulse that had made him announce to the others that he was going out. It was the same impulse that had made him announce himself for the bullfight. That had made him believe and hope that he could be an amateur matador. Now he was inspired by the example of Don Ricardo and he stood there looking both handsome and brave and he made his face scornful. But he could not speak.

"'Come, Don Faustino,' some one called from the line. 'Come, Don Faustino. Here is the biggest bull of all.'

"Don Faustino stood looking out and I think as he looked, that there was no pity for him on either side of the line. Still he looked both handsome and superb; but time was shortening and there was only one direction to go.

"'Don Faustino,' some one called. 'What are you waiting for, Don Faustino?'

"'He is preparing to vomit,' some one said and the lines laughed.

"'Don Faustino,' a peasant called. 'Vomit if it will give thee pleasure. To me it is all the same.'

"Then, as we watched, Don Faustino looked along the lines and across the square to the cliff and then when he saw the cliff and the emptiness beyond, he turned quickly and ducked back toward the entrance of the *Ayuntamiento*.

"All the lines roared and some one shouted in a high voice, 'Where do you go, Don Faustino? Where do you go?'

"'He goes to throw up,' shouted another and they all laughed again.

"Then we saw Don Faustino coming out again with Pablo behind him with the shotgun. All of his style was gone now. The sight of the lines had taken away his type and his style and he came out now with Pablo behind him as though Pablo were cleaning a street and Don Faustino was what he was pushing ahead of him. Don Faustino came out now and he was crossing himself and praying and then he put his hands in front of his eyes and walked down the steps toward the lines.

"'Leave him alone,' some one shouted. 'Don't touch him.'

"The lines understood and no one made a move to touch Don Faustino and, with his hands shaking and held in front of his eyes, and with his mouth moving, he walked along between the lines.

"No one said anything and no one touched him and, when he was halfway through the lines, he could go no farther and fell to his knees.

"No one struck him. I was walking along parallel to the line to see what happened to him and a peasant leaned down and lifted him to his feet and said, 'Get up, Don Faustino, and keep walking. The bull has not yet come out.'

"Don Faustino could not walk alone and the peasant in a black smock helped him on one side and another peasant in a black smock and herdsman's boots helped him on the other, supporting him by the arms and Don Faustino walking along between the lines with his hands over his eyes, his lips never quiet, and his yellow hair slicked on his head and shining in the sun, and as he passed the peasants would say, 'Don Faustino, *buen provecho*. Don Faustino, that you should have a good appetite,' and others said, 'Don Faustino, *a sus ordenes*. Don Faustino at your orders,' and one, who had failed at bullfighting himself, said, 'Don Faustino. *Matador, a sus ordenes*,' and another said, 'Don Faustino, there are beautiful girls in heaven, Don Faustino.' And they walked Don Faustino through the lines, holding him close on either side, holding him up as he walked, with him with his hands over his eyes. But he must have looked through his fingers, because when they came to the edge of the cliff with him, he knelt again, throwing himself down and clutching the ground and holding to the grass, saying, 'No. No. No. Please. NO. Please. Please. No. No.'

161

"Then the peasants who were with him and the others, the hard ones of the end of the line, squatted quickly behind him as he knelt, and gave him a rushing push and he was over the edge without ever having been beaten and you heard him crying loud and high as he fell.

"It was then I knew that the lines had become cruel and it was first the insults of Don Ricardo and second the cowardice of Don Faustino that had made them so.

"'Let us have another,' a peasant called out and another peasant slapped him on the back and said, 'Don Faustino! What a thing! Don Faustino!'

"'He's seen the big bull now,' another said. 'Throwing up will never help him, now.'

"'In my life,' another peasant said, 'in my life I've never seen a thing like Don Faustino.'

"'There are others,' another peasant said. 'Have patience. Who knows what we may yet see?'

"'There may be giants and dwarfs,' the first peasant said. 'There may be Negroes and rare beasts from Africa. But for me never, never will there be anything like Don Faustino. But let's have another one! Come on. Let's have another one!'

"The drunkards were handing around bottles of anis and cognac that they had looted from the bar of the club of the fascists, drinking them down like wine, and many of the men in the lines were beginning to be a little drunk, too, from drinking after the strong emotion of Don Benito, Don Federico, Don Ricardo and especially Don Faustino. Those who did not drink from the bottles of liquor were drinking from leather wineskins that were passed about and one handed a wineskin to me and I took a long drink, letting the wine run cool down my throat from the leather *bota* for I was very thirsty, too.

"'To kill gives much thirst,' the man with the wineskin said to me.

"'*Qué va*,' I said. 'Hast thou killed?'

"'We have killed four,' he said, proudly. 'Not counting the *civiles*. Is it true that thee killed one of the *civiles*, Pilar?'

"'Not one,' I said. 'I shot into the smoke when the wall fell, as did the others. That is all.'

"'Where got thee the pistol, Pilar?'

"'From Pablo. Pablo gave it to me after he killed the *civiles*.'

"'Killed he them with this pistol?'

"'With no other,' I said. 'And then he armed me with it.'

"'Can I see it, Pilar? Can I hold it?'

"'Why not, man?' I said, and I took it out from under the rope and handed it to him. But I was wondering why no one else had come out and just then who should come out but Don Guillermo Martín from whose store the flails, the herdsman's clubs, and the wooden pitchforks had been taken. Don Guillermo was a fascist but otherwise there was nothing against him.

"It is true he paid little to those who made the flails but he charged little for them too and if one did not wish to buy flails from Don Guillermo, it was possible to make them for nothing more than the cost of the wood and the leather. He had a rude way of speaking and he was undoubtedly a fascist and a member of their club and he sat at noon and at evening in the cane chairs of their club to read *El Debate*, to have his shoes shined, and to drink vermouth and seltzer and eat roasted almonds, dried shrimps, and anchovies. But one does not kill for that, and I am sure if it had not been for the insults of Don Ricardo Montalvo and the lamentable spectacle of Don Faustino, and the drinking consequent on the emotion of them and the others, some one would have shouted, 'That Don Guillermo should go in peace. We have his flails. Let him go.'

"Because the people of this town are as kind as they can be cruel and they have a natural sense of justice and a desire to do that which is right. But cruelty had entered into the lines and also drunkenness or the beginning of drunkenness and the lines were not as they were when Don Benito had come out. I do not know how it is in other countries, and no one cares more for the pleasure of drinking than I do, but in Spain drunkenness, when produced by other elements than wine, is a thing of great ugliness and the people do things that they would not have done. Is it not so in your country, *Inglés?*"

"It is so," Robert Jordan said. "When I was seven years old and going with my mother to attend a wedding in the state of Ohio at which I was to be the boy of a pair of boy and girl who carried flowers———"

"Did you do that?" asked Maria. "How nice!"

"In this town a Negro was hanged to a lamp post and later burned. It was an arc light. A light which lowered from the post to the pavement. And he was hoisted, first by the mechanism which was used to hoist the arc light but this broke———"

"A Negro," Maria said. "How barbarous!"

"Were the people drunk?" asked Pilar. "Were they drunk thus to burn a Negro?"

"I do not know," Robert Jordan said. "Because I saw it only looking out from under the blinds of a window in the house which stood on the corner where the arc light was. The street was full of people and when they lifted the Negro up for the second time———"

"If you had only seven years and were in a house, you could not tell if they were drunk or not," Pilar said.

"As I said, when they lifted the Negro up for the second time, my mother pulled me away from the window, so I saw no more," Robert Jordan said. "But since I have had experiences which demonstrate that drunkenness is the same in my country. It is ugly and brutal."

"You were too young at seven," Maria said. "You were too young for such things. I have never seen a Negro except in a circus. Unless the Moors are Negroes."

"Some are Negroes and some are not," Pilar said. "I can talk to you of the Moors."

"Not as I can," Maria said. "Nay, not as I can."

"Don't speak of such things," Pilar said. "It is unhealthy. Where were we?"

"Speaking of the drunkenness of the lines," Robert Jordan said. "Go on."

"It is not fair to say drunkenness," Pilar said. "For, yet, they were a long way from drunkenness. But already there was a change in them, and when Don Guillermo came out, standing straight, near-sighted, gray-headed, of medium height, with a shirt with a collar button but no collar, standing there and crossing himself once and looking ahead, but seeing little without his glasses, but walking forward well and calmly, he was an appearance to excite pity. But some one shouted from the line, 'Here, Don Guillermo. Up here, Don Guillermo. In this direction. Here we all have your products.'

"They had had such success joking at Don Faustino that they could not see, now, that Don Guillermo was a different thing, and if Don Guillermo was to be killed, he should be killed quickly and with dignity.

"'Don Guillermo,' another shouted. 'Should we send to the house for thy spectacles?'

"Don Guillermo's house was no house, since he had not much money and was only a fascist to be a snob and to console himself that he must work for little, running a wooden-implement shop. He was a fascist, too, from the religiousness of his wife which he accepted as his own due to his love for her. He lived in an apartment in the building three houses down the square and when Don Guillermo stood there, looking near-sightedly at the lines, the double lines he knew he must enter, a woman started to scream from the balcony of the apartment where he lived. She could see him from the balcony and she was his wife.

"'Guillermo,' she cried. 'Guillermo. Wait and I will be with thee.'

"Don Guillermo turned his head toward where the shouting came from. He could not see her. He tried to say something but he could not. Then he waved his hand in the direction the woman had called from and started to walk between the lines.

"'Guillermo!' she cried. 'Guillermo! Oh, Guillermo!' She was holding her hands on the rail of the balcony and shaking back and forth. 'Guillermo!'

"Don Guillermo waved his hand again toward the noise and walked into the lines with his head up and you would not have known what he was feeling except for the color of his face.

"Then some drunkard yelled, 'Guillermo!' from the lines, imitating the high cracked voice of his wife and Don Guillermo rushed toward the man, blindly, with tears now running down his cheeks and the man hit him hard across the face with his flail and Don Guillermo sat down from the force of the blow and sat there crying, but not from fear, while the drunkards beat him and one drunkard jumped on top of him, astride his shoulders, and beat him with a bottle. After this many of the men left the lines and their places were taken by the drunkards who had been jeering and saying things in bad taste through the windows of the *Ayuntamiento*.

"I myself had felt much emotion at the shooting of the *guardia civil* by Pablo," Pilar said. "It was a thing of great ugliness, but I had thought if this is how it must be, this is how it must be, and at least there was no cruelty, only the depriving of life which, as we all have learned in these years, is a thing of ugliness but also a necessity to do if we are to win, and to preserve the Republic.

"When the square had been closed off and the lines formed, I had admired and understood it as a conception of Pablo, although it seemed to me to be somewhat fantastic and that it would be necessary for all that was to be done to be done in good taste if it were not to be repugnant. Certainly if the fascists were to be executed by the people, it was better for all the people to have a part in it, and I wished to share the guilt as much as any, just as I hoped to share in the benefits when the town should be ours. But after Don Guillermo I felt a feeling of shame and distaste, and with the coming of the drunkards and the worthless ones into the lines, and the abstention of those who left the lines as a protest after Don Guillermo, I wished that I might disassociate myself altogether from the lines, and I walked away, across the square, and sat down on a bench under one of the big trees that gave shade there.

"Two peasants from the lines walked over, talking together, and one of them called to me, 'What passes with thee, Pilar?'

"'Nothing, man,' I told him.

"'Yes,' he said. 'Speak. What passes.'

"'I think that I have a belly-full,' I told him.

"'Us, too,' he said and they both sat down on the bench. One of them had a leather wineskin and he handed it to me.

"'Rinse out thy mouth,' he said and the other said, going on with the talking they had been engaged in, 'The worst is that it will bring bad luck. Nobody can tell me that such things as the killing of Don Guillermo in that fashion will not bring bad luck.'

"Then the other said, 'If it is necessary to kill them all, and I am not convinced of that necessity, let them be killed decently and without mockery.'

"'Mockery is justified in the case of Don Faustino,' the other said. 'Since he was always a farcer and was never a serious man. But to mock such a serious man as Don Guillermo is beyond all right.'

"'I have a belly-full,' I told him, and it was literally true because I felt an actual sickness in all of me inside and a sweating and a nausea as though I had swallowed bad sea food.

"'Then, nothing,' the one peasant said. 'We will take no further part in it. But I wonder what happens in the other towns.'

"'They have not repaired the telephone wires yet,' I said. 'It is a lack that should be remedied.'

"'Clearly,' he said. 'Who knows but what we might be better employed putting the town into a state of defense than massacring people with this slowness and brutality.'

"'I will go to speak with Pablo,' I told them and I stood up from the bench and started toward the arcade that led to the door of the *Ayuntamiento* from where the lines spread across the square. The lines now were neither straight nor orderly and there was much and very grave drunkenness. Two men had fallen down and lay on their backs in the middle of the square and were passing a bottle back and forth between them. One would take a drink and then shout, '*Viva la Anarquia!*' lying on his back and shouting as though he were a madman. He had a red-and-black handkerchief around his neck. The other shouted, '*Viva la Libertad!*' and kicked his feet in the air and then bellowed, '*Viva la Libertad!*' again. He had a red-and-black handkerchief too and he waved it in one hand and waved the bottle with the other.

"A peasant who had left the lines and now stood in the shade of the arcade looked at them in disgust and said, 'They should shout, "Long live drunkenness." That's all they believe in.'

"'They don't believe even in that,' another peasant said. 'Those neither understand nor believe in anything.'

166

"Just then, one of the drunkards got to his feet and raised both arms with his fists clenched over his head and shouted, 'Long live Anarchy and Liberty and I obscenity in the milk of the Republic!'

"The other drunkard who was still lying on his back, took hold of the ankle of the drunkard who was shouting and rolled over, so that the shouting drunkard fell with him, and they rolled over together and then sat up and the one who had pulled the other down put his arm around the shouter's neck and then handed the shouter a bottle and kissed the red-and-black handkerchief he wore and they both drank together.

"Just then, a yelling went up from the lines and, looking up the arcade, I could not see who it was that was coming out because the man's head did not show above the heads of those crowded about the door of the *Ayuntamiento*. All I could see was that some one was being pushed out by Pablo and Cuatro Dedos with their shotguns but I could not see who it was and I moved on close toward the lines where they were packed against the door to try to see.

"There was much pushing now and the chairs and the tables of the fascists' café had been overturned except for one table on which a drunkard was lying with his head hanging down and his mouth open and I picked up a chair and set it against one of the pillars and mounted on it so that I could see over the heads of the crowd.

"The man who was being pushed out by Pablo and Cuatro Dedos was Don Anastasio Rivas, who was an undoubted fascist and the fattest man in the town. He was a grain buyer and the agent for several insurance companies and he also loaned money at high rates of interest. Standing on the chair, I saw him walk down the steps and toward the lines, his fat neck bulging over the back of the collar band of his shirt, and his bald head shining in the sun, but he never entered them because there was a shout, not as of different men shouting, but of all of them. It was an ugly noise and was the cry of the drunken lines all yelling together and the lines broke with the rush of men toward him and I saw Don Anastasio throw himself down with his hands over his head and then you could not see him for the men piled on top of him. And when the men got up from him, Don Anastasio was dead from his head being beaten against the stone flags of the paving of the arcade and there were no more lines but only a mob.

"'We're going in,' they commenced to shout. 'We're going in after them.'

"'He's too heavy to carry,' a man kicked at the body of Don Anastasio, who was lying there on his face. 'Let him stay there.'

"'Why should we lug that tub of tripe to the cliff? Let him lie there.'

"'We are going to enter and finish with them inside,' a man shouted. 'We're going in.'

"'Why wait all day in the sun?' another yelled. 'Come on. Let us go.'

"The mob was now pressing into the arcade. They were shouting and pushing and they made a noise now like an animal and they were all shouting 'Open up! Open up!' for the guards had shut the doors of the *Ayuntamiento* when the lines broke.

"Standing on the chair, I could see in through the barred window into the hall of the *Ayuntamiento* and in there it was as it had been before. The priest was standing, and those who were left were kneeling in a half circle around him and they were all praying. Pablo was sitting on the big table in front of the Mayor's chair with his shotgun slung over his back. His legs were hanging down from the table and he was rolling a cigarette. Cuatro Dedos was sitting in the Mayor's chair with his feet on the table and he was smoking a cigarette. All the guards were sitting in different chairs of the administration, holding their guns. The key to the big door was on the table beside Pablo.

"The mob was shouting, 'Open up! Open up! Open up!' as though it were a chant and Pablo was sitting there as though he did not hear them. He said something to the priest but I could not hear what he said for the noise of the mob.

"The priest, as before, did not answer him but kept on praying. With many people pushing me, I moved the chair close against the wall, shoving it ahead of me as they shoved me from behind. I stood on the chair with my face close against the bars of the window and held on by the bars. A man climbed on the chair too and stood with his arms around mine, holding the wider bars.

"'The chair will break,' I said to him.

"'What does it matter?' he said. 'Look at them. Look at them pray.'

"His breath on my neck smelled like the smell of the mob, sour, like vomit on paving stones and the smell of drunkenness, and then he put his mouth against the opening in the bars with his head over my shoulder, and shouted, 'Open up! Open!' and it was as though the mob were on my back as a devil is on your back in a dream.

"Now the mob was pressed tight against the door so that those in front were being crushed by all the others who were pressing and from the square a big drunkard in a black smock with a red-and-black handkerchief around his neck, ran and threw himself against the press of the mob and fell forward onto the pressing men and then stood up and backed away and then ran forward again and threw himself against the backs of those men who were pushing, shouting, 'Long live me and long live Anarchy.'

"As I watched, this man turned away from the crowd and went and sat down and drank from a bottle and then, while he was sitting down, he saw Don Anastasio, who was still lying face down on the stones, but much trampled now, and the drunkard got up and went over to Don Anastasio and leaned over and poured out of the bottle onto the head of Don Anastasio and onto his clothes, and then he took a matchbox out of his pocket and lit several matches, trying to make a fire with Don Anastasio. But the wind was blowing hard now and it blew the matches out and after a little the big drunkard sat there by Don Anastasio, shaking his head and drinking out of the bottle and every once in a while, leaning over and patting Don Anastasio on the shoulders of his dead body.

"All this time the mob was shouting to open up and the man on the chair with me was holding tight to the bars of the window and shouting to open up until it deafened me with his voice roaring past my ear and his breath foul on me and I looked away from watching the drunkard who had been trying to set fire to Don Anastasio and into the hall of the *Ayuntamiento* again; and it was just as it had been. They were still praying as they had been, the men all kneeling, with their shirts open, some with their heads down, others with their heads up, looking toward the priest and toward the crucifix that he held, and the priest praying fast and hard and looking out over their heads, and in back of them Pablo, with his cigarette now lighted, was sitting there on the table swinging his legs, his shotgun slung over his back, and he was playing with the key.

"I saw Pablo speak to the priest again, leaning forward from the table and I could not hear what he said for the shouting. But the priest did not answer him but went on praying. Then a man stood up from among the half circle of those who were praying and I saw he wanted to go out. It was Don José Castro, whom every one called Don Pepe, a confirmed fascist, and a dealer in horses, and he stood up now small, neat-looking even unshaven and wearing a pajama top tucked into a pair of gray-striped trousers. He kissed the crucifix and the priest blessed him and he stood up and looked at Pablo and jerked his head toward the door.

"Pablo shook his head and went on smoking. I could see Don Pepe say something to Pablo but could not hear it. Pablo did not answer; he simply shook his head again and nodded toward the door.

"Then I saw Don Pepe look full at the door and realized that he had not known it was locked. Pablo showed him the key and he stood looking at it an instant and then he turned and went and knelt down again. I saw the priest look around at Pablo and Pablo grinned at him and showed him the key and the priest seemed to realize for the first time that the door was locked and he seemed as though he started to shake his head, but he only inclined it and went back to praying.

"I do not know how they could not have understood the door was locked unless it was that they were so concentrated on their praying and their own thoughts; but now they certainly understood and they understood the shouting and they must have known now that all was changed. But they remained the same as before.

"By now the shouting was so that you could hear nothing and the drunkard who stood on the chair with me shook with his hands at the bars and yelled, 'Open up! Open up!' until he was hoarse.

"I watched Pablo speak to the priest again and the priest did not answer. Then I saw Pablo unsling his shotgun and he reached over and tapped the priest on the shoulder with it. The priest paid no attention to him and I saw Pablo shake his head. Then he spoke over his shoulder to Cuatro Dedos and Cuatro Dedos spoke to the other guards and they all stood up and walked back to the far end of the room and stood there with their shotguns.

"I saw Pablo say something to Cuatro Dedos and he moved over two tables and some benches and the guards stood behind them with their shotguns. It made a barricade in that corner of the room. Pablo leaned over and tapped the priest on the shoulder again with the shotgun and the priest did not pay attention to him but I saw Don Pepe watching him while the others paid no attention but went on praying. Pablo shook his head and, seeing Don Pepe looking at him, he shook his head at Don Pepe and showed him the key, holding it up in his hand. Don Pepe understood and he dropped his head and commenced to pray very fast.

"Pablo swung his legs down from the table and walked around it to the big chair of the Mayor on the raised platform behind the long council table. He sat down in it and rolled himself a cigarette, all the time watching the fascists who were praying with the priest. You could not see any expression on his face at all. The key was on the table in front of him. It was a big key of iron, over a foot long. Then Pablo called to the guards something I could not hear and one guard went down to the door. I could see them all praying faster than ever and I knew that they all knew now.

"Pablo said something to the priest but the priest did not answer. Then Pablo leaned forward, picked up the key and tossed it underhand to the guard at the door. The guard caught it and Pablo smiled at him.

170

Then the guard put the key in the door, turned it, and pulled the door toward him, ducking behind it as the mob rushed in.

"I saw them come in and just then the drunkard on the chair with me commenced to shout 'Ayee! Ayee! Ayee!' and pushed his head forward so I could not see and then he shouted 'Kill them! Kill them! Club them! Kill them!' and he pushed me aside with his two arms and I could see nothing.

"I hit my elbow into his belly and I said, 'Drunkard, whose chair is this? Let me see.'

"But he just kept shaking his hands and arms against the bars and shouting, 'Kill them! Club them! Club them! that's it. Club them! Kill them! *Cabrones! Cabrones! Cabrones!*'

"I hit him hard with my elbow and said, '*Cabron!* Drunkard! Let me see.'

"Then he put both his hands on my head to push me down and so he might see better and leaned all his weight on my head and went on shouting, 'Club them! that's it. Club them!'

" 'Club yourself,' I said and I hit him hard where it would hurt him and it hurt him and he dropped his hands from my head and grabbed himself and said, '*No hay derecho, mujer.* This, woman, you have no right to do.' And in that moment, looking through the bars, I saw the hall full of men flailing away with clubs and striking with flails, and poking and striking and pushing and heaving against people with the white wooden pitchforks that now were red and with their tines broken, and this was going on all over the room while Pablo sat in the big chair with his shotgun on his knees, watching, and they were shouting and clubbing and stabbing and men were screaming as horses scream in a fire. And I saw the priest with his skirts tucked up scrambling over a bench and those after him were chopping at him with the sickles and the reaping hooks and then some one had hold of his robe and there was another scream and another scream and I saw two men chopping into his back with sickles while a third man held the skirt of his robe and the priest's arms were up and he was clinging to the back of a chair and then the chair I was standing on broke and the drunkard and I were on the pavement that smelled of spilled wine and vomit and the drunkard was shaking his finger at me and saying, '*No hay derecho, mujer, no hay derecho.* You could have done me an injury,' and the people were trampling over us to get into the hall of the *Ayuntamiento* and all I could see was legs of people going in the doorway and the drunkard sitting there facing me and holding himself where I had hit him.

"That was the end of the killing of the fascists in our town and I was

171

glad I did not see more of it and, but for that drunkard, I would have seen it all. So he served some good because in the *Ayuntamiento* it was a thing one is sorry to have seen.

"But the other drunkard was something rarer still. As we got up after the breaking of the chair, and the people were still crowding into the *Ayuntamiento*, I saw this drunkard of the square with his red-and-black scarf, again pouring something over Don Anastasio. He was shaking his head from side to side and it was very hard for him to sit up, but he was pouring and lighting matches and then pouring and lighting matches and I walked over to him and said, 'What are you doing, shameless?'

" '*Nada, mujer, nada,*' he said. 'Let me alone.'

"And perhaps because I was standing there so that my legs made a shelter from the wind, the match caught and a blue flame began to run up the shoulder of the coat of Don Anastasio and onto the back of his neck and the drunkard put his head up and shouted in a huge voice, 'They're burning the dead! They're burning the dead!'

" 'Who?' somebody said.

" 'Where?' shouted some one else.

" 'Here,' bellowed the drunkard. 'Exactly here!'

"Then some one hit the drunkard a great blow alongside the head with a flail and he fell back, and lying on the ground, he looked up at the man who had hit him and then shut his eyes and crossed his hands on his chest, and lay there beside Don Anastasio as though he were asleep. The man did not hit him again and he lay there and he was still there when they picked up Don Anastasio and put him with the others in the cart that hauled them all over to the cliff where they were thrown over that evening with the others after there had been a cleaning up in the *Ayuntamiento*. It would have been better for the town if they had thrown over twenty or thirty of the drunkards, especially those of the red-and-black scarves, and if we ever have another revolution I believe they should be destroyed at the start. But then we did not know this. But in the next days we were to learn.

"But that night we did not know what was to come. After the slaying in the *Ayuntamiento* there was no more killing but we could not have a meeting that night because there were too many drunkards. It was impossible to obtain order and so the meeting was postponed until the next day.

"That night I slept with Pablo. I should not say this to you, *guapa*, but on the other hand, it is good for you to know everything and at least what I tell you is true. Listen to this, *Inglés*. It is very curious.

"As I say, that night we ate and it was very curious. It was as after a storm or a flood or a battle and every one was tired and no one spoke much. I, myself, felt hollow and not well and I was full of shame and a sense of wrongdoing and I had a great feeling of oppression and of bad to come, as this morning after the planes. And certainly, bad came within three days.

"Pablo, when we ate, spoke little.

"'Did you like it, Pilar?' he asked finally with his mouth full of roast young goat. We were eating at the inn from where the buses leave and the room was crowded and people were singing and there was difficulty serving.

"'No,' I said. 'Except for Don Faustino, I did not like it.'

"'I liked it,' he said.

"'All of it?' I asked him.

"'All of it,' he said and cut himself a big piece of bread with his knife and commenced to mop up gravy with it. 'All of it, except the priest.'

"'You didn't like it about the priest?' because I knew he hated priests even worse than he hated fascists.

"'He was a disillusionment to me,' Pablo said sadly.

"So many people were singing that we had to almost shout to hear one another.

"'Why?'

"'He died very badly,' Pablo said. 'He had very little dignity.'

"'How did you want him to have dignity when he was being chased by the mob?' I said. 'I thought he had much dignity all the time before. All the dignity that one could have.'

"'Yes,' Pablo said. 'But in the last minute he was frightened.'

"'Who wouldn't be?' I said. 'Did you see what they were chasing him with?'

"'Why would I not see?' Pablo said. 'But I find he died badly.'

"'In such circumstances any one dies badly,' I told him. 'What do you want for your money? Everything that happened in the *Ayuntamiento* was scabrous.'

"'Yes,' said Pablo. 'There was little organization. But a priest. He has an example to set.'

"'I thought you hated priests.'

"'Yes,' said Pablo and cut some more bread. 'But a *Spanish* priest. A *Spanish* priest should die very well.'

"'I think he died well enough,' I said. 'Being deprived of all formality.'

"'No,' Pablo said. 'To me he was a great disillusionment. All day I had waited for the death of the priest. I had thought he would be the last to enter the lines. I awaited it with great anticipation. I expected something of a culmination. I had never seen a priest die.'

" 'There is time,' I said to him sarcastically. 'Only today did the movement start.'

" 'No,' he said. 'I am disillusioned.'

" 'Now,' I said. 'I suppose you will lose your faith.'

" 'You do not understand, Pilar,' he said. 'He was a *Spanish* priest.'

" 'What people the Spaniards are,' I said to him. And what a people they are for pride, eh, *Inglés*? What a people."

"We must get on," Robert Jordan said. He looked at the sun. "It's nearly noon."

"Yes," Pilar said. "We will go now. But let me tell you about Pablo. That night he said to me, 'Pilar, tonight we will do nothing.'

" 'Good,' I told him. 'That pleases me.'

" 'I think it would be bad taste after the killing of so many people.'

" '*Qué va,*' I told him. 'What a saint you are. You think I lived years with bullfighters not to know how they are after the Corrida?'

" 'Is it true, Pilar?' he asked me.

" 'When did I lie to you?' I told him.

" 'It is true, Pilar, I am a finished man this night. You do not reproach me?'

" 'No, *hombre,*' I said to him. 'But don't kill people every day, Pablo.'

"And he slept that night like a baby and I woke him in the morning at daylight but I could not sleep that night and I got up and sat in a chair and looked out of the window and I could see the square in the moonlight where the lines had been and across the square the trees shining in the moonlight, and the darkness of their shadows, and the benches bright too in the moonlight, and the scattered bottles shining, and beyond the edge of the cliff where they had all been thrown. And there was no sound but the splashing of the water in the fountain and I sat there and I thought we have begun badly.

"The window was open and up the square from the Fonda I could hear a woman crying. I went out on the balcony standing there in my bare feet on the iron and the moon shone on the faces of all the buildings of the square and the crying was coming from the balcony of the house of Don Guillermo. It was his wife and she was on the balcony kneeling and crying.

"Then I went back inside the room and I sat there and I did not wish to think for that was the worst day of my life until one other day."

"What was the other?" Maria asked.

"Three days later when the fascists took the town."

174

"Do not tell me about it," said Maria. "I do not want to hear it. This is enough. This was too much."

"I told you that you should not have listened," Pilar said. "See. I did not want you to hear it. Now you will have bad dreams."

"No," said Maria. "But I do not want to hear more."

"I wish you would tell me of it sometime," Robert Jordan said.

"I will," Pilar said. "But it is bad for Maria."

"I don't want to hear it," Maria said pitifully. "Please, Pilar. And do not tell it if I am there, for I might listen in spite of myself."

Her lips were working and Robert Jordan thought she would cry.

"Please, Pilar, do not tell it."

"Do not worry, little cropped head," Pilar said. "Do not worry. But I will tell the *Inglés* sometime."

"But I want to be there when he is there," Maria said. "Oh, Pilar, do not tell it at all."

"I will tell it when thou art working."

"No. No. Please. Let us not tell it at all," Maria said.

"It is only fair to tell it since I have told what we did," Pilar said. "But you shall never hear it."

"Are there no pleasant things to speak of?" Maria said. "Do we have to talk always of horrors?"

"This afternoon," Pilar said, "thou and *Inglés*. The two of you can speak of what you wish."

"Then that the afternoon should come," Maria said. "That it should come flying."

"It will come," Pilar told her. "It will come flying and go the same way and tomorrow will fly, too."

"This afternoon," Maria said. "This afternoon. That this afternoon should come."

Guerrilla Warfare

(from *For Whom the Bell Tolls*)

Agustín and Primitivo came up with the brush and Robert Jordan built
a good blind for the automatic rifle, a blind that would conceal the gun
from the air and that would look natural from the forest. He showed them
where to place a man high in the rocks to the right where he could see all
the country below and to the right, and another where he could command the only stretch where the left wall might be climbed.

"Do not fire if you see any one from there," Robert Jordan said.
"Roll a rock down as a warning, a small rock, and signal to us with thy
rifle, thus," he lifted the rifle and held it over his head as though guarding it. "Thus for numbers," he lifted the rifle up and down. "If they are
dismounted point thy rifle muzzle at the ground. Thus. Do not fire from
there until thou hearest the *máquina* fire. Shoot at a man's knees when
you shoot from that height. If you hear me whistle twice on this whistle
get down, keeping behind cover, and come to these rocks where the
máquina is."

Primitivo raised the rifle.

"I understand," he said. "It is very simple."

"Send first the small rock as a warning and indicate the direction and
the number. See that you are not seen."

"Yes," Primitivo said. "If I can throw a grenade?"

"Not until the *máquina* has spoken. It may be that cavalry will come
searching for their comrade and still not try to enter. They may follow the
tracks of Pablo. We do not want combat if it can be avoided. Above all
that we should avoid it. Now get up there."

"*Me voy*," Primitivo said, and climbed up into the high rocks with his
carbine.

"Thou, Agustín," Robert Jordan said. "What do you know of the gun?"

Agustín squatted there, tall, black, stubbly joweled, with his sunken
eyes and thin mouth and his big work-worn hands.

"*Pues*, to load it. To aim it. To shoot it. Nothing more."

176

"You must not fire until they are within fifty meters and only when you are sure they will be coming into the pass which leads to the cave," Robert Jordan said.

"Yes. How far is that?"

"That rock."

"If there is an officer shoot him first. Then move the gun onto the others. Move very slowly. It takes little movement. I will teach Fernando to tap it. Hold it tight so that it does not jump and sight carefully and do not fire more than six shots at a time if you can help it. For the fire of the gun jumps upward. But each time fire at one man and then move from him to another. At a man on a horse, shoot at his belly."

"Yes."

"One man should hold the tripod still so that the gun does not jump. Thus. He will load the gun for thee."

"And where will you be?"

"I will be here on the left. Above, where I can see all and I will cover thy left with this small *máquina*. Here. If they should come it would be possible to make a massacre. But you must not fire until they are that close."

"I believe that we could make a massacre. *Menuda matanza!*"

"But I hope they do not come."

"If it were not for thy bridge we could make a massacre here and get out."

"It would avail nothing. That would serve no purpose. The bridge is a part of a plan to win the war. This would be nothing. This would be an incident. A nothing."

"*Qué va*, nothing. Every fascist dead is a fascist less."

"Yes. But with this of the bridge we can take Segovia. The Capital of a Province. Think of that. It will be the first one we will take."

"Thou believest in this seriously? That we can take Segovia?"

"Yes. It is possible with the bridge blown correctly."

"I would like to have the massacre here and the bridge, too."

"Thou hast much appetite," Robert Jordan told him.

All this time he had been watching the crows. Now he saw one was watching something. The bird cawed and flew up. But the other crow still stayed in the tree. Robert Jordan looked up toward Primitivo's place high in the rocks. He saw him watching out over the country below but he made no signal. Robert Jordan leaned forward and worked the lock on the automatic rifle, saw the round in the chamber and let the lock down. The crow was still there in the tree. The other circled wide over the snow and then settled again. In the sun and the warm wind the snow was falling from the laden branches of the pines.

"I have a massacre for thee for tomorrow morning," Robert Jordan said. "It is necessary to exterminate the post at the sawmill."

"I am ready," Agustín said, "*Estoy listo.*"

"Also the post at the roadmender's hut below the bridge."

"For the one or for the other," Agustín said. "Or for both."

"Not for both. They will be done at the same time," Robert Jordan said.

"Then for either one," Agustín said. "Now for a long time have I wished for action in this war. Pablo has rotted us here with inaction."

Anselmo came up with the ax.

"Do you wish more branches?" he asked. "To me it seems well hidden."

"Not branches," Robert Jordan said. "Two small trees that we can plant here and there to make it look more natural. There are not enough trees here for it to be truly natural."

"I will bring them."

"Cut them well back, so the stumps cannot be seen."

Robert Jordan heard the ax sounding in the woods behind him. He looked up at Primitivo above in the rocks and he looked down at the pines across the clearing. The one crow was still there. Then he heard the first high, throbbing murmur of a plane coming. He looked up and saw it high and tiny and silver in the sun, seeming hardly to move in the high sky.

"They cannot see us," he said to Agustín. "But it is well to keep down. That is the second observation plane today."

"And those of yesterday?" Agustín asked.

"They are like a bad dream now," Robert Jordan said.

"They must be at Segovia. The bad dream waits there to become a reality."

The plane was out of sight now over the mountains but the sound of its motors still persisted.

As Robert Jordan looked, he saw the crow fly up. He flew straight away through the trees without cawing.

"Get thee down," Robert Jordan whispered to Agustín, and he turned his head and flicked his hand *Down, Down,* to Anselmo who was coming through the gap with a pine tree, carrying it over his shoulder like a Christmas tree. He saw the old man drop his pine tree behind a rock and then he was out of sight in the rocks and Robert Jordan was looking ahead across the open space toward the timber. He saw nothing and heard nothing but he could feel his heart pounding and then he heard

178

the clack of stone on stone and the leaping, dropping clicks of a small rock falling. He turned his head to the right and looking up saw Primitivo's rifle raised and lowered four times horizontally. Then there was nothing more to see but the white stretch in front of him with the circle of horse tracks and the timber beyond.

"Cavalry," he said softly to Agustín.

Agustín looked at him and his dark, sunken cheeks widened at their base as he grinned. Robert Jordan noticed he was sweating. He reached over and put his hand on his shoulder. His hand was still there as they saw the four horsemen ride out of the timber and he felt the muscles in Agustín's back twitch under his hand.

One horseman was ahead and three rode behind. The one ahead was following the horse tracks. He looked down as he rode. The other three came behind him, fanned out through the timber. They were all watching carefully. Robert Jordan felt his heart beating against the snowy ground as he lay, his elbows spread wide and watched them over the sights of the automatic rifle.

The man who was leading rode along the trail to where Pablo had circled and stopped. The others rode up to him and they all stopped.

Robert Jordan saw them clearly over the blued steel barrel of the automatic rifle. He saw the faces of the men, the sabers hanging, the sweat-darkened flanks of the horses, and the cone-like slope of the khaki capes, and the Navarrese slant of the khaki berets. The leader turned his horse directly toward the opening in the rocks where the gun was placed and Robert Jordan saw his young, sun- and wind-darkened face, his close-set eyes, hawk nose and the overlong wedge-shaped chin.

Sitting his horse there, the horse's chest toward Robert Jordan, the horse's head high, the butt of the light automatic rifle projecting forward from the scabbard at the right of the saddle, the leader pointed toward the opening where the gun was.

Robert Jordan sunk his elbows into the ground and looked along the barrel at the four riders stopped there in the snow. Three of them had their automatic rifles out. Two carried them across the pommels of their saddles. The other sat his horse with the rifle swung out to the right, the butt resting against his hip.

You hardly ever see them at such range, he thought. Not along the barrel of one of these do you see them like this. Usually the rear sight is raised and they seem miniatures of men and you have hell to make it carry up there; or they come running, flopping, running, and you beat a slope with fire or bar a certain street, or keep it on the windows; or far away you see them marching on a road. Only at the trains do you see them like this.

Only then are they like now, and with four of these you can make them scatter. Over the gun sights, at this range, it makes them twice the size of men.

Thou, he thought, looking at the wedge of the front sight placed now firm in the slot of the rear sight, the top of the wedge against the center of the leader's chest, a little to the right of the scarlet device that showed bright in the morning sun against the khaki cape. Though, he thought, thinking in Spanish now and pressing his fingers forward against the trigger guard to keep it away from where it would bring the quick, shocking, hurtling rush from the automatic rifle. Thou, he thought again, thou art dead now in thy youth. And thou, he thought, and thou, and thou. But let it not happen. Do not let it happen.

He felt Agustín beside him start to cough, felt him hold it, choke and swallow. Then as he looked along the oiled blue of the barrel out through the opening between the branches, his finger still pressed forward against the trigger guard, he saw the leader turn his horse and point into the timber where Pablo's trail led. The four of them trotted into the timber and Agustín said softly, "*Cabrones!*"

Robert Jordan looked behind him at the rocks where Anselmo had dropped the tree.

The gypsy, Rafael, was coming toward them through the rocks, carrying a pair of cloth saddlebags, his rifle slung on his back. Robert Jordan waved him down and the gypsy ducked out of sight.

"We could have killed all four," Agustín said quietly. He was still wet with sweat.

"Yes," Robert Jordan whispered. "But with the firing who knows what might have come?"

Just then he heard the noise of another rock falling and he looked around quickly. But both the gypsy and Anselmo were out of sight. He looked at his wrist watch and then up to where Primitivo was raising and lowering his rifle in what seemed an infinity of short jerks. Pablo has forty-five minutes' start, Robert Jordan thought, and then he heard the noise of a body of cavalry coming.

"*No te apures,*" he whispered to Agustín. "Do not worry. They will pass as the others."

They came into sight trotting along the edge of the timber in column of twos, twenty mounted men, armed and uniformed as the others had been, their sabers swinging, their carbines in their holsters; and then they went down into the timber as the others had.

"*Tu ves?*" Robert Jordan said to Agustín. "Thou seest?"

180

"There were many," Agustín said.

"These would we have had to deal with if we had destroyed the others," Robert Jordan said very softly. His heart had quieted now and his shirt felt wet on his chest from the melting snow. There was a hollow feeling in his chest.

The sun was bright on the snow and it was melting fast. He could see it hollowing away from the tree trunks and just ahead of the gun, before his eyes, the snow surface was damp and lácily fragile as the heat of the sun melted the top and the warmth of the earth breathed warmly up at the snow that lay upon it.

Robert Jordan looked up at Primitivo's post and saw him signal, "Nothing," crossing his two hands, palms down.

Anselmo's head showed above a rock and Robert Jordan motioned him up. The old man slipped from rock to rock until he crept up and lay down flat beside the gun.

"Many," he said. "Many!"

"I do not need the trees," Robert Jordan said to him. "There is no need for further forestal improvement."

Both Anselmo and Agustín grinned.

"This has stood scrutiny well and it would be dangerous to plant trees now because those people will return and perhaps they are not stupid."

He felt the need to talk that, with him, was the sign that there had just been much danger. He could always tell how bad it had been by the strength of the desire to talk that came after.

"It was a good blind, eh?" he said.

"Good," said Agustín. "To obscenity with all fascism good. We could have killed the four of them. Didst thou see?" he said to Anselmo.

"I saw."

"Thou," Robert Jordan said to Anselmo. "Thou must go to the post of yesterday or another good post of thy selection to watch the road and report on all movement as of yesterday. Already we are late in that. Stay until dark. Then come in and we will send another."

"But the tracks that I will make?"

"Go from below as soon as the snow is gone. The road will be muddied by the snow. Note if there has been much traffic of trucks or if there are tank tracks in the softness on the road. That is all we can tell until you are there to observe."

"With your permission?" the old man asked.

"Surely."

"With your permission, would it not be better for me to go into La

Granja and inquire there what passed last night and arrange for one to observe today thus in the manner you have taught me? Such a one could report tonight or, better, I could go again to La Granja for the report."

"Have you no fear of encountering cavalry?"

"Not when the snow is gone."

"Is there some one in La Granja capable of this?"

"Yes. Of this, yes. It would be a woman. There are various women of trust in La Granja."

"I believe it," Agustín said. "More, I know it, and several who serve for other purposes. You do not wish me to go?"

"Let the old man go. You understand this gun and the day is not over."

"I will go when the snow melts," Anselmo said. "And the snow is melting fast."

"What think you of their chance of catching Pablo?" Robert Jordan asked Agustín.

"Pablo is smart," Agustín said. "Do men catch a wise stag without hounds?"

"Sometimes," Robert Jordan said.

"Not Pablo," Agustín said. "Clearly, he is only a garbage of what he once was. But it is not for nothing that he is alive and comfortable in these hills and able to drink himself to death while there are so many others that have died against a wall."

"Is he as smart as they say?"

"He is much smarter."

"He has not seemed of great ability here."

"*Cómo qúe no?* If he were not of great ability he would have died last night. It seems to me you do not understand politics, *Inglés*, nor guerilla warfare. In politics and this other the first thing is to continue to exist. Look how he continued to exist last night. And the quantity of dung he ate both from me and from thee."

Now that Pablo was back in the movements of the unit, Robert Jordan did not wish to talk against him and as soon as he had uttered it he regretted saying the thing about his ability. He knew himself how smart Pablo was. It was Pablo who had seen instantly all that was wrong with the orders for the destruction of the bridge. He had made the remark only from dislike and he knew as he made it that it was wrong. It was part of the talking too much after a strain. So now he dropped the matter and said to Anselmo, "And to go into La Granja in daylight?"

"It is not bad," the old man said. "I will not go with a military band."

182

"Nor with a bell around his neck," Agustín said. "Nor carrying a banner."

"How will you go?"

"Above and down through the forest."

"But if they pick you up."

"I have papers."

"So have we all but thou must eat the wrong ones quickly."

Anselmo shook his head and tapped the breast pocket of his smock.

"How many times have I contemplated that," he said. "And never did I like to swallow paper."

"I have thought we should carry a little mustard on them all," Robert Jordan said. "In my left breast pocket I carry our papers. In my right the fascist papers. Thus one does not make a mistake in an emergency."

It must have been bad enough when the leader of the first patrol of cavalry had pointed toward the entry because they were all talking very much. Too much, Robert Jordan thought.

"But look, Roberto," Agustín said. "They say the government moves further to the right each day. That in the Republic they no longer say Comrade but Señor and Señora. Canst shift thy pockets?"

"When it moves far enough to the right I will carry them in my hip pocket," Robert Jordan said, "and sew it in the center."

"That they should stay in thy shirt," Agustín said. "Are we to win this war and lose the revolution?"

"Nay," Robert Jordan said. "But if we do not win this war there will be no revolution nor any Republic nor any thou nor any me nor anything but the most grand *carajo*."

"So say I," Anselmo said. "That we should win the war."

"And afterwards shoot the anarchists and the Communists and all this *canalla* except the good Republicans," Agustín said.

"That we should win this war and shoot nobody," Anselmo said. "That we should govern justly and that all should participate in the benefits according as they have striven for them. And that those who have fought against us should be educated to see their error."

"We will have to shoot many," Agustín said. "Many, many, many."

He thumped his closed right fist against the palm of his left hand.

"That we should shoot none. Not even the leaders. That they should be reformed by work."

"I know the work I'd put them at," Agustín said, and he picked up some snow and put it in his mouth.

"What, bad one?" Robert Jordan asked.

"Two trades of the utmost brilliance."

"They are?"

Agustín put some more snow in his mouth and looked across the clearing where the cavalry had ridden. Then he spat the melted snow out. "*Vaya.* What a breakfast," he said. "Where is the filthy gypsy?"

"What trades?" Robert Jordan asked him. "Speak, bad mouth."

"Jumping from planes without parachutes," Agustín said, and his eyes shone. "That for those that we care for. And being nailed to the tops of fence posts to be pushed over backwards for the others."

"That way of speaking is ignoble," Anselmo said. "Thus we will never have a Republic."

"I would like to swim ten leagues in a strong soup made from the *cojones* of all of them," Agustín said. "And when I saw those four there and thought that we might kill them I was like a mare in the corral waiting for the stallion."

"You know why we did not kill them, though?" Robert Jordan said quietly.

"Yes," Agustín said. "Yes. But the necessity was on me as it is on a mare in heat. You cannot know what it is if you have not felt it."

"You sweated enough," Robert Jordan said. "I thought it was fear."

"Fear, yes," Agustín said. "Fear and the other. And in this life there is no stronger thing than the other."

Yes, Robert Jordan thought. We do it coldly but they do not, nor ever have. It is their extra sacrament. Their old one that they had before the new religion came from the far end of the Mediterranean, the one they have never abandoned but only suppressed and hidden to bring it out again in wars and inquisitions. They are the people of the Auto de Fé; the act of faith. Killing is something one must do, but ours are different from theirs. And you, he thought, you have never been corrupted by it? You never had it in the Sierra? Nor at Usera? Nor through all the time in Estremadura? Nor at any time? *Qué va,* he told himself. At every train.

Stop making dubious literature about the Berbers and the old Iberians and admit that you have liked to kill as all who are soldiers by choice have enjoyed it at some time whether they lie about it or not. Anselmo does not like to because he is a hunter, not a soldier. Don't idealize him, either. Hunters kill animals and soldiers kill men. Don't lie to yourself, he thought. Nor make up literature about it. You have been tainted with it for a long time now. And do not think against Anselmo either. He is a Christian. Something very rare in Catholic countries.

But with Agustín I had thought it was fear, he thought. That natural fear before action. So it was the other, too. Of course, he may be bragging now. There was plenty of fear. I felt the fear under my hand. Well, it was time to stop talking.

"See if the gypsy brought food," he said to Anselmo. "Do not let him come up. He is a fool. Bring it yourself. And however much he brought, send back for more. I am hungry."

El Sordo's Last Stand

(from *For Whom the Bell Tolls*)

El Sordo was making his fight on a hilltop. He did not like this hill and when he saw it he thought it had the shape of a chancre. But he had had no choice except this hill and he had picked it as far away as he could see it and galloped for it, the automatic rifle heavy on his back, the horse laboring, barrel heaving between his thighs, the sack of grenades swinging against one side, the sack of automatic rifle pans banging against the other, and Joaquín and Ignacio halting and firing, halting and firing to give him time to get the gun in place.

There had still been snow then, the snow that had ruined them, and when his horse was hit so that he wheezed in a slow, jerking, climbing stagger up the last part of the crest, splattering the snow with a bright, pulsing jet, Sordo had hauled him along by the bridle, the reins over his shoulder as he climbed. He climbed as hard as he could with the bullets spatting on the rocks, with the two sacks heavy on his shoulders, and then, holding the horse by the mane, had shot him quickly, expertly, and tenderly just where he had needed him, so that the horse pitched, head forward down to plug a gap between two rocks. He had gotten the gun to firing over the horse's back and he fired two pans, the gun clattering, the empty shells pitching into the snow, the smell of burnt hair from the burnt hide where the hot muzzle rested, him firing at what came up to the hill, forcing them to scatter for cover, while all the time there was a chill in his back from not knowing what was behind him. Once the last of the five men had reached the hilltop the chill went out of his back and he had saved the pans he had left until he would need them.

There were two more horses dead along the slope and three more were dead here on the hilltop. He had only succeeded in stealing three horses last night and one had bolted when they tried to mount him bareback in the corral at the camp when the first shooting had started.

Of the five men who had reached the hilltop three were wounded.

Sordo was wounded in the calf of his leg and in two places in his left arm. He was very thirsty, his wounds had stiffened, and one of the wounds in his left arm was very painful. He also had a bad headache and as he lay waiting for the planes to come he thought of a joke in Spanish. It was, "*Hay que tomar la muerte como si fuera aspirina,*" which means, "You will have to take death as an aspirin." But he did not make the joke aloud. He grinned somewhere inside the pain in his head and inside the nausea that came whenever he moved his arm and looked around at what there was left of his band.

The five men were spread out like the points of a five-pointed star. They had dug with their knees and hands and made mounds in front of their heads and shoulders with the dirt and piles of stones. Using this cover, they were linking the individual mounds up with stones and dirt. Joaquín, who was eighteen years old, had a steel helmet that he dug with and he passed dirt in it.

He had gotten this helmet at the blowing up of the train. It had a bullet hole through it and every one had always joked at him for keeping it. But he had hammered the jagged edges of the bullet hole smooth and driven a wooden plug into it and then cut the plug off and smoothed it even with the metal inside the helmet.

When the shooting started he had clapped this helmet on his head so hard it banged his head as though he had been hit with a casserole and, in the last lung-aching, leg-dead, mouth-dry, bullet-spatting, bullet-cracking, bullet-singing run up the final slope of the hill after his horse was killed, the helmet had seemed to weigh a great amount and to ring his bursting forehead with an iron band. But he had kept it. Now he dug with it in a steady, almost machine-like desperation. He had not yet been hit.

"It serves for something finally," Sordo said to him in his deep, throaty voice.

"*Resistir y fortificar es vencer,*" Joaquín said, his mouth stiff with the dryness of fear which surpassed the normal thirst of battle. It was one of the slogans of the Communist party and it meant, "Hold out and fortify, and you will win."

Sordo looked away and down the slope at where a cavalryman was sniping from behind a boulder. He was very fond of this boy and he was in no mood for slogans.

"What did you say?"

One of the men turned from the building that he was doing. This man was lying flat on his face, reaching carefully up with his hands to put a rock in place while keeping his chin flat against the ground.

187

Joaquín repeated the slogan in his dried-up boy's voice without checking his digging for a moment.

"What was the last word?" the man with his chin on the ground asked.

"*Vencer*," the boy said. "Win."

"*Mierda*," the man with his chin on the ground said.

"There is another that applies to here," Joaquín said, bringing them out as though they were talismans, "Pasionaria says it is better to die on your feet than to live on your knees."

"*Mierda* again," the man said and another man said, over his shoulder, "We're on our bellies, not our knees."

"Thou. Communist. Do you know your Pasionaria has a son thy age in Russia since the start of the movement?"

"It's a lie," Joaquín said.

"*Qué va*, it's a lie," the other said. "The dynamiter with the rare name told me. He was of thy party, too. Why should he lie?"

"It's a lie," Joaquín said. "She would not do such a thing as keep a son hidden in Russia out of the war."

"I wish I were in Russia," another of Sordo's men said. "Will not thy Pasionaria send me now from here to Russia, Communist?"

"If thou believest so much in thy Pasionaria, get her to get us off this hill," one of the men who had a bandaged thigh said.

"The fascists will do that," the man with his chin in the dirt said.

"Do not speak thus," Joaquín said to him.

"Wipe the pap of your mother's breasts off thy lips and give me a hatful of that dirt," the man with his chin on the ground said. "No one of us will see the sun go down this night."

El Sordo was thinking: It is shaped like a chancre. Or the breast of a young girl with no nipple. Or the top cone of a volcano. You have never seen a volcano, he thought. Nor will you ever see one. And this hill is like a chancre. Let the volcanos alone. It's late now for the volcanos.

He looked very carefully around the withers of the dead horse and there was a quick hammering of firing from behind a boulder well down the slope and he heard the bullets from the submachine gun thud into the horse. He crawled along behind the horse and looked out of the angle between the horse's hindquarters and the rock. There were three bodies on the slope just below him where they had fallen when the fascists had rushed the crest under cover of the automatic rifle and submachine gunfire and he and the others had broken down the attack by throwing and rolling down hand grenades. There were other bodies that he could not see on the other sides of the hill crest. There was no dead ground by which attackers could approach the summit and Sordo knew that as long as his ammunition and grenades held out and he had as many as four men they could not get him out of there unless they brought up a trench mortar. He did not know whether they had sent to La Granja for a trench mortar. Perhaps they had not, because surely, soon, the planes would come. It had been four hours since the observation plane had flown over them.

This hill is truly like a chancre, Sordo thought, and we are the very pus of it. But we killed many when they made that stupidness. How could they think that they would take us thus? They have such modern armament that they lose all their sense with overconfidence. He had killed the young officer who had led the assault with a grenade that had gone bouncing and rolling down the slope as they came up it, running, bent half over. In the yellow flash and gray roar of smoke he had seen the officer dive forward to where he lay now like a heavy, broken bundle of old clothing marking the farthest point that the assault had reached. Sordo looked at this body and then, down the hill, at the others.

They are brave but stupid people, he thought. But they have sense enough now not to attack us again until the planes come. Unless, of course, they have a mortar coming. It would be easy with a mortar. The mortar was the normal thing and he knew that they would die as soon as a mortar came up, but when he thought of the planes coming up he felt as naked on that hilltop as though all of his clothing and even his skin had been removed. There is no nakeder thing than I feel, he thought. A flayed rabbit is as well covered as a bear in comparison. But why should they bring planes? They could get us out of here with a trench mortar easily. They are proud of their planes, though, and they will probably bring them. Just as they were so proud of their automatic weapons that they made that stupidness. But undoubtedly they must have sent for a mortar, too.

One of the men fired. Then jerked the bolt and fired again, quickly.

"Save thy cartridges," Sordo said.

"One of the sons of the great whore tried to reach that boulder," the man pointed.

"Did you hit him?" Sordo asked, turning his head with difficulty.

"Nay," the man said. "The fornicator ducked back."

"Who is a whore of whores is Pilar," the man with his chin in the dirt said. "That whore knows we are dying here."

"She could do no good," Sordo said. The man had spoken on the side of his good ear and he had heard him without turning his head. "What could she do?"

"Take these sluts from the rear."

"*Qué va*," Sordo said. "They are spread around a hillside. How would she come on them? There are a hundred and fifty of them. Maybe more now."

"But if we hold out until dark," Joaquín said.

"And if Christmas comes on Easter," the man with his chin on the ground said.

"And if thy aunt had *cojones* she would be thy uncle," another said to him. "Send for thy Pasionaria. She alone can help us."

"I do not believe that about the son," Joaquín said. "Or if he is there he is training to be an aviator or something of that sort."

"He is hidden there for safety," the man told him.

"He is studying dialectics. Thy Pasionaria has been there. So have Lister and Modesto and others. The one with the rare name told me."

"That they should go to study and return to aid us," Joaquín said.

"That they should aid us now," another man said. "That all the cruts of Russian sucking swindlers should aid us now." He fired and said, "*Me cago en tal*; I missed him again."

"Save thy cartridges and do not talk so much or thou wilt be very thirsty," Sordo said. "There is no water on this hill."

"Take this," the man said and rolling on his side he pulled a wineskin that he wore slung from his shoulder over his head and handed it to Sordo. "Wash thy mouth out, old one. Thou must have much thirst with thy wounds."

"Let all take it," Sordo said.

"Then I will have some first," the owner said and squirted a long stream into his mouth before he handed the leather bottle around.

"Sordo, when thinkest thou the planes will come?" the man with his chin in the dirt asked.

"Any time," said Sordo. "They should have come before."

"Do you think these sons of the great whore will attack again?"

"Only if the planes do not come."

He did not think there was any need to speak about the mortar. They would know it soon enough when the mortar came.

"God knows they've enough planes with what we saw yesterday."

"Too many," Sordo said.

His head hurt very much and his arm was stiffening so that the pain of moving it was almost unbearable. He looked up at the bright, high, blue early summer sky as he raised the leather wine bottle with his good arm. He was fifty-two years old and he was sure this was the last time he would see that sky.

He was not at all afraid of dying but he was angry at being trapped on this hill which was only utilizable as a place to die. If we could have gotten clear, he thought. If we could have made them come up the long valley or if we could have broken loose across the road it would have been all right. But this chancre of a hill. We must use it as well as we can and we have used it very well so far.

If he had known how many men in history have had to use a hill to die on it would not have cheered him any for, in the moment he was passing through, men are not impressed by what has happened to other men in similar circumstances any more than a widow of one day is helped by the knowledge that other loved husbands have died. Whether one has fear of it or not, one's death is difficult to accept. Sordo had accepted it but there was no sweetness in its acceptance even at fifty-two, with three wounds and him surrounded on a hill.

He joked about it to himself but he looked at the sky and at the far mountains and he swallowed the wine and he did not want it. If one must die, he thought, and clearly one must, I can die. But I hate it.

Dying was nothing and he had no picture of it nor fear of it in his mind. But living was a field of grain blowing in the wind on the side of a hill. Living was a hawk in the sky. Living was an earthen jar of water in the dust of the threshing with the grain flailed out and the chaff blowing. Living was a horse between your legs and a carbine under one leg and a hill and a valley and a stream with trees along it and the far side of the valley and the hills beyond.

Sordo passed the wine bottle back and nodded his head in thanks. He leaned forward and patted the dead horse on the shoulder where the muzzle of the automatic rifle had burned the hide. He could still smell the burnt hair. He thought how he had held the horse there, trembling, with the fire around them, whispering and cracking, over and around them like a curtain, and had carefully shot him just at the intersection of the cross-lines between the two eyes and the ears. Then as the horse pitched down he had dropped down behind his warm, wet back to get the gun to going as they came up the hill.

"*Eras mucho caballo,*" he said, meaning, "Thou wert plenty of horse."

El Sordo lay now on his good side and looked up at the sky. He was lying on a heap of empty cartridge hulls but his head was protected by the rock and his body lay in the lee of the horse. His wounds had stiffened badly and he had much pain and he felt too tired to move.

"What passes with thee, old one?" the man next to him asked.

"Nothing. I am taking a little rest."

"Sleep," the other said. "*They* will wake us when they come."

Just then some one shouted from down the slope.

"Listen, bandits!" the voice came from behind the rocks where the closest automatic rifle was placed. "Surrender now before the planes blow you to pieces."

"What is it he says?" Sordo asked.

Joaquín told him. Sordo rolled to one side and pulled himself up so that he was crouched behind the gun again.

"Maybe the planes aren't coming," he said. "Don't answer them and do not fire. Maybe we can get them to attack again."

"If we should insult them a little?" the man who had spoken to Joaquín about La Pasionaria's son in Russia asked.

"No," Sordo said. "Give me thy big pistol. Who has a big pistol?"

"Here."

"Give it to me." Crouched on his knees he took the big 9 mm. Star and fired one shot into the ground beside the dead horse, waited, then fired again four times at irregular intervals. Then he waited while he counted sixty and then fired a final shot directly into the body of the dead horse. He grinned and handed back the pistol.

"Reload it," he whispered, "and that every one should keep his mouth shut and no one shoot."

"*Bandidos!*" the voice shouted from behind the rocks.

No one spoke on the hill.

"*Bandidos!* Surrender now before we blow thee to little pieces."

"They're biting," Sordo whispered happily.

As he watched, a man showed his head over the top of the rocks. There was no shot from the hilltop and the head went down again. El Sordo waited, watching, but nothing more happened. He turned his head and looked at the others who were all watching down their sectors of the slope. As he looked at them the others shook their heads.

"Let no one move," he whispered.

"Sons of the great whore," the voice came now from behind the rocks again.

"Red swine. Mother rapers. Eaters of the milk of thy fathers."

Sordo grinned. He could just hear the bellowed insults by turning his good ear. This is better than the aspirin, he thought. How many will we get? Can they be that foolish?

The voice had stopped again and for three minutes they heard nothing and saw no movement. Then the sniper behind the boulder a hundred yards down the slope exposed himself and fired. The bullet hit a rock and ricocheted with a sharp whine. Then Sordo saw a man, bent double, run from the shelter of the rocks where the automatic rifle was across the open ground to the big boulder behind which the sniper was hidden. He almost dove behind the boulder.

Sordo looked around. They signalled to him that there was no movement on the other slopes. El Sordo grinned happily and shook his head. This is ten times better than the aspirin, he thought, and he waited, as happy as only a hunter can be happy.

Below on the slope the man who had run from the pile of stones to the shelter of the boulder was speaking to the sniper.

"Do you believe it?"

"I don't know," the sniper said.

"It would be logical," the man, who was the officer in command, said. "They are surrounded. They have nothing to expect but to die."

The sniper said nothing.

"What do you think?" the officer asked.

"Nothing," the sniper said.

"Have you seen any movement since the shots?"

"None at all."

The officer looked at his wrist watch. It was ten minutes to three o'clock.

"The planes should have come an hour ago," he said. Just then another officer flopped in behind the boulder. The sniper moved over to make room for him.

"Thou, Paco," the first officer said. "How does it seem to thee?"

The second officer was breathing heavily from his sprint up and across the hillside from the automatic rifle position.

"For me it is a trick," he said.

"But if it is not? What a ridicule we make waiting here and laying siege to dead men."

"We have done something worse than ridiculous already," the second officer said. "Look at that slope."

He looked up the slope to where the dead were scattered close to the top. From where he looked the line of the hilltop showed the scattered rocks, the belly, projecting legs, shod hooves jutting out, of Sordo's horse, and the fresh dirt thrown up by the digging.

"What about the mortars?" asked the second officer.

"They should be here in an hour. If not before."

"Then wait for them. There has been enough stupidity already."

"*Bandidos!*" the first officer shouted suddenly, getting to his feet and putting his head well up above the boulder so that the crest of the hill looked much closer as he stood upright. "Red swine! Cowards!"

The second officer looked at the sniper and shook his head. The sniper looked away but his lips tightened.

The first officer stood there, his head all clear of the rock and with his hand on his pistol butt. He cursed and vilified the hilltop. Nothing happened. Then he stepped clear of the boulder and stood there looking up the hill.

"Fire, cowards, if you are alive," he shouted. "Fire on one who has no fear of any Red that ever came out of the belly of the great whore."

This last was quite a long sentence to shout and the officer's face was red and congested as he finished.

The second officer, who was a thin sunburned man with quiet eyes, a thin, long-lipped mouth and a stubble of beard over his hollow cheeks, shook his head again. It was this officer who was shouting who had ordered the first assault. The young lieutenant who was dead up the slope had been the best friend of this other lieutenant who was named Paco Berrendo and who was listening to the shouting of the captain, who was obviously in a state of exaltation.

"Those are the swine who shot my sister and my mother," the captain said. He had a red face and a blond, British-looking moustache and there was something wrong about his eyes. They were a light blue and the lashes were light, too. As you looked at them they seemed to focus slowly. Then "Reds," he shouted. "Cowards!" and commenced cursing again.

He stood absolutely clear now and, sighting carefully, fired his pistol at the only target that the hilltop presented: the dead horse that had belonged to Sordo. The bullet threw up a puff of dirt fifteen yards below the horse. The captain fired again. The bullet hit a rock and sung off.

The captain stood there looking at the hilltop. The Lieutenant Berrendo was looking at the body of the other lieutenant just below the summit. The sniper was looking at the ground under his eyes. Then he looked up at the captain.

"There is no one alive up there," the captain said. "Thou," he said to the sniper, "go up there and see."

The sniper looked down. He said nothing.

"Don't you hear me?" the captain shouted at him.

"Yes, my captain," the sniper said, not looking at him.

"Then get up and go." The captain still had his pistol out. "Do you hear me?"

"Yes, my captain."

"Why don't you go, then?"

"I don't want to, my captain."

"You don't *want* to?" The captain pushed the pistol against the small of the man's back. "You don't *want* to?"

194

"I am afraid, my captain," the soldier said with dignity.

Lieutenant Berrendo, watching the captain's face and his odd eyes, thought he was going to shoot the man then.

"Captain Mora," he said.

"Lieutenant Berrendo?"

"It is possible the soldier is right."

"That he is right to say he is afraid? That he is right to say he does not *want* to obey an order?"

"No. That he is right that it is a trick."

"They are all dead," the captain said. "Don't you hear me say they are all dead?"

"You mean our comrades on the slope?" Berrendo asked him. "I agree with you."

"Paco," the captain said, "don't be a fool. Do you think you are the only one who cared for Julián? I tell you the Reds are dead. Look!"

He stood up, then put both hands on top of the boulder and pulled himself up, kneeing-up awkwardly, then getting on his feet.

"Shoot," he shouted, standing on the gray granite boulder and waved both his arms. "Shoot me! Kill me!"

On the hilltop El Sordo lay behind the dead horse and grinned.

What a people, he thought. He laughed, trying to hold it in because the shaking hurt his arm.

"Reds," came the shout from below. "Red canaille. Shoot me! Kill me!"

Sordo, his chest shaking, barely peeped past the horse's crupper and saw the captain on top of the boulder waving his arms. Another officer stood by the boulder. The sniper was standing at the other side. Sordo kept his eye where it was and shook his head happily.

"Shoot me," he said softly to himself. "Kill me!" Then his shoulders shook again. The laughing hurt his arm and each time he laughed his head felt as though it would burst. But the laughter shook him again like a spasm.

Captain Mora got down from the boulder.

"Now do you believe me, Paco?" he questioned Lieutenant Berrendo.

"No," said Lieutenant Berrendo.

"*Cojones!*" the captain said. "Here there is nothing but idiots and cowards."

The sniper had gotten carefully behind the boulder again and Lieutenant Berrendo was squatting beside him.

The captain, standing in the open beside the boulder, commenced to shout filth at the hilltop. There is no language so filthy as Spanish.

There are words for all the vile words in English and there are other words and expressions that are used only in countries where blasphemy keeps pace with the austerity of religion. Lieutenant Berrendo was a very devout Catholic. So was the sniper. They were Carlists from Navarra and while both of them cursed and blasphemed when they were angry they regarded it as a sin which they regularly confessed.

As they crouched now behind the boulder watching the captain and listening to what he was shouting, they both disassociated themselves from him and what he was saying. They did not want to have that sort of talk on their consciences on a day in which they might die. Talking thus will not bring luck, the sniper thought. Speaking thus of the *Virgen* is bad luck. This one speaks worse than the Reds.

Julián is dead, Lieutenant Berrendo was thinking. Dead there on the slope on such a day as this is. And this foul mouth stands there bringing more ill fortune with his blasphemies.

Now the captain stopped shouting and turned to Lieutenant Berrendo. His eyes looked stranger than ever.

"Paco," he said, happily, "you and I will go up there."

"Not me."

"What?" The captain had his pistol out again.

I hate these pistol brandishers, Berrendo was thinking. They cannot give an order without jerking a gun out. They probably pull out their pistols when they go to the toilet and order the move they will make.

"I will go if you order me to. But under protest," Lieutenant Berrendo told the captain.

"Then I will go alone," the captain said. "The smell of cowardice is too strong here."

Holding his pistol in his right hand, he strode steadily up the slope. Berrendo and the sniper watched him. He was making no attempt to take any cover and he was looking straight ahead of him at the rocks, the dead horse, and the fresh-dug dirt of the hilltop.

El Sordo lay behind the horse at the corner of the rock, watching the captain come striding up the hill.

Only one, he thought. We get only one. But from his manner of speaking he is *caza mayor.* Look at him walking. Look what an animal. Look at him stride forward. This one is for me. This one I take with me on the trip. This one coming now makes the same voyage I do. Come on, Comrade Voyager. Come striding. Come right along. Come along to meet it. Come on. Keep on walking. Don't slow up. Come right along. Come as thou art coming. Don't stop and look at those. That's right. Don't even look down. Keep on coming with your eyes forward. Look, he has a moustache. What do you think of that? He runs to a moustache, the Comrade Voyager. He is a captain. Look at his sleeves. I said he was *caza mayor*. He has the face of an *Inglés*. Look. With a red face and blond hair and blue eyes. With no cap on and his moustache is yellow. With blue eyes. With pale blue eyes. With pale blue eyes with something wrong with them. With pale blue eyes that don't focus. Close enough. Too close. Yes, Comrade Voyager. Take it, Comrade Voyager.

He squeezed the trigger of the automatic rifle gently and it pounded back three times against his shoulder with the slippery jolt the recoil of a tripoded automatic weapon gives.

The captain lay on his face on the hillside. His left arm was under him. His right arm that had held the pistol was stretched forward of his head. From all down the slope they were firing on the hill crest again.

Crouched behind the boulder, thinking that now he would have to sprint across that open space under fire, Lieutenant Berrendo heard the deep hoarse voice of Sordo from the hilltop.

"*Bandidos!*" the voice came. "*Bandidos!* Shoot me! Kill me!"

On the top of the hill El Sordo lay behind the automatic rifle laughing so that his chest ached, so that he thought the top of his head would burst.

"*Bandidos,*" he shouted again happily. "Kill me, *bandidos!*" Then he shook his head happily. We have lots of company for the Voyage, he thought.

He was going to try for the other officer with the automatic rifle when he would leave the shelter of the boulder. Sooner or later he would have to leave it. Sordo knew that he could never command from there and he thought he had a very good chance to get him.

Just then the others on the hill heard the first sound of the coming of the planes.

El Sordo did not hear them. He was covering the down-slope edge of the boulder with his automatic rifle and he was thinking: when I see him he will be running already and I will miss him if I am not careful. I could shoot behind him all across that stretch. I should swing the gun with him and ahead of him. Or let him start and then get on him and ahead of him. I will try to pick him up there at the edge of the rock and swing just ahead of him. Then he felt a touch on his shoulder and he turned and saw the gray, fear-drained face of Joaquín and he looked where the boy was pointing and saw the three planes coming.

At this moment Lieutenant Berrendo broke from behind the boulder and, with his head bent and his legs plunging, ran down and across the slope to the shelter of the rocks where the automatic rifle was placed.

Watching the planes, Sordo never saw him go.

"Help me to pull this out," he said to Joaquín and the boy dragged the automatic rifle clear from between the horse and the rock.

The planes were coming on steadily. They were in echelon and each second they grew larger and their noise was greater.

"Lie on your backs to fire at them," Sordo said. "Fire ahead of them as they come."

He was watching them all the time. "*Cabrones! Hijos de puta!*" he said rapidly.

"Ignacio!" he said. "Put the gun on the shoulder of the boy. Thou!" to Joaquín, "Sit there and do not move. Crouch over. More. No. More."

He lay back and sighted with the automatic rifle as the planes came on steadily.

"Thou, Ignacio, hold me the three legs of that tripod." They were dangling down the boy's back and the muzzle of the gun was shaking from the jerking of his body that Joaquín could not control as he crouched with bent head hearing the droning roar of their coming.

Lying flat on his belly and looking up into the sky watching them come, Ignacio gathered the legs of the tripod into his two hands and steadied the gun.

"Keep thy head down," he said to Joaquín. "Keep thy head forward."

"Pasionaria says 'Better to die on thy—'" Joaquín was saying to himself as the drone came nearer them. Then he shifted suddenly into "Hail Mary, full of grace, the Lord is with thee; Blessed art thou among women and Blessed is the fruit of thy womb, Jesus. Holy Mary, Mother of God, pray for us sinners now and at the hour of our death. Amen. Holy Mary, Mother of God," he started, then he remembered quickly as the roar came now unbearably and started an act of contrition racing in it, "Oh my God, I am heartily sorry for having offended thee who art worthy of all my love——"

Then there were the hammering explosions past his ears and the gun barrel hot against his shoulder. It was hammering now again and his ears were deafened by the muzzle blast. Ignacio was pulling down hard on the tripod and the barrel was burning his back. It was hammering now in the roar and he could not remember the act of contrition.

All he could remember was at the hour of our death. Amen. At the hour of our death. Amen. At the hour. At the hour. Amen. The others all were firing. Now and at the hour of our death. Amen.

Then, through the hammering of the gun, there was the whistle of the air splitting apart and then in the red black roar the earth rolled under his knees and then waved up to hit him in the face and then dirt and bits of rock were falling all over and Ignacio was lying on him and the gun was lying on him. But he was not dead because the whistle came again and the earth rolled under him with the roar. Then it came again and the earth lurched under his belly and one side of the hilltop rose into the air and then fell slowly over them where they lay.

The planes came back three times and bombed the hilltop but no one on the hilltop knew it. Then the planes machine-gunned the hilltop and went away. As they dove on the hill for the last time with their machine guns hammering, the first plane pulled up and winged over and then each plane did the same and they moved from echelon to V-formation and went away into the sky in the direction of Segovia.

Keeping a heavy fire on the hilltop, Lieutenant Berrendo pushed a patrol up to one of the bomb craters from where they could throw grenades onto the crest. He was taking no chances of any one being alive and waiting for them in the mess that was up there and he threw four grenades into the confusion of dead horses, broken and split rocks, and torn yellow-stained explosive-stinking earth before he climbed out of the bomb crater and walked over to have a look.

No one was alive on the hilltop except the boy Joaquín, who was unconscious under the dead body of Ignacio. Joaquín was bleeding from the nose and from the ears. He had known nothing and had no feeling since he had suddenly been in the very heart of the thunder and the breath had been wrenched from his body when the one bomb struck so close and Lieutenant Berrendo made the sign of the cross and then shot him in the back of the head, as quickly and as gently, if such an abrupt movement can be gentle, as Sordo had shot the wounded horse.

Lieutenant Berrendo stood on the hilltop and looked down the slope at his own dead and then across the country seeing where they had galloped before Sordo had turned at bay here. He noticed all the dispositions that had been made of the troops and then he ordered the dead men's horses to be brought up and the bodies tied across the saddles so that they might be packed in to La Granja.

"Take that one, too," he said. "The one with his hands on the automatic rifle. That should be Sordo. He is the oldest and it was he with the gun. No. Cut the head off and wrap it in a poncho." He considered a minute. "You might as well take all the heads. And of the others below on the slope and where we first found them. Collect the rifles and pistols and pack that gun on a horse."

Then he walked down to where the lieutenant lay who had been killed in the first assault. He looked down at him but did not touch him.

"*Qué cosa más mala es la guerra*," he said to himself, which meant, "What a bad thing war is."

Then he made the sign of the cross again and as he walked down the hill he said five Our Fathers and five Hail Marys for the repose of the soul of his dead comrade. He did not wish to stay to see his orders being carried out.

IV

At the Front Again:
The Allied Invasion of Europe

"This war is only a continuation of the last war. France was not beaten in 1940. France was beaten in 1917. Singapore was not really lost in 1942. It was lost at Gallipoli and on the Somme and in the mud of Passchendaele. Austria was not destroyed in 1938. Austria was destroyed in the battle of Vittorio-Veneto at the end of October in 1918. It was really lost and gone when it failed to beat Italy after Caporetto in the great Austrian victory offensive of the 15th of June, 1918."

—From *Men at War*

"Once we have a war there is only one thing to do. It must be won. For defeat brings on worse things than can ever happen in a war."

—From *Men at War*

Black Ass at the Cross Roads

We had reached the cross roads before noon and had shot a French civilian by mistake. He had run across the field on our right beyond the farmhouse when he saw the first jeep come up. Claude had ordered him to halt and when he had kept on running across the field Red shot him. It was the first man he had killed that day and he was very pleased.

We had all thought he was a German who had stolen civilian clothes, but he turned out to be French. Anyway his papers were French and they said he was from Soissons.

"*Sans doute c'était un Collabo,*" Claude said.

"He ran, didn't he?" Red asked. "Claude told him to halt in good French."

"Put him in the game book as a Collabo," I said. "Put his papers back on him."

"What was he doing up here if he comes from Soissons?" Red asked. "Soissons's way the hell back."

"He fled ahead of our troops because he was a collaborator," Claude explained.

"He's got a mean face." Red looked down at him.

"You spoiled it a little," I said. "Listen, Claude. Put the papers back and leave the money."

"Someone else will take it."

"*You* won't take it," I said. "There will be plenty of money coming through on Krauts."

Then I told them where to put the two vehicles and where to set up shop and sent Onèsime across the field to cross the two roads and get into the shuttered *estaminet* and find out what had gone through on the escape-route road.

Quite a little had gone through, always on the road to the right. I knew plenty more had to come through and I paced the distances back from the road to the two traps we had set up. We were using Kraut weapons so the noise would not alarm them if anyone heard the noise coming up on the cross roads. We set the traps well beyond the cross roads so that we would not louse up the cross roads and make it look like a shambles. We wanted them to hit the cross roads fast and keep coming.

"It is a beautiful *guet-apens*," Claude said and Red asked me what was that. I told him it was only a trap as always. Red said he must remember the word. He now spoke his idea of French about half the time and if given an order perhaps half the time he would answer in what he thought was French. It was comic and I liked it.

It was a beautiful late summer day and there were very few more to come that summer. We lay where we had set up and the two vehicles covered us from behind the manure pile. It was a big rich manure pile and very solid and we lay in the grass behind the ditch and the grass smelled as all summers smell and the two trees made a shade over each trap. Perhaps I had set up too close but you cannot ever be too close if you have fire power and the stuff is going to come through fast. One hundred yards is all right. Fifty yards is ideal. We were closer than that. Of course in that kind of thing it always seems closer.

Some people would disagree with this setup. But we had to figure to get out and back and keep the road as clean looking as possible. There was nothing much you could do about vehicles, but other vehicles coming would normally assume they had been destroyed by aircraft. On this day, though, there was no aircraft. But nobody coming would know there had not been aircraft through here. Anybody making their run on an escape route sees things differently too.

"*Mon Capitaine*," Red said to me. "If the point comes up they will not shoot the shit out of us when they hear these Kraut weapons?"

"We have observation on the road where the point will come from the two vehicles. They'll flag them off. Don't sweat."

"I am not sweating," Red said. "I have shot a proved collaborator. The only thing we have killed today and we will kill many Krauts in this setup. *Pas vrai*, Onie?"

Onèsime said, "*Merde*" and just then we heard a car coming very fast. I saw it come down the beech-tree bordered road. It was an overloaded grey-green camouflaged Volkswagen and it was filled with steel-helmeted people looking as though they were racing to catch a train. There were two aiming stones by the side of the road that I had taken from a wall by the farm, and as the Volkswagen crossed the notch of the cross roads and came toward us on the good straight escape road that crossed in front of us and led up a hill, I said to Red, "Kill the driver at the first stone." To Onèsime I said, "Traverse at body height."

The Volkswagen driver had no control of his vehicle after Red shot. I could not see the expression on his face because of the helmet. His hands relaxed. They did not grasp tight nor hold on the wheel. The machine gun started firing before the driver's hands relaxed and the car went into the ditch spilling the occupants in slow motion. Some were on the road and the second outfit gave them a small carefully hoarded burst. One man rolled over and another started to crawl and while I watched Claude shot them both.

"I think I got that driver in the head," Red said.

"Don't be too fancy."

"She throws a little high at this range," Red said. "I shot for the lowest part of him I could see."

"Bertrand," I called over to the second outfit. "You and your people get them off the road, please. Bring me all the *Feldbuchen* and you hold the money for splitting. Get them off fast. Go on and help, Red. Get them into the ditch."

I watched the road to the west beyond the *estaminet* while the cleaning up was going on. I never watched the cleaning up unless I had to take part in it myself. Watching the cleaning up is bad for you. It is no worse for me than for anyone else. But I was in command.

"How many did you get, Onie?"

"All eight, I think. Hit, I mean."

"At this range—"

"It's not very sporting. But after all it's their machine gun."

"We have to get set now fast again."

"I don't think the vehicle is shot up badly."

"We'll check her afterwards."

"Listen," Red said. I listened, then blew the whistle twice and everybody faded back, Red hauling the last Kraut by one leg with his head shuddering and the trap was set again. But nothing came and I was worried.

We were set up for a simple job of assassination astride an escape route. We were not astride, technically, because we did not have enough people to set up on both sides of the road and we were not technically prepared to cope with armored vehicles. But each trap had two German *Panzerfausten*. They were much more powerful and simpler than the general-issue American bazooka, having a bigger warhead and you could throw away the launching tube; but lately, many that we had found in the German retreat had been booby-trapped and others had been sabotaged. We used only those as fresh as anything in that market could be fresh and we always asked a German prisoner to fire off samples taken at random from the lot.

German prisoners who had been taken by irregulars were often as cooperative as head waiters or minor diplomats. In general we regarded the Germans as perverted Boy Scouts. This is another way of saying they were splendid soldiers. We were not splendid soldiers. We were specialists in a dirty trade. In French we said, *"un métier très sale."*

We knew, from repeated questionings, that all Germans coming through on this escape route were making for Aachen and I knew that all we killed now we would not have to fight in Aachen nor behind the West Wall. This was simple. I was pleased when anything was that simple.

The Germans we saw coming now were on bicycles. There were four of them and they were in a hurry too but they were very tired. They were not cyclist troops. They were just Germans on stolen bicycles. The leading rider saw the fresh blood on the road and then he turned his head and saw the vehicle and he put his weight hard down on his right pedal with his right boot and we opened on him and on the others. A man shot off a bicycle is always a sad thing to see, although not as sad as a horse shot with a man riding him nor a milk cow gut-shot when she walks into a fire fight. But there is something about a man shot off a bicycle at close range that is too intimate. These were four men and four bicycles. It was very intimate and you could hear the thin tragic noise the bicycles made when they went over onto the road and the heavy sound of men falling and the clatter of equipment.

"Get them off the road quick," I said. "And hide the four *vélos.*"

As I turned to watch the road one of the doors of the *estaminet* opened and two civilians wearing caps and working clothes came out each carrying two bottles. They sauntered across the cross roads and turned to come up in the field behind the ambush. They wore sweaters and old coats, corduroy trousers and country boots.

"Keep them covered, Red," I said. They advanced steadily and then raised the bottles high above their heads, one bottle in each hand as they came in.

"For Christ sake, get down," I called, and they got down and came crawling through the grass with the bottles tucked under their arms.

"Nous sommes des copains," one called in a deep voice, rich with alcohol.

"Advance, rum-dumb *copains*, and be recognized," Claude answered.

"We are advancing."

"What do you want out here in the rain?" Onèsime called.

"We bring the little presents."

"Why didn't you give the little presents when I was over there?" Claude asked.

"Ah, things have changed, *camarade.*"

"For the better?"

"*Rudement,*" the first rummy *camarade* said. The other, lying flat and handing us one of the bottles, asked in a hurt tone, "*On dit pas bonjour aux nouveaux camarades?*"

"*Bonjour,*" I said. "*Tu veux battre?*"

"If it's necessary. But we came to ask if we might have the *vélos.*"

"After the fight," I said. "You've made your military service?"

"Naturally."

"Okay. You take a German rifle each and two packs of ammo and go up the road two hundred yards on our right and kill any Germans that get by us."

"Can't we stay with you?"

"We're specialists," Claude said. "Do what the captain says."

"Get up there and pick out a good place and don't shoot back this way."

"Put on these arm bands," Claude said. He had a pocket full of arm bands. "You're *Franc-tireurs.*" He did not add the rest of it.

"Afterwards we can have the *vélos?*"

"One apiece if you don't have to fight. Two apiece if you fight."

"What about the money?" Claude asked. "They're using our guns."

"Let them keep the money."

"They don't deserve it."

"Bring any money back and you'll get your share. *Allez vite. Débine-toi.*"

"*Ceux sont des poivrots pourris,*" Claude said.

"They had rummies in Napoleon's time too."

"It's probable."

"It's certain," I said. "You can take it easy on that."

We lay in the grass and it smelled of true summer and the flies, the ordinary flies and the big blue flies started to come to the dead that were in the ditch and there were butterflies around the edges of the blood on the black-surfaced road. There were yellow butterflies and white butterflies around the blood and the streaks where the bodies had been hauled.

"I didn't know butterflies ate blood," Red said.

"I didn't either."

"Of course when we hunt it's too cold for butterflies."

"When we hunt in Wyoming the picket pin gophers and the prairie dogs are holed up already. That's the fifteenth of September."

"I'm going to watch and see if they really eat it," Red said.

"Want to take my glasses?"

He watched and after a while he said, "I'll be damned if I can tell. But it sure interests them." Then he turned to Onèsime and said, "Piss *pauvre* Krauts, Onie. *Pas de* pistol, *pas de binoculaire.* Fuck-all *rien.*"

"*Assez de sous,*" Onèsime said. "We're doing all right on the money."

"No fucking place to spend it."

"Some day."

"*Je veux* spend *maintenant,*" Red said.

Claude opened one of the two bottles with the cork screw on his Boy Scout German knife. He smelled it and handed it to me.

"*C'est du gnôle.*"

The other outfit had been working on their share. They were our best friends but as soon as we were split they seemed like the others and the vehicles seemed like the rear echelon. You split too easy, I thought. You want to watch that. That's one more thing you can watch.

I took a drink from the bottle. It was very strong raw spirits and all had was fire. I handed it back to Claude who gave it to Red. Tears came into his eyes when he swallowed it.

"What do they make it out of up here, Onie?"

"Potatoes, I think, and parings from horses' hooves they get at the blacksmith shop."

I translated to Red. "I taste everything but the potatoes," he said.

"They age it in rusty nail kegs with a few old nails to give it zest."

"I better take another to take the taste out of my mouth," Red said. "*Mon Capitaine*, should we die together?"

"*Bonjour, toute le monde,*" I said. This was an old joke we had about an Algerian who was about to be guillotined on the pavement outside the Santé who replied with that phrase when asked if he had any last words to say.

"To the butterflies," Onèsime drank.

"To the nail kegs," Claude raised the bottle.

"Listen," Red said and handed the bottle to me. We all heard the noise of a tracked vehicle.

"The fucking jackpot," Red said. "Along ongfong de la patree, le fucking jackpot ou le more." He sang softly, the nail keg juice no good to him now. I took another good drink of the juice as we lay and checked everything and looked up the road to our left. Then it came in sight. It was a Kraut half-track and it was crowded to standing room only.

When you set a trap on an escape route you have four or, if you can afford them, five Teller mines, armed, on the far side of the road. They lie like round checker counters wider than the biggest soup plates and toad squatted in their thick deadliness. They are in a semi-circle, covered with cut grass and connected by a heavy tarred line which may be procured at any ship chandler's. One end of this line is made fast to a kilometer marking, called a *borne*, or to a tenth of a kilometer stone, or any other completely solid object, and the line runs loosely across the road and is coiled in the first or second section of the trap.

The approaching overloaded vehicle was of the type where the driver looks out through slits and its heavy machine guns now showed high in anti-aircraft position. We were all watching it closely as it came nearer, so very overcrowded. It was full of combat S.S. and we could see the collars now and faces were clear then clearer.

"Pull the cord," I called to the second outfit and as the cord took up its slack and commenced to tighten the mines moved out of their semicircle and across the road looking. I thought, like nothing but green grasscovered Teller mines.

Now the driver would see them and stop or he would go on and hit them. You should not attack an armored vehicle while it was moving, but if he braked I could hit him with the big-headed German bazooka.

The half-track came on very fast and now we could see the faces quite clearly. They were all looking down the road where the point would come from. Claude and Onie were white and Red had a twitch in the muscle of his cheek. I felt hollow as always. Then someone in the halftrack saw the blood and the Volkswagen in the ditch and the bodies. They were shouting in German and the driver and the officer with him must have seen the mines across the road and they came to a tearing swerving halt and had started to back when the bazooka hit. It hit while both outfits were firing from the two traps. The people in the halftrack had mines themselves and were hurrying to set up their own road block to cover what had gone through because when the Kraut bazooka hit and the vehicle went up we all dropped our heads and everything rained down as from a fountain. It rained metal and other things. I checked on Claude and Onie and Red and they were all firing. I was firing too with a Smeizer on the slits and my back was wet and I had stuff all over my neck, but I had seen what fountained up. I could not understand why the vehicle had not been blown wide open or overturned. But it just blew straight up. The fifties from the vehicle were firing and there was so much noise you could not hear. No one showed from the halftrack and I thought it was over and was going to wave the fifties off, when someone inside threw a stick grenade that exploded just beyond the edge of the road.

"They're killing their dead," Claude said. "Can I go up and put a couple into her?"

"I can hit her again."

"No. Once was enough. My whole back's tattooed."

"Okay. Go on."

He crawled forward, snaking in the grass under the fire of the fifties and pulled the pin from a grenade and let the lever snap loose and held the grenade smoking grey and then lobbed it underhand up over the side of the half-track. It exploded with a jumping roar and you could hear the fragments whang against the armor.

"Come on out," Claude said in German. A German machine-gun pistol started shooting from the right-hand slit. Red hit the slit twice. The pistol fired again. It was obvious it was not being aimed.

"Come on out," Claude called. The pistol shot again, making a noise like children rattling a stick along a picket fence. I shot back making the same silly noise.

"Come on back, Claude," I said. "You fire on one slit, Red. Onie, you fire on the other."

When Claude came back fast I said, "Fuck that Kraut. We'll use up another one. We can get more. The point will be up anyway."

"This is their rear guard," Onie said. "This vehicle."

"Go ahead and shoot it," I said to Claude. He shot it and there was no front compartment and then they went in after what would be left of the money and the paybooks. I had a drink and waved to the vehicles. The men on the fifties were shaking their hands over their heads like fighters. Then I sat with my back against the tree to think and to look down the road.

They brought what paybooks there were and I put them in a canvas bag with the others. Not one of them was dry. There was a great deal of money, also wet, and Onie and Claude and the other outfit cut off a lot of S.S. patches and they had what pistols were serviceable and some that weren't and put it all in the canvas sack with the red stripes around it.

I never touched the money. That was their business and I thought it was bad luck to touch it anyway. But there was plenty of prize money. Bertrand gave me an Iron Cross, first class, and I put it in the pocket of my shirt. We kept some for a while and then we gave them all away. I never liked to keep anything. It's bad luck in the end. I had stuff for a while that I wished I could have sent back afterwards or to their families.

The outfit looked as though they had been showered by chunks and particles from an explosion in an abattoir and the other people did not look too clean when they came out from the body of the half-track. I did not know how badly I must have looked myself until I noticed how many flies there were around my back and neck and shoulders.

The half-track lay across the road and any vehicle passing would have to slow down. Everyone was rich now and we had lost no one and the place was ruined. We would have to fight on another day and I was sure this was the rear guard and all we would get now would be strays and unfortunates.

"Disarm the mines and pick up everything and we will go back to the farmhouse and clean up. We can interdict the road from there like in the book."

They came in heavily loaded and everyone was very cheerful. We left the vehicles where they were and washed up at the pump in the farm-yard and Red put iodine on the metal cuts and scratches and sifted Sulfa on Onie and Claude and me and then Claude took care of Red.

"Haven't they got anything to drink in that farmhouse?" I asked René.

"I don't know. We've been too busy."

"Get in and see."

He found some bottles of red wine that was drinkable and I sat around and checked the weapons and made jokes. We had very severe discipline but no formality except when we were back at Division or when we wanted to show off.

"*Encore un coup manqué,*" I said. That was a very old joke and it was a phrase that a crook we had with us for a while always uttered when I would let something worthless go by to wait for something good.

"It's terrible," said Claude.

"It's intolerable," said Michel.

"Me, I can go no further," Onèsime said.

"*Moi, je suis la France,*" Red said.

"You fight?" Claude asked him.

"*Pas moi,*" Red answered. "I command."

"You fight?" Claude asked me.

"*Jamais.*"

"Why is your shirt covered with blood?"

"I was attending the birth of a calf."

"Are you a midwife or a veterinary?"

"I give only the name, rank and serial number."

We drank some more wine and watched the road and waited for the point to come up.

"*Où est la* fucking point?" Red asked.

"I am not in their confidence."

"I'm glad it didn't come up while we had the little *accrochage,*" Onie said. "Tell me, *mon Capitaine,* how did you feel when you let the thing go?"

"Very hollow."

"What did you think about?"

"I hoped to Christ it would not trickle out."

"We were certainly lucky they were loaded with stuff."

"Or that they didn't back up and deploy."

"Don't ruin my afternoon," Marcel said.

"Two Krauts on bicycles," Red said. "Approaching from the west."

"Plucky chaps," I said.

"Encore un coup manqué," said Onie.

"Anybody want them?"

Nobody wanted them. They were pedaling steadily, slumped forward and their boots were too big for the pedals.

"I'll try one with the M-1," I said. Auguste handed it to me and I waited until the first German on the bicycle was past the half-track and clear of the trees and then had the sight on him, swung with him and missed.

"Pas bon," said Red and I tried it again swinging further ahead. The German fell in the same disconcerting heartbreaking way and lay in the road with the *vélo* upside down and a wheel still spinning. The other cyclist sprinted on and soon the *copains* were firing. We heard the hard *ta-bung* of their shots which had no effect on the cyclist who kept on pedaling until he was out of sight.

"Copains no bloody *bon,"* Red said.

Then we saw the *copains* falling back to retire onto the main body. The French of the outfit were ashamed and sore.

"On peut les fusiller?" Claude asked.

"No. We don't shoot rummies."

"Encore un coup manqué," said Onie and everybody felt better but not too good.

The first *copain* who had a bottle in his shirt which showed when he stopped and presented arms said, *"Mon Capitaine, on a fait un véritable massacre."*

"Shut up," said Onie. "And hand me your pieces."

"But we were the right flank," the *copain* said in his rich voice.

"You're shit," Claude said. "You venerable alcoholic. Shut up and fuck off."

"Mais on a battu."

"Fought, shit," Marcel said. *"Foute moi le camp."*

"On peut fusiller les copains?" Red asked. He had remembered it like a parrot.

"You shut up too," I said. "Claude, I promised them two *vélos.*"

"It's true," Claude said.

"You and I will go down and give them the worst two and remove the Kraut and the *vélo.* You others keep the road cut."

"It was not like this in the old days," one of the *copains* said.

"Nothing's ever going to be like it was in the old days. You were probably drunk in the old days anyway."

We went first to the German in the road. He was not dead but was shot through both lungs. We took him as gently as we could and laid him down as comfortable as we could and I took off his tunic and shirt and we sifted the wounds with Sulfa and Claude put a field dressing on him. He had a nice face and he did not look more than seventeen. He tried to talk but he couldn't. He was trying to take it the way he'd always heard you should.

Claude got a couple of tunics from the dead and made a pillow for him. Then he stroked his head and held his hand and felt his pulse. The boy was watching him all the time but he could not talk. The boy never looked away from him and Claude bent over and kissed him on the forehead.

"Carry that bicycle off the road," I said to the *copains*.

"*Cette putain guerre*," Claude said. "This dirty whore of a war."

The boy did not know that it was me who had done it to him and so he had no special fear of me and I felt his pulse too and I knew why Claude had done what he had done. I should have kissed him myself if I was any good. It was just one of those things that you omit to do and that stay with you.

"I'd like to stay with him for a little while," Claude said.

"Thank you very much," I said. I went over to where we had the four bicycles behind the trees and the *copains* were standing there like crows.

"Take this one and that one and *foute moi le camp*." I took off their brassards and put them in my pocket.

"But we fought. That's worth two."

"Fuck off," I said. "Did you hear me? Fuck off."

They went away disappointed.

A boy about fourteen came out from the *estaminet* and asked for the new bicycle.

"They took mine early this morning."

"All right. Take it."

"What about the other two?"

"Run along and keep off the road until the column gets up here."

"But you are the column."

"No," I said. "Unfortunately we are not the column."

The boy mounted the bicycle which was undamaged and rode down to the *estaminet*. I walked back under the hot summer sky to the farm-yard to wait for the point. I didn't know how I could feel any worse. But you can all right. I can promise you that.

"Will we go into the big town tonight?" Red asked me.

"Sure. They're taking it now, coming in from the west. Can't you hear it?"

"Sure. You could hear it since noon. Is it a good town?"

"You'll see it as soon as the column gets up and we fit in and go down that road past the *estaminet*." I showed him on the map. "You can see it in about a mile. See the curve before you drop down?"

"Are we going to fight any more?"

"Not today."

"You got another shirt?"

"It's worse than this."

"It can't be worse than this one. I'll wash this one out. If you have to put it on wet it won't hurt on a hot day like this. You feeling bad?"

"Yeah. Very."

"What's holding Claude up?"

"He's staying with the kid I shot until he dies."

"Was it a kid?"

"Yeah."

"Oh shit," Red said.

After a while Claude came back wheeling the two *vélos*. He handed me the boy's *Feldbuch*.

"Let me wash your shirt good too, Claude. I got Onie's and mine washed and they're nearly dry."

"Thanks very much, Red," Claude said. "Is there any of the wine left?"

"We found some more and some sausage."

"Good," Claude said. He had the black ass bad too.

"We're going in the big town after the column overruns us. You can see it only a little more than a mile from here," Red told him.

"I've seen it before," Claude said. "It's a good town."

"We aren't going to fight any more today."

"We'll fight tomorrow."

"Maybe we won't have to."

"Maybe."

"Cheer up."

"Shut up. I'm cheered up."

"Good," Red said. "Take this bottle and the sausage and I'll wash the shirt in no time."

"Thank you very much," Claude said. We were splitting it even between us and neither of us liked our share.

214

The Taking of Paris

(from *Across the River and Into the Trees*)

"Tell me about the last war," the girl said. "Then we will ride in our gondola in the cold wind."

"It was not very interesting," the Colonel said. "To us, of course, such things are always interesting. But there were only three, maybe four, phases that really interested me."

"Why?"

"We were fighting a beaten enemy whose communications had been destroyed. We destroyed many divisions on paper, but they were ghost divisions. Not real ones. They had been destroyed by our tactical aviation before they ever got up. It was only really difficult in Normandy, due to the terrain, and when we made the break for Georgie Patton's armour to go through and held it open on both sides."

"How do you make a break for armour to go through? Tell me, please."

"First you fight to take a town that controls all the main roads. Call the town St. Lo. Then you have to open up the roads by taking other towns and villages. The enemy has a main line of resistance, but he cannot bring up his divisions to counter-attack because the fighter-bombers catch them on the roads. Does this bore you? It bores the hell out of me."

"It does not bore me. I never heard it said understandably before."

"Thank you," the Colonel said. "Are you sure you want more of the sad science?"

"Please," she said. "I love you, you know, and I would like to share it with you."

"Nobody shares this trade with anybody," the Colonel told her. "I'm just telling you how it works. I can insert anecdotes to make it interesting, or plausible."

"Insert some, please."

"The taking of Paris was nothing," the Colonel said. "It was only an emotional experience. Not a military operation. We killed a number of typists and the screen the Germans had left, as they always do, to cover

215

their withdrawal. I suppose they figured they were not going to need a hell of a lot of office workers any more and they left them as soldiers."

"Was it not a great thing?"

"The people of Leclerc, another jerk of the third or fourth water, whose death I celebrated with a magnum of Perrier-Jouet Brut 1942, shot a great number of rounds to make it seem important and because we had given them what they had to shoot with. But it was not important."

"Did you take part in it?"

"Yes," the Colonel said. "I think I could safely say, yes."

"Did you have no great impressions of it? After all, it was Paris and not everyone has taken it."

"The French, themselves, had taken it four days before. But the grand plan of what we called SHAEF, Supreme, get that word, Headquarters of the Allied Expeditionary Forces, which included all the military politicians of the rear, and who wore a badge of shame in the form of a flaming something, while we wore a four-leafed clover as a designation, and for luck, had a master plan for the envelopment of the city. So we could not simply take it.

"Also we had to wait for the possible arrival of General or Field Marshal Bernard Law Montgomery who was unable to close, even, the gap at Falaise and found the going rather sticky and could not quite get there on time."

"You must have missed him," the girl said.

"Oh, we did," the Colonel said. "No end."

"But was there nothing noble or truly happy about it?"

"Surely," the Colonel told her. "We fought from Bas Meudon, and then the Porte de Saint Cloud, through streets I knew and loved and we had no deads and did as little damage as possible. At the Étoile I took Elsa Maxwell's butler prisoner. It was a very complicated operation. He had been denounced as a Japanese sniper. A new thing. Several Parisians were alleged to have been killed by him. So we sent three men to the roof where he had taken refuge and he was an Indo-China boy."

"I begin to understand a little. But it is disheartening."

"It is always disheartening as hell. But you are not supposed to have a heart in this trade."

"But do you think it was the same in the time of the Grand Captains?"

"I am quite sure it was worse."

"But you got your hand honorably?"

"Yes. Very honorably. On a rocky, bare-assed hill."

"Please let me feel it," she said.

"Just be careful around the center," the Colonel said. "It's split there and it still cracks open."

"You ought to write," the girl said. "I mean it truly. So someone would know about such things."

"No," the Colonel disagreed. "I have not the talent for it and I know too much. Almost any liar writes more convincingly than a man who was there."

"But other soldiers wrote."

"Yes. Maurice de Saxe. Frederick the Great. Mr. T'sun Su."

"But soldiers of our time."

"You use the word our with facility. I like it though."

"But didn't many modern soldiers write?"

"Many. But did you ever read them?"

"No. I have read mostly the classics and I read the illustrated papers for the scandals. Also, I read your letters."

"Burn them," the Colonel said. "They are worthless."

"Please. Don't be rough."

"I won't. What can I tell you that won't bore you?"

"Tell me about when you were a General."

"Oh, that," he said and motioned to the *Gran Maestro* to bring champagne. It was Roederer Brut '42 and he loved it.

"When you are a general you live in a trailer and your Chief of Staff lives in a trailer, and you have bourbon whisky when other people do not have it. Your G's live in the C.P. I'd tell you what G's are, but it would bore you. I'd tell you about G1, G2, G3, G4, G5 and on the other side there is always Kraut-6. But it would bore you. On the other hand, you have a map covered with plastic material, and on this you have three regiments composed of three battalions each. It is all marked in colored pencil.

"You have boundary lines so that when the battalions cross their boundaries they will not then fight each other. Each battalion is composed of five companies. All should be good, but some are good, and some are not so good. Also you have divisional artillery and a battalion of tanks and many spare parts. You live by co-ordinates."

He paused while the *Gran Maestro* poured the Roederer Brut '42.

"From Corps," he translated, unlovingly, *cuerpo d'Armata*, "they tell you what you must do, and then you decide how to do it. You dictate the orders or, most often, you give them by telephone. You ream out people you respect, to make them do what you know is fairly impossible, but is ordered. Also, you have to think hard, stay awake late and get up early."

"And you won't write about this? Not even to please me?"

"No," said the Colonel. "Boys who were sensitive and cracked and kept all their valid first impressions of their day of battle, or their three days, or even their four, write books. They are good books but can be dull if you have been there. Then others write to profit quickly from the war they never fought in. The ones who ran back to tell the news. The news is hardly exact. But they ran quickly with it. Professional writers who had jobs that prevented them from fighting wrote of combat that they could not understand, as though they had been there. I do not know what category of sin that comes under."

*   *   *

"I don't know what to tell you," the Colonel said. "Everything about war bores those who have not made it. Except the tales of the liars."

"I would like to know about the taking of Paris."

"Why? Because I told you that you looked like Marie Antoinette in the tumbril?"

"No. I was complimented by that and I know we are a little alike in profile. But I have never been in any tumbril, and I would like to hear about Paris. When you love someone and he is your hero, you like to hear about the places and the things."

"Please turn your head," the Colonel said, "and I will tell you. *Gran Maestro* is there any more in that wretched bottle?"

"No," the *Gran Maestro* answered.

"Then bring another."

"I have one already iced."

"Good. Serve it. Now, Daughter, we parted from the column of the General Leclerc at Clamart. They went to Montrouge and the Porte d'Orléans and we went directly to Bas Meudon and secured the bridge of the Porte de Saint Cloud. Is this too technical and does it bore you?"

"No."

"It would be better with a map."

"Go on."

"We secured the bridge and established a bridge-head on the other side of the river and we threw the Germans, living and dead, who had defended the bridge, into the Seine River," he stopped. "It was a token defense of course. They should have blown it. We threw all these Germans into the River Seine. They were nearly all office workers, I believe."

"Go on."

"The next morning, we were informed that the Germans had strong points at various places, and artillery on Mount Valérien, and that tanks

218

were roaming the streets. A portion of this was true. We were also requested not to enter too rapidly as the General Leclerc was to take the city. I complied with this request and entered as slowly as I could."

"How do you do that?"

"You hold up your attack two hours and you drink champagne whenever it is offered to you by patriots, collaborators or enthusiasts."

"But was there nothing wonderful nor great, the way it is in books?"

"Of course. There was the city itself. The people were very happy. Old general officers were walking about in their mothballed uniforms. We were very happy, too, not to have to fight."

"Did you not have to fight at all?"

"Only three times. Then not seriously."

"But was that all you had to fight to take such a city?"

"Daughter, we fought twelve times from Rambouillet to enter the city. But only two of them were worth describing as fights. Those at Toussus le Noble and at LeBuc. The rest was the necessary garnishing of a dish. I really did not need to fight at all except at those two places."

The Valhalla Express

(from *Across the River and Into the Trees*)

Death is a lot of shit, he thought. It comes to you in small fragments that hardly show where it has entered. It comes, sometimes, atrociously. It can come from unboiled water; an un-pulled-up mosquito boot, or it can come with the great, white-hot, clanging roar we have lived with. It comes in small cracking whispers that precede the noise of the automatic weapon. It can come with the smoke-emitting arc of the grenade, or the sharp, cracking drop of the mortar.

I have seen it come, loosening itself from the bomb rack, and falling with that strange curve. It comes in the metallic rending crash of a vehicle, or the simple lack of traction on a slippery road.

It comes in bed to most people, I know, like love's opposite number. I have lived with it nearly all my life and the dispensing of it has been my trade. But what can I tell this girl now on this cold, windy morning in the Gritti Palace Hotel?

"What would you like to know, Daughter?" he asked her.

"Everything."

"All right," the Colonel said. "Here goes."

They lay on the pleasantly hard, new-made bed with their legs pressed tight against one another, and her head was on his chest, and her hair spread across his old hard neck; and he told her.

"We landed without much opposition. They had the true opposition at the other beach. Then we had to link up with the people who had been dropped, and take and secure various towns, and then we took Cherbourg. This was difficult, and had to be done very fast, and the orders were from a General called Lightning Joe that you never would have heard of. Good General."

"Go on, please. You spoke about Lightning Joe before."

"After Cherbourg we had everything. I took nothing but an Admiral's compass because I had a small boat at that time on Chesapeake Bay. But we had all the Wehrmacht stamped Martell and some people had as much as six million German printed French francs. They were good until a year ago, and at that time they were worth fifty to the dollar, and many a man has a tractor now instead of simply one mule who knew how to send them home through his Esses, or sometimes his G's.

"I never stole anything except the compass because I thought it was bad luck to steal, unnecessarily, in war. But I drank the cognac and I used to try to figure out the different corrections on the compass when I had time. The compass was the only friend I had, and the telephone was my life. We had more wire strung than there are cunts in Texas."

"Please keep telling me and be as little rough as you can. I don't know what the word means and I don't want to know."

"Texas is a big state," the Colonel said. "That is why I used it and its female population as a symbol. You cannot say more cunts than Wyoming because there are less than thirty thousand there, perhaps, hell, make it fifty, and there was a lot of wire, and you kept stringing it and rolling it up, and stringing it again."

"Go on."

"We will cut to the break-through," the Colonel said. "Please tell me if this bores you."

"No."

"So we made the mucking break-through," the Colonel said, and now his head was turned to her head, and he was not lecturing; he was confessing.

"The first day most of them came over and dropped the Christmas tree ornaments that confuse the other people's radar and it was called off. We were ready to go but they called it off. Quite properly I am sure. I love the very highest brass like I love the pig's you know."

"Tell it to me and don't be bad."

"Conditions were not propitious," the Colonel said. "So the second day we were for it, as our British cousins, who could not fight their way out of a wet tissue towel, say, and over came the people of the wild, blue yonder.

"They were still taking off from the fields where they lived on that green-grassed aircraft carrier that they called England, when we saw the first of them.

"Shining, bright and beautiful, because they had scraped the invasion paint by then, or maybe they had not. My memory is not exact about this part.

"Anyway, Daughter, you could see the line of them going back toward the east further than you could see. It was like a great train. They were high in the sky and never more beautiful. I told my S-2 that we should call them the Valhalla Express. Are you tired of it?"

"No. I can see the Valhalla Express. We never saw it in such numbers. But we saw it. Many times."

"We were back two thousand yards from where we were to take off from. You know what two thousand yards is, Daughter, in a war when you are attacking?"

"No. How could I?"

"Then the front part of the Valhalla Express dropped coloured smoke and turned and went home. This smoke was dropped accurately, and clearly showed the target which was the Kraut positions. They were good positions and it *might* have been impossible to move him out of them without something mighty and picturesque such as we were experiencing.

"Then, Daughter, the next sections of the Valhalla Express dropped everything in the world on the Krauts and where they lived and worked to hold us up. Later it looked as though all of the earth had erupted and the prisoners that we took shook as a man shakes when his malaria hits him. They were very brave boys from the Sixth Parachute Division and they all shook and could not control it though they tried.

"So you can see it was a good bombing. Just the thing we always need in this life. Make them tremble in the fear of justice and of might.

"So then daughter, not to bore you, the wind was from the east and the smoke began to blow back in our direction. The heavies were bombing on the smoke line and the smoke line was now over us. Therefore they bombed us the same as they had bombed the Krauts. First it was the heavies, and no one need ever worry about hell who was there that day. Then, to really make the break-through good and to leave as few people as possible on either side, the mediums came over and bombed who was left. Then we made the break-through as soon as the Valhalla Express had gone home, stretching in its beauty and its majesty from that part of France to all over England."

If a man has a conscience, the Colonel thought, he might think about air-power some time.

"Give me a glass of that Valpolicella," the Colonel said, and remembered to add, "please."

"Excuse me," he said. "Be comfortable, honey dog, please. You asked me to tell you."

"I'm not your honey dog. That must be someone else."

"Correct. You're my last and true and only love. Is that correct? But you asked me to tell you."

222

"Please tell me," the girl said. "I'd like to be your honey dog if I knew how to do it. But I am only a girl from this town that loves you."

"We'll operate on that," the Colonel said. "And I love you. I probably picked up that phrase in the Philippines."

"Probably," the girl said. "But I would rather be your straight girl."

"You are," the Colonel said. "Complete with handles and with the flag on top."

"Please don't be rough," she said. "Please love me true and tell me as true as you can, without hurting yourself in any way."

"I'll tell you true," he said. "As true as I can tell and let it hurt who it hurts. It is better that you hear it from me, if you have curiosity on this subject, than that you read it in some book with stiff covers."

"Please don't be rough. Just tell me true and hold me tight and tell me true until you are purged of it; if that can be."

"I don't need to purge," he said. "Except heavies being used tactically. I have nothing against them if they use them right even if they kill you. But for ground support give me a man like Pete Quesada. There is a man who will boot them in."

"Please."

"If you ever want to quit a beat-up character like me that guy could give you ground support."

"You are not beat-up, whatever that is, and I love you."

"Please give me two tablets from that bottle and pour the glass of Valpolicella that you neglected to pour, and I will tell you some of the rest of it."

"You don't have to. You don't have to tell me and I know now it is not good for you. Especially not the Valhalla Express day. I am not an inquisitor; or whatever the female of inquisitor is. Let us just lie quietly and look out of the window, and watch and see what happens on our Grand Canal."

"Maybe we better. Who gives a damn about the war anyway."

The Pistol-Slappers

(from *Across the River and Into the Trees*)

"There were more maps in the room than Our Lord could read on his best day," the Colonel continued. "There were the Big Picture, the Semi-Big Picture and the Super-Big-Picture. All these people pretended to understand them, as did the boys with the pointers, a sort of half-assed billiard cue that they used for explanation."

"Don't say rough words. I don't know, even, what half-assed means."

"Shortened, or abbreviated in an inefficient manner," the Colonel explained. "Or deficient as an instrument, or in character. It's an old word. You could probably find it in Sanskrit."

"Please tell me."

"What for? Why should I perpetuate ignominy just with my mouth?"

"I'll write it if you want. I can write truly what I hear or think. I would make mistakes of course."

"You are a lucky girl if you can write truly what you hear or think. But don't you ever write one word of this."

He resumed, "The place is full of correspondents dressed according to their taste. Some are cynical and some are extremely eager.

"To ride herd on them, and to wield the pointers, there is a group of pistol-slappers. We call a pistol-slapper a nonfighting man, disguised in uniform, or you might even call it costume, who gets an erection every time the weapon slaps against his thighs. Incidentally, Daughter, the weapon, not the old pistol, the real pistol, has missed more people in combat than probably any weapon in the world. Don't ever let anyone give you one unless you want to hit people on the head with it in Harry's Bar."

"I never wanted to hit anyone; except perhaps Andrea."

"If you ever hit Andrea, hit him with the barrel; not with the butt. The butt is awfully slow, and it misses and if it lands you get blood on your hands when you put the gun away. Also please do not ever hit Andrea because he is my friend. I do not think he would be easy to hit either."

"No. I do not think so either. Please tell me some more about the meeting, or the assembly. I think I could recognize a pistol slapper now. But I would like to be checked out more thoroughly."

"Well, the pistol-slappers, in all the pride of their pistol-slappery, were awaiting the arrival of the great General who was to explain the operation.

"The correspondents were muttering, or twittering, and the intelligent ones were glum or passively cheerful. Everybody sat on folding chairs as for a Chautauqua lecture. I'm sorry about these local terms; but we are a local people.

"In comes the General. He is no pistol-slapper, but a big businessman; an excellent politician, the executive type. The Army is the biggest business, at that moment, in the world. He takes the half-assed pointer, and he shows us, with complete conviction, and without forebodings, exactly what the attack will be, why we are making it, and how facilely it will succeed. There is no problem."

"Go on," the girl said. "Please let me fill your glass and you, please look at the light on the ceiling."

"Fill it and I'll look at the light and I will go on.

"This high pressure salesman, and I say this with no disrespect, but with admiration for all his talents, or his talent, also told what we would have of the necessary. There would be no lack of anything. The organization called SHAEF was then based on a town named Versailles outside of Paris. We would attack to the east of Aachen a distance of some 380 kilometers from where they were based.

"An army can get to be huge; but you can close up a little bit. They finally went as far forward as Rheims which was 240 kilometers from the fighting. That was many months later.

"I understand the necessity of the big executive being removed from contact with his working people. I understand about the size of the army and the various problems. I even understand logistics which is not difficult. But no one ever commanded from that far back in history."

The Chain of Command

(from *Across the River and Into the Trees*)

"Listen, Daughter," the Colonel said. "Now we will cut out all references to glamour and to high brass, even from Kansas, where the brass grows higher than osage-orange trees along your own road. It bears a fruit you can't eat and it is purely Kansan. Nobody but Kansans ever had anything to do with it; except maybe us who fought. We ate them every day. Osage oranges," he added. "Only we called them K Rations. They weren't bad. C Rations were bad. Ten in ones were good.

"So we fought. It is dull but it is informative. This is the way it goes if anyone is ever interested; which I doubt.

"It goes like this: 1300 Red S-3: White jumped off on time. Red said they were waiting to tie in behind White. 1305 (that is one o'clock and five minutes after in the afternoon, if you can remember that, Daughter) Blue S-3, you know what an S-3 is I hope, says, 'Let us know when you move.' Red said they were waiting to tie in behind White.

"You can see how easy it is," the Colonel told the girl. "Everybody ought to do it before breakfast."

"We cannot all be combat infantrymen," the girl told him softly. "I respect it more than anything except good, honest fliers. Please talk, I'm taking care of you."

"Good fliers are very good and should be respected as such," the Colonel said.

He looked up at the light on the ceiling and he was completely desperate at the remembrance of his loss of his battalions, and of individual people. He could never hope to have such a regiment, ever. He had not built it. He had inherited it. But, for a time, it had been his great joy. Now every second man in it was dead and the others nearly all were wounded. In the belly, the head, the feet or the hands, the neck, the back, the lucky buttocks, the unfortunate chest and the other places. Tree burst wounds hit men where they would never be wounded in open country. And all the wounded were wounded for life.

226

"It was a good regiment," he said. "You might even say it was a beautiful regiment until I destroyed it under other people's orders."

"But why do you have to obey them when you know better?"

"In our army you obey like a dog," the Colonel explained. "You always hope you have a good master."

"What kind of masters do you get?"

"I've only had two good ones so far. After I reached a certain level of command, many nice people, but only two good masters."

"Is that why you are not a General now? I would love it if you were a General."

"I'd love it too," the Colonel said. "But maybe not with the same intensity."

"Would you try to sleep, please, to please me?"

"Yes," the Colonel said.

"You see, I thought that if you slept you might get rid of them, just being asleep."

"Yes. Thank you very much," he said.

There was nothing to it, gentlemen. All a man need ever do is obey.

The Ivy Leaf

(from *Across the River and Into the Trees*)

The girl was asleep, still holding his bad hand, that he despised, and he could feel her breathe, as the young breathe when they are easily asleep.

The Colonel told her all about it; but he did not utter it.

So after I had the privilege of hearing General Walter Bedell Smith explain the facility of the attack, we made it. There was the Big Red One, who believed their own publicity. There was the Ninth, which was a better Division than we were. There was us, who had always done it when they asked for you to do it.

We had no time to read comic books, and we had no time for practically nothing, because we always moved before first light. This is difficult and you have to throw away the Big Picture and be a division.

We wore a four-leaf clover, which meant nothing except among ourselves, who all loved it. And every time I ever see it the same thing happens in my inner guts. Some people thought that it was ivy. But it was not. It was a four-leaf clover disguised as ivy.

The orders were that we would attack with the Big Red One, the First Infantry Division of the Army of the United States, and they, and their Calypso singing PRO never let you forget it. He was a nice guy. And it was his job.

But you get fed up with horse-shit unless you like the aroma or the taste. I never liked it. Although I loved to walk through cow-shit when I was a kid and feel it between my toes. But horse-shit bores you. It bores me very rapidly, and I can detect it at over one thousand yards.

So we attacked, the three of us in line, exactly where the Germans wished us to attack. We will not mention General Walter Bedell Smith any further. He is not the villain. He only made the promises and explained how it would go. There are no villains, I presume, in a Democracy. He was only just as wrong as hell. Period, he added in his mind.

The patches had all been removed even as far back as the rear eche-

228

lon so that no Kraut would know that it was us, the three he knew so well, who were going to attack. We were going to attack with the three of us in line and nothing in reserve. I won't try to explain what that means, Daughter. But it isn't any good. And the place we were going to fight in, which I had taken a good look at, was going to be Passchendaele with tree bursts. I say that too much. But I think it too much.

The poor bloody twenty-eighth which was up on our right had been bogged down for some time and so there was pretty accurate information available about what conditions in those woods were going to be like. I think we could conservatively describe them as unfavorable.

Then we were ordered to commit one regiment before the attack started. That means that the enemy will get at least one prisoner which makes all the taking off of the Divisional patches silly. They would be waiting for us. They would be waiting for the old four leaf clover people who would go straight to hell like a mule and do it for one hundred and five days. Figures of course mean nothing to civilians. Nor to the characters from SHAEF we never saw ever in these woods. Incidentally, and of course these occurrences are always incidental at the SHAEF level, the regiment was destroyed. It was no one's bloody fault, especially not the fault of the man who commanded it. He was a man I would be glad to spend half my time in hell with; and may yet.

It certainly would be odd if instead of going to hell, as we always counted on, we should go to one of those Kraut joints like Valhalla and not be able to get along with the people. But maybe we could get a corner table with Rommel and Udet and it would be just like any winter-sports hotel. It will probably be hell though and I don't even believe in hell.

Well anyway this regiment was rebuilt as American regiments always are by the replacement system. I won't describe it since you can always read about it in a book by somebody who was a replacement. It boils down, or distills, to the fact you stay in until you are hit badly or killed or go crazy and get section-eighted. But I guess it is logical and as good as any other, given the difficulties of transport. However it leaves a core of certain un-killed characters who know what the score is and no one of these characters liked the look of these woods much.

You could sum up their attitude in this phrase, "Don't shit me, Jack."

And since I had been an un-killed character for around twenty-eight years I could understand their attitude. But they were soldiers, so most of them got killed in those woods and when we took the three towns that looked so innocent and were really fortresses. They were just built to tempt us and we had no word on them at all. To continue to use the silly parlance of my trade: this could or could not be faulty intelligence.

"I feel terribly about the regiment," the girl said. She had wakened and spoken straight from sleep.

"Yes," said the Colonel. "So do I. Let's drink to it once. Then you go to sleep, Daughter, please. The war is over and forgotten."

The Dead

(from *Across the River and Into the Trees*)

The first day there, we lost the three battalion commanders. One killed in the first twenty minutes and the other two hit later. This is only a statistic to a journalist. But good battalion commanders have never yet grown on trees; not even Christmas trees which was the basic tree of that woods. I do not know how many times we lost company commanders how many times over. But I could look it up.

They aren't made, nor grown, as fast as a crop of potatoes is either. We got a certain amount of replacements but I can remember thinking that it would be simpler, and more effective, to shoot them in the area where they detrucked, than to have to try to bring them back from where they would be killed and bury them. It takes men to bring them back, and gasoline, and men to bury them. These men might just as well be fighting and get killed too.

There was snow, or something, rain or fog, all the time and the roads had been mined as many as fourteen mines deep in certain stretches, so when the vehicles churned down to a new string deeper, in another part of the mud, you were always losing vehicles and, of course, the people that went with them.

Besides just mortaring it all to hell and having all the firelanes taped for machine gun, and automatic weapon fire, they had the whole thing worked out and canalized so however you out-thought them you ran right into it. They also shelled you with heavy artillery fire and with at least one railway gun.

It was a place where it was extremely difficult for a man to stay alive even if all he did was be there. And we were attacking all the time, and every day.

Let's not think about it. The hell with it. Maybe two things I will think about and get rid of them. One was a bare-assed piece of hill that you had to cross to get into Grosshau.

Just before you had to make this run, which was under observation with fire by 88's, there was a little piece of dead ground where they could only hit you with a howitzer, only interdicting fires, or, from the right by mortar. When we cleaned it up we found they had good observation for their mortars there too.

This was a comparatively safe place, I'm really not lying, not me nor anybody else. You can't fool those that were in Hurtgen, and if you lied they would know it the minute you opened your mouth, Colonel or no Colonel.

We met a truck at this place and slowed up, and he had the usual grey face and he said, "Sir, there is a dead GI in the middle of the road up ahead, and every time any vehicle goes through they have to run over him, and I'm afraid it is making a bad impression on the troops."

"We'll get him off the road."

So we got him off the road.

And I can remember just how he felt, lifting him, and how he had been flattened and the strangeness of his flatness.

Then there was one other thing, I remember. We had put an awful lot of white phosphorus on the town before we got in for good, or whatever you would call it. That was the first time I ever saw a German dog eating a roasted German kraut. Later on I saw a cat working on him too. It was a hungry cat, quite nice looking, basically. You wouldn't think a good German cat would eat a good German soldier, would you, Daughter? Or a good German dog eat a good German soldier's ass which had been roasted by white phosphorus.

How many could you tell like that? Plenty, and what good would they do? You could tell a thousand and they would not prevent war. People would say we are not fighting the krauts and besides the cat did not eat me nor my brother Gordon, because he was in the Pacific. Maybe land crabs ate Gordon. Or maybe he just deliquesced.

In Hurtgen they just froze up hard; and it was so cold they froze up with ruddy faces. Very strange. They all were grey and yellow like waxworks, in the summer. But once the winter really came they had ruddy faces.

Real soldiers never tell any one what their own dead looked like, he told the portrait. And I'm through with this whole subject. And what about that company dead up the draw? What about them, professional soldier?

They're dead, he said. And I can hang and rattle.

Now who would join me in a glass of Valpolicella? What time do you think I should wake your opposite number, you girl? We have to get to that jewelry place. And I look forward to making jokes and to talking of the most cheerful things.

What's cheerful, portrait? You ought to know. You're smarter than I am, although you haven't been around as much.

All right, canvas girl, the Colonel told her, not saying it aloud, we'll drop the whole thing and in eleven minutes I will wake the live girl up, and we will go out on the town, and be cheerful and leave you here to be wrapped.

I didn't mean to be rude. I was just joking roughly. I don't wish to be rude ever because I will be living with you from now on. I hope, he added, and drank a glass of the wine.

Losing Your Son to War

(from *Islands in the Stream*)

"Look, darling, I go to sea occasionally because I am a painter of marine life for the Museum of Natural History. Not even war must interfere with our studies."

"They are sacred," she said. "I'll remember that lie and stick with it. Tom, you truly don't care for her at all?"

"Not at all."

"You still love me?"

"Didn't I give any signs of it?"

"It could have been a role. The one of the always faithful lover no matter what whores I find you with. Thee hasn't been faithful to me, Cynara, in thy fashion."

"I always told you that you were too literate for your own good. I was through with that poem when I was nineteen."

"Yes, and I always told you that if you would paint and work at it as you should, instead of making fantasies and falling in love with other people—"

"Marrying them, you mean."

"No. Marrying them is bad enough. But you fall in love with them and then I don't respect you."

"That's that old lovely one I remember. 'And then I don't respect you.' I'll buy that one at any price you put on it and take it out of circulation."

"I respect you. And you don't love her, do you?"

"I love you and respect you and I don't love her."

"That's wonderful. I'm so glad I'm so ill and that I missed the plane."

"I really do respect you, you know, and I respect every damned fool thing you do or did."

"And you treat me wonderfully and keep all your promises."

"What was the last one?"

"I don't know. If it was a promise you broke it."

"Would you want to skip it, beauty?"

"I'd like to have skipped it."

"Maybe we could. We skipped most things."

"No. That's untrue. There's visible evidence on that. But you think making love to a woman is enough. You never think about her wanting to be proud of you. Nor about small tendernesses."

"Nor about being a baby like the men you love and care for."

"Couldn't you be more needing and make me necessary and not be so damned give it and take it and take it away I'm not hungry."

"What did we come out here for? Moral lectures?"

"We came out here because I love you and I want you to be worthy of yourself."

"And of you and God and all other abstractions. I'm not even an abstract painter. You'd have asked Toulouse-Lautrec to keep away from brothels and Gauguin not to get the syphilis and Baudelaire to get home early. I'm not as good as they were but the hell with you."

"I never was like that."

"Sure you were. Along with your work. Your goddam hours of work."

"I would have given it up."

"Sure, I know you would. And sung in night clubs and I could be the bouncer. Do you remember when we planned that?"

"What have you heard from Tom?"

"He's fine," the man said and felt the strange prickling go over his skin.

"He hasn't written me in three weeks. You'd think he'd write his mother. He always was so good about writing."

"You know how it is with kids in a war. Or maybe they're holding up all mail. Sometimes they do."

"Do you remember when he couldn't speak any English?"

"And he had his gang at Gstaad? And up in the Engadine and at Zug?"

"Do you have any new pictures of him?"

"Only that one you have."

"Could we have a drink? What do you drink here?"

"Anything you want. I'll go and find the boy. The wine is in the cellar."

"Please don't be gone long."

"That's a funny thing to say to each other."

"Please don't be gone long," she repeated. "Did you hear it? And I never asked you to get in early. That wasn't the trouble and you know it."

"I know it," he said. "And I won't be gone long."

"Maybe the boy could make something to eat, too."

"Maybe he could," Thomas Hudson said. Then to the cat, "You stay with her, Boise."

Now, he thought. Why did I say that? Why did I lie? Why did I do that breaking it gently thing? Did I want to keep my grief for myself, as Willie said? Am I that sort of guy?

Well, you did it, he thought. How do you tell a mother that her boy is dead when you've just made love to her again? How do you tell yourself your boy is dead? You used to know all the answers. Answer me that.

There aren't any answers. You should know that by now. There aren't any answers at all.

"Tom," her voice called. "I'm lonely and the cat isn't you, even though he thinks he is."

"Put him on the floor. The boy's gone to the village and I'm getting ice."

"I don't care about the drink."

"Neither do I," he said and came back into the room walking on the tiled floor until he felt the matting. He looked at her and she was still there.

"You don't want to talk about him," she said.

"No."

"Why? I think it's better."

"He looks too much like you."

"That isn't it," she said. "Tell me. Is he dead?"

"Sure."

"Please hold me tight. I *am* ill now." He felt her shaking and he knelt by the chair and held her and felt her tremble. Then she said, "And poor you. Poor, poor you."

After a time she said, "I'm sorry for everything I ever did or said."

"Me, too."

"Poor you and poor me."

"Poor everybody," he said and did not add, "poor Tom."

"What can you tell me?"

"Nothing. Just that."

"I suppose we'll learn how to take it."

"Maybe."

"I wish I could break down but I'm just hollow sick."

"I know."

"Does it happen to everybody?"

"I suppose so. Anyway it can only happen to us once."

"And now it's like in a house of the dead."

"I'm sorry I didn't tell you when I saw you."

"That's all right," she said. "You always put things off. I'm not sorry."

"I wanted you so damned much and I was selfish and stupid."

"You weren't selfish. We always loved each other. We only made mistakes."

"I made the worst ones."

"No. We both made them. Let's not fight anymore ever, though." Something was happening to her and then finally she cried and said, "Oh, Tommy, all of a sudden I just can't stand it."

"I know," he said. "My sweet, good lovely beauty. I can't stand it either."

"We were so young and stupid and we were both beautiful and Tommy was so damned beautiful—"

"Like his mother."

"And now there'll never be any visible evidence."

"My poor dearest love."

"And what will we do?"

"You do what you're doing and I'll do what I'm doing."

"Couldn't we be together for a while?"

"Only if this wind keeps up."

"Then let it blow. Do you think making love is wicked?"

"I don't think Tom would disapprove."

"No. Surely no."

"Do you remember skiing with him on your shoulders and how we'd sing coming down through the orchard behind the inn in the dusk?"

"I remember everything."

"So do I," she said. "And why were we so stupid?"

"We were rivals as well as lovers."

"I know it and we shouldn't have been. But you don't love anyone else, do you? Now that that's all we have?"

"No. Truly."

"I don't either really. Do you think we could take each other back?"

"I don't know whether it would work. We could try it."

"How long will the war be?"

"Ask the man who owns one."

"Will it be years?"

"A couple, anyway."

"Are you liable to be killed too?"

"Very."

"That's not good."

"And if I'm not?"

"I don't know. Now Tom's gone we wouldn't start being bitter and bad again?"

"I could try not to. I'm not bitter and I've learned how to handle the bad. Really."

237

"What? With whores?"

"I guess so. But I wouldn't need them if we were together."

"You always did put things so prettily."

"See? Let's not start it."

"No. Not in the house of the dead."

"You said that once."

"I know," she said. "I'm sorry. But I don't know how to put it any other way and mean the same thing. It's started to get numb already."

"It will get number," he said. "Numb is as bad as at the start. But it will get number."

"Will you tell me every bad thing you know about it so mine will get numb quicker?"

"Sure," he said. "Christ, I love you."

"You always did," she said. "Now tell me."

He was sitting at her feet and he did not look at her. He looked at Boise the cat, who was lying in a patch of sunlight on the matting. "He was shot down by a flak ship in a routine sweep off Abbeville."

"Did he bail out?"

"No. The kite burned. He must have been hit."

"I hope he was," she said. "I hope so much he was."

"It's almost sure he was. He had time to bail out."

"You're telling me the truth? His chute didn't burn?"

"No," he lied, thinking that was enough for today.

"Who did you hear it from?"

He told her the name of the man. "Then it's true," she said. "I don't have a son anymore and neither do you. I suppose we can learn about that. Do you know anything else?"

"No," he told her, as truly as possible.

"And we just go on?"

"That's it."

"With what?"

"With nothing," he said.

SELECTED WAR
CORRESPONDENCE

V

World War I and Its Aftermath

"You know they say there isn't anything funny about this war and there isn't. I wouldn't say it was hell, because that's been a bit overworked since Gen. Sherman's time, but there have been about 8 times when I would have welcomed Hell. Just on the chance that it couldn't come up to the phase of war I was experiencing. For example. In the trenches during an attack when a shell makes a direct hit in a group where you are standing. Shells aren't bad except direct hits. You must take chances on the fragments of the bursts. But when there is a direct hit your pals get spattered all over you. Spattered is literal. During the six days I was up in the Front line trenches, only 50 yds from the Austrians, I got the rep. of having a charmed life. The rep of having one doesn't mean much but having one does! I hope I have one."

—To his family, while recovering
from trench mortar wounds,
Milan, August 18, 1918

Popular in Peace—Slacker in War

The Toronto Star Weekly
MARCH 13, 1920

During the late friction with Germany a certain number of Torontonians of military age showed their desire to assist in the conduct of the war by emigrating to the States to give their all to laboring in munition plants. Having amassed large quantities of sheckels through their patriotic labor, they now desire to return to Canada and gain fifteen percent on their United States money.

Through a desire to aid these morally courageous souls who supplied the sinews of war we have prepared a few hints on "How to Be Popular Although a Slacker."

It were wise, of course, for the returning munitioneer to come back to a different town than the one he left. Citizens of his own city might have misunderstood his motives in exposing himself to the dangers of the munition works.

The first difficulty to be surmounted will be the C.E.F. [Canadian Expeditionary Force] overseas badge. This is easily handled, however. If anyone asks you why you do not wear your button, reply haughtily: "I do not care to advertise my military service!"

This reply will make the man who was out since Mons and is brazenly wearing his button feel very cheap.

When you are asked by a sweet young thing at a dance if you ever met Lieut. Smithers, of the R.A.F., in France or if you happened to run into Maj. MacSwear, of the C.M.R.'s, merely say "No," in a distant tone. That will put her in her place, and, besides, it is all that any of us can say.

A good plan is to go to one of the stores handling secondhand army goods and purchase yourself a trench coat. A trench coat worn in wintertime is a better advertisement of military service than an M.C. [Military Cross]. If you cannot get a trench coat buy a pair of army shoes. They will convince everyone you meet on a streetcar that you have seen service.

The trench coat and the army issue shoes will admit you at once into that camaraderie of returned men which is the main result we obtained from the war. Your far-seeing judgment in going to the States is now vindicated, you have all the benefits of going to war and none of its drawbacks.

A very good plan would be to learn the tunes of "Mademoiselle from Armentières" and "Madelon." Whistle these religious ballads as you stand in the back platform of the streetcar and you will be recognized by all as a returned man. Unless you are of hardy temperament do not attempt to learn the words of either of those two old hymns.

Buy or borrow a good history of the war. Study it carefully and you will be able to talk intelligently on any part of the front. In fact, you will more than once be able to prove the average returned veteran a pinnacle of inaccuracy if not unveracity. The average soldier has a very abominable memory for names and dates. Take advantage of this. With a little conscientious study you should be able to prove to the man who was at first and second Ypres that he was not there at all. You, of course, are aided in this by the similarity of one day to another in the army. This has been nobly and fittingly expressed by the recruiting sergeant in these words: "Every day in the army is like Sunday on the farm."

Now that you have firmly established by suggestion your status as an ex-army man and possible hero the rest is easy. Be modest and unassuming and you will have no trouble. If anyone at the office addresses you as "major" wave your hand, smile deprecatingly and say, "No; not quite major."

After that you will be known to the office as captain.

Now you have service at the front, proven patriotism and a commission firmly established, there is only one thing left to do. Go to your room alone some night. Take your bankbook out of your desk and read it through. Put it back in your desk.

Stand in front of your mirror and look yourself in the eye and remember that there are fifty-six thousand Canadians dead in France and Flanders. Then turn out the light and go to bed.

Fascisti Party Half-Million

The Toronto Daily Star
JUNE 24, 1922

MILAN.—Benito Mussolini, head of the Fascisti movement, sits at his desk at the fuse of the great powder magazine that he has laid through all Northern and Central Italy and occasionally fondles the ears of a wolf-hound pup, looking like a short-eared jackrabbit, that plays with the papers on the floor beside the big desk. Mussolini is a big, brown-faced man with a high forehead, a slow smiling mouth, and large, expressive hands.

"The Fascisti are now half a million strong," he told me. "We are a political party organized as a military force."

Talking slowly in Italian and choosing his words in order that he might be sure that I understood everything he said, he went on to tell how the Fascisti have 250,000 troops organized into squads of *Camicie Nere*, or black shirts, as shock troops of the political party. "Garibaldi had red shirts," he smiled deprecatingly.

"We are not out to oppose any Italian government. We are not against the law," Mussolini explained in carefully accented words, leaning back in his editorial chair and emphasizing his points with his great brown hands. "But," he enunciated very slowly and carefully, "we have force enough to overthrow any government that might try to oppose or destroy us."

"How about the Guardia Regia?" I asked. (The Guardia Regia are the recently organized force of troops from the South of Italy formed by Ex-Premier Nitti to keep the peace in case of civil war.)

"The Guardia Regia will never fight us!" Mussolini said.

Now that situation needs a bit of examination and comparison. The Fascisti platform is one of extreme conservatism. Imagine the Conservative party of Canada with 250,000 men under arms, "a political party organized as a military force," with their leader declaring that they have force enough to overthrow any Liberal or other government that might oppose them. It makes quite a picture, doesn't it? At the same time imagine a special military police force having been created to prevent the Conservatives from battling in the streets with the Liberals, and you have a good angle of observation on the present Italian political situation. Mussolini was a great surprise. He is not the monster he has been pictured. His face is intellectual, it is the typical "Bersagliere" face, with its large, brown, oval shape, dark eyes and big, slow-speaking mouth. Mussolini is often described as a "renegade Socialist," but he seems to have had a very good reason for his renunciation of the party.

Born 37 years ago in the Romagna in a little town called Foli, he started life in a hotbed of revolution. It was near his birthplace that the revolution of 1913 occurred, the "red wig" revolt in which Malatesta, the famous Italian anarchist, attempted to establish a republic. Mussolini began his career as a schoolteacher when he was under twenty. He drifted into journalism and made his first prominent appearance in Trento as an associate of Cesare Battisti on the *Libertà*. Cesare Battisti was the Italian who was captured, wounded by the Austrians while he was an officer of Alpini, and hanged in the Castle of Trento because he was born in the part of Italy held by the Austrians.

When war broke out in 1914 Mussolini was editor of *Avanti*, the Socialist daily paper of Milan. He worked for Italy going into the war on the side of the Allies so strongly that the management of his paper dispensed with his services and Mussolini founded his own paper, the *Popolo d'Italia*, to set forth his views. He sank all his money in this enterprise and as soon as Italy entered the war enlisted in the crack "Bersagliere" corps as a private.

Severely wounded in the fighting on the Carso plateau and several times decorated for valor, Mussolini, a patriot above all things, saw what he regarded as the fruits of Italy's victory being swept away from her in 1919 by a wave of communism that covered all of Northern Italy and threatened all private property rights. As a protest against this he organized the Fascisti or anti-Communist shock troops. The history of their activities in the next two years has been told very often.

Now Mussolini stands at the head of an organization of 500,000 members. It comprises men of almost every trade in Italy, several hundreds of thousand workers disgusted with the communism, having turned to the Fascisti as an armed force who might do something for them. Fascism thus enters its third phase. First it was an organization of counterattackers against the Communist demonstrations, second it became a political party, and now it is a political and military party that is enlisting the workers of Italy and invading the field of labor organizations. It is dominating Italy from Rome to the Alps.

The question is now, what does Mussolini, sitting at his desk in the office of the *Popolo d'Italia* and fondling the ears of his wolfhound pup, intend to do with his "political party organized as a military force"?

A Veteran Visits the Old Front

The Toronto Daily Star
JULY 22, 1922

PARIS.—Don't go back to visit the old front. If you have pictures in your head of something that happened in the night in the mud at Paschendaele or of the first wave working up the slope of Vimy, do not try and go back to verify them. It is no good. The front is as different from the way it used to be as your highly respectable shin, with a thin, white scar on it now, is from the leg that you sat and twisted a tourniquet around while the blood soaked your puttee and trickled into your boot, so that when you got up you limped with a "squidge" on your way to the dressing station.

Go to someone else's front, if you want to. There your imagination will help you out and you may be able to picture the things that happened. But don't go back to your own front, because the change in everything and the supreme, deadly, lonely dullness, the smooth green of the fields that were once torn up with shell holes and slashed with trenches and wire, will combine against you and make you believe that the places and happenings that had been the really great events to you were only fever dreams or lies you had told to yourself. It is like going into the empty gloom of a theater where the charwomen are scrubbing. I know because I have just been back to my own front.

Not only is it battlefields that have changed in quality and feeling and gone back into a green smugness with the shell holes filled up, the trenches filled in, the pillboxes blasted out and smoothed over and the wire all rolled up and rotting in a great heap somewhere. That was to be expected, and it was inevitable that the feelings in the battlefields would change when the dead that made them both holy and real were dug up and reburied in big, orderly cemeteries miles away from where they died. Towns where you were billeted, towns unscarred by war, are the ones where the changes hit you hardest. For there are many little towns that you love, and after all, no one but a staff officer could love a battlefield.

There may be towns back of the old Canadian front, towns with queer Flemish names and narrow, cobbled streets, that have kept their magic. There may be such towns. I have just come from Schio, though. Schio was the finest town I remember in the war, and I wouldn't have recognized it now—and I would give a lot not to have gone.

Schio was one of the finest places on earth. It was a little town in the Trentino under the shoulder of the Alps, and it contained all the good cheer, amusement and relaxation a man could desire. When we used to be in billets there, everyone was perfectly contented and we were always talking about what a wonderful place Schio would be to come and live after the war. I particularly recall a first-class hotel called the Due Spadi, where the food was superb and we used to call the factory where we were billeted the "Schio Country Club."

The other day Schio seemed to have shrunk. I walked up one side of the long, narrow main street looking in shop windows at the fly-speckled shirts, the cheap china dishes, the postcards showing about seven different varieties of a young man and a young girl looking into each other's eyes, the stiff, fly-speckled pastry, the big, round loaves of sour bread. At the end of the street were the mountains, but I had walked over the St. Bernard Pass the week before and the mountains, without snow caps, looked rain-furrowed and dull; not much more than hills. I looked at the mountains a long time, though, and then walked down the other side of the street to the principal bar. It was starting to rain a little and shopkeepers were lowering the shutters in front of their shops.

"The town is changed since the war," I said to the girl, she was red-cheeked and black-haired and discontented-looking, who sat on a stool, knitting behind the zinc-covered bar.

"Yes?" she said without missing a stitch.

"I was here during the war," I ventured.

"So were many others," she said under her breath, bitterly.

"Grazie, Signor," she said with mechanical, insolent courtesy as I paid for the drink and went out.

That was Schio. There was more, the way the Due Spadi had shrunk to a small inn, the factory where we used to be billeted now was humming, with our old entrance bricked up and a flow of black muck polluting the stream where we used to swim. All the kick had gone out of things. Early next morning I left in the rain after a bad night's sleep.

249

There was a garden in Schio with the wall matted with wisteria where we used to drink beer on hot nights with a bombing moon making all sorts of shadows from the big plane tree that spread above the table. After my walk in the afternoon I knew enough not to try and find that garden. Maybe there never was a garden.

Perhaps there never was any war around Schio at all. I remember lying in the squeaky bed in the hotel and trying to read by an electric light that hung high up from the center of the ceiling and then switching off the light and looking out the window down the road where the arc light was making a dim light through the rain. It was the same road that the battalions marched along through the white dust in 1916. They were the Brigata Ancona, the Brigata Como, the Brigata Tuscana and ten others brought down from the Carso to check the Austrian offensive that was breaking through the mountain wall of the Trentino and beginning to spill down the valleys that led to the Venetian and Lombardy plains. They were good troops in those days and they marched through the dust of the early summer, broke the offensive along the Galio-Asiago-Canoev line, and died in the mountain gullies, in the pine woods on the Trentino slopes, hunting cover on the desolate rocks and pitched out in the soft-melting early summer snow of the Pasubio.

It was the same old road that some of the same old brigades marched along through the dust of June of 1918, being rushed to the Piave to stop another offensive. Their best men were dead on the rocky Carso, in the fighting around Goritzia, on Mount San Gabrielle, on Grappa and in all the places where men died that nobody ever heard about. In 1918 they didn't march with the ardor that they did in 1916, some of the troops strung out so badly that, after the battalion was just a dust cloud way up the road, you would see poor old boys hoofing it along the side of the road to ease their bad feet, sweating along under their packs and rifles and the deadly Italian sun in a long, horrible, never-ending stagger after the battalion.

So we went down to Mestre, that was one of the great railheads for the Piave, traveling first class with an assorted carriageful of evil-smelling Italian profiteers going to Venice for vacations. In Mestre we hired a motorcar to drive out to the Piave and leaned back in the rear seat and studied the map and the country along the long road that is built through the poisonous green Adriatic marshes that flank all the coast near Venice.

Near Porto Grande, in the part of the lower Piave delta where Austrians and Italians attacked and counterattacked waist-deep in the swamp water, our car stopped in a desolate part of the road that ran like a causeway across the green marshy waste. It needed a long, grease-smearing job of adjustment on the gears and while the driver worked, and got a splinter of steel in his finger that my wife [Hadley] dug out with a needle from our rucksack, we baked in the hot sun. Then a wind blew the mist away from the Adriatic and we saw Venice way off across the swamp and the sea standing gray and yellow like a fairy city.

Finally the driver wiped the last of the grease off his hands into his over-luxuriant hair, the gears took hold when he let the clutch in and we went off along the road through the swampy plain. Fossalta, our objective, as I remembered it, was a shelled-to-pieces town that even rats couldn't live in. It had been within trench-mortar range of the Austrian lines for a year and in quiet times the Austrian had blown up anything in it that looked as though it ought to be blown up. During active sessions it had been one of the first footholds the Austrian had gained on the Venice side of the Piave, and one of the last places he was driven out of and hunted down in and very many men had died in its rubble- and debris-strewn streets and been smoked out of its cellars with *flammenwerfers* during the house-to-house work.

We stopped the car in Fossalta and got out to walk. All the shattered, tragic dignity of the wrecked town was gone. In its place was a new, smug, hideous collection of plaster houses, painted bright blues, reds and yellows. I had been in Fossalta perhaps fifty times and I would not have recognized it. The new plaster church was the worst-looking thing. The trees that had been splintered and gashed showed their scars if you looked for them and had a stunted appearance, but you could not have told in passing, unless you had known, how they had been torn. Everything was so abundantly green and prosperous-looking.

I climbed the grassy slope and above the sunken road where the dugouts had been to look at the Piave and looked down an even slope to the blue river. The Piave is as blue as the Danube is brown. Across the river were two new houses where the two rubble heaps had been just inside the Austrian lines.

I tried to find some trace of the old trenches to show my wife, but there was only the smooth green slope. In a thick prickly patch of hedge we found an old rusty piece of shell fragment. From the cast-iron look of the smoothly burst fragment I could tell it was an old bit of gas shell. That was all there was left of the front.

On our way back to the motorcar we talked about how jolly it is that Fossalta is all built up now and how fine it must be for all the families to have their homes back. We said how proud we were of the way the Italians had kept their mouths shut and rebuilt their devastated districts while some other nations were using their destroyed towns as showplaces and reparation appeals. We said all the things of that sort that as decent-thinking people we thought—and then we stopped talking. There was nothing more to say. It was so very sad.

For a reconstructed town is much sadder than a devastated town. The people haven't their homes back. They have new homes. The home they played in as children, the room where they made love with the lamp turned down, the hearth where they sat, the church they were married in, the room where their child died, these rooms are gone. A shattered village in the war always had a dignity, as though it had died for something. It had died for something and something better was to come. It was all part of the great sacrifice. Now there is just the new, ugly futility of it all. Everything is just as it was—except a little worse.

So we walked along the street where I saw my very good friend killed, past the ugly houses toward the motorcar, whose owner would never have had a motorcar if it had not been for the war, and it all seemed a very bad business. I had tried to recreate something for my wife and had failed utterly. The past was as dead as a busted Victrola record. Chasing yesterdays is a bum show—and if you have to prove it, go back to your old front.

Did Poincaré Laugh
in Verdun Cemetery?

The Toronto Daily Star
AUGUST 12, 1922

PARIS.—Did Premier Poincaré really laugh in the cemetery at Verdun when the United States government decorated the martyred city?

Whether M. Poincaré laughed or not, the pictures taken of him at the time caused the French Communist party to launch a bitter attack on the premier, brought forth a white-hot denial from M. Poincaré, caused a debate in the Chamber of Deputies, threw France into an uproar and also resulted in the country being flooded with postcards.

The picture published with this article was issued by the French Communist party in the form of a postcard, and first made its appearance at one of the Sunday Communist meetings held in the country outside of Paris. It shows M. Poincaré and United States Ambassador Herrick walking in the cemetery at Verdun and shows both M. Poincaré and the ambassador apparently laughing heartily. The Communists, who had always accused M. Poincaré of a great share in the responsibility for the war, issued the card with a flamboyant inscription, calling it "The Man Who Laughs" and saying that "Poincaré, like other murderers, returns to the scene of his crimes."

In a short time the Communist headquarters had sold over 100,000 of the postcards. The matter came to a head in the Chamber of Deputies when a young Communist deputy smiled at some remark of M. Poincaré's in regard to Communist propaganda in the French colonies in Northern Africa.

"You smile?" said M. Poincaré.

"Yes, I smile," said Vaillant-Coutourier, the young deputy who was one of the great war heroes of France, "but I do not laugh in the cemetery of Verdun!"

M. Poincaré went white with rage, and denounced the postcard as a fake and demanded that the entire matter be cleared up with an inter-pellation. That is, that the Communists accuse him publicly from the floor, and that he answer.

"I never laughed in the cemetery at Verdun," M. Poincaré said, denying the charge absolutely and categorically. "The explanation of the matter is that the sun got into my eyes and twisted my face so that it looked as though I were laughing."

M. Poincaré has stuck to this explanation through thick and thin.

An interesting Toronto angle to the story appears here in the fact that the *Star* on July 22, in their picture page, published, long before there was any controversy or before the Communists had issued their postcard, a picture of Ambassador Herrick and M. Poincaré, taken at the same cer-emony as the picture that has caused the great trouble. The *Star*'s pic-ture shows Ambassador Herrick obviously laughing but whether M. Poincaré is smiling must be left to the judgment of the reader.

According to the French papers, Ambassador Herrick gave two expla-nations of the affair. The papers first quote him as saying that of course he did not laugh, and after being shown the picture as saying, "Perhaps something I said to M. Poincaré made him laugh."

There are two divergent explanations already. M. Poincaré says he did not laugh. Ambassador Herrick says perhaps something he said to M. Poincaré made him laugh.

Now comes a third explanation. A movie photographer who was present on the occasion says that he was hurrying to get in front of Poin-caré and Herrick and was running along with his tripod when he slipped and fell sprawling and both the French premier and the ambassador laughed heartily at his ridiculous plight.

Whatever the explanation, the incident, the debate in the Chamber of Deputies, and the postal card have raised a furor in France. Over 200,000 of the postcards have been sold and they are selling at present at the rate of 15,000 a day. Communists charge that those sent through the mail are being destroyed, but those familiar with the French policy of complete freedom of speech in politics doubt this. At any rate they have made their appearance in England.

"What if M. Poincaré did laugh at the cemetery?" many people will ask. "Anyone might have laughed accidentally. What is all the furor about anyway?"

To understand all that you must realize the French attitude toward the dead. It is safe to say that no living man in France today commands as much respect as any dead man does.

Marshal Foch, Anatole France, Henri Barbusse, M. Poincaré or the Pope could never, any one of them, receive the united respect of all the people they would meet if they drove two blocks down the Champs-Elysées. There are too many people with too many divergent political, religious and ethical views in France for any one person to be a complete national hero. But everyone in a motor bus, regardless of religion or politics, takes off their hats when the bus passes a hearse, even if it is a draggled black hearse with only one mourner walking behind. Even the caps of the motormen and chauffeurs come off when they pass a funeral.

It is that great spirit of respect for the dead, coupled with the significance of Verdun, that has given the question of whether M. Poincaré laughed or not the national prominence that it holds.

Mussolini, Europe's Prize Bluffer
(an excerpt)

The Toronto Daily Star
JANUARY 27, 1923

Mussolini is the biggest bluff in Europe. If Mussolini would have me taken out and shot tomorrow morning I would still regard him as a bluff. The shooting would be a bluff. Get hold of a good photo of Signor Mussolini sometime and study it. You will see the weakness in his mouth which forces him to scowl the famous Mussolini scowl that is imitated by every 19-year-old Fascisto in Italy. Study his past record. Study the coalition that Fascismo is between capital and labor and consider the history of past coalitions. Study his genius for clothing small ideas in big words. Study his propensity for dueling. Really brave men do not have to fight duels, and many cowards duel constantly to make themselves believe they are brave. And then look at his black shirt and his white spats. There is something wrong, even histrionically, with a man who wears white spats with a black shirt.

There is not space here to go into the question of Mussolini as a bluff or as a great and lasting force. Mussolini may last fifteen years or he may be overthrown next spring by Gabriele D'Annunzio, who hates him. But let me give two true pictures of Mussolini at Lausanne.

The Fascist dictator had announced he would receive the press. Everybody came. We all crowded into the room. Mussolini sat at his desk reading a book. His face was contorted into the famous frown. He was registering Dictator. Being an ex-newspaperman himself he knew how many readers would be reached by the accounts the men in the room would write of the interview he was about to give. And he remained absorbed in his book. Mentally he was already reading the lines of the two thousand papers served by the two hundred correspondents. "As we entered the room the Black Shirt Dictator did not look up from the book he was reading, so intense was his concentration, etc."

I tiptoed over behind him to see what the book was he was reading with such avid interest. It was a French-English dictionary—held upside down.

The other picture of Mussolini as Dictator was on the same day when a group of Italian women living in Lausanne came to the suite of rooms at the Beau Rivage Hotel to present him with a bouquet of roses. There were six women of the peasant class, wives of workmen living in Lausanne, and they stood outside the door waiting to do honor to Italy's new national hero who was their hero. Mussolini came out of the door in his frock coat, his gray trousers and his white spats. One of the women stepped forward and commenced her speech. Mussolini scowled at her, sneered, let his big-whited African eyes roll over the other five women and went back into the room. The unattractive peasant women in their Sunday clothes were left holding their roses. Mussolini had registered Dictator.

Half an hour later he met Clare Sheridan, who has smiled her way into many interviews, and had time for half an hour's talk with her.

Of course the newspaper correspondents of Napoleon's time may have seen the same things in Napoleon, and the men who worked on the *Giornale d'Italia* in Caesar's day may have found the same discrepancies in Julius, but after an intimate study of the subject there seems to be a good deal more of Bottomley, an enormous, warlike, duel-fighting, successful Italian Horatio Bottomley, in Mussolini than there does of Napoleon.

It isn't really Bottomley though. Bottomley was a great fool. Mussolini isn't a fool and he is a great organizer. But it is a very dangerous thing to organize the patriotism of a nation if you are not sincere, especially when you work its patriotism to such a pitch that it offers to loan money to the government without interest. Once the Latin has sunk his money in a business, he wants results and he is going to show Signor Mussolini that it is much easier to be the opposition to a government than to run the government yourself.

A new opposition will rise, it is forming already, and it will be led by that old, bald-headed, perhaps a little insane but thoroughly sincere, divinely brave swashbuckler, Gabriele D'Annunzio.

257

War Medals for Sale

The Toronto Star Weekly
DECEMBER 8, 1923

What is the market price of valor? In a medal and coin shop on Adelaide street the clerk said: "No, we don't buy them. There isn't any demand."

"Do many men come in to sell medals?" I asked.

"Oh, yes. They come in every day. But we don't buy medals from this war."

"What do they bring in?"

"Victory medals mostly, 1914 stars, a good many M.M.'s, and once in a while a D.C.M., or an M.C. We tell them to go over to the pawnshops where they can get their medal back if they get any money for it."

So the reporter went up to Queen street and walked west past the glittering windows of cheap rings, junk shops, two-bit barber shops, second-hand clothing stores, and street hawkers, in search of the valor mart.

Inside the pawnshop it was the same story.

"No, we don't buy them," a young man with shiny hair said from behind a counter of unredeemed pledges. "There is no market for them at all. Oh, yes. They come in here with all sorts. Yes, M.C.'s. And I had a man in here the other day with a D.S.O. I send them over to the second-hand stores on York street. They buy anything."

"What would you give me for an M.C.?" asked the reporter.

"I'm sorry, Mac. We can't handle it."

Out on to Queen street went the reporter, and into the first second-hand shop he encountered. On the window was a sign, "We Buy and Sell Everything."

The opened door jangled a bell. A woman came in from the back of the shop. Around the counter were piled broken door bells, alarm clocks, rusty carpenters' tools, old iron keys, kewpies, crap shooters' dice, a broken guitar and other things.

"What do you want?" said the woman.

"Got any medals to sell?" the reporter asked.

"No. We don't keep them things. What do you want to do? Sell me things?"

"Sure," said the reporter. "What'll you give me for an M.C.?"

"What's that?" asked the woman, suspiciously, tucking her hands under her apron.

"It's a medal," said the reporter. "It's a silver cross."

"Real silver?" asked the woman.

"I guess so," the reporter said.

"Don't you know?" the woman said. "Ain't you got it with you?"

"No," answered the reporter.

"Well, you bring it in. If it's real silver maybe I'll make you a nice offer on it." The woman smiled. "Say," she said, "it ain't one of them war medals, is it?"

"Sort of," said the reporter.

"Don't you bother with it, then. Them things are no good!"

In succession the reporter visited five more second-hand stores. None of them handled medals. No demand.

In one store the sign outside said, "We Buy and Sell Everything of Value. Highest Prices Paid."

"What you want to sell?" snapped the bearded man back of the counter.

"Would you buy any war medals?" the reporter asked.

"Listen, maybe those medals were all right in the war. I ain't saying they weren't, you understand? But with me business is business. Why should I buy something I can't sell?"

The merchant was being very gentle and explanatory.

"What will you give me for that watch?" asked the reporter.

The merchant examined it carefully, opened the case and looked in the works. Turned it over in his hand and listened to it.

"It's got a good tick," suggested the reporter.

"That watch now," said the heavily bearded merchant judicially, laying it down on the counter. "That watch now, is worth maybe sixty cents."

The reporter went on down York street. There was a second-hand shop every door or so now. The reporter got, in succession, a price on his coat, another offer of seventy cents on his watch, and a handsome offer of 40 cents for his cigarette case. But no one wanted to buy or sell medals.

"Every day they come in to sell those medals. You're the first man ever ask me about buying them for years," a junk dealer said.

Finally, in a dingy shop, the searcher found some medals for sale. The woman in charge brought them out from the cash till.

They were a 1914–15 star, a general service medal and a victory medal. All three were fresh and bright in the boxes they had arrived in. All bore the same name and number. They had belonged to a gunner in a Canadian battery.

The reporter examined them.

"How much are they?" he asked.

"I only sell the whole lot," said the woman, defensively.

"What do you want for the lot?"

"Three dollars."

The reporter continued to examine the medals. They represented the honor and recognition his King had bestowed on a certain Canadian. The name of the Canadian was on the rim of each medal.

"Don't worry about those names, Mister," the woman urged. "You could easy take off the names. Those would make you good medals."

"I'm not sure these are what I'm looking for," the reporter said.

"You won't make no mistake if you buy those medals, Mister," urged the woman, fingering them. "You couldn't want no better medals than them."

"No, I don't think they're what I want," the reporter demurred.

"Well, you make me an offer on them."

"No."

"Just make me an offer. Make me any offer you feel like."

"Not to-day."

"Make me any kind of an offer. Those are good medals, mister. Look at them. Will you give me a dollar for all the lot?"

Outside the shop the reporter looked in the window. You could evidently sell a broken alarm-clock. But you couldn't sell an M.C.

You could dispose of a second-hand mouth-organ. But there was no market for a D.C.M.

You could sell your old military puttees. But you couldn't find a buyer for a 1914 Star.

So the market price of valor remained undetermined.

VI

The Greco-Turkish War

"It is hard to believe this rich pleasant farming country is the bleak-sounding Balkans. It is, though, and as you ride through it you can see how the love of the land can make men fight wars. It is a matter of land, of fields of corn and yellowing tobacco, of flocks of sheep and herds of cattle, of heaps of yellow pumpkins in the shocked corn, of beech groves and peat smoke from chimneys, a matter of mine and thine that is the cause of all just wars—and there can never be peace in the Balkans as long as one people holds the lands of another people—no matter what the political excuse may be."

—From "Balkans: A Picture of Peace, Not War,"
The Toronto Daily Star, October 16, 1922

Christians Leave Thrace to Turks

The Toronto Daily Star
OCTOBER 16, 1922

CONSTANTINOPLE.—Thousands of Christians, many hungry and with all their earthly belongings packed on their backs, trudged out of Thrace today as the cross made way for the crescent. Aged men and women, many carrying children, walked toward the Balkan peninsula, leaving forever the homes that they have occupied for years.

Some loaded their household goods in ox carts. Others left everything behind and fled in order to be out of Thrace in fifteen days, the time limit set by the Allied generals and Turkish representatives at the Mudania Conference.

Most of the trains in Thrace have been commandeered by the Greek government to carry soldiers, who will be loaded on transports when they reach the ports. The civilian population had to depend on the rickety carts or walk.

Rodosto, on the Balkan peninsula, was choked with refugees. The suffering and foodless Greeks and Armenians awaited some means to carry them into Greece.

Little relief, it is believed, will greet the refugees when they arrive in Greece. The food supplies there are very inadequate because of the thousands of refugees that are already dependent on the government and charitable agencies for food.

Four British and three French battalions were entering Thrace today on the heels of the departing Greeks.

Waiting for an Orgy

The Toronto Daily Star
OCTOBER 19, 1922

CONSTANTINOPLE.—There is a tight-drawn, electric tension in Constantinople such as only people who live in a city that has never been invaded can imagine.

Take the tension that comes when the pitcher steps into the box before the packed stands at the first game of the world series, multiply it by the tension that comes when the barrier snaps up, the gong clangs and they're off at the King's Plate at the Woodbine [Toronto racetrack], add to it the tension in your mind when you walk the floor downstairs as you wait frightened and cold for someone you love, while a doctor and a nurse are doing something in a room above that you cannot help in any way, and you have something comparable to the feeling in Constantinople now.

It is we correspondents who have nothing at stake that get the selfish world series thrill. Even at that, I never lay awake all night in October before a world series because it was too hot to sleep, nor fought mosquitoes and bedbugs in the best New York or Chicago hotels.

It is the collection of cutthroats, robbers, bandits, thugs and Levantine pirates who have gathered here from Batum to Bagdad, and from Singapore to Sicily, that are getting the Woodbine thrill. They are waiting for the looting to begin. And they are ready to begin it on their own account as soon as the triumphal entry of Mustapha Kemal Pasha's troops starts the riotous orgy of celebration that will permit them to fire the wooden tenement quarter which will burn like a gasoline-soaked matchbox.

If the Allied and Turkish police prevent the orgy that has been planned for the celebration of the Kemal entry it will be one of the finest achievements in the world, because the tough element of all the Near

East, of the Balkans, and of the Mediterranean are gathered in Constantinople like jackals waiting for the lion to make his kill.

The people who are getting the sickening, cold, crawling fear-thrill are the Armenians, Greeks and Macedonians, who cannot get away or who have elected to stay. Those who stay are arming themselves and talking desperately.

The landlord of my hotel is a Greek. He has bought the place with his life's savings. Everything he has in the world is invested in it. I am now the only guest.

"I tell you, sir," he said last night. "I'm going to fight. We are armed and there are plenty of Christians armed too. I am not going to leave all my life's work here just because the French force the Allies to give Constantinople to that bandit Kemal. Why do they do it? Greece fought for the Allies in the war and now they desert us. We cannot understand it."

There are many Greeks talking that way. And all those who are staying are arming. That, of course, increases the danger of trouble still further, because if some Greek in a nervous hysteria takes a potshot at some Turkish celebrators the whole pot will boil over in an instant.

Russian refugees are still another class that are tremendously affected by the coming entry of the Kemalist army. Up till now Constantinople has been the great place of refuge for those of the old regime in Russia who fled from the Soviets.

Many of them have death sentences pending which will be executed if they are handed over to the Soviet government. Kemal is hand in glove with the Soviets and his entry will wipe out the greatest Russian sanctuary.

Fully a fourth of the uniforms you see on the streets are Russian, either the old Imperial army or the troops of Wrangel, Denikin and Yudenitch. Their wearers fled to Constantinople or were evacuated with the remnants of the counterrevolutionary forces, and have not had enough money since to buy any other clothes. Just how Kemal, and his allies of the cheka, will dispose of these men in the high-booted, loosely bloused, worn old Russian uniforms who have been fighting against the Soviets and cannot disguise the fact, is not a pleasant problem.

I would hate to be Kemal with all the dangerous prestige of a great victory behind me and these problems ahead. All the East says that Mustapha Kemal Pasha is a great man. At least he is a successful man, but his entry into Constantinople will be the first indication of whether his fame is to be merely the bubble of military reputation, always burst by the first defeat, or the greatness of a man who can deal with the problems his victory has brought him.

The cards look stacked against him in Constantinople, but if he can accomplish a peaceful entry, keep his troops in hand, and see there is no reign of terror, it will be of greater permanent value to Turkey than many victories in Thrace.

A Silent, Ghastly Procession

The Toronto Daily Star
OCTOBER 20, 1922

ADRIANOPLE.—In a never-ending, staggering march, the Christian population of Eastern Thrace is jamming the roads toward Macedonia. The main column crossing the Maritza River at Adrianople is twenty miles long. Twenty miles of carts drawn by cows, bullocks and muddy-flanked water buffalo, with exhausted, staggering men, women and children, blankets over their heads, walking blindly along in the rain beside their worldly goods.

This main stream is being swelled from the back country. They don't know where they are going. They left their farms, villages and ripe, brown fields and joined the main stream of refugees when they heard the Turk was coming. Now they can only keep their places in the ghastly procession while mud-splashed Greek cavalry herd them along like cow-punchers driving steers.

It is a silent procession. Nobody even grunts. It is all they can do to keep moving. Their brilliant peasant costumes are soaked and draggled. Chickens dangle by their feet from the carts. Calves nuzzle at the draught cattle wherever a jam halts the stream. An old man marches under a young pig, a scythe and a gun, with a chicken tied to his scythe. A husband spreads a blanket over a woman in labor in one of the carts to keep off the driving rain. She is the only person making a sound. Her little daughter looks at her in horror and begins to cry. And the procession keeps moving.

At Adrianople where the main stream moves through, there is no Near East Relief at all. They are doing very good work at Rodosto on the coast, but can only touch the fringe.

There are 250,000 Christian refugees to be evacuated from Eastern Thrace alone. The Bulgarian frontier is shut against them. There is only

Macedonia and Western Thrace to receive the fruit of the Turk's return to Europe. Nearly half a million refugees are in Macedonia now. How they are to be fed nobody knows, but in the next month all the Christian world will hear the cry: "Come over into Macedonia and help us!"

Turks Distrust Kemal Pasha

The Toronto Daily Star
OCTOBER 24, 1922

CONSTANTINOPLE.—Mustapha Kemal Pasha a few months ago was regarded as a new Saladin by the Moslem world. He was to lead Islam into battle against Christianity and to spread a holy war through all the East. Now the East is beginning to distrust him. Mohammedans I have talked to say: "Kemal has betrayed us." There is no talk now of the holy war.

This has happened because Kemal, the conquering general, has shown himself to be Kemal the businessman. He is now in something of the position Arthur Griffith and Michael Collins occupied in Ireland just before their death. That is, he is taking the tangible gains offered him, making what appear to the Pan-Islamites to be humiliating compromises, and trying to salt down his winnings—always planning to try for more when these are consolidated.

As yet his de Valera has not appeared. But if he continues to play a waiting game, there will be a de Valera sooner or later. And this possibility of a split in the Turkish forces may be the saving of the western power in the Orient.

One thing that may bring it about is the report that is current that the heads of the Turkish nationalist movement, which it should always be remembered is the Kemalist party, are many of them atheists and French Freemasons rather than good Mohammedans. That is the report you get as gossip when the Mohammedans talk politics and it is bringing about a distrust that is growing up in regard to Kemal in the minds of those people who had regarded him as a conquering Messiah for the Mohammedan peoples.

The Jews claim that Kemal is a Jew. His thin, intense, rigid face does look Jewish. But the Jews also claim Gabriele D'Annunzio and Christopher Columbus and a thousand years or so from now may even be claiming Henry Ford. At any rate that rumor about Kemal is doing him no harm and gaining very little credence; the charge of atheism is much more dangerous, for that is the one crime that any Turk is prepared to believe any other Turk is guilty of but there is no blacker crime in the Mohammedan world.

The Kemalists have a treaty and an alliance with Bolshevist Russia. They also have a treaty and something very like an alliance with France. As I explained in my last article, one of these alliances must go. Whichever alliance Turkey drops clears the air very little, because the one big aim of the Kemalists, the aim for which they are being criticized now in their own circles for not having fulfilled, the aim which does not appear in any published pacts but that everyone in the country understands is the possession of Mesopotamia. [Editor's note: A cable dispatch received yesterday says it is understood the Turks will claim Mesopotamia at the peace conference.] Turkey is bound to have Mesopotamia. If France is her ally when she goes after it or if, having broken with France, she is backed by Russia, the situation is equally dangerous. If there is war in Mesopotamia between Great Britain and Turkey, and I give Mustapha Kemal twenty months to consolidate his present gains before he provokes such a war, it may be the blaze that will start the holy war that the Pan-Islamites are praying for to destroy all western domination in the east. France, if she is Kemal's ally at that time, will probably remain neutral. Russia might not remain neutral.

It is oil that Kemal and company want Mesopotamia for, and it is oil that Great Britain wants to keep Mesopotamia for, so the East that is disappointed in Kemal the Saladin because he shows no inclination to plunge into a fanatical holy war may yet get their war from Kemal the businessman.

Afghans: Trouble for Britain

The Toronto Daily Star
OCTOBER 31, 1922

CONSTANTINOPLE.—Afghanistan is another weapon that is being forged against the British Empire by Kemal and his Pan-Eastern friends. For over a year Kemalist officers have been training Afghan troops, getting them ready for the moment to strike. Now they are ready.

I happen to know something about the inside history of contemporary Afghanistan with its aims and hatreds. It came to me from Shere Mohamet Khan, who lived in Rome for a while and is now Afghan minister for war.

Shere Mohamet—the Khan is the Afghan suffix meaning prince—was tall, dark-haired, hawk-faced, as straight as a lance, with the bird-of-prey eyes and the hooked nose that mark the Afghan. He looked like a man out of the Renaissance, though his breed are the original Semites and go back as an unconquered people to the days of the Medes and Persians.

The old Amir of Afghanistan was Abderahman Khan. All his life he hated the English, who were using Afghanistan as a buffer state between India and Russia, and who forbade them to have diplomatic relations with any country except England, runs Shere Mohamet's story.

He was a great man, was Abderahman, a hard man, a farseeing man and an Afghan. He spent his life consolidating Afghanistan into a strong nation, and in training his son. His son was to carry on his work, to make war on the English.

The old man died. The son, Habibullah Khan, became Amir. The English invited him to come down to India, on a state visit, and he went to see what manner of people these English were. There the English got him. First they entertained him royally. They showed him many delights and they taught him to drink. I do not say he was not an apt learner. He was no longer a man and an Afghan.

He came back to Kabul, that was just after the armistice in 1918, and

271

the Afghans killed him. He was assassinated. It was really an execution. Then there was a meeting of the Great Council in Kabul and Nasirullah Khan, the oldest grandson of the old Amir, was questioned.

"Will you defend Afghanistan if you are chosen king?" they asked him.

"I will defend Afghanistan," he answered.

"Will you make war on the English?"

"I will try," he answered.

They let him go out of the council room.

Aminullah, the next grandson, was brought in.

"What will you do if you are chosen king?" they asked him.

"I will do two things," Aminullah answered. "I will defend Afghanistan and I will make war on the English."

So they chose him king, and a few weeks later he led his troops over the pass into India.

That is Shere Mohamet's story.

Very few people even remember that there was an Afghan war, just after the armistice. It was the Royal Air Force that won it by bombing out the Afghan cities back of the lines and destroying the mud forts where the hill men, having had no experience with planes before, congregated. At any rate it was a British victory and so announced.

But when they signed the treaty of peace, Great Britain gave up every right that she had always fought for in Afghanistan. Other countries were permitted by treaty to have diplomatic and consular representatives in Afghanistan, arms were permitted to be imported, arms were even permitted to be imported through India. The war may have been a British victory but the peace was certainly an Afghan victory. The Afghans had always hated England but now they felt contempt for her.

So now there are Soviet Russian consulates in all the Afghan cities, the Afghans are armed with modern arms and are trained by Kemalist officers. Aminullah, "my great king," Shere Mohamet calls him, has not forsworn his oath to make war on the English—and he has not gone down to the fleshpots of India.

When Kemal attacks Mesopotamia, and sooner or later he will, there will be a well-equipped, well-trained Afghan army come down the Khyber Pass that will not be the ill-equipped, unschooled band of hill men that were defeated in 1919. They have an alliance with Mustapha Kemal now. They are elated over the Kemalist successes and even their existence is a perpetual threat against the British rule in India that prevents her from drawing a single regiment from there in case of trouble elsewhere.

The Afghans will fight. It is their métier. Shere Mohamet has a story that illustrates the Afghan spirit.

"When I came home to my house in Kabul from the council that decided on the last war, my wife and my daughter had my pistols and my sword and all my kit laid out for me.

" 'What is this?' I said.

" 'Your things for the war. There is going to be a war, is there not?' said my wife.

" 'Yes. But I am the minister of war. I do not go to this war. The minister of war does not go to the war itself.'

"My wife shook her head. 'I do not understand it,' she said very haughtily. 'If you are this minister of war who cannot go to war, you must resign. That is all. We would be disgraced if you did not go.'"

That is the spirit the Kemalists trained, and armed by the Russians it makes another Eastern problem that does not look easy of solution.

The Greek Revolt

The Toronto Daily Star
NOVEMBER 3, 1922

MURADLI, EASTERN THRACE.—As I write, the Greek troops are commencing their evacuation of Eastern Thrace. In their ill-fitting U.S. uniforms, they are trekking across the country, cavalry patrols out ahead, the soldiers marching sullenly but occasionally grinning at us as we pass their strung-out, straggling columns. They have cut all the telegraph wires behind them; you see them dangling from the poles like Maypole ribbons. They have abandoned their thatched huts, their camouflaged gun positions, their machine-gun nests, and all the heavily wired, strung-out, fortified ridges where they had planned to make a last stand against the Turks.

Heavy wheeled baggage carts drawn by muddy-flanked buffalo with slanted-back horns drag along the dusty road. Some soldiers lie on top of the mounds of baggage, while others goad the buffalo along. Ahead and behind the baggage carts are strung out the troops. This is the end of the great Greek military adventure.

Might-have-beens are a sad business and the end of Greek military power is sad enough as it is, but there is no blame for it to be given to the Greek common soldier. Even in the evacuation the Greek soldiers looked like good troops. There was a sturdy doggedness about them that would have meant a hard time for the Turk if Kemal's army would have had to fight for Thrace instead of having it handed to them as a gift at Mudania.

Captain Wittal of the Indian cavalry, who was attached to the Greek army in Anatolia as an observer during the Greek war with Kemal, told me the inside story of the intrigue that led to the breakdown of the Greek army in Asia Minor.

"The Greek soldiers were first-class fighting men," Captain Wittal said. "They were well officered by men who had served with the British and French at Salonika and they outclassed the Kemalist army. I believe they would have captured Angora and ended the war if they had not been betrayed.

"When Constantine came into power all the officers of the army in the field were suddenly scrapped, from the commander-in-chief down to platoon commanders. These officers had many of them been promoted from the ranks, were good soldiers and splendid leaders. They were removed and their places filled with new officers of the Tino [Constantine] party, most of whom had spent the war in Switzerland or Germany and had never heard a shot fired. That caused a complete breakdown of the army and was responsible for the Greek defeat."

Captain Wittal told me how artillery officers who had no experience at all took over the command of batteries and massacred their own infantry. He told about infantry officers who used powder, face powder not gun-powder, and rouge, and about staff work which was criminal in its ignorance and negligence.

"In one show in Anatolia," Wittal said, "the Greek infantry were doing an absolutely magnificent attack and their artillery was doing them in. Major Johnson [the other British observer who later acted as liaison officer with the press at Constantinople] is a gunner, you know. He's a fine gunner too. Well, Major Johnson cried at what those gunners were doing to their infantry. He was wild to take over the artillery. But he couldn't do a thing. We had orders to preserve strict neutrality—and he couldn't do a thing."

That is the story of the Greek army's betrayal by King Constantine. And that is the reason the revolution in Athens was not just a fake as many people have claimed. It was the rising of an army that had been betrayed against the man who had betrayed it.

The old Venizelist officers came back after the revolution and reorganized the army in Eastern Thrace. Greece looked on Thrace as a Marne where she must fight and make a final stand or perish. Troops were rushed in. Everybody was at a white heat. Then the Allies at Mudania handed Eastern Thrace over to the Turk and gave the Greek army three days to start getting out.

The army waited, not believing that their government would sign the Mudania convention, but it did, and the army, being soldiers, are getting out.

All day I have been passing them, dirty, tired, unshaven, wind-bitten soldiers hiking along the trails across the brown, rolling, barren Thracian countryside. No bands, no relief organizations, no leave areas, nothing but lice, dirty blankets, and mosquitoes at night. They are the last of the glory that was Greece. This is the end of their second siege of Troy.

Kemal's One Submarine

The Toronto Daily Star
NOVEMBER 10, 1922

CONSTANTINOPLE.—Before the British fleet steamed into the Sea of Marmora, Constantinople was in a state of panic, the Turkish pound rocketing and falling, the European population panic-stricken, and ugly talk of massacres was blowing about everywhere.

Then the great, gray fleet came in one day and the town settled back in relief. There was no more massacre talk, for it was made known to Hamid Bey, Kemal's Constantinople representative, that if there was any massacre of Christians started, Stamboul would be razed to the ground. It may have been a bluff but the Turks believed it.

Perhaps it is because of the navy's treatment of war correspondents that it so effectively remains the Silent Service. It has a way with war correspondents, a most definite way. It divides them into friends and enemies.

Enemies receive the treatment the *Daily Mail* man got after Northcliffe's attack on Admiral Jellicoe, the idol of the Navy. He shared every hardship with his men and was loved like a father. The *Daily Mail* came out with an attack on him and shortly after the man who wrote it was assigned to the Grand Fleet. The journalist arrived armed with a letter from the admiralty ordering the commanders of all ships to give him transportation wherever he desired to go. He presented himself to a certain admiral.

"You can't come on board," said the admiral.

The *Daily Mail* man produced his letter. The admiral read it.

"Good," he growled. "This is a definite order. Where do you wish to go and when?"

The *Daily Mail* man told him.

"Good," said the admiral. "Send for Lieutenant Wilson."

Lieutenant Wilson arrived and saluted.

"This man has a letter from the admiralty ordering us to give him transportation. It is a definite order. But it says nothing about comfort, aid or anything else. You will take this man where he wishes to go on your destroyer but do not allow him off the deck or in the wardroom."

Lieutenant Wilson saluted again.

When the journalist went aboard no one spoke to him except the destroyer commander. "Oh, by the way, Paddock, [that is not his name] "this letter doesn't say anything about food. If you want to eat you'd better dig yourself up some grub ashore and bring it aboard."

That is the way the navy has with enemies. Its friends it entertains so amply, completely, thoroughly and enthusiastically that they retain only a vague and idyllic picture of the visit.

Kemal's only submarine was the principal problem and joy of the fleet at Constantinople. This submarine was given to Mustapha Kemal by Soviet Russia and sent out from Odessa. The captain was not enthusiastic about going and the Bolshevists told him he would be hanged if he came back to Odessa without having sunk a British warship.

British naval intelligence officers were advised of the undersea boat's departure and orders were given to sink it on sight with no questions asked or answered as soon as it crossed an imaginary line drawn across the Black Sea entrance to the Bosporus. Destroyer commanders were also instructed that this line was to be fairly elastic and subject to a little stretching.

As soon as the submarine was sighted, two destroyers were to put out into the Black Sea and get behind him so he couldn't go back. Four others were to proceed along the narrow channel of the Bosporus dropping depth charges at regular intervals.

Destroyers sighted the submarine on six different occasions, but he was always too far at sea for them to go after him, even allowing for extreme stretching of the imaginary deadline. Then the submarine disappeared.

He next turned up off Trebizond as a full-fledged pirate, halting ships, searching the passengers and crew and doing a very good business. He is still under the "Jolly Roger" and the captain is laying away plunder enough to enable him to retire if he escapes the gallows that are waiting for him at Odessa and the six lean gray destroyers cruise up and down the Bosporus waiting for him to appear.

The destroyer patrols have exciting times in the Bosporus. At one time, during the Mudania Conference, a destroyer was running a night patrol along the Asiatic side of the straits. No one knew whether there was going to be peace or war, and the destroyer had been picking up small boats with armed Turks in them who were making their way across to Constantinople.

Their searchlight showed something suspicious-looking in a cove near Belcos, not twelve miles from Constantinople, and a boat put ashore to investigate.

As the boat neared the beach, it was fired upon. It kept on going and after the first ragged volley there was no shooting. As the boat landed on the beach a horseman rode out of the black shadow at the side of the searchlight beam and spoke in French.

"We are a squadron of Kemalist cavalry," he said, and the officer in charge of the boat could see the horses huddled back of the little hill. "We have come here to show we could if we want to. Now we are going back."

There was nothing for the British officer to do. The cavalry were some thirty miles inside the neutral zone—but all the British army and navy's efforts in those days were directed to avoiding war instead of accepting provocations for making it. The officer went back with his boat to his destroyer.

Another night a destroyer patrol near the suburb of Bebek stopped a boatload of Turkish women who were crossing from Asia Minor after the ferries were stopped. On being searched for arms or contraband it turned out all the women were men. They were all armed—and later proved to be Kemalist officers sent over to organize the Turkish population in the suburbs in case of an attack on Constantinople.

But whether they were checking the infiltration of Kemalist troops, seizing Russian gold rubles and propaganda tracts that were being brought up the straits in crazy old fishing smacks from Batum, or simply seeing that the Turkish boats kept their riding lights lit, the destroyer flotilla remained a part of the Silent Service. Now with the censorship off, this is the first account of their activities or of the sad career of Kemal's Bolshevik submarine.

VII

The Spanish Civil War

"*It is very dangerous to write the truth in war and the truth is very dangerous to come by. . . . When a man goes to seek the truth in war he may find death instead. But if twelve go and only two come back, the truth they bring will be the truth, and not the garbled hearsay that we pass as history.*"

—From a speech to the American Writers' Congress,
New York, June 4, 1937

A New Kind of War

NANA Dispatch
APRIL 14, 1937

MADRID.—The window of the hotel is open and, as you lie in bed, you hear the firing in the front line seventeen blocks away. There is a rifle fire all night long. The rifles go tacrong, capong, craang, tacrong, and then a machine gun opens up. It has a bigger calibre and is much louder, rong, cararong, rong, rong. Then there is the incoming boom of a trench mortar shell and a burst of machine gun fire. You lie and listen to it and it is a great thing to be in bed with your feet stretched out gradually warming the cold foot of the bed and not out there in University City or Carabanchel. A man is singing hard-voiced in the street below and three drunks are arguing when you fall asleep.

In the morning, before your call comes from the desk, the roaring burst of a high explosive shell wakes you and you go to the window and look out to see a man, his head down, his coat collar up, sprinting desperately across the paved square. There is the acrid smell of high explosive you hoped you'd never smell again, and, in a bathrobe and bedroom slippers, you hurry down the marble stairs and almost into a middle-aged woman, wounded in the abdomen, who is being helped into the hotel entrance by two men in blue workmen's smocks. She has her two hands crossed below her big, old-style Spanish bosom and from between her fingers the blood is spurting in a thin stream. On the corner, twenty yards away, is a heap of rubble, smashed cement and thrown up dirt, a single dead man, his torn clothes dusty, and a great hole in the sidewalk from which the gas from a broken main is rising, looking like a heat mirage in the cold morning air.

"How many dead?" you ask a policeman.

"Only one," he says. "It went through the sidewalk and burst below. If it would have burst on the solid stone of the road there might have been fifty."

281

A policeman covers the top of the trunk, from which the head is missing; they send for someone to repair the gas main and you go in to breakfast. A charwoman, her eyes red, is scrubbing the blood off the marble floor of the corridor. The dead man wasn't you nor anyone you know and everyone is very hungry in the morning after a cold night and a long day the day before up at the Guadalajara front.

"Did you see him?" asked someone else at breakfast.

"Sure," you say.

"That's where we pass a dozen times a day. Right on that corner." Someone makes a joke about missing teeth and someone else says not to make that joke. And everyone has the feeling that characterizes war. It wasn't me, see? It wasn't me.

The Italian dead up on the Guadalajara front weren't you, although Italian dead, because of where you had spent your boyhood, always seemed, still, like our dead. No. You went to the front early in the morning in a miserable little car with a more miserable little chauffeur who suffered visibly the closer he came to the fighting. But at night, sometimes late, without lights, with the big trucks roaring past, you came on back to sleep in a bed with sheets in a good hotel, paying a dollar a day for the best rooms on the front. The smaller rooms in the back, on the side away from the shelling, were considerably more expensive. After the shell that lit on the sidewalk in front of the hotel you got a beautiful double corner room on that side, twice the size of the one you had had, for less than a dollar. It wasn't me they killed. See? No. Not me. It wasn't me anymore.

Then, in a hospital given by the American Friends of Spanish Democracy, located out behind the Morata front along the road to Valencia, they said, "Raven* wants to see you."

"Do I know him?"

"I don't think so," they said, "but he wants to see you."

"Where is he?"

"Upstairs."

In the room upstairs they are giving a blood transfusion to a man with a very gray face who lay on a cot with his arm out, looking away from the gurgling bottle and moaning in a very impersonal way. He moaned mechanically and at regular intervals and it did not seem to be him that made the sound. His lips did not move.

"Where's Raven?" I asked.

"I'm here," said Raven.

*J. Robert Raven

The voice came from a high mound covered by a shoddy gray blanket. There were two arms crossed on the top of the mound and at one end there was something that had been a face, but now was a yellow scabby area with a wide bandage cross where the eyes had been.

"Who is it?" asked Raven. He didn't have lips, but he talked pretty well without them and with a pleasant voice.

"Hemingway," I said. "I came up to see how you were doing."

"My face was pretty bad," he said. "It got sort of burned from the grenade, but it's peeled a couple of times and it's doing better."

"It looks swell," I said. "It's doing fine."

I wasn't looking at it when I spoke.

"How are things in America?" he asked. "What do they think of us over there?"

"Sentiment's changed a lot," I said. "They're beginning to realize the government is going to win this war."

"Do you think so?"

"Sure," I said.

"I'm awfully glad," he said. "You know, I wouldn't mind any of this if I could just watch what was going on. I don't mind the pain, you know. It never seemed important really. But I was always awfully interested in things and I really wouldn't mind the pain at all if I could just sort of follow things intelligently. I could even be some use. You know, I didn't mind the war at all. I did all right in the war. I got hit once before and I was back and rejoined the battalion in two weeks. I couldn't stand to be away. Then I got this."

He had put his hand in mine. It was not a worker's hand. There were no callouses and the nails on the long, spatulate fingers were smooth and rounded.

"How did you get it?" I asked.

"Well, there were some troops that were routed and we went over to sort of reform them and we did and then we had quite a fight with the fascists and we beat them. It was quite a bad fight, you know, but we beat them and then someone threw this grenade at me."

Holding his hand and hearing him tell it, I did not believe a word of it. What was left of him did not sound like the wreckage of a soldier somehow. I did not know how he had been wounded, but the story did not sound right. It was the sort of way everyone would like to have been wounded. But I wanted him to think I believed it.

"Where did you come from?" I asked.

"From Pittsburgh. I went to the University there."

"What did you do before you joined up here?"

"I was a social worker," he said. Then I knew it couldn't be true and I wondered how he had really been so frightfully wounded and I didn't care. In the war that I had known, men often lied about the manner of their wounding. Not at first; but later. I'd lied a little myself in my time. Especially late in the evening. But I was glad he thought I believed it, and we talked about books, he wanted to be a writer, and I told him about what happened north of Guadalajara and promised to bring some things from Madrid next time we got out that way. I hoped maybe I could get a radio.

"They tell me Dos Passos and Sinclair Lewis are coming over, too," he said.

"Yes," I said. "And when they come I'll bring them up to see you."

"Gee, that will be great," he said. "You don't know what that will mean to me."

"I'll bring them," I said.

"Will they be here pretty soon?"

"Just as soon as they come I'll bring them."

"Good boy, Ernest," he said. "You don't mind if I call you Ernest, do you?"

The voice came very clear and gentle from that face that looked like some hill that had been fought over in muddy weather and then baked in the sun.

"Hell, no," I said. "Please. Listen, old-timer, you're going to be fine. You'll be a lot of good, you know. You can talk on the radio."

"Maybe," he said. "You'll be back?"

"Sure," I said. "Absolutely."

"Goodbye, Ernest," he said.

"Goodbye," I told him.

Downstairs they told me he'd lost both eyes as well as his face and was also badly wounded all through the legs and in the feet.

"He's lost some toes, too," the doctor said, "but he doesn't know that."

"I wonder if he'll ever know it."

"Oh, sure he will," the doctor said. "He's going to get well."

And it still isn't you that gets hit but it is your countryman now. Your countryman from Pennsylvania, where once we fought at Gettysburg.

Then, walking along the road, with his left arm in an airplane splint, walking with the gamecock walk of the professional British soldier that neither ten years of militant party work nor the projecting metal wings of the splint could destroy, I met Raven's commanding officer, Jock Cunningham, who had three fresh rifle wounds through his upper left arm (I looked at them, one was septic) and another rifle bullet under his shoulder blade that had entered his left chest, passed through, and lodged there. He told me, in military terms, the history of the attempt to rally retiring troops on his battalion's right flank, of his bombing raid down a trench which was held at one end by the fascists and at the other end by the government troops, of the taking of this trench and, with six men and a Lewis gun, cutting off a group of some eighty fascists from their own lines, and of the final desperate defense of their impossible position his six men put up until the government troops came up and, attacking, straightened out the line again. He told it clearly, completely convincingly, and with a strong Glasgow accent. He had deep, piercing eyes sheltered like an eagle's, and, hearing him talk, you could tell the sort of soldier he was. For what he had done he would have had a V.C. in the last war. In this war there are no decorations. Wounds are the only decorations and they do not award wound stripes.

"Raven was in the same show," he said. "I didn't know he'd been hit. Ay, he's a good mon. He got his after I got mine. The fascists we'd cut off were very good troops. They never fired a useless shot when we were in that bad spot. They waited in the dark there until they had us located and then opened with volley fire. That's how I got four in the same place."

We talked for a while and he told me many things. They were all important, but nothing was as important as what Jay Raven, the social worker from Pittsburgh with no military training, had told me was true. This is a strange new kind of war where you learn just as much as you are able to believe.

The Chauffeurs of Madrid

NANA Dispatch
MAY 22, 1937

We had a lot of different chauffeurs in Madrid. The first one was named Tomás, was four feet eleven inches high and looked like a particularly unattractive, very mature dwarf out of Velásquez put into a suit of blue dungarees. He had several front teeth missing and seethed with patriotic sentiments. He also loved Scotch whisky.

We drove up from Valencia with Tomás and, as we sighted Madrid rising like a great white fortress across the plain from Alcalá de Henares, Tomás said, through missing teeth, "Long live Madrid, the Capital of my Soul!"

"And of my heart," I said, having had a couple myself. It had been a long cold ride.

"Hurray!" shouted Tomás and abandoned the wheel temporarily in order to clap me on the back. We just missed a lorry full of troops and a staff car.

"I am a man of sentiment," said Tomás.

"Me, too," I said, "but hang on to that wheel."

"Of the noblest sentiment," said Tomás.

"No doubt of it, comrade," I said, "but just try to watch where you are driving."

"You can place all confidence in me," said Tomás.

But the next day we were stalled on a muddy road up near Brihuega by a tank, which had lurched around a little too far on a hairpin bend, and held up six other tanks behind it. Three rebel planes sighted the tanks and decided to bomb them. The bombs hit the wet hillside above us, lifting mud geysers in sudden, clustered, bumping shocks. Nothing hit us and the planes went on over their own lines. In the field glasses, standing by the car, I could see the little Fiat fighter planes that protected the bombers, very shining looking, hanging up in the sun. We thought some more bombers were coming and everybody got away from there as fast as possible. But no more came.

Next morning Tomás couldn't get the car to start. And every day when anything of that sort happened, from then on, no matter how well the car had run coming home at night, Tomás never could start her in the morning. The way he felt about the front became sort of pitiful, finally, along with his size, his patriotism, and his general inefficiency, and we sent him back to Valencia, with a note to the press department thanking them for Tomás, a man of the noblest sentiments and the finest intentions; but could they send us something just a little braver.

So they sent one with a note certifying him as the bravest chauffeur in the whole department. I don't know what his name was because I never saw him. Sid Franklin (the Brooklyn bullfighter), who bought us all our food, cooked breakfasts, typed articles, wangled petrol, wangled cars, wangled chauffeurs, and covered Madrid and all its gossip like a human dictaphone, evidently instructed this chauffeur very strongly. Sid put forty liters of petrol in the car, and petrol was the correspondents' main problem, being harder to obtain than Chanel's and Molyneux's perfumes or Bols gin, took the chauffeur's name and address, and told him to hold himself ready to roll whenever he was called. We were expecting an attack.

Until we called him he was free to do whatever he wanted. But he must leave word at all times where we could reach him. We did not want to use up the precious petrol riding around Madrid in the car. We all felt good now, because we had transport.

The chauffeur was to check in at the hotel the next night at seven-thirty to see if there were any new orders. He didn't come and we called up his rooming house. He had left that same morning for Valencia with the car and the forty liters of petrol. He is in jail in Valencia now. I hope he likes it.

Then we got David. David was an Anarchist boy from a little town near Toledo. He used language that was so utterly and inconceivably foul that half the time you could not believe what your ears were hearing. Being with David has changed my whole conception of profanity.

He was absolutely brave and he had only one real defect as a chauffeur. He couldn't drive a car. He was like a horse which has only two gaits; walking and running away. David could sneak along, in second speed, and hit practically no one in the streets, due to his clearing a swathe ahead of him with his vocabulary. He could also drive with the car wide open, hanging to the wheel, in a sort of fatalism that was, however, never tinged with despair.

287

We solved the problem by driving for David ourselves. He liked this and it gave him a chance to work with his vocabulary. His vocabulary was terrific.

He liked the war and he thought shelling was beautiful. "Look at that! Olé! That's the stuff to give the unmentionable, unspeakable, absolutely unutterables," he would say in delight. "Come on, let's get closer!" He was watching his first battle in the Casa del Campo and it was like a super-fireworks show to him. The spouting clouds of stone and plaster dust that pulsed up as the Government shells landed on a house the Moors held with machine guns and the great, tremendous, slither automatic rifles, machine guns and rapid fire combine into at the moment of the assault moved David very deeply. "Ayee! Ayee!" he said. "That's war. That's really war!"

He liked the tearing rush of the incomers just as much as the crack and the chu-chu-chu-ing air-parting rustle of sound that came from the battery which was firing over our heads on to the rebel positions.

"Olé," said David as a 75 burst a little way down the street. "Listen," I said. "Those are the bad ones. Those are the ones that kill us."

"That's of no importance," David said. "Listen to that unspeakable unmentionable noise."

Well, I went back to the hotel, finally, to write a dispatch and we sent David around to a place near the Plaza Mayor to get some petrol. I had almost finished the dispatch when in came David.

"Come and look at the car," he said. "It's full of blood. It's a terrible thing." He was pretty shaky. He had a dark face and his lips trembled.

"What was it?"

"A shell hit a line of women waiting to buy food. It killed seven. I took three to the hospital."

"Good boy."

"But you can't imagine it," he said. "It's terrible. I did not know there were such things."

"Listen, David," I said. "You're a brave boy. You must remember that. But all day you have been being brave about noises. What you see now is what those noises do. Now you must be brave about the noises knowing what they can do."

"Yes, man," he said. "But it is a terrible thing just the same to see."

David was brave, though. I don't think he ever thought it was quite as beautiful again as he did that first day; but he never shirked any of it. On the other hand he never learned to drive a car. But he was a good, if fairly useless, kid and I loved to hear his awful language. The only thing that developed in David was his vocabulary. He went off to the village where the motion picture outfit was making a film and, after having one more particularly useless chauffeur that there is no point in going into, we got Hipolito. Hipolito is the point of this story.

Hipolito was not much taller than Tomás, but he looked carved out of a granite block. He walked with a roll, putting his feet down flat at each stride; and he had an automatic pistol so big it came halfway down his leg. He always said "Salud" with a rising inflection as though it were something you said to hounds. Good hounds that knew their business. He knew motors, he could drive and if you told him to show up at six a.m., he was there at ten minutes before the hour.

He had fought at the taking of Montana barracks in the first days of the war and he had never been a member of any political party. He was a trade union man for the last twenty years in the Socialist Union, the U.G.T. He said, when I asked him what he believed in, that he believed in the Republic.

He was our chauffeur in Madrid and at the front during a nineteen-day bombardment of the capital that was almost too bad to write anything about. All the time he was as solid as the rock he looked to be cut from, as sound as a good bell and as regular and accurate as a railway man's watch. He made you realize why Franco never took Madrid when he had the chance.

Hipolito and the others like him would have fought from street to street, and house to house, as long as any one of them was left alive; and the last ones left would have burned the town. They are tough and they are efficient. They are the Spaniards that once conquered the Western World. They are not romantic like the Anarchists and they are not afraid to die. Only they never mention it. The Anarchists talk a little bit too much about it, the way the Italians do.

On the day we had over 300 shells come into Madrid so the main streets were a glass-strewn, brick-dust powdered, smoking shambles, Hipolito had the car parked in the lee of a building in a narrow street beside the hotel. It looked like a good safe place and after he had sat around the room while I was working until he was thoroughly bored, he said he'd go down and sit in the car. He hadn't been gone ten minutes when a six-inch shell hit the hotel just at the junction of the main floor and the sidewalk. It went deep in out of sight and didn't explode. If it had burst, there would not have been enough left of Hipolito and the car to take a picture of. They were about fifteen feet away from where the shell hit. I looked out of the window, saw he was all right, and then went downstairs.

"How are you?" I was fairly average breathless.

289

"Fine," he said.

"Put the car further down the street."

"Don't be foolish," he said. "Another one wouldn't drop there in a thousand years. Besides it didn't explode."

"Put it farther along the street."

"What's the matter with you?" he asked. "You getting windy?"

"You've got to be sensible."

"Go ahead and do your work," he said. "Don't worry about me."

The details of that day are a little confused because after nineteen days of heavy shelling some of the days get merged into others; but at one o'clock the shelling stopped and we decided to go to the Hotel Gran Via, about six blocks down, to get some lunch. I was going to walk by a very tortuous and extremely safe way I had worked out utilizing the angles of least danger, when Hipolito said, "Where are you going?"

"To eat."

"Get in the car."

"You're crazy."

"Come on, we'll drive down the Gran Via. It's stopped. They are eating their lunch too."

Four of us got into the car and drove down the Gran Via. It was solid with broken glass. There were great holes all down the sidewalks. Buildings were smashed and we had to walk around a heap of rubble and a smashed stone cornice to get into the hotel. There was not a living person on either side of the street, which had been, always, Madrid's Fifth Avenue and Broadway combined. There were many dead. We were the only motor car.

Hipolito put the car up a side street and we all ate together. We were still eating when Hipolito finished and went up to the car. There was some more shelling sounding, in the hotel basement, like muffled blasting, and when we finished the lunch of bean soup, paper thin sliced sausage and an orange, we went upstairs, the streets were full of smoke and clouds of dust. There was new smashed cement work all over the sidewalk. I looked around a corner for the car. There was rubble scattered all down that street from a new shell that had hit just overhead. I saw the car. It was covered with dust and rubble.

"My God," I said, "they've got Hipolito."

He was lying with his head back in the driver's seat. I went up to him feeling very badly. I had got very fond of Hipolito.

Hipolito was asleep.

"I thought you were dead," I said. He woke and wiped a yawn on the back of his hand.

"Qué va, hombre," he said. "I am always accustomed to sleep after lunch if I have time."

"We are going to Chicote's Bar," I said.

"Have they got good coffee there?"

"Excellent."

"Come on," he said. "Let's go."

I tried to give him some money when I left Madrid.

"I don't want anything from you," he said.

"No," I said. "Take it. Go on. Buy something for the family."

"No," he said. "Listen, we had a good time, didn't we?"

You can bet on Franco, or Mussolini, or Hitler, if you want. But my money goes on Hipolito.

Dying, Well or Badly

Ken
APRIL 21, 1938

It has been going on now, in Spain, all day and all night long for over a year and a half. So you are all tired of it. Even the word doesn't mean anything anymore. War is not a word that frightens people any longer. They are getting used to it now. You even hear that we have been promised one if business does not pick up. Though nobody believes that of course.

So now, before you read any further in this, look across the page and you will see two pictures of Italian soldiers who died well in battle. They look pretty good, don't they?

The boy at the bottom of the page was shot through the head. The man at the top was hit in the hand, had bandaged that wound, and then was killed by a bullet in the chest. The man at the top of the next page was shot through the legs and the chest. There was nothing very odd nor very extraordinary about any of those wounds; and in this last year one has seen many people that one knew die in the same way.

But at the bottom of the next page, and on the page opposite you see three photographs of three Italian soldiers who came to Spain to die but did not have quite such good luck at it.

The man at the bottom of the left-hand page was hit by high explosive. There are no feet to his legs.

The man at the bottom of the other page was hit by a tank shell which exploded in the little pile of rocks where he was working an automatic rifle. The other man, who was helping serve the gun, is dead on the left from the same shell. He does not show in the picture; but he looks all right. There's nothing very startling about him; but he is quite dead.

The man at the top of the right-hand page was hit by a light bomb dropped from a pursuit plane which was ground-strafing. He is rather

292

impressive to those who are not accustomed to a battle-field. But in your time you've seen good friends look as bad or worse.

You remember this man quite well because you turned him over to look at his papers and among them was a letter from his wife that you kept until you lost it. She wrote how badly things were going in the village, how pleased she was to get his pay allotment; but that she cried every night because he was not there. She also told how many times she prayed each day to keep him safe and that she had never ceased to thank St. Joseph for sending her such a good husband.

These are photographs of what happens to the men sent to die in a fascist invasion of a democratic country; a country with a republican form of government.

The men who are defending that country against the Moors, the Italians and the Germans, die in the same way. They die in as strange ways, in as ugly ways, as do the invaders. But they die knowing why they die; they die fighting for *you* now; knowing that unless they beat the fascists now *you* will have to fight them later. Many of them came a long way to die in Spain and none of them who fought on the ground got more than 50¢ a day. They, the men of the International Brigades, were not soldiers of fortune or adventurers. They were just very clear thinkers. No one sent them. They came to Spain to fight fascism because they saw, long before the diplomats, how dangerous it was.

Before this is published, the Italians will have attacked again. In the last three months while discussing the withdrawal of volunteers, Italy has sent 50,000 more troops to Spain. She has also sent three full brigades of artillery, and Germany, hiding behind the Italians, has sent between three and four hundred new planes and much new artillery and tanks. The fascist nations act while the democratic nations talk, vacillate connive and betray.

If the democratic nations allow Spain to be over-run by the fascists through their refusal to allow the legal Spanish government to buy and import arms to combat a military insurrection and fascist invasion, they will deserve whatever fate that brings them. The majority of the career diplomats of England, France, and the United States, are fascist, and it is they who supply the erroneous information on which their foreign offices and state departments act. But no matter what excuse the democratic countries may have for their ignorance of the necessity for beating the fascists in Spain, history will label their actions in 1936 and 1937, when they refused to allow Spain to arm herself to fight *their* enemies, as criminal stupidity.

Meantime all day, and all night, it goes on. The resistance of the republican government in Spain against the first combined fascist invasion is the great holding attack to save what we call civilization. If Italy could be beaten in Spain, as Napoleon was beaten there, the Berlin-Rome-Tokyo axis would be broken before it ever had a chance to make the war it threatens. But because it has gone on so long the people who do not have to go hungry, fight and die in it, get quite tired of the whole thing. They do not even want to hear about it. Perhaps these pictures will make it seem a little more real. Because those pictures are what you will look like if we let the next war come.

A Program for U.S. Realism

Ken
AUGUST 11, 1938

Question: What is War?

Answer: War is an act of violence intended to compel our opponent to fulfill our will.

Question: What is the primary aim of war?

Answer: The primary aim of war is to disarm the enemy.

Question: What are the necessary steps to achieve this?

Answer: First; the military power must be destroyed, that is, reduced to such a state that it will not be able to carry on the war. Second; the country must be conquered. For out of the country a new military force may be formed. Third; the will of the enemy must be subdued.

Question: Are there any ways of imposing our will on the enemy without fulfilling these three conditions?

Answer: Yes. There is invasion, that is the occupation of the enemy's territory, not with a view to keeping it, but in order to levy contributions on it, or to devastate it.

Question: Can a country which remains on the defensive hope to win a war?

Answer: Yes. This negative intention, which constitutes the principle of the pure defensive, is also the natural means of overcoming the enemy by the duration of the combat, that is of wearing him out. If then, the negative purpose, that is the concentration of all the means into a state of pure resistance, affords a superiority in the contest, and if this advantage is sufficient to balance whatever superiority in numbers the adversary may have, then the mere duration of the contest will suffice gradually to bring the loss of force on the part of the adversary to a point *at which the political object can no longer be an equivalent*, a point at which, therefore, he must give up the contest. We see then that this class of means, the wearing out of the enemy, includes the great number of cases in which the weaker resists the stronger.

Frederick the Great, during the Seven Years' War, was never strong enough to overthrow the Austrian monarchy. If he had tried to do so after the fashion of Charles the 12th, he would inevitably have had to succumb himself. But after his skillful application of the system of husbanding his resources had shown the powers allied against him, through a seven years' struggle, that the actual expenditure of strength far exceeded what they had at first anticipated, they made peace.

The answers are all by Clausewitz, who knew the answers very well. They make dry, hard reading, but there is so much nonsense written, thought and spoken about war that it is necessary to go back to the old Einstein of battles to see the military precedent by which the Spanish Republic continues to fight. If you study those two paragraphs by Clausewitz on the power of the defensive, you will see why there will be war in Spain for a long time.

There has been war in Spain, now, for two years. There has been war in China for a year. War is due in Europe by next summer at the latest.

It nearly came on May 21. It is possible that it will come now, in August. Or it may be delayed until next summer. But it is coming.

Now what is war again? We say war is murder, that it is inexcusable, that it is indefensible, that no objective can justify an offensive war. But what does Clausewitz say? He calls war "a continuation of state policy by other means."

Just when will this new war come? You may be sure that every detail of the starting of it is planned now. But just when is it coming?

"If two parties have armed themselves for strife, then a feeling of animosity must have moved them to it. As long now as they continue armed, that is, do not come to terms of peace, this feeling must exist. And it can only be brought to a standstill by either side by one single motive alone, which is, *that he waits for a more favorable moment for action.*

That is Clausewitz again.

"The Statesman, who, knowing his instrument to be ready, and seeing war inevitable, hesitates to strike first, is guilty of a crime against his country."

That is by Von Der Goltz. And that is something to read over.

There is a great demand now by Mr. Neville Chamberlain and the mouthpieces of his policy in our state department, that we should be realists.

Why not be realists? Not Chamberlain realists, who are merely the exponents of a stop-gap British policy which will be scrapped as soon as the British are armed, but American realists.

There is going to be war in Europe. What are we going to do about it as realists?

First, we want to stay out of it. We have nothing to gain in a European war except the temporary prosperity it will bring.

One way to stay out is to have nothing to do with it, not sell war materials to either side. And if you do that the British and the pro-British state department boys will be pulling you into it just the same; only it will not be for sordid ends, it will be on the highest and noblest humanitarian grounds. The other side will be working on us too; but the British are the most skillful and the most plausible.

The Germans have a genius for irritating people, for offending nations and for supplying pretexts. The Hohenzollerns were bad enough, but the Nazis will be worse, and where there was one *Lusitania* the last time you can figure on half a dozen this time. You can't expect the savages that bombed Guernica and the civilian population of Barcelona to resist a crack at the *Normandie* and the *Queen Mary*. So when war comes Americans will have to try American ships for a change. Or else make up their minds to fight for the French Line and for Cunard.

No. If you are going to be a realist you have to make up your mind beforehand whether you are going to go to war or not. There will be plenty of pretexts to get us in. And there is going to be a war.

So let us make up our minds to stay out. But why stay out and go broke? If we are realists why not sell to both sides, anything they want, anything we can manufacture? But sell it all for cash. Nothing should be sold for credit, so that we will be dragged in to help one side win so they can pay us what they owe us, and then go through the whole farce of war debts again.

There is going to be a war in Europe. Why not make something out of it if we are realists? But all sales should be for cash and the cash should be gold.

Then, to ensure our not being dragged in, nothing should be shipped to any belligerent country in American ships. Nor should any American ships carry war materials. Let the belligerent countries who can buy, send their own ships, pay cash for what they buy, and then, if their ships are sunk, it is their lookout. The more that are sunk the better.

At that point we sell them ships, also for cash; good, fast-built, cheap bottoms such as we turned out during the last war. All these we sell and build for cash. Cash down with the order; the ship the property of the country that buys it from the minute that the keels are laid.

Then when the Gestapo lads sabotage and burn ship-yards we do not go to war about that either. We are insured, see. The more sabotage the better. And if their liners are sunk too, we will build them some others too; for cash.

Let the gentlemen of Europe fight and, if they pay cash, see how long it will last. Why not be realists, Mr. Chamberlain? Why not be realists? Or don't you want to play?

VIII
World War II

"*I have decided, or rather I decided several months before it started, or may be several years say, not to write propaganda in this war at all. I am willing to go to it and will send my kids to it and will give what money I have to it but I want to write just what I believe all the way through it and after it. It was the writers in the last war who wrote propaganda that finished themselves off that way. There is plenty of stuff that you believe absolutely that you can write which is useful enough without having to write propaganda. . . . If we are fighting for what we believe in we might as well always keep on believing in what we have believed, and for me this is to write nothing that I do not think is the absolute truth.*"

—To Maxwell Perkins, Finca Vigía, Cuba,
May 30, 1942

Notes on the Next War:
A Serious Topical Letter

Esquire
SEPTEMBER 1935

Not this August, nor this September; you have this year to do in what you like. Not next August, nor next September; that is still too soon; they are still too prosperous from the way things pick up when armament factories start at near capacity; they never fight as long as money can still be made without. So you can fish that summer and shoot that fall or do whatever you do, go home at nights, sleep with your wife, go to the ball game, make a bet, take a drink when you want to, or enjoy whatever liberties are left for anyone who has a dollar or a dime. But the year after that or the year after that they fight. Then what happens to you?

First you make a lot of money; maybe. There is a chance now that you make nothing; that it will be the government that makes it all. That is what, in the last analysis, taking the profits out of war means. If you are on relief you will be drafted into this great profitless work and you will be a slave from that day.

If there is a general European war we will be brought in if propaganda (think of how the radio will be used for this), greed, and the desire to increase the impaired health of the state can swing us in. Every move that is made now to deprive the people of their decision on all matters through their elected representatives and to delegate those powers to the executive brings us that much nearer war.

It removes the only possible check. No one man nor group of men incapable of fighting or exempt from fighting should in any way be given the power, no matter how gradually it is given them, to put this country or any country into war.

The first panacea for a mismanaged nation is inflation of the currency; the second is war. Both bring a temporary prosperity; both bring a permanent ruin. But both are the refuge of political and economic opportunists.

No European country is our friend nor has been since the last war and no country but one's own is worth fighting for. Never again should this country be put into a European war through mistaken idealism, through propaganda, through the desire to back our creditors, or through the wish of anyone through war, notoriously the health of the state, to make a going concern out of a mismanaged one.

Now let us examine the present set-up and see what chance there is of avoiding war.

No nations, anymore, pay their debts. There is no longer even a pretense of honesty between nations or of the nation toward the individual. Finland pays us still; but she is a new country and will learn better. We were a new country once and we learned better. Now when a country does not pay its debts you cannot take its word on anything. So we may discard any treaties or declarations of intentions by any countries which do not coincide completely and entirely with the immediate and most cynical national aims of those countries.

A few years ago, in the late summer, Italy and France mobilized along their border to fight over Italy's desire for colonial expansion in North Africa. All references to this mobilization were censored out of cables and radiograms. Correspondents who mentioned it in mailed stories were threatened with expulsion. That difference has now been settled by Mussolini's shift of ambition to East Africa where he has obviously made a deal with the French to abandon his North African plans in return for France allowing him to make war on a free sovereign state under the protection of membership in the League of Nations.

Italy is a country of patriots and whenever things are going badly at home, business bad, oppression and taxation too great, Mussolini has only to rattle the saber against a foreign country to make his patriots forget their dissatisfaction at home in their flaming zeal to be at the throats of the enemy. By the same system, early in his rule, when his personal popularity waned and the opposition was strengthened, an attempted assassination of the Duce would be arranged which would put the populace in such a frenzy of hysterical love for their nearly lost leader that they would stand for anything and patriotically vote the utmost repressive measures against the opposition.

Mussolini plays on their admirable patriotic hysteria as a violinist on his instrument but when France and Jugo-Slavia were the possible enemy he could never really give them the full Paganini because he did not want war with those countries; only the threat of war. He still remembers Caporetto, where Italy lost 320,000 men in killed, wounded and missing, of which amount 265,000 were missing, although he has trained a generation of young Italians who believe Italy to be an invincible military power.

Now he is setting out to make war on a feudal country, whose soldiers fight barefooted and with the formations of the desert and the middle ages; he plans to use planes against a people who have none and machine guns, flame projectors, gas, and modern artillery against bows and arrows, spears, and native cavalry armed with carbines. Certainly the stage is as nearly set as it ever can be for an Italian victory and such a victory as will keep Italians' minds off things at home for a long time. The only flaw is that Abyssinia has a small nucleus of trained, well armed troops.

France is glad to see him fight. In the first place anyone who fights may be beaten; Italy's Black Caporetto, her second greatest military debacle, was administered by these same Ethiopians at Adowa when fourteen thousand Italian troops were killed or driven from the field by a force which Mussolini now describes as 100,000 Ethiopians. Certainly it is unfair to ask fourteen thousand troops to fight one hundred thousand but the essence of war is not to confront your force of fourteen thousand with a hundred thousand of anything. Actually the Italians lost more than 4500 white and 2000 native troops, killed and wounded. Sixteen hundred Italians were taken prisoners. The Abyssinians admitted losing 3000 men.

The French remember Adowa and less possibly though more recently, Baer and Braddock (who knows but what Owney Madden may have bought a piece of the Ethiopians?), and they know that anybody who fights may be beaten. Dysentery, fever, the sun, bad transport, many things can defeat an army. There are also a number of tropical diseases which can only become epidemic when given the opportunity afforded by an invading army of men unused to the climate and possessing no immunity against them. Anyone who fights near the equator can be beaten by the mere difficulty of keeping an army in the field.

Then France feels that if Italy wins or loses, the war will cost her so much that she will be in no position to make trouble in Europe. Italy has never been a serious problem unless she has allies, because she has no coal and no iron. No nation can make war without coal and iron. Lately Italy has tried to overcome this by building up an enormous air-force and it is her air-force that makes her the threat she is in Europe today.

England is glad to see Italy fight Ethiopia. First she may be whipped which, they figure, will teach her a lesson and lengthen the peace of Europe. Secondly if she wins that removes the annoyance of Abyssinian raids along the northern frontier province of Kenya and gives some one else the responsibility of suppressing the perennial Abyssinian slave trade across to Arabia. Next England must undoubtedly have an arrangement with the possible victor about the water power project in northeastern Ethiopia which she has long coveted for the watering of the Sudan. It is only logical that Anthony Eden should have arranged about that when he was in Rome recently. Lastly she knows that anything Italy finds and brings out of Ethiopia must come through the Suez Canal or, taking the long way around, the straits of Gibraltar, while if Japan had been permitted to penetrate into Ethiopia and thus gain a foothold in Africa what she took would go direct to Japan and in time of necessity there would be no control over it.

Germany is glad to have Mussolini try to gobble Ethiopia. Any change in the African status quo provides an opening for her soon-to-be-made demands for return of her African colonial possessions. This return, if made, will probably delay war for a long time. Germany, under Hitler, wants war, a war of revenge, wants it fervently, patriotically and almost religiously. France hopes that it will come before Germany is too strong. But the people of France do not want war.

There is the great danger and the great difference. France is a country and Great Britain is several countries but Italy is a man, Mussolini, and Germany is a man, Hitler. A man has ambitions, a man rules until he gets into economic trouble; he tries to get out of this trouble by war. A country never wants war until a man through the power of propaganda convinces it. Propaganda is stronger now than it has ever been before. Its agencies have been mechanized, multiplied and controlled until in a state ruled by any one man truth can never be presented.

War is no longer made by simply analysed economic forces if it ever was. War is made or planned now by individual men, demagogues and dictators who play on the patriotism of their people to mislead them into a belief in the great fallacy of war when all their vaunted reforms have failed to satisfy the people they misrule. And we in America should see that no man is ever given, no matter how gradually or how noble and excellent the man, the power to put this country into a war which is now being prepared and brought closer each day with all the premeditation of a long planned murder. For when you give power to an executive you do not know who will be filling that position when the time of crisis comes.

They wrote in the old days that it is sweet and fitting to die for one's country. But in modern war there is nothing sweet nor fitting in your dying. You will die like a dog for no good reason. Hit in the head you will die quickly and cleanly even sweetly and fittingly except for the white blinding flash that never stops, unless perhaps it is only the frontal bone or your optic nerve that is smashed, or your jaw carried away, or your nose and cheek bones gone so you can still think but you have no face to talk with. But if you are not hit in the head you will be hit in the chest, and choke in it, or in the lower belly, and feel it all slip and slide loosely as you open, to spill out when you try to get up, it's not supposed to be so painful but they always scream with it, it's the idea I suppose, or have the flash, the slamming clang of high explosive on a hard road and find your legs are gone above the knee, or maybe just below the knee, or maybe just a foot gone and watch the white bone sticking through your puttee, or watch them take a boot off with your foot a mush inside it, or feel an arm flop and learn how a bone feels grating, or you will burn, choke and vomit, or be blown to hell a dozen ways, without sweetness or fittingness; but none of this means anything. No catalogue of horrors ever kept men from war. Before the war you always think that it's not you that dies. But you will die, brother, if you go to it long enough.

The only way to combat the murder that is war is to show the dirty combinations that make it and the criminals and swine that hope for it and the idiotic way they run it when they get it so that an honest man will distrust it as he would a racket and refuse to be enslaved into it.

If war was fought by those who wanted to fight it and knew what they were doing and liked it, or even understood it, then it would be defensible. But those who want to go to the war, the élite, are killed off in the first months and the rest of the war is fought by men who are enslaved into the bearing of arms and are taught to be more afraid of sure death from their officers if they run than possible death if they stay in the line or attack. Eventually their steadily increasing terror overcomes them, given the proper amount of bombardment and a given intensity of fire, and they all run and, if they get far enough out of hand, for that army it is over. Was there any allied army which did not, sooner or later, run during the last war? There is not room here to list them.

No one wins a modern war because it is fought to such a point that everyone must lose. The troops that are fighting at the end are incapable of winning. It is only a question of which government rots the first or which side can get in a new ally with fresh troops. Sometimes the allies are useful. Sometimes they are Rumania.

In a modern war there is no Victory. The allies won the war but the regiments that marched in triumph were not the men who fought the war. The men who fought the war were dead. More than seven million of them were dead and it is the murder of over seven million more that an ex-corporal in the German army and an ex-aviator and former morphine addict drunk with personal and military ambition and fogged in a blood-stained murk of misty patriotism look forward hysterically to today. Hitler wants war in Europe as soon as he can get it. He is an ex-corporal and he will not have to fight in this one; only to make the speeches. He himself has nothing to lose by making war and everything to gain.

Mussolini is an ex-corporal, too, but he is also an ex-anarchist, a great opportunist, and a realist. He wants no war in Europe. He will bluff in Europe but he never means to fight there. He can still remember what the war was like himself and how he left it after being wounded in an accident with an Italian trench mortar and went back to newspaper work. He does not want to fight in Europe because he knows that anyone who fights may lose, unless of course one can arrange to fight Rumania, and the first dictator who provokes a war and loses it puts a stop to dictators, and their sons, for a long time.

Because the development of his regime calls for a war he chooses Africa as the place to fight and the only surviving free African state as his opponent. The Abyssinians unfortunately are Christians so it cannot be a Holy war. But while he is making Ethiopia Fit for Fiats he can, of course, suppress slavery on paper, and doubtless in the Italian War College, it looks like a foolproof, quick and ideal campaign. But it may be that a regime and a whole system of government will fall because of this foolproof war in less than three years.

A German colonel named Von Lettow-Vorbeck with an original force of 5000 troops, only two hundred and fifty of whom were whites, fought 130,000 allied troops for a period of over four years in Tanganyika and Portuguese Africa and caused the expenditure of 72,000,000 pounds sterling. At the end of the war he was still at large carrying on guerrilla warfare.

If the Abyssinians choose to fight on in guerrilla warfare rather than make peace Italy may find that Ethiopia will be an unhealing wound in her side that will drain away her money, her youth and her food supplies and return men broken in health and disgusted with suffering and the government that sent them to suffer with promises of glory. It is the disillusioned soldiers who overthrow a regime.

It may be that this war in Africa will prolong the temporary peace in Europe. In the meantime something may happen to Hitler. But of the hell broth that is brewing in Europe we have no need to drink. Europe has always fought, the intervals of peace are only Armistices. We were fools to be sucked in once on a European war and we should never be sucked in again.

The Malady of Power:
A Second Serious Letter
(an excerpt)

Esquire
NOVEMBER 1935

If you tell it to them once they think it is marvelous. When you tell it to them again they say, "We heard that before somewhere. Where do you suppose he got that from?" If you tell it to them a third time they are bored to death and they won't listen to it. It may be truer every time. But they get tired of hearing it.

So this month we wrap it all up in a series of anecdotes so that perhaps you will not taste the castor-oil in the chop suey sandwich. But having read the President's reported statement to a group of Representatives that he could, if he would, put the U.S. into war in ten days, this one is still about the next war.

In the old days, when your correspondent was a working newspaper man, he had a friend named Bill Ryall, then a European correspondent for the Manchester *Guardian*. This Ryall had a white, lantern-jawed face of the sort that is supposed to haunt you if seen suddenly in a London fog, but on a bright windy day in Paris meeting him on the boulevard wearing a long fur-collared great coat he had the never-far-from-tragic look of a ham Shakespearean actor. None of us thought of him as a genius then and I do not think he thought of himself as one either, being too busy, too intelligent, and, then, too sardonic to go in for being a genius in a city where they were a nickel a dozen and it was much more distinguished to be hard working. He was a South African and had been very badly blown up in the war while commanding infantry.

*   *   *

It was Ryall's theory that a politician or a patriot as soon as given a supreme position in a state, unless he was without ambition and had not sought the office, always began to show the symptoms of what power was doing to him. He said you could see it very clearly in all the men of the French Revolution, too, and it was because our forefathers in America knew how power affected men that they had limited the term of the executive.

Ryall said one of the first symptoms of the malady of power was suspicion of the man's associates, then came great touchiness on all matters, inability to receive criticism, belief that he was indispensable, and that nothing had ever been done rightly until he came into power and that nothing would ever be done rightly again unless he stayed in power. He said that the better and more disinterested the man, the quicker this attacked him. He said that a man who was dishonest would last much longer because his dishonesty made him either cynical or humble in a way, and that protected him.

That night I remember him quoting the example of a Lord of the British Admiralty who had been getting steadily more advanced in the malady of power. It had become impossible for almost anyone to work with him and the final smash came at a meeting at which they were discussing how to get a better class of cadets for the navy. This admiral had hammered on a table with his fist and said, "Gentlemen if you do not know where to get them, by God I will make them for you!"

Since that evening your correspondent has studied various politicians, statesmen and patriots in the light of Bill Ryall's theory and he believes that the fate of our country for the next hundred years or so depends on the extent of Franklin D. Roosevelt's ambition. If he is ambitious only to serve his country, as Cleveland was, we, and our children, and their children will be very fortunate. If he is ambitious personally, to leave a great name, or to eclipse the luster of the name he bears, which was made famous by another man, we will be out of luck because the sensational improvements that can be made legally in the country in time of peace are being rapidly exhausted.

War is coming in Europe as surely as winter follows fall. If we want to stay out now is the time to decide to stay out. Now, before the propaganda starts. Now is the time to make it impossible for any one man, or any hundred men, or any thousand men, to put us in a war in ten days—in a war they will not have to fight.

In the next ten years there will be much fighting, there will be opportunities for the United States to again swing the balance of power in Europe; she will again have a chance to save civilization; she will have a chance to fight another war to end war.

Whoever heads the nation will have a chance to be the greatest man in the world for a short time—and the nation can hold the sack once the excitement is over. For the next ten years we need a man without ambition, a man who hates war and knows that no good ever comes of it, and a man who has proved his beliefs by adhering to them. All candidates will need to be measured against these requirements.

Russo-Japanese Pact

PM
JUNE 10, 1941

HONG KONG.—On the day the Japanese-Soviet neutrality pact was signed in Moscow, Dr. H. H. Kung, who is both Prime Minister and Minister of Finance for his brother-in-law, Generalissimo Chiang Kai-shek, was dining with Soviet Ambassador Paniushkin in Chungking.

"We hear that a pact is going to be signed," the Chinese statesman said.

"Yes," the Soviet Ambassador answered. "That is true."

"What will be the effect of such a pact on Russian aid to China?"

"None," answered the Soviet Ambassador.

"Will you withdraw any troops from the Manchukuo frontier?"

"We will reinforce our divisions there," the Soviet Ambassador said, and the head of the Soviet military advisers in China, a Lieutenant General, nodded agreement.

At the time that incident happened I did not care to write it because diplomats rarely impart bad news over the dinner table and it was possible that very different news might come out of Moscow. But since then I have heard directly from both Dr. Kung and Mme. Chiang Kai-shek that Russian aid is continuing to arrive and that no Soviet staff officers, aviation instructors, or military advisers have been withdrawn from the Generalissimo's army.

My wife and I had lunched with Mme. Chiang Kai-shek the day the pact was announced and during the conversation she said, "But how will we know whether they will really withdraw aid or not?"

"If they are going to withdraw aid," I told her, remembering how it had happened in Spain, "the first move will be to withdraw the military advisers, the instructors and the staff officers. As long as they stay on, it means the aid will continue."

Last week a letter from Mme. Chiang Kai-shek contained these three paragraphs:

"I am fulfilling my promise to inform you of the Generalissimo's reaction to the neutrality pact between the USSR and Japan.

"The Generalissimo declares that this pact will not have the slightest effect on China's determination to continue national resistance. We began it single-handedly and if necessary, we shall end it the same way. What other nations, friendly or otherwise, may or may not do, will not influence. We will fight on until victory is won. Outer Mongolia and Manchuria are parts of China and the people of these regions themselves feel that they are indissolubly linked with the National Government, which recognizes no alienation of territory, and does not intend to, whatever happens.

"So far there is no indication that the USSR will withdraw its advisers from China, or will cease supplying us with war materials."

Soviet Russia has given China more aid than any other country has supplied. She has provided planes, pilots, trucks, some artillery, gasoline, military instructors and staff officers who act as military advisers. She has lent Chiang Kai-shek's government something over the equivalent of 200,000,000 U.S. dollars.

Most of this huge loan was attained on a barter basis and has been repaid in tea, wolfram (tungsten ore) and other products. The Russians drove a hard bargain when the barter terms were made and at present the Chinese have a difficult time buying the tea at prices agreed on with Russia. But they are still making deliveries.

Feeling between Chinese Communists and the Central Government is so bitter on both sides that I was amazed at first to find Soviet staff officers still serving in an advisory capacity with Chiang Kai-shek's armies and Soviet aid to China still coming in steadily. While I was at the front with Chinese Central Army troops I encountered Soviet staff officers and I saw new Russian planes which had come in; both bombardment and pursuit. In the officers' club where I lived at Chengtu in Northern Szechwan Province the room numbers on all the rooms were in Russian and various delicacies we had for breakfasts, including cocoa and tinned butter, had come by way of Vladivostok and Chita.

This Vladivostok route was using the Trans-Siberian Railroad to haul freight to Chita. From Chita to Urga, all transport was by truck and bus. From Urga to Ninghsia, camel caravans carried the freight to the Chinese roadhead where it was loaded onto trucks again for the haul to Chungking and Chengtu.

311

No visitors are allowed to see the Russian military advisers, instructors and pilot instructors, but I had run into three Russian staff officers out at the front on an impassable muddy road where all transport was stalled. So I greeted one of them whom I knew with, "How are you doing, Tovarich?" It was evidently decided after that encounter that there was very little point in concealing from me the Russians' presence and from then on the subject was always discussed very frankly. Consequently, I had a good chance to compare the Chinese field staff and general officers' opinions on the various foreign military advisers they had fought under.

Almost unanimously they ranked the Germans first as soldiers and staff officers and the Russians second. Their complaint against the Russians was that they rarely worked out any offensive action on a large or small scale in sufficient force.

To simplify the explanation to the utmost, using men in terms of money: if a position was purchasable for 50 cents, the Russians would try to take it for a dime. They would fail at that and finally have to pay $1.15 for it because there no longer was any element of surprise. On the other hand, if a position was worth 50 cents, the Germans would smack it with $1.50. After it was taken you would often find that only a quarter out of the $1.50 had been spent.

Chinese generals, if they are convinced that you know what you are talking about, are extraordinarily frank, straight talking, intelligent and articulate. I have spent some time on various British maneuvers. The atmosphere at the Chinese front with the men who had fought the war lords for five years, the Communists for 10 and the Japanese for nearly four was as different from that of a British staff as the locker room of the Green Bay Packers professional football team would be from even such a good prep school as Choate.

One Chinese general asked me what the British in Hong Kong thought of them. We were a couple of days riding together after the opening formal politenesses. We had drunk numerous cups of rice wine and worked late over the map.

"Does the General really want to know what they said?"

"Yes, truly."

"The General will not be offended?"

"Of course not."

"'Well, we don't think very much of the Chinese, you know.'" I tried to reproduce it. "'Johnny's all right and a very good fellow and all that. But he's absolutely hopeless on the offensive, you know. We have absolutely no confidence in him ever taking the offensive. Truly none. No. Too bad. We can't count on Johnny.'"

"Johnny?" asked the General.

"John Chinaman," I said.

"Very interesting," the General said. "Very interesting."

Then he went on, "We have no artillery to speak of, you know. No planes. Or very few. You know that, of course. Do you think the British would go on the offensive without artillery or aerial support anywhere? Any time?

"No," he interrupted me. "Let me tell you a Chinese story. A new Chinese story. Not an old Chinese story. Do you know why the British staff officer wears a single glass in his eye?"

"No," I said.

"Ho," he said. "It is a very new Chinese story. He wears a single glass in his eye so he will not see more than he can understand."

"I will tell that officer when I see him," I said.

"Very good," he said. "Tell him it is a little message from Johnny."

Voyage to Victory

Collier's
JULY 22, 1944

No one remembers the date of the Battle of Shiloh. But the day we took Fox Green beach was the sixth of June, and the wind was blowing hard out of the northwest. As we moved in toward land in the gray early light, the 36-foot coffin-shaped steel boats took solid green sheets of water that fell on the helmeted heads of the troops packed shoulder to shoulder in the stiff, awkward, uncomfortable, lonely companionship of men going to a battle. There were cases of TNT, with rubber-tube life preservers wrapped around them to float them in the surf, stacked forward in the steel well of the LCV(P), and there were piles of bazookas and boxes of bazooka rockets encased in water-proof coverings that reminded you of the transparent raincoats college girls wear.

All this equipment, too, had the rubber-tube life preservers strapped and tied on, and the men wore these same gray rubber tubes strapped under their armpits.

As the boat rose to a sea, the green water turned white and came slamming in over the men, the guns and the cases of explosives. Ahead you could see the coast of France. The gray booms and derrick-forested bulks of the attack transports were behind now, and, over all the sea, boats were crawling forward toward France.

As the LCV(P) rose to the crest of a wave, you saw the line of low, silhouetted cruisers and the two big battlewagons lying broadside to the shore. You saw the heat-bright flashes of their guns and the brown smoke that pushed out against the wind and then blew away.

"What's your course, coxswain?" Lieutenant (jg) Robert Anderson of Roanoke, Virginia, shouted from the stern.

"Two-twenty, sir," the coxswain, Frank Currier of Saugus, Massachusetts, answered. He was a thin-faced, freckled boy with his eyes fixed on the compass.

"Then steer two-twenty, damn it!" Anderson said. "Don't steer all over the whole damn' ocean!"

"I'm steering two-twenty, sir," the coxswain said patiently.

"Well, steer it, then," Andy said. He was nervous, but the boat crew, who were making their first landing under fire, knew this officer had taken LCV(P)s in to the African landing, Sicily and Salerno, and they had confidence in him.

"Don't steer into that LCT," Andy shouted, as we roared by the ugly steel hull of a tank landing craft, her vehicles sea-lashed, her troops huddling out of the spray.

"I'm steering two-twenty," the coxswain said.

"That doesn't mean you have to run into everything on the ocean," Andy said. He was a handsome, hollow-cheeked boy with a lot of style and a sort of easy petulance. "Mr. Hemingway, will you please see if you can see what that flag is over there, with your glasses?"

I got my old miniature Zeiss glasses out of an inside pocket, where they were wrapped in a woolen sock with some tissue to clean them, and focused them on the flag. I made the flag out just before a wave drenched the glasses.

"It's green."

"Then we are in the mine-swept channel," Andy said. "That's all right. Coxswain, what's the matter with you? Can't you steer two-twenty?"

I was trying to dry my glasses, but it was hopeless the way the spray was coming in, so I wrapped them up for a try later on and watched the battleship Texas shelling the shore. She was just off on our right now and firing over us as we moved in toward the French coast, which was showing clearer all the time on what was, or was not, a course of 220 degrees, depending on whether you believed Andy or Currier the coxswain.

The low cliffs were broken by valleys. There was a town with a church spire in one of them. There was a wood that came down to the sea. There was a house on the right of one of the beaches. On all the headlands, the gorse was burning, but the northwest wind held the smoke close to the ground.

Those of our troops who were not wax-gray with seasickness, fighting it off, trying to hold onto themselves before they had to grab for the steel side of the boat, were watching the Texas with looks of surprise and happiness. Under the steel helmets they looked like pikemen of the Middle Ages to whose aid in battle had suddenly come some strange and unbelievable monster.

There would be a flash like a blast furnace from the 14-inch guns of the Texas, that would lick far out from the ship. Then the yellow-

315

brown smoke would cloud out and, with the smoke still rolling, the concussion and the report would hit us, jarring the men's helmets. It struck your near ear like a punch with a heavy, dry glove.

Then up on the green rise of a hill that now showed clearly as we moved in would spout two tall black fountains of earth and smoke.

"Look what they're doing to those Germans," I leaned forward to hear a G.I. say above the roar of the motor. "I guess there won't be a man alive there," he said happily.

That is the only thing I remember hearing a G.I. say all that morning. They spoke to one another sometimes, but you could not hear them with the roar the 225-horsepower high-speed gray Diesel made. Mostly, though, they stood silent without speaking. I never saw anyone smile after we left the line of firing ships. They had seen the mysterious monster that was helping them, but now he was gone and they were alone again.

I found if I kept my mouth open from the time I saw the guns flash until after the concussion, it took the shock away.

I was glad when we were inside and out of the line of fire of the Texas and the Arkansas. Other ships were firing over us all day and you were never away from the sudden, slapping thud of naval gunfire. But the big guns of the Texas and Arkansas that sounded as though they were throwing whole railway trains across the sky were far away as we moved on in. They were no part of our world as we moved steadily over the gray, white-capped sea toward where, ahead of us, death was being issued in small, intimate, accurately administered packages. They were like the thunder of a storm that is passing in another county whose rain will never reach you. But they were knocking out the shore batteries, so that later the destroyers could move in almost to the shore when they had to come in to save the landing.

Now ahead of us we could see the coast in complete detail. Andy opened the silhouette map with all the beaches and their distinguishing features reproduced on it, and I got my glasses out and commenced drying and wiping them under the shelter of the skirts of my burberry. As far as you could see, there were landing craft moving in over the gray sea. The sun was under at this time, and smoke was blowing all along the coast.

The map that Andy spread on his knees was in ten folded sheets, held together with staples, and marked Appendix One to Annex A. Five different sheets were stapled together and, as I watched Andy open his map, which spread, open, twice as long as a man could reach with outstretched arms, the wind caught it, and the section of the map showing

Dog White, Fox Red, Fox Green, Dog Green, Easy Red and part of Sector Charlie snapped twice gaily in the wind and blew overboard.

I had studied this map and memorized most of it, but it is one thing to have it in your memory and another thing to see it actually on paper and be able to check and be sure.

"Have you got a small chart, Andy?" I shouted. "One of those one-sheet ones with just Fox Green and Easy Red?"

"Never had one," said Andy. All this time we were approaching the coast of France, which looked increasingly hostile.

"That the only chart?" I said, close to his ear.

"Only one," said Andy, "and it disintegrated on me. A wave hit it, and it disintegrated. What beach do you think we are opposite?"

"There's the church tower that looks like Colleville," I said. "That ought to be on Fox Green. Then there is a house like the one marked on Fox Green and the timber that runs down to the water in a straight line, like on Easy Red."

"That's right," said Andy. "But I think we're too far to the left."

"Those are the features, all right," I said. "I've got them in my head but there shouldn't be any cliffs. The cliffs start to the left of Fox Green where Fox Red beach starts. If that's true, then Fox Green has to be on our right."

"There's a control boat here somewhere," Andy said. "We'll find out what beach we're opposite."

"She can't be Fox Green if there are cliffs," I said.

"That's right," Andy said. "We'll find out from a control boat. Steer for that PC, coxswain. No, not there! Don't you see him? Get ahead of him. You'll never catch him that way."

We never did catch him, either. We slammed into the seas instead of topping them, and the boat pulled away from us. The LCV(P) was bow-heavy with the load of TNT and the weight of the three-eighth-inch steel armor, and where she should have lifted easily over the seas she banked into them and the water came in solidly.

"The hell with him!" Andy said. "We'll ask this LCI."

Landing Craft Infantry are the only amphibious operations craft that look as though they were made to go to sea. They very nearly have the lines of a ship, while the LCV(P)s look like iron bathtubs, and the LCTs like floating freight gondolas. Everywhere you could see, the ocean was covered with these craft but very few of them were headed toward shore. They would start toward the beach, then sheer off and circle back. On the beach itself, in from where we were, there were lines of what looked like tanks, but my glasses were still too wet to function.

"Where's Fox Green beach?" Andy cupped his hands and shouted up at the LCI that was surging past us, loaded with troops.

"Can't hear," someone shouted. We had no megaphone.

"What beach are we opposite?" Andy yelled.

The officer on the LCI shook his head. The other officers did not even look toward us. They were looking over their shoulders at the beach.

"Get her close alongside, coxswain," Andy said. "Come on, get in there close."

We roared up alongside the LCI, then cut down the motor as she slipped past us.

"Where's Fox Green beach?" Andy yelled, as the wind blew the words away.

"Straight in to your right," an officer shouted.

"Thanks." Andy looked astern at the other two boats and told Ed Banker, the signalman, "Get them to close up. Get them up."

Ed Banker turned around and jerked his forearm, with index finger raised, up and down. "They're closing up, sir," he said.

Looking back you could see the other heavily loaded boats climbing the waves that were green now the sun was out, and pounding down into the troughs.

"You wet all through, sir?" Ed asked me.

"All the way."

"Me, too," Ed said. "Only thing wasn't wet was my belly button. Now it's wet, too."

"This has got to be Fox Green," I said to Andy. "I recognize where the cliff stops. That's all Fox Green to the right. There is the Colleville church. There's the house on the beach. There's the Ruquet Valley on Easy Red to the right. This is Fox Green absolutely."

"We'll check when we get in closer," Andy said. "You really think it's Fox Green?"

"It has to be."

Ahead of us, the various landing craft were all acting in the same confusing manner—heading in, coming out and circling.

"There's something wrong as hell," I said to Andy. "See the tanks? They're all along the edge of the beach. They haven't gone in at all."

Just then one of the tanks flared up and started to burn with thick black smoke and yellow flame. Farther down the beach, another tank started burning. Along the line of the beach, they were crouched like big yellow toads along the high water line. As I stood up, watching, two more started to burn. The first ones were pouring out gray smoke now, and the wind was blowing it flat along the beach. As I stood up, trying to see if there was anyone in beyond the high water line of tanks, one of the burning tanks blew up with a flash in the streaming gray smoke.

"There's a boat we can check with," Andy said. "Coxswain, steer for that LC over there. Yes, that one. Put her hard over. Come on. Get over there!"

This was a black boat, fast-looking, mounting two machine guns and wallowing slowly out away from the beach, her engine almost idling.

"Can you tell us what beach this is?" Andy shouted.

"Dog White," came the answer.

"Are you sure?"

"Dog White beach," they called from the black boat.

"You checked it?" Andy called.

"It's Dog White beach," they called back from the boat, and their screw churned the water white as they slipped into speed and pulled away from us.

I was discouraged now, because ahead of us, inshore, was every landmark I had memorized on Fox Green and Easy Red beaches. The line of the cliffs that marked the left end of Fox Green beach showed clearly. Every house was where it should be. The steeple of the Colleville church showed exactly as it had in the silhouette. I had studied the charts, the silhouettes, the data on the obstacles in the water and the defenses all one morning, and I remember having asked our captain, Commander W. I. Leahy of the attack transport Dorothea M. Dix, if our attack was to be a diversion in force.

"No," he had said. "Absolutely not. What makes you ask that question?"

"Because these beaches are so highly defensible."

"The Army is going to clear the obstacles and the mines out in the first thirty minutes," Captain Leahy had told me. "They're going to cut lanes in through them for the landing craft."

I wish I could write the full story of what it means to take a transport across through a mine-swept channel; the mathematical precision of maneuver; the infinite detail and chronometrical accuracy and split-second timing of everything from the time the anchor comes up until the boats are lowered and away into the roaring, sea-churning assembly circle from which they break off into the attack wave.

The story of all the teamwork behind that has to be written, but to get all that in would take a book, and this is simply the account of how it was in a LCV(P) on the day we stormed Fox Green beach.

Right at this moment, no one seemed to know where Fox Green

beach was. I was sure we were opposite it, but the patrol boat had said this was Dog White beach which should be 4.295 yards to our right, if we were where I knew we were.

"It can't be Dog White, Andy," I said. "Those are the cliffs where Fox Red starts on our left."

"The man says it's Dog White," Andy said.

In the solid-packed troops in the boat, a man with a vertical white bar painted on his helmet was looking at us and shaking his head. He had high cheekbones and a rather flat, puzzled face.

"The lieutenant says he knows it, and we're on Fox Green," Ed Banker shouted back at us. He spoke again to the lieutenant but we could not hear what they said.

Andy shouted at the lieutenant, and he nodded his helmeted head up and down.

"He says it's Fox Green," Andy said.

"Ask him where he wants to go in," I said.

Just then another small black patrol boat with several officers in it came toward us from the beach, and an officer stood up in it and megaphoned, "Are there any boats here for the seventh wave on Fox Green beach?"

There was one boat for that wave with us, and the officer shouted to them to follow their boat.

"Is this Fox Green?" Andy called to them.

"Yes. Do you see that ruined house? Fox Green beach runs for eleven hundred and thirty-five yards to the right of that ruined house."

"Can you get into the beach?"

"I can't tell you that. You will have to ask a beach control boat."

"Can't we just run in?"

"I have no authority on that. You must ask the beach control boat."

"Where is it?"

"Way out there somewhere."

"We can go in where an LCV(P) has been in or an LCI," I said. "It's bound to be clear where they run in, and we can go in under the lee of one."

"We'll look for the control boat," Andy said, and we went banging out to sea through the swarming traffic of landing craft and lighters.

"I can't find her," Andy said. "She isn't here. She ought to be in closer. We have to get the hell in. We're late now. Let's go in."

"Ask him where he is supposed to land," I said.

Andy went down and talked to the lieutenant. I could see the lieutenant's lips moving as he spoke, but could hear nothing above the engine noise.

"He wants to run straight in for that ruined house," Andy said, when he came back.

We headed in for the beach. As we came in, running fast, the black patrol boat swung over toward us again.

"Did you find the control boat?" they megaphoned.

"No!"

"What are you going to do?"

"We're going in," Andy said.

"Well, good luck to you fellows," the megaphone said. It came over, slow and solemn like an elegy. "Good luck to all of you fellows."

That included Thomas E. Nash, engineer, from Seattle with a good grin and two teeth out of it. It included Edward F. Banker, signalman, of Brooklyn, and Lacey T. Shiflet of Orange, Virginia, who would have been the gunner if we had had room for guns. It included Frank Currier, the coxswain, of Saugus, Massachusetts, and it included Andy and me. When we heard the lugubrious tone of that parting benediction we all knew how bad the beach really was.

As we came roaring in on the beach, I sat high on the stern to see what we were up against. I had the glasses dry now and I took a good look at the shore. The shore was coming toward us awfully fast, and in the glasses it was coming even faster.

On the beach on the left where there was no sheltering overhang of shingled bank, the first, second, third, fourth and fifth waves lay where they had fallen, looking like so many heavily laden bundles on the flat pebbly stretch between the sea and the first cover. To the right, there was an open stretch where the beach exit led up a wooden valley from the sea. It was here that the Germans hoped to get something very good, and later we saw them get it.

To the right of this, two tanks were burning on the crest of the beach, the smoke now gray after the first violent black and yellow billows. Coming in I had spotted two machine-gun nests. One was firing intermittently from the ruins of the smashed house on the right of the small valley. The other was two hundred yards to the right and possibly four hundred yards in front of the beach.

The officer commanding the troops we were carrying had asked us to head directly for the beach opposite the ruined house.

"Right in there," he said. "That's where."

"Andy," I said, "that whole sector is enfiladed by machine-gun fire. I just saw them open twice on that stranded boat."

An LCV(P) was slanted drunkenly in the stakes like a lost gray steel bathtub. They were firing at the water line, and the fire was kicking up sharp spurts of water.

"That's where he says he wants to go," Andy said. "So that's where we'll take him."

"It isn't any good," I said. "I've seen both those guns open up."

"That's where he wants to go," Andy said. "Put her ahead straight in." He turned astern and signaled to the other boats, jerking his arm, with its upraised finger, up and down.

"Come on, you guys," he said, inaudible in the roar of the motor that sounded like a plane taking off. "Close up! Close up! What's the matter with you? Close up, can't you? Take her straight in, coxswain!"

At his point, we entered the beaten zone from the two machine-gun points, and I ducked my head under the sharp cracking that was going overhead. Then I dropped into the well in the stern sheets where the gunner would have been if we had any guns. The machine-gun fire was throwing water all around the boat, and an antitank shell tossed up a jet of water over us.

The lieutenant was talking, but I couldn't hear what he said. Andy could hear him. He had his head down close to his lips.

"Get her the hell around and out of here, coxswain!" Andy called. *"Get her out of here!"*

As we swung round on our stern in a pivot and pulled out, the machine-gun fire stopped. But individual sniping shots kept cracking over or spitting into the water around us. I'd got my head up again with some difficulty and was watching the shore.

"It wasn't cleared, either," Andy said. "You could see the mines on all those stakes."

"Let's coast along and find a good place to put them ashore," I said. "If we stay outside of the machine-gun fire, I don't think they'll shoot at us with anything big because we're just an LCV(P), and they've got better targets than us."

"We'll look for a place," Andy said.

"What's he want now?" I said to Andy.

The lieutenant's lips were moving again. They moved very slowly and as though they had no connection with him or with his face.

Andy got down to listen to him. He came back into the stern. "He wants to go out to an LCI we passed that has his commanding officer on it."

"We can get him ashore farther up toward Easy Red," I said.

"He wants to see his commanding officer," Andy said. "Those people in that black boat were from his outfit."

Out a way, rolling in the sea, was a Landing Craft Infantry, and as we came alongside of her I saw a ragged shellhole through the steel plates forward of her pilothouse where an 88-mm. German shell had punched through. Blood was dripping from the shiny edges of the hole into the sea with each roll of the LCI. Her rails and hull had been befouled by seasick men, and her dead were laid forward of her pilothouse. Our lieutenant had some conversation with another officer while we rose and fell in the surge alongside the black iron hull, and then we pulled away.

Andy went forward and talked to him, then came aft again, and we sat up on the stern and watched two destroyers coming along toward us from the eastern beaches, their guns pounding away at targets on the headlands and sloping fields behind the beaches.

"He says they don't want him to go in yet; to wait," Andy said. "Let's get out of the way of this destroyer."

"How long is he going to wait?"

"He says they have no business in there now. People that should have been ahead of them haven't gone in yet. They told him to wait."

"Let's get in where we can keep track of it," I said. "Take the glasses and look at that beach, but don't tell them forward what you see."

Andy looked. He handed the glasses back to me and shook his head.

"Let's cruise along it to the right and see how it is up at that end," I said. "I'm pretty sure we can get in there when he wants to get in. You're sure they told him he shouldn't go in?"

"That's what he says."

"Talk to him and get it straight."

Andy came back. "He says they shouldn't go in now. They're supposed to clear the mines away, so the tanks can go, and he says nothing is in there to go yet. He says they told him it is all fouled up and to stay out yet awhile."

The destroyer was firing point blank at the concrete pillbox that had fired at us on the first trip into the beach, and as the guns fired you heard the bursts and saw the earth jump almost at the same time as the empty brass cases clanged back onto the steel deck. The five-inch guns of the destroyer were smashing at the ruined house at the edge of the little valley where the other machine gun had fired from.

"Let's move in now that the can has gone by and see if we can't find a good place," Andy said.

"That can punched out what was holding them up there, and you can see some infantry working up that draw now," I said to Andy. "Here, take the glasses."

Slowly, laboriously, as though they were Atlas carrying the world on their shoulders, men were working up the valley on our right. They were not firing. They were just moving slowly up the valley like a tired pack train at the end of the day, going the other way from home.

"The infantry had pushed up to the top of the ridge at the end of that valley," I shouted to the lieutenant.

"They don't want us yet," he said. "They told me clear they didn't want us yet."

"Let me take the glasses—or Hemingway," Andy said. Then he handed them back. "In there, there's somebody signaling with a yellow flag, and there's a boat in there in trouble, it looks like. Coxswain, take her straight in."

We moved in toward the beach at full speed, and Ed Banker looked around and said, "Mr. Anderson, the other boats are coming, too."

"Get them back!" Andy said. "*Get them back!*"

Banker turned around and waved the boats away. He had difficulty making them understand, but finally the wide waves they were throwing subsided and they dropped astern.

"Did you get them back?" Andy asked, without looking away from the beach where we could see a half-sunken LCV(P) foundered in the mined stakes.

"Yes, sir," Ed Banker said.

An LCI was headed straight toward us, pulling away from the beach after having circled to go in. As it passed, a man shouted with a megaphone, "There are wounded on that boat and she is sinking."

"Can you get in to her?"

The only words we heard clearly from the megaphone as the wind snatched the voice away were "machine-gun nest."

"Did they say there was or there wasn't a machine-gun nest?" Andy said.

"I couldn't hear."

"Run alongside of her again, coxswain," he said. "Run close alongside."
"*Did you say there was a machine-gun nest?*" he shouted.

An officer leaned over with the megaphone. "A machine-gun nest has been firing on them. They are sinking."

"Take her straight in, coxswain," Andy said.

It was difficult to make our way through the stakes that had been sunk as obstructions, because there were contact mines fastened to them that looked like large double pie plates fastened face to face. They looked as though they had been spiked to the pilings and then assembled. They were the ugly, neutral gray-yellow color that almost everything is in war.

We did not know what other stakes with mines were under us, but the ones that we could see we fended off by hand and worked our way to the sinking boat.

It was not easy to bring on board the man who had been shot through the lower abdomen, because there was no room to let the ramp down the way we were jammed in the stakes with the cross sea.

I do not know why the Germans did not fire on us unless the destroyer had knocked the machine-gun pillbox out. Or maybe they were waiting for us to blow up with the mines. Certainly the mines had been a great amount of trouble to lay and the Germans might well have wanted to see them work. We were in the range of the antitank gun that had fired on us before, and all the time we were maneuvering and working in the stakes I was waiting for it to fire.

As we lowered the ramp the first time, while we were crowded in against the other LCV(P), but before she sank, I saw three tanks coming along the beach, barely moving, they were advancing so slowly. The Germans let them cross the open space where the valley opened onto the beach, and it was absolutely flat with a perfect field of fire. Then I saw a little fountain of water jut up, just over and beyond the lead tank. Then smoke broke out of the leading tank on the side away from us, and I saw two men dive out of the turret and land on their hands and knees on the stones of the beach. They were close enough so that I could see their faces, but no more men came out as the tank started to blaze up and burn fiercely.

By then, we had the wounded man and the survivors on board, the ramp back up, and were feeling our way out through the stakes. As we cleared the last of the stakes, and Currier opened up the engine wide as we pulled out to sea, another tank was beginning to burn.

We took the wounded boy out to the destroyer. They hoisted him aboard it in one of those metal baskets and took on the survivors. Meantime, the destroyers had run in almost to the beach and were blowing every pillbox out of the ground with their five-inch guns. I saw a piece of German about three feet long with an arm on it sail high up into the air in the fountaining of one shellburst. It reminded me of a scene in Petrouchka.

The infantry had now worked up the valley on our left and had gone on over that ridge. There was no reason for anyone to stay out now. We ran in to a good spot we had picked on the beach and put our troops and their TNT and their bazookas and their lieutenant ashore, and that was that.

The Germans were still shooting with their antitank guns, shifting them around in the valley, holding their fire until they had a target they wanted. Their mortars were still laying a plunging fire along the beaches. They had left people behind to snipe at the beaches, and when we left, finally, all these people who were firing were evidently going to stay until dark at least.

The heavily loaded ducks that had formerly sunk in the waves on their way in were now making the beach steadily. The famous thirty-minute clearing of the channels through the mined obstacles was still a myth, and now, with the high tide, it was a tough trip in with the stakes submerged.

We had six craft missing, finally, out of the twenty-four LCV(P)s that went in from the Dix, but many of the crews could have been picked up and might be on other vessels. It had been a frontal assault in broad daylight, against a mined beach defended by all the obstacles military ingenuity could devise. The beach had been defended as stubbornly and as intelligently as any troops could defend it. But every boat from the Dix had landed her troops and cargo. No boat was lost through bad seamanship. All that were lost were lost by enemy action. And we had taken the beach.

There is much that I have not written. You could write for a week and not give everyone credit for what he did on a front of 1,135 yards. Real war is never like paper war, nor do accounts of it read much the way it looks. But if you want to know how it was in an LCV(P) on D-Day when we took Fox Green beach and Easy Red beach on the sixth of June, 1944, then this is as near as I can come to it.

How We Came to Paris

Collier's
OCTOBER 7, 1944

Never can I describe to you the emotions I felt on the arrival of the armored column of General Leclerc southeast of Paris. Having just returned from a patrol which scared the pants off of me and having been kissed by all the worst element in a town which imagined it had been liberated through our fortuitous entry, I was informed that the general himself was just down the road and anxious to see us. Accompanied by one of the big shots of the resistance movement and Colonel B, who by that time was known throughout Rambouillet as a gallant officer and a *grand seigneur* and who had held the town ever since we could remember, we advanced in some state toward the general. His greeting—unprintable—will live in my ears forever.

"Buzz off, you unspeakables," the gallant general said, in effect, in something above a whisper, and Colonel B, the resistance king and your armored-operations correspondent withdrew.

Later the G-2 of the division invited us to dinner and they operated next day on the information Colonel B had amassed for them. But for your correspondent that was the high point of the attack on Paris.

In war, my experience has been that a rude general is a nervous general. At this time I drew no such deductions but departed on another patrol where I could keep my own nervousness in one jeep and my friends could attempt to clarify the type of resistance we could encounter on the following day between Toussus le Noble and Le Christ de Saclay.

Having found out what this resistance would be, we returned to the Hotel du Grand Veneur in Rambouillet and passed a restless night. I do not remember exactly what produced this restlessness but perhaps it was the fact that the joint was too full of too many people, including, actually, at one time two military police. Or perhaps it was the fact that we had proceeded too far ahead of our supply of Vitamin B$_1$, and the ravages of alcohol were affecting the nerves of the hardier guerrillas who had liberated too many towns in too short a time. At any rate I was restless and I think, without exaggeration, I may truly state that those whom Colonel B and I by then referred to as "our people" were restless.

The guerrilla chief, the actual fighting head of "our people," said, "We want to take Paris. What the hell is the delay?"

"There is no delay, Chief," I answered. "All this is part of a giant operation. Have patience. Tomorrow we will take Paris."

"I hope so," the guerrilla chief said. "My wife has been expecting me there for some time. I want to get the hell into Paris to see my wife, and I see no necessity to wait for a lot of soldiers to come up."

"Be patient," I told him.

That fateful night we slept. It might be a fateful night but tomorrow would certainly be an even more fateful day. My anticipations of a really good fight on the morrow were marred by a guerrilla who entered the hotel late at night and woke me to inform me that all the Germans who could do so were pulling out of Paris. We knew there would be fighting the next day by the screen the German army had left. But I did not anticipate any heavy fighting, since we knew the German dispositions and could attack or by-pass them accordingly, and I assured our guerrillas that if they would only be patient, we would have the privilege of entering Paris with soldiers ahead of us instead of behind us.

This privilege did not appeal to them at all. But one of the big shots of the underground insisted that we do this, as he said it was only courteous to allow troops to precede and by the time we had reached Toussus le Noble, where there was a short but sharp fight, orders were given that neither newspapermen nor guerrillas were to be allowed to proceed until the column had passed.

The day we advanced on Paris it rained heavily and everyone was soaked to the skin within an hour of leaving Rambouillet. We proceeded through Chevreuse and St. Rémy-lès-Chevreuses where we had formerly run patrols and were well known to the local inhabitants, from whom we had collected information and with whom we had downed considerable quantities of armagnac to still the ever-present discontent of our guerrillas, who were very Paris-conscious at this time. In those days I had found that the production of an excellent bottle of any sort of alcoholic beverage was the only way of ending an argument.

After we had proceeded through St. Rémy-lès-Chevreuses, where we were wildly acclaimed by the local *charcutier,* or pork butcher, who had participated in previous operations and been cockeyed ever since, we made a slight error in preceding the column to a village called Courcelle. There we were informed that there were no vehicles ahead of us and, greatly to the disgust of our people who wished to proceed on what they believed to be the shortest route into Paris, we returned to St. Rémy-lès-Chevreuses to join the armored column which was proceeding toward Châteaufort. Our return was viewed with considerable alarm by the local *charcutier.* But when we explained the situation to him he acclaimed us wildly again and, downing a couple of quick ones, we advanced resolutely toward Toussus le Noble where I knew the column would have to fight.

At this point I knew there would be German opposition just ahead of us and also on our right at Le Christ de Saclay. The Germans had dug and blasted out a series of defense points between Châteaufort and Toussus le Noble and beyond the crossroads. Past the airdrome toward Buc they had 88s that commanded all that stretch of road. As we came closer to where the tanks were operating around Trappes I became increasingly apprehensive.

The French armor operated beautifully. On the road toward Toussus le Noble, where we knew there were Germans with machine guns in the wheat shocks, the tanks deployed and screened both of our flanks and we saw them rolling ahead through the cropped wheat field as though they were on maneuvers. No one saw the Germans until they came out with their hands up after the tanks had passed. It was a beautiful use of armor, that problem child of war, and it was lovely to see.

When we ran up against the seven tanks and four 88s the Germans had beyond the airfield, the French handled the fight prettily, too. Their artillery was back in another open wheat field, and when the German guns—four of which had been brought up during the night and were firing absolutely in the open—cut loose on the column, the French mechanized artillery slammed into them. You could not hear with the German shells coming in, the 20-mm. firing, and the machine-gun fire cracking overhead, but the French underground leader who had correlated the information on the German dispositions shouted in French into my ear, "The contact is beautiful. Just where we said. Beautiful."

It was much too beautiful for me, who had never been a great lover of contact anyway, and I hit the deck as an 88 shell burst alongside the road. Contact is a very noisy business and, since our column was held up at this point, the more forceful and active of the guerrillas aided in reconstructing the road which had been churned into soup by the armor. This kept their minds from the contact taking place all around us. They filled in the mudholes with bricks and tiles from a smashed house, and passed along chunks of cement and pieces of house from hand to hand. It was raining hard all this time, and by the time the contact was over, the column had two dead and five wounded, one tank burned up, and had knocked out two of the seven enemy tanks and silenced all of the 88s.

"*C'est un bel accrochage,*" the underground leader said to me jubilantly.

This means something like "We have grappled with them prettily" or "We tied into them beautifully," searching in mind for the exact meaning of *accrochage*, which is what happens when two cars lock bumpers.

I shouted, "Prettily! Prettily!"

At which a young French lieutenant, who did not have the air of having been mixed up in too many *accrochages* in his time but who, for all I know, may have participated in hundreds of them, said to me, "Who the hell are you and what are you doing here in our column?"

"I am a war correspondent, monsieur," I replied.

The lieutenant shouted: "Do not let any war correspondents proceed until the column has passed. And especially do not let this one proceed."

"Okay, my lieutenant," the M.P. said. "I will keep an eye on them."

"And none of that guerrilla rabble, either," the lieutenant ordered. "None of that is to pass until all the column has gone through."

"My lieutenant," I said, "the rabble will be removed from sight once this little *accrochage* is finished and the column has proceeded."

"What do you mean—this little *accrochage?*" he demanded, and I feared hostility might be creeping into his voice.

Since we were not to advance farther with the column, I took evasive action at this point and waded down the road to a bar. Numerous guerrillas were seated in it singing happily and passing the time of day with a lovely Spanish girl from Bilbao whom I had last met on the famous two-way, or wide-open patrol point just outside the town of Cognières. This was the town we used to take from the Germans whenever one of their vehicles pulled out of it, and they would return whenever we stepped off the road. This girl had been following wars and preceding troops since she was fifteen and she and the guerrillas were paying no attention to the *accrochage* at all.

A guerrilla chief named C said, "Have a drink of this excellent white wine." I took a long drink from the bottle and it turned out to be a highly alcoholic liqueur tasting of oranges and called Grand Marnier.

A stretcher was coming back with a wounded man on it. "Look," a guerrilla said, "these military are constantly suffering casualties. Why do they not allow us to proceed ahead in a sensible manner?"

"Okay, okay," said another guerrilla in G.I. fatigue clothes, with the brassard of the *francs-tireurs* on his sleeve. "What about the comrades who were killed yesterday on the road?"

Another said, "But today we're going into Paris."

"Let's go back and see if we can make it by Le Christ de Saclay," I said. "The law has arrived and they won't let us go on any farther until the column has passed. The roads are too muddy and torn up here. We could push the light touring cars through, but the truck might bog down and stall things."

"We can push through by a side road," the guerrilla chief named C said. "Since when do we have to follow columns?"

"I think it is best to go back as far as Châteaufort," I said. "Maybe we can go much faster that way."

On the crossroads outside Châteaufort we found Colonel B and Commander A, who had become detached from us before we had run into the *accrochage*, and told them about the beautiful contact up the road. The artillery was still firing in the open wheat field, and the two gallant officers had found some lunch in a farmhouse. French troops from the column were burning the wooden boxes that had held the shells the artillery had been blasting with, and we took off our wet clothes and dried them at the fire. German prisoners were drifting in, and an officer in the column asked us to send the guerrillas up to where a group of Germans had just surrendered in the wheat shocks. They brought them back in good military style, all the prisoners alive and well.

"This is idiotic, you know, my captain," the oldest one of the band said. "Now someone has to feed them."

The prisoners said they were office workers in Paris and had only been brought out and put in the positions at one o'clock this morning.

"Do you believe that sort of stuff?" asked the oldest guerrilla.

"It could be possible. They weren't here yesterday," I said.

"This entire military nonsense disgusts me," the oldest guerrilla said. He was forty-one and had a thin, sharp face with clear blue eyes, and a rare but fine smile. "Eleven of our group were tortured and shot by these Germans. I have been beaten and kicked by them, and they would have shot me if they knew who I was. Now we are asked to guard them carefully and respectfully."

"They are not your prisoners," I explained. "The military took them."

The rain turned to a light drifting mist and then the sky cleared. The prisoners were sent back to Rambouillet in the big German truck that the underground big shot quite rightly was anxious to get out of the column for the moment. Leaving word with the M.P. on the crossroads where the truck could rejoin us, we drove on after the column.

We caught up with the tanks on a side road this side of the main Versailles-Paris highway and moved with them down into a deeply wooded valley and out into green fields where there was an old château. We watched the tanks deploy again, like watching dogs outside a moving band of sheep. They had fought once up ahead of us while we had gone back to see if the road through Le Christ de Saclay was free, and we passed a burned-out tank and three dead Germans. One of these had been run over and flattened out in a way that left no doubt of the power of armor when properly used.

On the main Versailles-Villacoublay highway the column proceeded past the wrecked airdrome of Villacoublay to the crossroads of the Porte Clamart. Here, while the column was stopped, a Frenchman came running up and reported a small German tank on the road that led into the woods. I searched the road with my glasses but could not see anything. In the meantime, the German vehicle, which was not a tank but a lightly armored German jeep mounting a machine gun and a 20-mm. gun, made a turn in the woods and came tearing up the road, firing at the crossroads.

Everyone started shooting at it, but it wheeled and regained the woods. Archie Pelkey, my driver, got in two shots at it but could not be sure that he had hit. Two men were hit and were carried into the lee of the corner building for first aid. The guerrillas were happy now that shooting had started again.

"We have nice work ahead of us. Good work ahead of us," the guerrilla with the sharp face and the light blue eyes said. "I'm happy some of the b——s are still here."

"Do you think we will have much more chance to fight?" the guerrilla named C asked.

"Certainly," I said. "There's bound to be some of them in the town."

My own war aim at this moment was to get into Paris without being shot. Our necks had been out for a long time. Paris was going to be taken. I took cover in all the street fighting—the solidest cover available—and with someone covering the stairs behind me when we were in houses or the entrances to apartment houses.

From now on, the advance of the column was something to see. Ahead of us would be a barricade of felled trees. The tanks would pass around them or butt them around like elephants handling logs. You would see the tanks charge into a barricade of old motorcars and go smashing on ahead with a jalopy bouncing along, its smashed fenders entangled in the tracks. Armor, which can be so vulnerable and so docile in the close hedgerow country where it is a prey to antitank guns, bazookas and anyone who does not fear it, was smashing round like so many drunken elephants in a native village.

Ahead and on our left, a German ammunition dump was burning, and the varicolored antiaircraft projectiles were bursting in the continuous rattle and pop of the exploding 20-mm. stuff. The larger projectiles started to explode as the heat increased, and gave the impression of a bombardment. I couldn't locate Archie Pelkey, but later I found he had advanced on the burning munitions dump, thinking it was a fight.

"There wasn't nobody there, Papa," he said; "it was just a lot of ammunition burning."

"Don't go off by yourself," I said. "How did you know we didn't want to roll?"

"Okay, Papa. Sorry, Papa. I understand, Papa. Only, Mr. Hemingway, I went off with *Frère*—the one who is my brother—because I thought he said there was a fight."

"Oh, hell!" I said. "You've been ruined by guerrillas."

We ran through the road where the munitions dump was exploding, with Archie, who has bright red hair, six years of regular Army, four words of French, a missing front tooth, and a *Frère* in a guerrilla outfit, laughing heartily at the noise the big stuff was making as it blew.

"Sure is popping off, Papa," he shouted. His freckled face was completely happy. "They say this Paris is quite a town, Papa. You ever been into it?"

"Yeah."

We were going downhill now, and I knew that road and what we would see when we made the next turn.

"*Frère*, he was telling me something about it while the column was held up, but I couldn't make it out," Archie said. "All I could make out was it must be a hell of a place. Something about he was going to *Paname*, too. This place hasn't got anything to do with Panama, has it?"

"No, Arch," I said, "the French call it *Paname* when they love it very much."

"I see," Archie said. "*Compris*. Just like something you might call a girl that wouldn't be her right name. Right?"

"Right."

"I couldn't make out what the hell *Frère* was saying," Archie said. "I guess it's like they call me Jim. Everybody in the outfit calls me Jim, and my name is Archie."

"Maybe they like you," I said.

"They're a good outfit," Archie said. "Best outfit I ever been with. No discipline. Got to admit that. Drinking all the time. Got to admit that. But plenty fighting outfit. Nobody gives a damn if they get killed or not. *Compris?*"

"Yeah," I said. I couldn't say anything more then, because I had a funny choke in my throat and I had to clean my glasses because there now, below us, gray and always beautiful, was spread the city I love best in all the world.

War in the Siegfried Line

Collier's
NOVEMBER 18, 1944

A lot of people will tell you how it was to be first into Germany and how it was to break the Siegfried Line and a lot of people will be wrong. So this will not be held up by the censor while all the claims are threshed out. We do not claim anything. No claims, see? You get it? No claims at all. Let them decide and then we will see who was in there first. I mean which outfit. Not which people.

The infantry cracked the Siegfried Line. They cracked it on a cold rainy morning when even the crows weren't flying, much less the Air Force. Two days before, on the last day before the weather broke for the bad, we had come to the end of the rat race. It had been a fine rat race from Paris up as far as Le Cateau, with bitter fighting at Landrecies that few saw and fewer still are left to remember. Then there had been the forcing of the passes of the Ardennes Forest in country like the illustrations for Grimm's Fairy Tales only a lot grimmer.

Then the rat race went on again through rolling, forested country. Sometimes we would be half an hour behind the retreating enemy's mechanized force. Sometimes we would get up to within five minutes of them. Sometimes we would overrun them and, from the point of the recon, you would hear the fifties hammering behind you and the 105-millimeter Wump guns going on the tank destroyers and the merging roar and rattle of enemy fire, and the word would come along: "Enemy tanks and half-tracks in the rear of the column. Pass the word along."

Then, suddenly the rat race was over, and we were on a high hill, out of the forest, and all the rolling hills and forests that you saw ahead of you were Germany. There was a heavy, familiar roar from the creek valley below as the bridge was blown, and beyond the black cloud of smoke and debris that rose, you saw two enemy half-tracks tearing up the white road that led into the German hills.

Our artillery was blasting yellow-white clouds of smoke and road dust ahead of them. You watched one half-track slither sideways across the road. The other stopped on the turn of the road after trying twice to move like a wounded animal. Another shell pounded up a fountain of dust and smoke alongside the crippled half-track and when the smoke cleared, you could see the bodies on the road. That was the end of the rat race, and we came down a trail in the woods and into the ford over the river and across the slab-stoned river bed and up the far bank into Germany.

We passed the unmanned old-fashioned pillboxes that many unfortunate people were to think constituted the Siegfried Line, and got up into good high ground that night. The next day we were past the second line of concrete fortified strong points that guarded road junctions and approaches to the main Westwall, and that same night we were up on the highest of the high ground before the Westwall, ready to assault in the morning.

The weather had broken. It was cold and raining and blowing half a gale, and ahead of us was the dark forest wall of the Schnee Eifel range where the dragon lived, and behind us on the first hill behind was a German reviewing stand that had been built for high officers to occupy when they watched the maneuvers that proved that the Westwall never could be broken. We were hitting it on the point that the Germans had chosen to prove, in sham battles, that it was impregnable.

The rest of this story is told in the words of Captain Howard Blazzard of Arizona. It may give you a little idea of what happens in combat.

"That night we got L Company into that town to hold it. It was practically unoccupied. Six Jerries, and we shot them. *(This was the town, or small village rather, from which the attack started in the morning up the hill and across the level field of fire over a cropped wheatfield, the wheat shocks stacked, to assault the main fortifications of the Westwall which were in the thick pine forest of the dark hill beyond.)*

"The Colonel, of Washington, D. C., got the three battalion commanders together and the S-2 and the S-3 and planned the breakthrough for in the morning. Where this break was going to be made *(you notice the phrasing 'Going to be made,' not 'Going to be attempted')* we were supposed to have one company of tanks and one company of T.D.s (Tank Destroyers) but they only gave us one platoon of tanks (five). We were supposed to have twelve T.D.s and we had only nine. You remember how everything was then and how the gas was short and all.

"The way it was supposed to be now *(There is a great difference in combat between the way it is supposed to be and the way it is—as great as the dif-*

ference in how life is supposed to be and how it is): L Company, that had moved into town the night before, was going to be on the right flank, and they were going to make the holding attack with fire.

"K Company had started walking early, before six A.M., and they were going to ride the tanks and the T.D.s. While they were coming up we got the T.D.s up into town and finally by twelve-thirty we got one platoon of tanks. Five of them. All five of them.

"Now I Company was back so far they couldn't get up. You remember everything that was happening that day. *(Plenty. Plenty was happening.)* So the Colonel, he took a company away from the First Battalion and threw them in, so he'd have three companies to make the attack.

"That was around one o'clock. The Colonel and I went up this left fork that was sort of drawn off on the left, to watch the attack get started. It started fine. K Company started riding the tanks and the T.D.s, and then they moved up and got just below the crest and fanned out. Just as they should. Just as they hit that little crest, L Company on their right opened up with machine guns and 60-millimeter mortars and all that fire, to attract attention from K Company.

"The tanks and T.D.s got up the hill and the flak guns *(German anti-aircraft guns, which fire almost as rapidly as machine guns, being used for direct fire on the ground against the attacking troops)* opened up first. The 88 which we knew was in there held its fire. When the ack-ack and the machine guns opened up, the men started to dismount from the tanks, just as they should, and they went on up and they went fine till they got out in the open on that big bare field and almost to the edge of the last field in front of the woods.

"About that time they really opened up with the 88s—the 88s and all that flak. One T.D. hit a mine over on the left by that little road, you remember, just before it goes into the woods, and the tanks began to run. Lost a T.D. and a tank and they all started backing up. You know how they are when they start backing up.

"They started coming back down across the field, dragging a few wounded and a few limping. You know how they look coming back. Then the tanks started coming back and the T.D.s coming back and the men coming back plenty. They couldn't stay in that bare field, and the ones who weren't hit started yelling for the medicos for those who were hit, and you know how that excites everybody.

"The Colonel and I were sitting by the house and we could see the fight and the way it started fine and good. We thought they'd got right through. But then this stuff starts. Then come four tankers tearing along on foot and yelling and hollering how everything was knocked out.

"Then I asked the Colonel—I'd been in the Third Battalion a long time—and I said, 'Sir, I can go out there and kick those bastards in the tail and take that place.' And he said, 'You're S-2 in a staff function and you stay where you are.' That chewed my tail out. That made me unhappy.

"We sat there another ten or fifteen minutes, and the wounded kept drifting along back, and we were just there and I thought we're going to lose this battle. Then the Colonel says, 'Let's get up there. This thing has got to move. Those chickenspits aren't going to break down this attack.'

"So we started up the hill and we passed little groups here and there—you know how they drift together—and you know how the Colonel looks, and he is carrying his forty-five and walking up that hill. There is a sort of little terrace at the top where the hill starts to come down; under the cover of that little terrace were all the tanks and the T.D.s, and K Company was lined up along in a sort of skirmish line and they were all just sort of dead, and the attack was gone.

"The Colonel came up the hill and out over this terrace where they were all lying and he said, 'Let's go get these Krauts. Let's kill these chickenspitters. Let's get up over this hill now and get this place taken.'

"He had his goddam forty-five and he shot three-four times at where the Kraut fire was coming from, and he said, 'Goddam, let's go get these Krauts! Come on! Nobody's going to stop here now!' They were plenty cold as hell but he kept talking to them and telling them, and pretty soon he got some of them, and in fifteen minutes he got most of them moving. Once he got them moving, the Colonel and I and Smith *(Sergeant James C. Smith from Tullahoma, Tennessee)*, we went on ahead of them and the attack was going again and we headed into the woods. It was bad in the woods but they went in good now.

"When we got into the woods *(The woods were close-planted fir trees, and the shell-bursts tore and smashed them, and the splinters from the tree bursts were like javelins in the half-light of the forest, and the men were shouting and calling now to take the curse off the darkness of the forest and shooting and killing Krauts and moving ahead now)* it was pretty thick for the tanks, and so they went to the outside. They were shooting into the woods, but we had to stop them now because K Company had pushed through ahead of them way into the woods.

"The Colonel and I and Smith, we went on ahead and found a hole in the timber where we could get a T.D. in. Now the attack was going good on ahead and all of a sudden we saw a bunker right beside us, and they started shooting at us. We decided there were Krauts in it. *(The bunker was completely hidden by fir trees planted over it and grass growing over it and was a subterranean fort on the Maginot Line style with automatic ventilation, con-*

cussion-proof doors, bunks fifteen feet underground for the men, special exit pro-
visions so that it could be run over and then its occupants attack the enemy from
the rear, and it held fifty SS troops whose mission was to let the attack pass and
then come out and fire on it.)

"All there was left with us now was the Colonel, I and Smith and Roger, this French boy who had been with us ever since St. Poix, I never knew his last name but he was a wonderful Frenchman. Best boy in a fight you ever saw. These Krauts in the bunker started shooting at us. So we started walking over toward it and we decided we'd got to get them out.

"There was an embrasure over on our side, but we couldn't see that, the way it was all planted over. I had only one grenade because I wasn't expecting what we were going to do. We got over within about ten yards of the pillbox, coming in this side of it. We couldn't see the aperture at the bottom of it. It all looked like a wooded hillock.

"They're shooting sort of scattered all the while. The Colonel and Smith were at the right of it. Roger was going in right toward the aperture. You couldn't see the fire.

"I yelled at Roger to get down, and right then they shot him. I saw the goddam hole then and I threw the grenade to go in, but you know how those apertures are beveled, and it hit and bounced out. Smith grabbed the Frenchman by the heels and started to drag him clear because he was still alive. In that slit trench on the left, there was a Kraut and he stood up, and Smith shot him with his carbine. You can tell how fast this happened because just then the grenade went off, and we all ducked.

"Then we started to get a lot of fire from the field out in front of the woods—the field we'd crossed to get into the woods—and Smith said, 'Colonel, you better get down in that hole because here come those Krauts.'

"They were firing from the wheat shocks in the field right there in front of the woods and in that little tongue of brush. The Krauts started shooting at us from out there, which should have been our rear.

"The Colonel dropped one Kraut with his forty-five. Smith shot two with his carbine; I was in back of the pillbox and I shot the one who was in back of us across the road about fifteen yards away. I had to shoot at him three times before he stopped and then I didn't kill him good because when the T.D. came up finally he was lying right across the middle of the road and, seeing the T.D. coming up, he sort of scrounged up and tried to get out of the way, and the T.D. went over him and flattened him out.

"The rest of the Krauts sort of took off across the field and we didn't have any real trouble with that lot. Just sort of long-range fire. We know we killed three and we wounded some more that took off.

"We didn't have any more hand grenades and the bastards in the bunker wouldn't come out when we yelled at them. So the Colonel and I were waiting for them to come out, and Smith went off to the left and found a T.D. and brought it up. That was the T.D. that ran over the Kraut I had to shoot three times with that little old German pistol.

"The Krauts still wouldn't come out when talked to, so we pulled that T.D. right up to the back of that steel door we had located by now, and that old Wump gun fired about six rounds and blasted that door in, and then you ought to have heard them want to come out. You ought to have heard them yell and moan and moan and scream and yell '*Kamerad!*'

"The T.D. had that old Wump gun pointed right in the door, and they started to come out, and you never saw such a mess. Every one of them was wounded in five or six different places, from pieces of concrete and steel. About eighteen good ones came out, and all the time inside there was the most piteous moaning and screaming, and there was one fellow with both his legs cut off by the steel door. I went down to see how everything was and got a suitcase with a couple of quarts of whisky in it and a couple of boxes of cigars and a pistol for the Colonel.

"One of the prisoners was in pretty good shape, not really good shape but he could travel. He was a noncom. The rest of them were lying down outside, all moaning, wounded and shot up.

"This noncom showed us where the next bunker was. By then, we knew what they looked like, and you could spot them by any sort of rise of ground. So we took the T.D. and went down the road about seventy-five yards to this second bunker—you know which one—and had this bird ask them to surrender. You ought to have seen this Kraut. He was a Wehrmacht, regular army, and he kept saying, 'Bitty. S.S.S.' He meant they were those real bad ones and they would kill him if he asked them to surrender. He yelled at them to come out, and they wouldn't come. They wouldn't answer. So we pulled the Wump gun up to the back door just like the other time and yelled to them to come out, and they wouldn't come. So we put in about ten shots from the Wump gun and then they came out—what was left of them. They were a sad and bedraggled lot. Every one of them was in awful shape.

"They were SS boys, all of them, and they got down in the road, one by one, on their knees. They expected to get shot. But we were obliged to disappoint them. There were about twelve that got out. The rest were all blown to pieces and wounded all to hell. There were legs and arms and heads scattered all over that goddamn place.

"We had so many prisoners and nobody to guard them but the Colonel and I and Smith and the Wump gun, so we sort of sat around there until things sort of clarified. After a while a medical aide came up and looked at the French boy, Roger. He was lying there all the time and when they came to dress him, he said, '*Mon colonel, je suis content.* I am happy to die on German soil.'

"They put a tag on him reading 'Free French' and I said, 'The hell with that,' and changed the tag to read 'Company L.'

"Every time I think about that Frenchman, it makes me want to get to killing Krauts again. . . ."

There is a lot more to the story. Maybe that is as much as you can take today. I could write you just what I Company did, what the other two battalions did. I could write for you, if you could take it, what happened at the third bunker and the fourth bunker and at fourteen other bunkers. They were all taken.

If you want to know something, get someone who was there to tell you. If you wish, and I can still remember, I will be glad to tell you sometime what it was like in those woods for the next ten days; about all the counterattacks and about the German artillery. It is a very, very interesting story if you can remember it. Probably it has even epic elements. Doubtless sometime you will even see it on the screen.

It probably is suitable for screen treatment, because I remember the Colonel saying, "Ernie, a lot of the time I felt as though I were at a Grade B picture and kept saying to myself, 'This is where I came in.' "

The only thing that will probably be hard to get properly in the picture is the German SS troops, their faces black from the concussion, bleeding at the nose and mouth, kneeling in the road, grabbing their stomachs, hardly able to get out of the way of the tanks, though probably the cinema will be able to make this even more realistic. But a situation like that is the fault of the engineers who, when they designed those concussion-proof doors, did not expect to have 105-mm. Wump guns come up and fire point-blank at them from behind.

That was not provided for when the specifications were laid down. And sometimes, observing such sad sights and such elaborate preparations gone wrong, I have a feeling that it really would have been better for Germany not to have started this war in the first place.

341

A Bibliography of Ernest Hemingway's Writings on War

There is a wealth of unpublished writing by Ernest Hemingway at the Hemingway Archives of the John F. Kennedy Library in Boston, including letters, pages from journals, and a number of stories and articles in various stages of completion, as well as family scrapbooks and other ephemera.

The following is a selected chronological list of Hemingway's published writings on war.

Three Stories & Ten Poems. Paris: Contact Publishing Company, 1923.

in our time. Paris: Three Mountains Press, 1924.

In Our Time. New York: Boni & Liveright, 1925.

Men Without Women. New York: Charles Scribner's Sons, 1927.

A Farewell to Arms. New York: Charles Scribner's Sons, 1929.

To Have and Have Not. New York: Charles Scribner's Sons, 1937.

The Spanish Earth. With an Introduction by Jasper Wood and Illustrations by Frederick K. Russell. Cleveland: The J. B. Savage Company, 1938.

The Fifth Column, and the First Forty-nine Stories. New York: Charles Scribner's Sons, 1938.

Preface to *All the Brave*, a volume of paintings by the Spanish artist Luis Quintanilla with text by Elliot Paul and Jay Allen. New York: Modern Age Books, 1938.

Foreword to *Men in the Ranks: The Story of 12 Americans in Spain*, by Joseph North. New York: Friends of the Abraham Lincoln Brigade, 1939.

For Whom the Bell Tolls. New York: Charles Scribner's Sons, 1940.

Preface to *The Great Crusade*, by Gustav Regler. New York and Toronto: Longmans, Green, 1940.

Men at War: The Best War Stories of All Time. Edited with an Introduction by Ernest Hemingway. New York: Crown Publishers, 1942.

Introduction to *Studio: Europe*, written and illustrated by John Groth. New York: Vanguard Press, 1945.

Foreword to *Treasury for the Free World,* edited by Ben Raeburn. New York: Arco, 1946.

A Farewell to Arms. With an Introduction by Ernest Hemingway and Illustrations by Daniel Rasmusson. New York: Charles Scribner's Sons, 1948.

Across the River and Into the Trees. New York: Charles Scribner's Sons, 1950.

Islands in the Stream. New York: Charles Scribner's Sons, 1970.

Ernest Hemingway: 88 Poems. Edited by Nicholas Gerogiannis. New York and London: Harcourt Brace Jovanovich/Bruccoli Clark, 1979.

The Complete Short Stories of Ernest Hemingway. The Finca Vigía Edition. New York: Scribner, 1987.

Hemingway's writings as a reporter and war correspondent are some of our most compelling accounts of historical conflicts. In the following publications may be found, among other writings, his earliest articles relating to World War I and its aftermath when he was a reporter for *The Toronto Star,* his dispatches as a correspondent for the North American Newspaper Alliance during the Spanish Civil War, and his articles written for various magazines during the Spanish Civil War and World War II.

"The Spanish War," *Fact,* no. 16 (15 July 1938): 7–72.

By-Line: Ernest Hemingway. Selected Articles and Dispatches of Four Decades. Edited by William White. New York: Charles Scribner's Sons, 1961.

Ernest Hemingway, Dateline: Toronto. The Complete Toronto Star Dispatches, 1920–1924. Edited by William White. New York: Scribner, 1985.

Numerous references to war also may be found in the published letters, in which Hemingway sometimes writes of his works, or describes his experiences and feelings having to do with war.

Ernest Hemingway, Selected Letters, 1917–1961. Edited by Carlos Baker. New York: Scribner, 1981.

Hemingway in Cuba by Norberto Fuentes. Introduction by Gabriel García Márquez. Translated by Consuelo E. Corwin and edited by Larry Alson. Secaucus, N.J.: Lyle Stuart, 1984.

The Only Thing That Counts: The Ernest Hemingway/Maxwell Perkins Correspondence, 1925–1947. Edited by Matthew J. Bruccoli. Columbia, S.C.: University of South Carolina Press, 1996.

CPSIA information can be obtained at www.ICGtesting.com
Printed in the USA
LVOW06s1301111213

364857LV00001B/111/P